Celebrate the

PENNY
JORDAN

Phenomenally successful author of more than 200 books with sales of over 100 million copies!

Penny Jordan's novels are read and loved by millions of readers all around the word in many different languages. This beautiful collection of six volumes offers a chance to recapture the pleasure of a special selection of her fabulous stories.

As an extra treat, each volume also includes an introductory letter by a different author. Some of the most popular names in romantic fiction share their personal thoughts and memories, which we hope you will enjoy.

Wedding nights

A set of three Penny Jordan novels, first seen as *The Bride's Bouquet* and set around a wedding, collected together just for your pleasure—passion and seduction at your fingertips!

**Mills & Boon® proudly presents
a very special tribute**

PENNY
JORDAN
COLLECTION

DESERT NIGHTS
Available in August 2012

WEDDING NIGHTS
Available in September 2012

MEDITERRANEAN NIGHTS
Available in October 2012

CHRISTMAS NIGHTS
Available in November 2012

PASSIONATE NIGHTS
Available in December 2012

SINFUL NIGHTS
Available in January 2013

PENNY
JORDAN
COLLECTION

Wedding
nights

MILLS &
BOON

Published in Great Britain 2012
Mills & Boon, an imprint of Harlequin (UK) Limited,
Eton House, 18-24 Paradise Road, Richmond, Surrey TW9 1SR

WEDDING NIGHTS © Harlequin Enterprises II B.V./S.à.r.l. 2012

Woman to Wed? © Penny Jordan 1996
Best Man to Wed? © Penny Jordan 1996
Too Wise to Wed? © Penny Jordan 1996

ISBN: 978 0 263 90212 9

028-0912

Harlequin (UK) policy is to use papers that are natural, renewable and recyclable products and made from wood grown in sustainable forests. The logging and manufacturing processes conform to the legal environmental regulations of the country of origin.

Printed and bound
by CPI Group (UK) Ltd, Croydon, CR0 4YY

Dear Reader,

It's a bittersweet honour for me to be asked to write a letter to go in the front of this beautiful new collection of Penny Jordan's 'Bride's Bouquet' books. On one hand it's given me a brilliant excuse to drop everything else and lose myself in Claire, Poppy and Star's stories, which has been a joy. On the other it is a fresh reminder of the great sadness that Penny is no longer here to introduce them herself.

The books are now fifteen and sixteen years old and yet they retain the freshness and sparkle that are the hallmarks of Penny's writing. The characters are sharply observed, and each of the three stories that spring from the initial confetti-strewn, champagne-sealed pact between the heroines is fabulously distinctive and sizzling with its own unique chemistry. Reading them, I was reminded firstly what a truly wonderful, natural storyteller Penny was (in fact I was so wrapped up in devouring them it was a job to remember anything else!) and also that, although I can't pick up the phone and speak to her or share a gossipy lunch, I can still hear her voice in her books. In them, she has left a legacy and a gift that will be enjoyed by generations to come.

Writing was Penny's passion, and she spoke very often of her gratitude to every one of her readers for enabling her to make her living doing the thing she loved. She'd be really cross with me if I didn't end this by saying thank you on her behalf for picking up this book, and I really hope you enjoy it.

India

Penny Jordan is one of Mills & Boon's most popular authors. Sadly Penny died from cancer on 31st December 2011, aged sixty-five. She leaves an outstanding legacy, having sold over a hundred million books around the world. She wrote a total of a hundred and eighty-seven novels for Mills & Boon, including the phenomenally successful *A Perfect Family, To Love, Honour & Betray, The Perfect Sinner* and *Power Play*, which hit the *Sunday Times* and *New York Times* bestseller lists. Loved for her distinctive voice, her success was in part because she continually broke boundaries and evolved her writing to keep up with readers' changing tastes. *Publishers Weekly* said about Jordan: 'Women everywhere will find pieces of themselves in Jordan's characters' and this perhaps explains her enduring appeal.

Although Penny was born in Preston, Lancashire, and spent her childhood there, she moved to Cheshire as a teenager and continued to live there for the rest of her life. Following the death of her husband she moved to the small traditional Cheshire market town on which she based her much-loved Crighton books.

Penny was a member and supporter of the Romantic Novelists' Association and the Romance Writers of America—two organisations dedicated to providing support for both published and yet-to-be published authors. Her significant contribution to women's fiction was recognised in 2011, when the Romantic Novelists' Association presented Penny with a Lifetime Achievement Award.

Woman to Wed?

PENNY JORDAN

PROLOGUE

THERE has been a long tradition at weddings that the one to catch the bride's bouquet as she throws it will be the next to marry.

The bride emerged from the hotel bedroom, giving her skirts a final shake, turning round to check on the long, flowing satin length of her train before turning to smile lovingly into the eyes of her new husband.

Her two adult bridesmaids—her best friend and her husband's young cousin—and her stepmother had been dismissed for this, her final appearance in her wedding gown. Chris could be her attendant on this occasion, she had told them.

'Come on; we'd better go down,' he warned her. 'Otherwise everyone will be wondering what on earth we're doing.'

Laughing, they walked to the top of the stairs and then paused to stand and watch the happy crowd in the room below them. The reception was in full swing.

The bride turned to her husband and whispered emotionally, 'This has been the happiest day of my life.'

'And mine too,' Chris returned, squeezing Sally's hand and bending his head to kiss her.

Arm in arm they started to walk down the stairs, and

then, somehow or other, Sally missed her footing and slipped. The small group of people clustered at the foot of the stairs waiting for them, alerted to what was happening by Sally's frightened cry, rushed forward, James, the best man, Chris's elder brother and two of the ushers going to the aid of the bride, whilst the two bridesmaids and the bride's stepmother reacted immediately and equally instinctively, quickly reaching out to protect the flowers that the bride had dropped as she'd started to fall.

As three pairs of equally feminine but very different hands reached out to grasp the bouquet, the bride, back on her feet now, smiled mischievously down at them and warned, 'That's it! There'll be three more weddings now.'

'No!'

'Never!'

'Impossible!'

Three very firm and determined female voices made the same immediate denial; three pairs of female eyes all registered an immediate and complete rejection of the bride's triumphant assertion.

Marry? Them? Never.

The three of them looked at one another and then back at the bride.

It was just a silly old superstition. It meant nothing, and besides, each of them knew that no matter what the other two chose to do she was most definitely not going to get married.

The bride was still laughing as she swept down the few remaining stairs on her husband's arm.

Her two bridesmaids had both already separately and jointly informed her that they had no intention of taking part in any silly old rituals which involved the degradation of them vying for possession of her wedding bouquet, and as for her stepmother...

A tiny frown pleated Sally's forehead. When would Claire accept that, at a mere thirty-four and widowed, she was not, as she always insisted, too mature to want to share her life with a new partner?

While Sally and Chris made sure that they spoke with every guest once the speeches were over, the two bridesmaids and Claire worked together to gather up the scattered wedding presents. Poppy, Chris's cousin, suddenly spotted Sally's wedding bouquet lying on one of the tables. Unable to help herself, she went over to it and picked it up, tears filling her eyes.

'Forget it,' Star, her fellow bridesmaid, instructed her, grimly removing the flowers from her tense grip. 'It's just a stupid superstition. It means nothing, and I for one intend to prove it by saying publicly and unequivocally here and now that I never intend to marry.'

As her eye was caught by an unopened bottle of champagne, she reached for it, opened it deftly and poured the foaming liquid into three empty glasses, challenging the other two, 'I'm willing to make a vow not to marry. What about you two?'

'I certainly have no plans to remarry,' Claire, Sally's stepmother, agreed more gently.

Tearfully Poppy nodded. 'I shan't marry now. Not now that Chris... Not now...' Fresh tears filled her eyes as she solemnly joined the other two in a pledge of solidarity.

All three of them raised their glasses, none of them aware that their conversation had been overheard...

CHAPTER ONE

CLAIRE MARSHALL gave a rueful look at the now empty, still confetti-strewn reception area of the hotel.

Was it really less than a couple of hours since her step-daughter and her new husband had run laughing down those stairs, trying to dodge the happy bombardment of rose petals?

Most of the guests had left now, just a small nucleus remaining in the hotel lounge. She had only come back in here to check that nothing had inadvertently been left behind.

It had been a lovely day, a perfect wedding, marred only by the fact that her husband, Sally's father, had not been with them.

It was over two years now since his death but she still missed him; he had been a good husband—kind, loving, protective. As she bent to touch the bouquet which Sally had so cleverly tricked the three women into catching, Claire acknowledged that the adjectives she was using to describe her husband were more those that she would use to describe a loving father.

'You should marry again,' Sally had urged her more than once recently. Sadness darkened her eyes. She had been lucky to find one loving and understanding man; she doubted that she would ever be lucky enough to find a second. And besides, she didn't really want to marry a second time—to make explanations, excuses or apologies.

She was distracted from her thoughts as both the adult bridesmaids came to join her. Poppy, the bridegroom's cousin, glowered angrily at the bridal bouquet and curtly echoed Star's earlier bitter comment.

'No one pays any attention to those silly old superstitions these days anyway...'

Claire gave her a gentle smile. Sally had confided to her that it was an open secret in her new husband's family that his cousin had been hopelessly in love with him for years.

Poor girl, Claire thought compassionately. No wonder she looked so pale and strained; the whole day must have been an unbearable ordeal for her, and the bridegroom's brother hadn't made things any easier for her. She had accidentally come across the pair of them deep in the middle of a very angry quarrel earlier and she suspected now that at some point in the day Poppy had been crying.

'I never want to get married—never!' Poppy announced savagely now.

'A statement with which I fully concur,' the third member of the trio murmured calmly.

Claire turned her head to smile at her stepdaughter's closest and oldest friend. Claire could remember quite vividly how as a young teenager Star had always insisted that she never intended to marry and that her career was going to be the most important thing in her life.

'Such a shame that none of us truly appreciated Sally's gesture,' Claire commented ruefully as she picked up the bouquet and studied it.

'Careful,' Star warned her drily. 'You don't know what effect holding it could have...'

Claire laughed but she still replaced the bouquet. 'It is only a tradition,' she reminded the other two.

'Mmm…but perhaps for safety's sake we ought to do something constructive to ensure that we stick to the vow we made earlier and remain unmarried,' said Star.

'Such as what?' Poppy demanded, adding bitterly, 'Not that I shall ever change my mind…if I can't…' Tears were already filling her eyes. Angrily she blinked them away.

'Look, why don't we agree to meet, say, once every three months just to remind each other that we intend to stay husband-free? Then if one of us does start slipping we've always got the others to turn to for support,' Star suggested.

'I won't need any support,' Poppy declared.

But Claire, who could sense already how Sally's marriage was bound to alter the relationship they each had with her and one another, said firmly, 'I think that's a very good idea. Let's make a date to meet here three months from now. We can have lunch together…my treat.'

'Great, I'll put it in my diary,' Star confirmed.

Claire looked across at Poppy. She didn't know her as well as she did Star, who had been Sally's best friend ever since they had started senior school together, but she could sense how unhappy the younger girl was. It must have been hard for her, seeing the man she loved marrying someone else.

Sally had confessed that when she had first heard about Poppy she had been inclined to feel very wary of her but that once she had met her, and knowing how strong Chris's love was for her, she had simply felt desperately sad for her.

'It must be so awful loving someone who can't love you back in the same way,' Sally had said. 'Chris likes her, of course—she's his cousin—but…'

'But he loves you,' Claire had agreed.

Sally had come over to her and given her a quick hug. They had always got on well together from the moment

John had introduced them. Sally had been a pupil at the huge comprehensive where Claire had done her teacher-training practice.

She had often wondered if one of the reasons why Sally had accepted her so lovingly and so readily as her stepmother had been that she had never known her own mother. Sally's mother, John's first wife, had died just after Sally's birth.

'Paula will always be part of my...of our lives. I shall always love her,' John had told her seriously when he had proposed to her.

She had accepted that, felt warmed by it, almost reassured... Knowing how much he had loved his first wife and still loved her made her feel...safe.

Sally had once asked innocently when Claire was going to have children of her own and when she was going to have a little brother or sister. Claire had had to turn away from her, leaving it to John to answer, to defuse the situation.

She sighed faintly now. Of course she would have liked children, if things had been different. As a girl she had always imagined that one day she would have them.

'I think we ought to be going now,' she told the two bridesmaids. 'I don't think we've left anything behind. I can't see anything, can you, Poppy?'

'No. There's nothing left,' Poppy agreed drearily. 'Not now.'

Claire gave her a quick look but said nothing. It seemed kinder not to.

'So now that the wedding is over, what do you intend to do with the rest of your life?'

'Oh, I don't plan to make any major changes,' Claire told

her sister-in-law. 'I'm thinking of putting in a few more hours at the school but apart from that...'

Claire worked part-time as a volunteer at a local school for mentally and physically handicapped children. John had left her very well provided for financially but, as she had explained to his sister, Irene, when she had first started working at the school, she felt that she wanted to put something back into the community, and since she had originally trained as a teacher...

'Mmm, you wouldn't be interested in taking a lodger, I suppose?'

'A lodger?' Claire stared at her.

'Mmm...a colleague of Tim's who wants somewhere "home-like" to stay. A service flat is out of the question. He doesn't care for that kind of anonymity. He's an American and from a large family and he doesn't want to live alone.'

Irene went on to give her details of his background, before concluding, 'He's in his late thirties, not a young student, and it simply wouldn't be appropriate to put him in to just any kind of lodgings. He holds quite a high position in the company,' Irene said. 'In fact his family own it.'

'How high?' Claire asked her, alarm bells ringing.

'He's Tim's boss,' Irene told her a little stiffly.

'Ah, I see.' Claire grinned. 'He's Tim's boss and it's down to Tim to come up with somewhere suitable for him to stay, is that it? I can't see why you don't move him into your house, Irene,' Claire told her mock-innocently. 'After all, you've got the room, with Peter away at university and Louise working in Japan.'

'No, I don't think that would be a good idea. Things aren't going all that well for Tim at the moment—sales have dropped and there have been problems with delivery and installation. I keep telling Tim that he should be tougher, more assertive—' She broke off, shaking her head.

'Would you do it, Claire?' she asked with unfamiliar humility. 'Tim is getting himself in a dreadful state about the whole thing. Apparently this American, his new boss, is something of an...individual—'

'An individual...? What does that mean?' Claire asked her warily.

Irene started to frown. As Claire knew from past experience, likeable though her sister-in-law was, she was inclined to steamroller people in order to get her own way when it suited her, and Claire could tell that she wasn't particularly pleased at having been interrupted and questioned.

'I'm sure he's not an awkward character. Oh, Claire, I wouldn't ask you,' Irene pleaded, 'but Tim is feeling so vulnerable about his job at the moment. He has convinced himself that this American is coming in very much as a new broom; psychologically it will make him feel so much more confident if he feels that he's done something constructive ahead of his arrival...'

'"Something constructive"? Are you sure this man is going to want to be my lodger? From the sound of it, it seems to me that he's used to a far more luxurious lifestyle than I enjoy. You know how quietly I live, Irene. I've never been a keen socialiser.'

'No, maybe not, but people like you, Claire; they feel drawn to you—your house is always full of callers, your phone never stops ringing.'

Claire digested her comment in silence, knowing that it was an argument she could not refute.

John had often remonstrated with her about her tendency to attract people who needed a shoulder to cry on. The only time the big Edwardian house had ever really been quiet had been during those pitifully brief weeks leading up to John's death, and then only because Claire had specifically asked people not to call. She still missed him dreadfully—his support, his wise counsel, his protection.

His protection.

A tiny tremor shook her body.

'Irene, I don't think that it would be a good idea... I—'

'Oh, Claire, please.'

As Claire looked at her sister-in-law she could see that her anxiety was genuine. She gave a small sigh.

'Very well, then,' she agreed. 'But I doubt that this man, Tim's new boss, is going to be very thrilled when he discovers—'

'Nonsense. Your house complies with all his stipulations,' Irene told her, then proceeded to tick them off on her fingers as she listed them.

'It's a proper home right in the centre of the community—well, at least in the best residential part of the town. You've got a proper guest suite—or at least you will have now that Sally's gone. He can have her old room and bathroom and he can use one of the other bedrooms as an office. After all, you have got five of them.

'There's a garden with adequate space for his car. He'll be part of a large family network—'

'What? There's only me,' Claire protested.

'No, there's not; there's Sally and Chris and all his family and us, and you've got enough friends to fill a fair-sized church hall twice over. You're a member at the sports club so you'll be able to take him there and—'

'I'll be able to take him where? Hang on a minute, Irene...' Claire started to protest, but her sister-in-law wasn't listening to her any more.

She was standing up, reaching out to hug her affectionately and gratefully as she told her warmly and, Claire was sure, slightly triumphantly, 'I knew you'd do it… It's the perfect solution, after all. Tim will be so pleased and relieved. He was terrified that you might not agree, poor dear, especially since…'

'Especially since what?' Claire demanded suspiciously.

'Well, it's nothing really; it's just that this man is due to arrive tomorrow and of course he's going to expect Tim to have worked out his accommodation requirements. We've booked him into an hotel for the first couple of days…'

'He's arriving tomorrow?' Claire protested, and demanded, 'Irene, just how long have you known—?'

'I must run,' Irene interrupted her. 'I've promised Mary I'll give her a hand sorting out the cricket teas and I'm already late.

'We're picking Brad up from the airport when he arrives, and naturally we thought we ought to have him for dinner tomorrow evening. You'll join us, of course. It will be an ideal opportunity for him to meet you and for you to make arrangements to show him the house…'

'Irene…' Claire started to remonstrate, but it was too late. Her sister-in-law was already beating a strategic retreat.

'What on earth are you doing?'

Claire raised her flushed face from her kneeling position in the bathroom adjacent to the spare bedroom and put down her damp cloth.

She hadn't heard her friend and next-door neighbour Hannah come in.

'Clearing out this room ready for my new lodger,' she told Hannah breathlessly, and quickly explained to her what had happened.

'Oh, trust Irene; she really has pulled a fast one on

you this time, hasn't she?' Hannah commented wryly. 'A lodger, and single too, I imagine, otherwise he would be looking for a house to rent. Mmm…that's going to cause a bit of excitement in the close… Wonder what he looks like…?'

'I don't know and I don't care,' Claire told her firmly, standing up and surveying the tiles she had just finished polishing with an abstracted frown, pushing one hand into her hair to lift its heavy weight off the nape of her neck.

Thick and naturally curly, its rich dark exuberance was the bane of her life. Sally often teased her enviously that, with her petite, small-boned frame and her small, heart-shaped face, framed by her glossy chestnut curls, she looked young enough to be her peer rather than almost a decade her senior.

'You should be being one of my bridesmaids,' Sally had teased her. 'You certainly look young enough to get away with it.'

Claire had shaken her head over such foolishness. She was, she had reminded her stepdaughter, a mature woman of thirty-four.

'A mature woman?' Sally had scoffed unrepentantly. 'You look more like a young girl. It's odd, you know,' she had added more seriously, 'but, despite the fact that you'd been married to Dad for over ten years when he died, there's still something almost…almost—well, virginal about you.'

She had given Claire a wry look as she'd spoken. 'I know it sounds crazy but it's true, there is, and I'm not the only one to think so. Chris noticed it as well…'

'You're unreal, do you know that?' Hannah told her fondly now. 'Here you are, an adult, fully functioning woman in the full power of her womanhood…without a man, and you turn round and tell me…'

As she saw the look Claire was giving her Hannah backed off, apologising.

'All right, all right… So I know how close you and John were and how much you must still miss him. It just seems such a waste, that's all. One thing does puzzle me, though; if this guy is Tim's boss, what on earth is he doing looking for lodgings? Why doesn't he—?'

'He wants to live in a family home,' Claire explained patiently, repeating what Irene had told her.

'Apparently he's used to having a large family around him. According to Irene, he and his brothers and sisters were orphaned when his parents were killed in an accident. He was just eighteen at the time and he stepped in as a surrogate parent, put himself and all of them through college, then took a job locally with the family business to keep the family together.'

'Oh, I see, and I suppose he was too busy taking care of his siblings to have time to marry and have his own family… Mmm…I wonder what he is like? He sounds…'

'Incredibly dull and worthy,' Claire supplied wryly for her.

Both of them started to giggle.

'I wasn't going to say that,' Hannah protested. 'Oh, by the way, what's all this about you and Sally's two bridesmaids making a pact to stay single?'

'What?'

Claire gave her a confused look and then realised what she meant.

'Oh, that… It wasn't so much of a pact, rather an act of feminine solidarity,' she explained ruefully.

'I felt so sorry for poor Poppy, Hannah. It's no secret how she feels about Chris. Sally was in two minds about whether or not to ask her to be her bridesmaid, not because she didn't want her, but because she was worried about the strain it would place her under. But, as she and Poppy agreed, for her not to have done so could have placed Poppy in an even more invidious position.

'And as for Star—well, you know her background; her mother has been divorced several times and is currently having an affair with a boy who's younger than Star and her father has, at the last count, nine children from four different relationships, none of whom he seems to have any real time for. It's no wonder that Star is so anti-marriage...'

'So it isn't true, then, that the three of you took a vow to support one another in withstanding the famous power of the bride's wedding bouquet?' Hannah teased her archly.

Claire stared at her.

'Who told you that?'

'Ah...so it is true... Someone—and I'm afraid I simply cannot reveal my source—happened to be walking past the door and overheard you.

'I don't know if it's true, but I have heard rumours that there are plans to run a book on the odds of the three of you being unattached by the time Sally and Chris celebrate their first anniversary.'

'Oh, there are, are there?' Claire retorted fiercely. 'Well, for your information... I shall never marry again, Hannah,' she said, more quietly and seriously. The laughter died from her friend's eyes as she listened to her. 'John was a wonderful husband and I loved him dearly.'

'You've only been widowed for two years,' Hannah reminded her gently. 'One day some man is going to walk into your life, set your heart pounding and make you realize that you're still very much a woman. Who knows? It could even be this American,' she teased wickedly.

'Never,' Claire declared firmly, and she meant it.

She had her own reasons for knowing that there could never be a second marriage or any other kind of intimate relationship for her, but that was something she could not talk about to Hannah, or to anyone else. That was something she had only been able to share with John, and was just one of the reasons why she still missed him so desperately.

John had known her as no one else, man or woman, had or ever could, especially no other man—most especially another man.

As he boarded his flight for Heathrow Brad Stevenson was frowning. He hadn't wanted to take up this appointment in Britain; in fact he had done every damn thing he could to try to get out of it, and in the end it had taken the combined appeal of the president of the company himself and the retired chairman to persuade him to change his mind.

As he had faced his two uncles across the boardroom table he had protested that he was quite happy where he was, that the last thing he wanted was to be sent across the Atlantic to sort out the problems they were having with the British-based offshoot of their air-conditioning company, which they had insisted on buying into, against his advice.

'OK,' he had said at the time, 'so right now Britain is sweltering in a heatwave and everyone wants air-conditioning. Next summer could be a different story and you'll be left with a warehouse full of unwanted conditioners and a long, long haul until the next hot spot.'

It had taken all his powers of persuasion then to get certain British organisations to agree to fit the air-conditioning systems in their business premises, and by doing so he had managed to avert the financial disaster with their British distribution outlet which he had predicted, but enough was enough. The thought of spending God alone knew how much time rescuing the ailing outlet to get it running efficiently and profitably was enough to make him grind his teeth in angry frustration.

How the hell had those two old guys guessed that he had intended to take the easy way out and oh, so slowly ease himself out of the business and out of the task of eventually having to step into their shoes, which he could see looming ominously ahead of him?

He was thirty-eight years old and there were things that he wanted to do, things he needed to do, that did not involve running a transatlantic company.

There was that boat out on the lake that he still had only half built, for instance; that voyage he had been promising himself that he would make ever since his high-school days when he had earnestly traced the voyage of Christopher Columbus through the Indies and the rich, Spanish-owned lands of South America.

Yes, there were things he wanted to do, a life he wanted to live, now that he was finally able to do so—now that the last of his siblings had finally left home and got settled.

'You watch; you'll be the next,' Sheri, the second youngest of the family, had teased him. 'Now that you've not got all of us at home to fuss over you'll be looking around for a wife…raising a family with her, starting the whole thing over again…'

'Never,' he had said firmly. 'I've done all the child-raising I plan to do with you five.'

Sheri had given him a serious look. 'Has it really been so bad?' she had asked him quietly, and then, answering her own question, had said softly, 'Yeah, I guess at times it must have been. Not from our point of view but from yours. We've given you a hard time over the years but you've always stood by all of us, supported us…loved us… It hasn't really put you off finding someone of your own, though, has it, Brad? Having your own kids?

'I mean, look at all of us… All of us married and all of us with kids except for Doug, and he's only just got married. My bet is, though, that he and Lucille won't want to wait very long. You've been so good to all of us; I hate to think—'

'Then don't,' Brad had advised her firmly, and after one look at him Sheri had acknowledged that there were times when, for all his great love for them, it was best not to push her eldest brother too far.

She didn't care to think what would have happened to them if Brad hadn't been there to take charge when Mom and Dad had been killed. There were six years between him and Amy, the next eldest, who had been twelve then, but no more than a year to eighteen months between Amy and the rest of them, going right down to Doug, who had been only just five. The accident had happened twenty years ago.

Brad had tried his best to get out of going to Britain to act as his uncle's right arm and troubleshooter, even resorting to what he had privately admitted was the unfairly underhanded ploy of laying down a set of criteria on how he wanted to live whilst he was in Britain, which he'd known full well would be virtually impossible to fulfil. Or, rather, which he had assumed would be virtually impossible to fulfil. He had not reckoned with the British distributor having a widowed sister-in-law who could, apparently, provide him with exactly the homely living accommodation he had specified.

Brad was grimacing to himself as he took his seat on the plane, but the stewardess still cast a dazzling and very approving smile in his direction. Unusually for a first-class passenger, he was wearing a pair of soft, well-worn denims and an immaculate white T-shirt that revealed the firm, tanned muscles of his arms—and hid what she suspected would prove to be the equally tanned and certainly equally firm muscles of his torso.

Generally speaking, she didn't care for such dark-haired and formidable-looking men; macho was all very well in its way, but she preferred something a little softer, a little more malleable. In this particular hunk's case, however, she was willing to make an exception, she decided enthusiastically.

It was true that those grey eyes looked as though they could hold a certain stern frostiness if required to do so, but there was no denying the sexual appeal of those thickly curling dark eyelashes or the hawkish, downright sexiness of that male profile with its warmly curved bottom lip.

'Miss, miss...we're Row F; where is that, please...?' Reluctantly she turned her attention to the middle-aged couple approaching her. Just her luck, she thought—it was a busy, fully booked flight and she doubted that she would get any spare time to flirt with their sexy solitary passenger.

Brad was aware of the stewardess's interest but chose to ignore it. He was not in the market for a relationship right now—of any kind. What he wanted more than anything else was to get this business in Britain all cleared up and functioning profitably so that he could hightail it back to the States and tell his uncles politely but firmly that there was no point in them looking to him to step into their shoes.

He wanted out. What he had in mind for his future was not another twenty-odd years worrying over the fate of the family business and its employees, but the freedom to pursue his own life and his own dreams.

What he had in mind was to leave work altogether, to finish building that boat of his, and then, who knew what...? To sail it around the world, maybe...? To do, in short, all the things he had never had the opportunity to do when he was younger, when he had been busy and too preoccupied with raising his brothers and sisters. He deserved some time for himself, didn't he?

He wondered briefly what the elderly widow would be like. Not too fussy and house-proud, he hoped. He was beginning to regret using that particular delaying tactic and he wondered how quickly he would be able to make his excuses to his landlady and explain that he had changed his mind and decided that it might be better if he rented himself an apartment. He had certainly never expected Tim Burbridge to come up so quickly with someone who so closely fitted all his criteria.

Worrying about hurting his prospective landlady's feelings by telling her that he had changed his mind should have been the last thing on his mind, he told himself as the plane started to lift into the sky.

Somewhere over the Atlantic he fell asleep. The stewardess paused to watch him, wondering enviously if there was already a woman in his life and how it must feel to wake up beside him every morning. Sighing regretfully, she moved further down the aisle.

CHAPTER TWO

CLAIRE was having a bad day. In fact, it had been a bad day from the moment she had woken up and remembered that this evening she was due to meet her prospective lodger for the first time. Irene had rung to stress to her how important it was that Tim's new boss was made to feel welcome and at home.

'I'll do my best,' Claire had promised meekly, but she had felt that Irene was going a touch too far when she'd informed her that she had borrowed from a friend with American connections a recipe book containing favourite traditional American recipes.

'There's a recipe in it for pot-roast, which, apparently, they love, and one for pecan pie and—'

Hurriedly thanking her, Claire had quickly brought the telephone conversation to an end. In the brief time which had elapsed since Irene had used strong-arm tactics to make her agree to help she had already begun to regret her decision, but, as yet, she had been unable to find the courage or the excuse to rescind it.

She liked Tim, who was a gentle, amiable man, technically brilliant in his field but slow to express himself verbally, unaggressive in his approach to others. She liked Irene as well, of course, but...

The small hand tugging on her arm distracted her from

her private thoughts. She smiled lovingly and patiently as
she waited for Paul to say something to her. He was the
oldest of the children who attended the school, and whilst
mentally extremely clever and quick, suffered very badly
from cerebral palsy.

All the children were special in their own way but she
had a particularly soft spot for Paul.

It was a lovely, warm, sunny spring day and, knowing
how much they enjoyed the treat, she had taken Paul and
one other child for a walk in the local park.

Everything had been all right until Janey, a Down's
syndrome girl, had seen the ice-cream van parked by one
of the exits from the park.

Both of them, of course, had wanted an ice cream, especially Janey, whose wide, loving smile touched Claire's
heart every time she saw her, as did her loving hugs and
cuddles.

Several other children and adults had already clustered
around the van, waiting to be served, and Claire had had
no inkling of what was to come as she'd joined them, although, as she had told herself bitterly later, she should
have done. She was not, after all, completely unfamiliar
with the cruelty with which people could sometimes treat
those whom they perceived as different from themselves.

It had been a young woman who'd started it, quickly
pulling her own child out of the way when pretty, brown-
eyed Janey had tried to reach out and touch the girl's
blonde ringlets.

'Keep away; don't you dare touch her,' she had
screamed, her daughter now frightened and screaming
too. Janey had also started to cry, but it had been the look
of resigned knowingness in Paul's eyes that had hurt Claire
most of all—that and the awareness that she could not protect him from that knowledge.

As the other woman had led her screaming child away she'd turned round and shouted to Claire.

'You ought to be ashamed of yourself. Kids like that should be with their own sort, not allowed to mix with normal kids.'

It had been Paul—bright, clever and pitifully physically limited Paul—who had asked her on the way back, 'What did she mean, Claire—our own sort...?'

She had wanted to cry then. But not in front of them. To have done so would have demeaned everything that they struggled so hard to achieve, everything that they were, but she would cry later in the privacy of the staff loo.

Now, as she walked Janey and Paul back through the park to their respective homes, Janey 'helping' to push Paul's chair, she hesitated when Paul asked if they could stop for a while to watch several children playing football.

Janey was starting to get tired and they still had several minutes before Paul's mother would be home from her part-time job, so they headed for a nearby bench.

A man was seated on it, watching the young footballers. A parent? Claire wondered. An odd feeling, unfamiliar and, because of that, all the more disconcerting, threw her very much off balance as she glanced at him. It wasn't, surely, those warmly tanned, hard-muscled male forearms revealed by the immaculate white T-shirt that were having such an extraordinary effect on her, was it?

Hastily she assured herself that it couldn't possibly be. Other women might be susceptible to that kind of arrant male sexuality, but she most certainly wasn't. Quite the opposite. Open male sexuality was something she invariably found distasteful, alarming...sometimes even threatening.

It certainly didn't normally have the effect of making her glance want to linger and examine...to explore...

A sudden flush of embarrassed, self-conscious heat

flooded her body. What on earth had come over her? No
wonder the man was frowning as he looked from the children to her and then back again to the children, watching
them, studying them…his frown deepening as he started
to stand up and walk away from them.

At her side Paul made a small, distressed sound, focusing Claire's thoughts and emotions on his feelings rather
than her own, and a huge fierce wave of protective anger
swamped her as she recognised the reason for Paul's pain.

Without giving herself time to think, she told Janey
quietly but firmly to wait with Paul and then ran after
the man, catching hold of his arm so that he stopped and
turned round to look at her.

'How dare you do that?' she exploded. 'How dare you
walk away from us like that…? Hurt them like that? They
are human beings, you know, just like us. No, better than
us, because they accept and love us. Have you any idea
how much it hurts them when people do what you've just
done? Have you no compassion…no understanding…?'

To Claire's horror she could feel her eyes starting to
flood with tears, her anger starting to die away as quickly
as it had arisen. What on earth had got into her? She had
never in her whole life behaved so aggressively to anyone
as she was to this man. It was simply not in her nature—
or so she had always thought.

Thoroughly shaken by her own behaviour, and ashamed
of her outburst, she turned to go but, to her shock, instead
of letting her walk away the man reached out and took
hold of her, imprisoning her shoulders with his strong grip.

Later, reflecting on the incident, her face burning with
chagrined dismay and guilt, she wouldn't be able to understand or explain her own lack of reaction at being thus
confined, or her own lack of fear, because she certainly
didn't feel any.

Shock, yes. Outrage, yes. But fear? No.

'Let go of me,' she demanded, struggling to break free.

But he refused to comply, giving her a gentle little shake and telling her in a soft, slow American accent, 'Will you quit yelling at me for a breath, woman, and listen to me...?'

Listen to him.

'No, I will not,' Claire stormed back at him, her rage flooding back. 'Let me go!'

'Not until you've let me have my say, you little fire-brand. You've had yours and now it's my turn...'

'Let me go,' Claire insisted, glowering up at him.

He had the most amazingly warm grey eyes, thickly fringed with dark, curly lashes. Her breath caught in a small gasp, the look in his eyes somehow mesmerising her, so that when he cursed softly under his breath and lowered his head—his mouth—towards her own she simply stood there, her own lips softly parted...waiting...knowing...

Just before his lips touched hers, she thought she heard him mutter, 'Seems to me like there's only one way to silence a feisty lady like you,' but, since her attention was focused far more on what he was doing rather than what he was saying, she couldn't be too sure.

It was a long time since she had been kissed by a man as if she was a woman, Claire acknowledged—a very, very long time. In fact, she couldn't remember ever being kissed quite so...quite so...

Her heart started to hammer frantically against her ribs as the firm, warm pressure of a kiss meant to impose silence on her somehow or other became the slow and deliberate exploration of her mouth by lips that seemed to sense, to know...to understand... She felt herself starting to respond, her own lips suddenly pliant and soft.

With a small, outraged cry Claire wrenched herself away, her face burning not just with indignation and shock but with something far more intimate and far more worrying.

'Look, I'm sorry... I never meant... I didn't intend...' he started to apologise.

'You had no right,' Claire stormed, but he wouldn't let her finish, shaking his head and agreeing firmly.

'No, I didn't, and I'm sorry. I overstepped the mark... It should never have happened... It's just that you made me so damned mad, ripping up at me like that...

'I didn't walk away from you because of the kids,' he told her quietly. 'Or at least not in the way that you meant. That bench over there is pretty small—not much room for me and the three of you, and so I did what I thought was the gentlemanly thing and decided to move on to give you your own space. It's the kinda thing we do where I come from,' he told her pointedly.

Claire could feel her flush deepening. She had never felt more mortified or embarrassed in her life, and not just because she had totally misjudged his actions.

She turned to walk back to the children, who were still waiting patiently and anxiously by the bench, and as she did so she realised that the man had fallen into step beside her. As they reached Paul's wheelchair he crouched down beside him and, giving him a warm smile, told him conversationally, 'I spent a few months in one of those a good while back.'

Whilst Claire watched, Paul's small, thin face glowed with happy colour as he slowly showed his new friend all the things his chair could do.

Janey didn't miss out on the unexpected attention either, disengaging her hand from Claire's and going up to Paul's chair, flirting coyly.

It was only later, when Claire had delivered both children to their respective homes and she had time to her-

self to review the entire incident, that a horrid thought
struck her.

That man, the American, he couldn't possibly be Tim's
new boss and her prospective lodger, could he? No, of
course he couldn't, she reassured herself. Tim's boss
wouldn't be sitting on his own in a small park watching
children, dressed in a T-shirt and a pair of faded jeans...
He wouldn't, would he?

If it had been him—if it had been—she had probably
solved the problem of trying to wriggle out of her agreement to offer him a temporary home. Irene would probably kill her, she decided faintly. No, not probably—Irene
would kill her!

'You look very...er...formal. Where on earth are you
going?' Hannah asked curiously, surveying the heavy calf-
length black skirt that Claire was wearing, and its equally
businesslike and repressive-looking tailored black jacket.

'Dinner at Irene and Tim's to meet my prospective
lodger,' Claire told her.

'Help! Poor man!' Hannah exclaimed, gulping back
laughter. 'One look at you in that outfit and he'll think
he's moving in with a Victorian matron. Where on earth
did you get that suit...?'

'I bought it for John's funeral,' Claire told her quietly,
adding quickly when she saw the guilty chagrin in her
friend's eyes, 'Oh, it's all right... I was in such a state
at the time I just bought the first black suit I could find.'

'Yes...well...for a funeral...but why are you wearing it
tonight? You'll be boiled alive in it, for one thing.'

'Irene wants me to make a good impression on Tim's
new boss,' Claire explained.

'In that? You'll terrify the life out of him,' Hannah protested. 'You can't possibly wear it. What about that pretty

knitted three-piece—the one with the little waistcoat? You look lovely in that...'

The oatmeal knitted outfit in question did suit her, Claire acknowledged. Sally had been with her when she had bought it and had insisted on her getting it, even though Claire herself had been inclined at first to think that it was too sexy for her.

'I don't think Irene would totally approve,' Claire told Hannah hastily.

'Irene might not but I'll bet your new lodger certainly will,' Hannah countered forthrightly. 'The honour of the close is at stake here, Claire; there is no way I can allow you to go out of here wearing that suit. No way at all...'

Claire gave a faint sigh, smiling ruefully at her friend.

'All right,' she agreed. 'I'll go and get changed...'

'Into the knit,' Hannah prompted.

'Into something,' Claire prevaricated.

'Into the knit,' Hannah said emphatically. 'And I shall come with you to make sure that you do.'

It was going to be easier to give in than to argue, Claire recognised, and if she didn't she was going to be late, which would really please Irene.

'Very well, then, the knit,' she agreed cravenly.

There was absolutely no logical reason at all for her to fear that her American—the American of the park—might be Tim's boss, Claire assured herself firmly as she parked her car in her sister-in-law's drive, behind Tim's large Volvo and the unexpectedly ordinary Ford which she assumed must belong to the American. After all, he had hardly looked as though he might be Tim's boss and an important, high-ranking executive with a successful go-getting American company, did he? He had looked... He had looked...

Hastily Claire dismissed the startlingly explicit and detailed printout that her brain immediately produced of the American's physical attributes and concentrated instead on the probable appearance of Tim's boss. He would in all likelihood be an American version of Tim—middle-aged, well fed, business-suited, going slightly bald.

A kind enough man, she was sure, she acknowledged quickly. He must be, given the brief, potted history that Irene had given her, but hardly the sort to wear the casual garb of youth with such devastating sexiness—which her American had, and with far more masculinity than the vast majority of those young men who did wear it, Claire admitted as she wove her way between the closely parked cars and headed for the house.

Irene had obviously been waiting for her because she was opening the door even before Claire knocked, beckoning her inside, telling her in a low voice that Tim and Brad were in the garden.

'Brad, apparently, is a keen gardener, so at least that's one thing you'll have in common,' she told Claire firmly as she led the way through the house to the small sitting room at the back where French windows led out onto a sunken patio with steps up onto the lawn.

Two pairs of male legs were currently descending those steps, both of them suit-trouser-clad. One pair—the bulkier pair—Claire immediately recognised as belonging to Tim; the other, she decided in relief, obviously belonged to his boss.

The navy wool with the fine, barely discernible chalk stripe running through it was such a reassuring contrast to the well-washed, snug-fitting jeans that were now beginning to haunt her that she almost laughed out aloud. How could her protagonist from the park possibly be...?

Claire literally felt the blood draining from her face

as the two men finally stepped down onto the patio and came into full view.

She could feel the sharp, questioning look that Irene was giving her as she inadvertently drew in her breath in a short hiss of horror, but she refused to look back at her. She dared not do so.

Her face felt as though it was burning hot with chagrined embarrassment and dismay and she knew too that he had recognised her just as instantly as she had him, even though he gave no indication to the others—thankfully—as he extended his hand towards her and said formally, 'Mrs...?'

'Oh, good heavens, there's no need for such formality. Claire—Brad,' Irene announced, quickly introducing them.

'Tim, get everyone a drink, will you, whilst I go and check on dinner...?'

'I...I'll come with you and give you a hand,' Claire offered, desperate to escape.

But Irene wouldn't let her, shaking her head firmly and telling her pointedly, 'No, you stay and talk to Brad. We'll drive you over to see the house tomorrow,' she told their other guest. 'But in the meantime, if there are any questions you want to ask Claire...'

Claire could feel her heart starting to thump unevenly and heavily as he gave her a long, steady look. Her face, her whole body felt so suffused with colour that she was surprised that Irene hadn't commented on it.

'I understand you're a widow...' was his only comment as Tim, obedient to his wife's commands, bustled about getting them drinks.

'Yes...yes. John, my husband, died some time ago...'

'And you've lived on your own since then?'

Claire gave him a sharp look, made faintly uncomfortable by some undercurrent to his words. What was he trying to imply? Did he assume that just because...just because he had caught her momentarily off guard this afternoon with his...his unforgivably arrogant male behaviour in taking hold of her and kissing her...and just because, for the briefest possible smidgen of time, she might actually have involuntarily and inexplicably responded to him... that she was some kind of...that she...that her widowhood had been filled with a series of relationships...men...?

Indignation as well as a certain amount of self-conscious guilt coloured her face a soft, pretty pink, but when she opened her mouth to refute his subtle condemnation to her own shock she heard herself saying almost coyly, 'Well, no, as a matter of fact...until recently there was someone...'

It was left to Tim, returning with their drinks, to rescue her from the potential consequences of her own folly by picking up the tail-end of their conversation and telling Brad jovially, 'Claire's only been on her own a matter of days. Sally, her late husband's daughter, was living with her until she got married—'

'Your stepdaughter,' Brad elucidated, turning to take his drink from Tim with a brief smile that was far, far warmer than the one he had given her but nothing like as warm as the one he had bestowed on Paul and Janey in the park this afternoon, Claire registered, wondering at the same time why on earth she should feel so ridiculously forlorn and shut out somehow because she was excluded from that warmth.

Well, at least one thing was pretty sure, Claire decided fatalistically; now that he had recognised her and knew who she was, Brad Stevenson was hardly likely to want to stay with her.

For some reason, instead of the security and relief she

would have expected to feel at such knowledge she felt a small and astonishingly painful stab of regret.

Regret...for what? Or would it be more appropriate to ask herself for whom?

'Yes...yes. Sally, my stepdaughter,' she agreed, flushing a little more pinkly under the look he was giving her.

'Claire is the sort of person that others just naturally gravitate towards,' Irene added, coming into the room to announce that dinner was ready. 'She always seems to have a house full of people. If John hadn't been so much older than her I'm sure she would have filled their home with children—'

'Your husband was a good deal older than you?' Brad interjected, looking even more assessingly at Claire.

What on earth was wrong with the man? Why did he have to make every question he asked her sound not merely like an accusation but virtually like a denunciation? Listening to him just then, she had heard quite clearly the disapproval and the cynicism in his voice, and she could see herself quite clearly through his eyes: the young, calculating woman deliberately enticing a much more financially well off and vulnerably older man into falling for her.

The truth was that her relationship with John had been nothing like that...nothing at all.

'He was older, yes,' she confirmed quietly now. Suddenly she felt very tired and drained. She was the one who should be questioning him, not the other way round, she told herself indignantly. How could she possibly allow him to move into her home after what he had done?

But, no matter how hard she tried to stir up a sense of injustice as they made their way to the dining room, honesty compelled her to admit that the last thing she had experienced in his arms was her normal lack of interest in sensual intimacy between a man and a woman and that she had, disconcertingly, actually responded to him.

Brad might have broken all the rules by kissing her but, startled though she had been by his behaviour, it had been her own unfamiliar and totally unexpected response to him which had really thrown her.

After years of passively accepting that she was simply not a very sexual person it had not been a pleasant experience to discover that she was in danger of responding to a totally unknown man with the kind of sensual hunger that she had always associated with books and films and with having far more to do with fiction than reality.

She still wasn't quite sure which aspect of her own behaviour she found the least palatable—the fact that she had been so unexpectedly sensually aware of and aroused by him or the fact that her behaviour had made her question if she knew herself as well as she had always thought.

Both led to the kind of in-depth thinking about herself and her past which she found easier to avoid than to face, which was probably why, right now, she found herself not just embarrassed to have met Brad again but almost antagonistic towards him as well.

Once they were sitting down and eating, to Claire's mild irritation and embarrassment, Irene started to list enthusiastically Claire's domestic abilities for Brad's benefit.

'Claire is a wonderful cook,' she told him when he had commented on her own cooking. 'Of course, my brother, John, was an extremely fussy eater and he never really approved of the fact that Claire insisted on growing her own vegetables...'

'Oh?' Brad gave Claire a curious look. 'Most health-conscious people these days take the view that home-grown produce is the best.'

'Oh, it wasn't that he disapproved of that,' Irene ex-

plained. 'No, John simply thought that that kind of gardening wasn't really suitable for a woman. He—'

'My husband would have preferred me to hire someone to look after our vegetable plot.' Claire felt compelled
to interrupt Irene and explain. 'He didn't think that sort
of gardening was... He felt I should confine myself to—'

'John was a very old-fashioned man,' Tim cut in, giving Claire an affectionate, supportive smile. 'He believed
that a woman's role in the garden should be confined to
the picking and arranging of flowers.'

'John simply didn't want Claire overtaxing herself.'
Irene bristled, quick to defend her brother.

'And besides, our mother always had someone in to
do the heavy work. Of course, you know, Tim, that John
always blamed you for Claire's interest in her vegetable
garden. You were the one, after all, who encouraged her,
going round there virtually every weekend to help her.'

Whilst Claire and Tim exchanged slightly guilty and
conspiratorial looks Irene sighed and shook her head,
grumbling about the amount of time that Tim gave to his
precious garden.

Then Tim commented enthusiastically to Claire, 'I'm
going to have another try with the asparagus, dig out a
new bed, and I was thinking... That south wall of yours—
there's no reason why we shouldn't try a grapevine on it.
There are some new strains now that are far more hardy.'

'You prefer the domestic environment, then, do you,
Claire?' Brad overrode Tim, his voice somehow unexpectedly hard-edged as he looked almost challengingly at her.
'You've never had any desire to have a career?' he asked
pointedly, or so it seemed to Claire.

'Being a stepmother to Sally and John's wife was my
career,' Claire told him stiffly.

'A career which is now over,' Brad said silkily. 'Haven't

you been tempted, as so many modern women are, to take up the challenge of making a place for yourself in the commercial arena? After all, these days there is no such thing as a job for life. All of us have to be flexible, adaptable and to accept that sometimes, for our own good, we have to change career paths.'

Claire could see how nervous Brad's comments were making Tim. Was he simply trying to get at her, she wondered, or was he using her as a means of warning Tim of what lay ahead?

Either way there was something she intended to point out to him.

'I did train as a teacher,' she told him coolly. 'That's how I met John and—'

'John wanted Claire to be at home for Sally once they were married,' Irene intervened. 'She works part-time now on a voluntary basis at a special school for disadvantaged children...'

'I see... Such work must be very emotionally draining. I should have thought you would prefer the...tranquillity of your gardening.'

'Plants can be as quarrelsome and awkward in their way as children,' Claire told him with unusual sharpness as she watched the way he looked from Tim's face to her own. 'And besides, it isn't the children I find hard to deal with so much as the way that other people treat them...'

'No matter how well intentioned they are or how well drawn up, no amount of anti-discrimination laws can genuinely legislate against people's prejudices—what they feel gut-deep inside themselves,' Brad told her quietly, his earlier sharpness subsiding.

'No,' Claire agreed. 'They can't.'

'I realise that it may not necessarily be of any comfort to you, but there is a school of thought that suggests that we can and do choose what we will and will not be when we are reincarnated on this earth, and that such children bring with them special gifts of courage and understanding.'

Claire gave him a surprised look. In view of what had happened between them she had not expected him to want to offer her any kind of emotional comfort.

As though he had read her mind, he told her calmly and unexpectedly openly, 'I went through a very bad time when my folks were killed. I was very angry, very resentful, very bitter. We were never what you would call a religious family but out local pastor did his best to help. He told me that some people found it helped to view such tragedies as indications that they were stronger than others, that somehow they must be and that they would find strength to overcome whatever had happened to them. Or perhaps he simply judged that I would react better that way.'

Instead of lapsing into silence and so escaping from the extremely odd and disturbing sensations, both emotional and physical, that Brad was somehow arousing inside her—sensations which were not unlike the unpleasantness of pins and needles experienced when feeling finally started to return to a formerly numb limb, she recognised warily—she heroically subdued her instinct to retreat into herself and said firmly to Brad, 'I understand that one of the reasons you want to lodge in a family home is because you have a large family back at home in America...'

'Yes,' Brad agreed. 'I'm the eldest of six. They've all left home and established lives and families of their own now—all but the youngest... He got married a short while back. But it doesn't stop there. Ours is a small town by American standards, and at times it feels like I can't so much as walk down Main Street without bumping into an aunt or a cousin or some other relative.

'My father and his two brothers set up an air-conditioning plant in the town in the early fifties. Until recently both my uncles still worked in the business. One of them retired on doctor's orders last fall and the other...'

He paused, his eyes suddenly becoming shadowed, and Claire wondered what it was he was thinking to have caused that look of mingled anger and pain.

It was gone eleven o'clock when she eventually left, and when Brad stood up politely as she said her goodbyes and came towards her she suddenly discovered that instead of holding out her hand for him to shake she was virtually on the point of lifting her face to his... For what...? For him to kiss... And not decorously and socially on the cheek either, but as he had done this afternoon—on her lips, on her mouth, slowly caressing and exploring, making her feel...making her want.

Hot-faced, she took a quick step back from him and almost barged into Irene, who was watching her frowningly.

'Well, don't forget that we're bringing Brad round to see the house in the morning, will you?' Irene reminded her bossily as Claire turned to her. 'Will eleven suit you?'

'Eleven...yes. Eleven's fine,' Claire agreed jerkily.

She couldn't understand why on earth Brad hadn't already said that he had changed his mind. This evening they had made polite conversation with one another but it must be as obvious to him as it was to her that it would be impossible for them to live under the same roof.

She found him far too...disturbing...far too...male, and underneath her hard struggle for an air of calm she could feel her nerve-ends bristling with anxiety-induced aggression.

Just sitting there this evening on the opposite side of the dinner table to him had mentally and emotionally ex-

hausted her, although quite why he should be having such
an extraordinary effect on her she didn't really know.

Be honest with yourself, she told herself firmly as she
drove home; you never wanted to have him lodging with
you. Irene caught you at a weak moment and now that
you've actually met him...

Now that she had actually met him...what? Guiltily
she realised that the traffic lights had changed colour and
that the driver behind her was hooting impatiently for her
to move off.

It wasn't dignified for a woman of her widowed status to
experience emotions and physical sensations which more
properly belonged to the early years of a woman's sexual
burgeoning, although in her case her sexual burgeoning
had been delayed so that she had assumed that it would
never happen. Had been delayed—did that mean—?

Hastily she censored her thoughts.

Suddenly, she was defensively resentful of the way
Brad's unwanted intrusion into her quiet, well-ordered
life had brought to the surface issues, emotions and feelings that she had long, long ago thought safely buried.

It was a relief to get home, to walk into the familiar
warmth and smell of her own kitchen.

John had originally bought the house on his marriage
to Sally's mother, and, as he had explained to Claire, since
it had always been Sally's home he felt it would be unfair
to her to sell it and move somewhere else, especially since
it was such a large and comfortable house situated in the
most sought-after area of the town.

Claire had agreed with him—genuinely so. She herself had liked the house from the first moment she had
walked into it, from that very first night when John had
taken her there. It had felt right somehow—welcoming,

warm, protective, reaching out to hold her in its sturdy Edwardian embrace.

She had known, of course, that there were other reasons why John didn't want to move. He had loved his first wife very, very much indeed. The house was a part of her, her home. Even now there were still photographs of her in the drawing room, and an oil painting of her hung at the bend in the stairs, revealing how very like her Sally was.

Some of the rooms were still furnished with the pieces of antique furniture she had inherited from her family.

Down the years Claire had lovingly cared for and polished them and when Sally had announced her engagement she had immediately offered them to her.

'No, thanks,' Sally had told her, wrinkling her nose. 'Just thinking of how much it would cost to insure them makes me feel ill.'

'But they are yours,' Claire had insisted. 'Your father left them to you. They were your mother's...'

'The best and most important gift my father ever gave me, the most valued asset he left, is you,' Sally had told her emotionally, hugging her fiercely, making them both cry.

'Until you came into my life, into this house, I can only remember how dull and dark my life was—how shadowed. When you came you brought the sunshine with you. When I hear people talking about wicked stepmothers I want to stand up and shout that it doesn't have to be that way, that there are "steps" who are genuinely loved and valued.

'Don't you dare even think of going out of my life, Claire,' she had told her stepmother fiercely. 'When I eventually have my children I want you there for them just like you were there for me. You will be their grandmother... you...and I will need you to be there for me and for them so much.

'I still wish that you and Dad had had children of your

own, you know. I know that Dad always felt that it wasn't
fair to me but he was wrong. You were the one he wasn't
fair to, and I would have loved a brother or a sister or, even
better, both...'

'Sometimes these things just aren't meant to be,' Claire
had told her huskily.

She loved her stepdaughter as though she were her own
child—had loved her from the moment John had introduced them. Sally had then been a solemn, too serious
and mature child, who had stood out from her peers with
her too big school uniform and the neat plaits which John
had copied from photographs he'd had of Sally's mother
at the same age.

It had been left to Claire to explain gently to him that
Sally felt self-conscious and different because of them,
that such a hairstyle was out of date and could tempt other
children to pick on her and bully her.

Those first years of her marriage had been happy, productive years. Years when she had eagerly reached out
to embrace the opportunity to put the past behind her—
something she felt she had done very successfully and
thoroughly.

So why had it now started to force its way past all the
careful barriers she had erected to protect herself from
it? And, more importantly, why was it Brad who was
somehow responsible for the unwanted turbulence and
disturbance of her normally calm and easily controlled
emotions?

CHAPTER THREE

'So COME on, then, tell me. What was he like...?'

'You'll be able to judge for yourself soon enough,' Claire told her neighbour placidly. 'Irene's bringing him round at eleven to look over the house.'

Hannah had called round ostensibly to show Claire a photograph of the hotel where she would be staying on holiday in Turkey, but Claire was more amused than deceived by her old friend's ploy to satisfy her curiosity.

'I'll go if you want me to,' Hannah offered, but without making any real attempt to dislodge herself from her comfortable seat at Claire's kitchen table.

In order to dispel some of her unwanted nervous energy Claire had been trying out a new biscuit recipe. The results of her work would be eaten by the children at the school, but there was a deeper purpose to her self-imposed task than merely the execution of her culinary skills.

The school, which was privately and voluntarily funded, with some council aid, took, in the main, children from backgrounds where for one reason or another there were certain social deprivations.

In many cases these sprang solely from the fact that the child's mother had to work and could not be there full-time, and one of the things Claire enjoyed doing was showing the children and teaching them when she could, the kind of simple domestic tasks which they would have learned as a matter of course in a different age.

The biscuit recipe she had been trying out this morning was of the very simplest variety and one she was sure that her children would thoroughly enjoy trying for themselves.

'Mmm...these are good,' Hannah opined as she sampled the first of the batch to be removed from the oven.

'I thought you were supposed to be on a diet,' Claire reminded her.

'Tomorrow,' Hannah muttered through a second mouthful of warm biscuit, turning her head in the direction of the kitchen door as they both heard a car pull up onto the drive.

'Oh, Hannah...were you just about to leave?' Irene demanded bossily as Claire opened the door to let her and Brad into the kitchen.

Hannah and Irene were old adversaries, probably because Irene knew that she couldn't boss the other woman about in the same way as she could Claire, Claire admitted wryly, mentally acknowledging that that was, perhaps, one of the reasons why she had not encouraged Hannah to leave. She didn't care to think of herself as being manipulative, but there were times...

'You must be Brad,' Hannah announced, ignoring Irene's suggestion to get up and go and shaking Brad's hand. 'I'm one of Claire's neighbours... Your neighbour too, I understand. You'll love living here with Claire; she'll spoil you to death,' she declared. 'She's a wonderful cook.'

'Mmm...smells like it,' Brad agreed pleasantly.

He was more casually dressed this morning, although not in the jeans and T-shirt in which she had first seen him. This time he was wearing a pair of plain, casual, neutral linen trousers with a white linen shirt and a soft knit neutral unbuttoned waistcoat. On another man such clothes might have looked too stylish and uncomfortable but Brad wore them so easily that they seemed; to be an intrinsic part of him.

There was something about a man who took an interest in his appearance but at the same time managed to look as if he didn't care if sticky little fingers touched his clothes that was infinitely appealing, Claire recognised. Too appealing, she warned herself hastily as she became aware that Brad had turned his head and was watching her watching him.

'I...er... Where would you like to start...? The bedroom?' she suggested quickly, and then for no reason that she could think of immediately blushed so hard and so colourfully that she felt completely humiliated by her ridiculous reaction.

What on earth had got into her? She was behaving like a...like a... She didn't know what she was behaving like, only that she didn't care for it, she acknowledged as Irene frowned at her and told her firmly, 'Brad will want to see the whole of the house, of course.

'My brother bought this house in the early days of his first marriage,' she told Brad informatively as Claire dutifully walked towards the kitchen door. 'It was very run-down then and he and Paula completely renovated it. Paula had very, very good taste and of course John was well off enough to indulge her.

'It was her idea to use some of the spare bedroom space to give each of the four main bedrooms its own bathroom, wasn't it, Claire?' Without waiting for Claire to reply she continued talking to Brad.

They were in the hallway now, all of them, Claire noticed in mild exasperation as she opened the double doors into the drawing room so that Brad could see for himself the colour scheme that Irene was describing.

Claire could remember the first time she had walked

into this room—how overawed she had felt by its pristine beauty and, at the same time, how protected and at peace. The whole room breathed serenity and beauty.

Without being conscious of what she was doing Claire frowned as she realised that the large, silver-framed photograph of John and Paula's wedding had been pushed to the rear of the display on the pretty Regency sofa table and her own much simpler wedding photograph pushed to the fore.

Sally, had done that, of course; she had had a bit of a thing about her father's insistence on giving prominence to his first wife's photographs, but Claire hadn't minded.

'Your late husband's first wife?'

Claire paused as Brad stepped past her and picked up the photograph she had just moved.

'Yes,' she agreed. 'Sally, my stepdaughter, is very like her mother...just as pretty, although John would never have it. In his eyes no one could ever measure up to Paula...'

She missed the frowning look that Brad gave her as he heard the conviction and warmth in her voice.

Didn't it bother her to know that her husband had loved her predecessor so much and, if not, why not? She was either an extraordinarily unusual woman or...

As he glanced around the beautiful, serenely immaculate room his eyes were caught by something that looked glaringly out of place—a very amateurishly stitched sampler which was framed and had pride of place on one of the walls.

Intrigued, he moved closer to study it.

'Paula's hobby was tapestry work,' Claire told him quietly. 'She stitched the cushions in here whilst she was pregnant with Sally. There were complications with her pregnancy which meant she had to rest.'

A small shadow touched her face. 'Unfortunately it wasn't enough and after Sally's birth... John lost her when

Sally was less than three days old. It was the most terrible tragedy...'

So tragic, Brad thought, that her husband had never got
over it, even though, eventually, he had found and married
her, and even though, from all that Irene and Tim had told
him, and from what he could see with his own eyes, she
was very obviously the kind of woman whom it would be
easy for any man to love... Too easy...

Brad's frown deepened. He didn't like the direction
his thoughts were taking—and kept taking, in fact, ever
since that incident in the park when, for God alone knew
what mad, impulsive reason, he had seized hold of her and
kissed her. Kissed her and felt her mouth soften into the
kind of quivering, softly feminine response that he couldn't
remember experiencing since he had left the heady days
of his early teens behind...

'We were all thoroughly relieved when he married
Claire,' Irene told him. 'There was a time when we were
beginning to worry that John was trying to turn Sally into
a carbon copy of Paula.'

'He was just trying to do his best for her,' Claire protested. 'He loved Paula so much...thought she was so perfect—'

She broke off as she saw the way that Brad was looking
at her—the mingled pity and curiosity she thought were
in his eyes. Pride and rejection of his unwanted compassion sparkled in her own eyes as she lifted her head and
looked back at him.

Her upbringing had had its share of pain, like Sally's.
Orphaned whilst she was still a toddler, she had been
brought up by a maiden aunt of her father's—a retired
schoolteacher who had had very strong views on the way
that children and most especially girls should behave.

Under her tutelage Claire had developed into an intelligent but socially shy and uncertain girl with very little in common with her peers.

Her great-aunt had died unexpectedly from a fatal heart attack whilst Claire was coming to the end of her teacher training. She had first met John a few weeks later, just after...

Brad, who was still watching her, wondered what it was that had suddenly made her look so haunted.

Despite the obvious tension it was causing between them, he couldn't bring himself to regret totally what had happened at their first meeting, but the passionately vibrant woman she had been then seemed curiously at odds with the woman she appeared to be now—a woman who seemed quite content passively to accept her role as a very poor second best to her husband's first wife.

She was such an obviously sensual and loving woman that he couldn't imagine how she could ever have been happy with a man who, from what he had heard about him, could not possibly have met and satisfied her emotional needs—or her physical ones either.

He frowned, angry with himself for the probing intimacy of his thoughts.

But he had seen for himself how warm and womanly she was, both with the children and with Tim, her gentle smile taking the edge off Irene's almost acerbic comments to her husband.

It was, perhaps, no wonder that Tim should choose to spend so much of his free time helping Claire with her gardening.

His frown deepened as he wondered if the relationship between them was as innocent as it had first seemed.

There had been nothing so far in Irene's manner towards either her husband or her sister-in-law to suggest that she suspected anything, but she was being remarkably insistent that Claire's home was the perfect place for him to lodge. Why? Because she felt that a third party living there would put a stop to any untoward intimacy between her husband and Claire?

If Claire was having a relationship with Tim, that would explain her shocked reaction to her brief response to his kiss—and the anger he had sensed in her both at dinner and again now.

He frowned again, unwilling to delve too deeply into why he should feel almost a personal sense of disappointment and loss at the thought of her being involved with another man.

What was really bugging him? The thought that his own judgement was at fault, that his first impression of her as a warm, open and very loving woman was wrong, or was it something more than mere pique at the possibility of having misjudged her?

What was Brad thinking about? Claire wondered as she saw the way he frowned. Did he, perhaps, not care for the house, or was it her he didn't like?

'If you'd like to follow me...' she told him, determined to sound businesslike and in control.

As he followed her up the stairs and along the landing Brad acknowledged that there was something about Claire that he found profoundly compelling; there was such a dramatic contrast between the warm, emotional woman who had flown at him with such fury to protect the feelings of her young charges and the cool, hostile person he was seeing now.

Claire had stopped outside one of the bedroom doors and was waiting for him to join her. Irene and Hannah had

both come with them and Irene frowned as she saw which
door Claire had opened.

'But that's your bedroom—yours and John's,' she protested. 'I thought you were going to give Brad Sally's bedroom.'

'This is larger and more...more suitable,' Claire told
Irene quietly.

'But where will you sleep...?' Irene demanded.

'I—'

'Look, the last thing I want is to deprive you of your
bedroom...' Brad began.

But Claire shook her head quickly, her face flushing
slightly as she told him, 'I...I had already decided to...to
move to another bedroom. This one...John's...John's and
mine,' she amended quickly, 'is too... The decor is much
more suitable for a man. It has an ensuite bathroom and
there's already a desk in the dressing room. John sometimes worked in there himself... I—'

'You've moved out of your own bedroom?' Irene was
persisting, apparently oblivious to Claire's lack of enthusiasm for pursuing the subject. She looked, Brad decided,
rather like a guilty schoolgirl caught out in some forbidden act.

Why? Why shouldn't she change bedroom if she
wished? It was, after all, her home...her house. He remembered the look in her eyes as she had talked about her
late husband's love for his first wife, the woman whose
"home" it had actually been.

'I was thinking of having it redecorated. It's never been
my favourite room, and—'

'But it's the master bedroom,' Irene protested.

'Yes,' Claire agreed with a quiet irony in her voice
which was obviously lost on Irene but which Brad picked
up on. So she was passionate and quick-witted too—a

dangerously alluring combination in a woman—or so he
had always felt.

The room was a good size, he acknowledged as he
stepped into it, with what looked like plenty of solidly
built dark wood closet space and a generously propor-
tioned, sensibly constructed bed. As he studied it Brad
let out a small sigh of relief. British standard-sized double
beds did not easily accommodate a man used to the luxury
of an American king-size, as he had already discovered.
This bed was the only one he had seen in Britain so far
that came anywhere near the spacious comfort of his own
at home, even if it was a little on the high side.

As he cast his eye appreciatively and approvingly over
the immaculate percale bedlinen, he acknowledged that it
would be hard for him to find anything to surpass the comfort that such a bed promised. From behind him he could
hear Irene saying almost accusingly to Claire, 'You've
changed the bedding...'

He could sense from Claire's response that Irene's comment had embarrassed her and guessed that the new bedlinen had been bought specifically for him. She really was
the most extraordinarily sensitive woman, he thought as
she showed him through to the well-planned bathroom
with its large bath and separate shower.

The dressing room was small, but plenty large enough
for the desk and chair already installed in it, and as she
waited for him to rejoin her on the landing he admitted
to himself that in terms of comfort and convenience it
wouldn't be easy to match the facilities of this house.

From the bedroom window he could see out into the
garden. Long and wide, it was split into a series of areas
by a variety of cleverly intermingled structures and plant-
ings, and a rueful smile curled his mouth as he espied

the smallest of the enclosed gardens with its swing and scuffed grass.

There was an area of equally stubborn baldness on his own lawn back home. When he had threatened to have the swing removed and the area reseeded the previous fall, the whole family had been up in arms, protesting against the removal of one of their sacred childhood haunts. The house was far too large for him now, of course. He really ought to sell it...

Outside on the landing Claire could feel her face start to flush defensively as Irene reiterated, 'Claire, I thought you were going to give him Sally's old room...'

'I...I didn't think it would be very suitable. The decor is so very feminine,' Claire told her, unwilling to admit that she had not wanted her stepdaughter to return from her honeymoon to find that someone else had taken over her old bedroom.

Sensitively she wanted Sally to be able to feel that the house was still her home, that her room was still her own and that she could return to it whenever she wished. Not that she anticipated that Sally would ever do so—nor did she want her to: her place, her home now was with her new husband.

'But to move out of your own bedroom...' Irene protested.

'It isn't my room,' Claire told her. 'It was John's room—our room,' she amended hurriedly as she saw Brad walking towards them. How could she explain to Irene—to anyone—how, after John had died, instead of finding comfort in remaining in the room—the bed—that they had shared during their marriage she had found it...empty and that she much preferred the smaller, prettier, warmer guest room that she had now appropriated as her own?

It hadn't been totally unfamiliar to her, after all; there

had been nights during her marriage when she had woken up and, unable to get back to sleep, afraid of waking John, had crept quietly into the solitude of the guest bedroom.

'So, Brad, what do you think?' Irene demanded with the confidence of one who already knew the answer she was going to get.

'I'm sure I shall be very comfortable here,' he declared, before turning to Claire and saying, 'We haven't had an opportunity to discuss the financial details yet, I know. Would it be OK with you if I called back later...say, this evening...to do so?'

'This evening? Oh, no, I'm afraid I can't; I'm going out.'

'You're going out?' Irene frowned. 'Where...who with?'

Claire had started to walk down the stairs, and as they reached the bottom Hannah appeared in the hall just in time to catch Irene's question and to comment, with a sly smile in Claire's direction, 'Well, it can't be with a man— not unless you're cheating already...'

Cheating? Brad frowned. Did that mean that there was someone in her life? It must be a man whom she didn't want Irene to know anything about, to judge from Claire's uncomfortable and slightly hunted expression.

'It's parents' evening at school,' she explained.

'But they can't expect you to be there,' Irene said. 'You only work on a voluntary basis.'

'No, they don't expect it,' Claire agreed, her voice and her manner suddenly a good deal firmer. She could be firm and indeed almost aggressive in her defence of those whom she deemed vulnerable and in need of her protection, Brad guessed—be it a child or an adult. 'However, I want to be there. I'm sorry I can't see you tonight,' she apologised to Brad. 'Perhaps tomorrow evening.'

The effects of his long flight were beginning to catch up on him and he still had to go out to the warehouse to see Tim, although he didn't intend to start any in-depth investigations into the difficulties of the British distribution and sales side of the business as yet.

He was already aware of how on edge Tim was in his presence and he could guess why; the spectre of redundancy haunted them all these days. Just as it no doubt would have haunted him were he married with a not quite fully adult and independent family.

'You should get married,' Laura, one of his sisters, had scolded him the previous Thanksgiving. She and the rest of them had certainly done their best to find him a suitable wife. He found himself wondering for a moment what they would make of Claire and then quickly caught himself up, warily aware of how unusual it was for him to have such a thought.

It was her differentness that intrigued him so much, he reassured himself—the complexity and contrast of what he had so far witnessed of her personality.

'Wow. Now that's what I call a real man,' Hannah commented, greedily munching another purloined biscuit when she and Claire had the kitchen to themselves once again. 'He's not at all what I expected. I thought he'd be all crew-cut and loud checked suit.

'He's got the teeth, though,' she added thoughtfully. 'Americans always have good, strong teeth...all the better to eat you with, my dear,' she added mischievously, grinning widely when Claire gave her a suspicious look. 'And he does look as though he'd be rather good at that sort of thing...'

'If you're suggesting what I think you're suggesting—' Claire began primly, but then gave up, shaking her head as Hannah interrupted her.

'I'm not suggesting anything. I'm simply saying that

he's a very…sexy man. Perhaps there is something in that old myth about catching the bride's bouquet, after all,' she murmured thoughtfully.

'Hannah!' Claire warned her direfully.

'All right, all right, I know—you've taken a vow of celibacy and I shan't say another word; it just seems such a pity that it's all such a waste…'

After Hannah had gone, taking the rest of the biscuits with her, Claire walked slowly upstairs and then paused outside the door to the master bedroom, pushing it open slowly, with reluctance almost, pausing on the threshold before eventually walking inside.

This was the room she had shared with John throughout their marriage—as a bride and a young wife—but when she stood still in its centre there were no echoes of those years to ruffle its almost sterile blankness.

There was no sense, no awareness, no feeling in this room of people having lived intimately within the protection of its walls, of having laughed and cried, fought and made up, of having shared intimacies…of having loved. She had seen the way that Brad had frowned as he had studied the room and had worried anxiously that he too might have picked up on the room's lack of those intimate vibrations.

It was strange how one became accustomed to things, adapted to them, accepted them and eventually came to think of them as the norm. It took something—someone different to make one see things from a different perspective—to make one realise.

As she smoothed down the already smooth cover on the bed Claire realised that her hand was trembling. Her marriage…her life…her…her privacy…they belonged to her and to no one else. There was no need for her to worry

that someone else—that anyone else—would ever discover
them, she reassured herself firmly.

The only way he…they could ever do so would be if
she chose to tell them, and since she was certainly not
going to do that…

Brad was halfway through his meeting with Tim when he
realised that his wallet was missing. Mentally reviewing
the events of the day, rerunning them through his mind's
eye, he pinned down its possible loss to the moment when
he had leaned forward and then bent down to inspect the
workings on the shower on his tour of Claire's house.
Glancing at his watch, he decided that it would probably
be quicker and simpler to drive straight over than to waste
time telephoning to announce his arrival.

Breaking gently into Tim's long-winded description of
the vagaries of the British weather and its effect on the
sales of air-conditioning systems, he explained that there
was an urgent task he needed to perform.

As Brad parked his car in the drive he saw that Claire's
back door was slightly open in the homely way he remembered from his own childhood, and without thinking he
pushed it wider and walked in.

He found Claire in the drawing room, gently dusting
the face of one of the silver-framed photographs. When
she saw him she put it down quickly, guiltily almost, and
for some reason the defensiveness of her action angered
him, making him demand brusquely as he gestured towards the photograph, 'Wasn't there ever a time when you
were jealous of her, when you resented her and wished
that you came first, instead of always having to stand in
her shadow?'

Claire's flush, initially caused by a mixture of shock

at the unexpected arrival and embarrassment at the way
he had caught her behaving in her own home almost as
though she felt that she had no real right to be there, darkened to one of outraged anger.

'In your country it might be perfectly acceptable to
make personal criticisms and to ask intimate questions,
to pry into people's personal thoughts and lives, but in
this country it isn't,' she reprimanded him sharply. 'My
marriage—'

'Your marriage!' Brad interrupted her. 'In my country we don't classify the type of relationship you seemed
to have with your husband as very much of a marriage,'
he told her scornfully. 'In my country,' he stressed, 'no
woman worthy of the name would tamely accept being
pushed so obviously into second place by accepting second-best—'

'My marriage was not second-best,' Claire denied furiously. 'I knew when I married John how much he loved
Paula. I knew then that...'

'That what? All he wanted you for was to care for the
shrine to her that he had turned this place into? And you
were happy with that...you accepted that...?'

The contemptuous disbelief in his voice stung Claire
into defending herself. 'You don't know the first thing
about marriage.'

'Don't I?' Brad challenged her softly. 'I know as much
as any other man about what it feels like to be a man. Why
did you move out of your—sorry, John's—bedroom?' he
asked her.

'I... After John died...I didn't...'

'You didn't what? Like sharing your bed with a ghost?
Funny that, since all your married life you'd already been
sharing it with the ghost of his first wife.'

Brad didn't need to hear Claire's shocked gasp or to see

the anguish in her eyes to know that he had gone too far, said too much. He had realised it almost as soon as the cruel words had left his mouth but, of course, it was too late to recall them now; too late too to curse himself under his breath and to question what on earth had prompted him, driven him—him of all men, who had surely learned years ago to deal gently with other people's vulnerable emotions; you couldn't raise four sisters without doing so—to tear away another human being's defences so ruthlessly and so angrily.

Why? Why? What was it about this one particular woman that made him react so challengingly, so malely aggressively?

'I'm sorry,' he apologised quietly. 'You're right...I was out of line. It's just...' He gestured towards the photograph and told her, 'I guess it's just that I can't help thinking how I'd feel if you were one of my sisters. It can't have been easy for you...married to a man who...'

'Who what?' Claire challenged him. 'Who loved his first wife more than he loved me?' Her mouth twisted slightly as she saw the way he looked away from her. So she had embarrassed him. Well, it served him right. He was the one who had brought up the subject of her marriage, not her, and a little embarrassment was the least he deserved to suffer after what he had said to her...done to her.

'Well, I'm not one of your sisters,' she told him fiercely, 'and my relationship with John—our marriage was...' She paused, her eyes suddenly filling with tears.

'You must have loved him very much,' she heard Brad saying gruffly, whilst he wondered how and where Tim fitted into her life.

In a way what he had said was true, Claire acknowledged inwardly, only it wasn't so much John she had loved as what he had done for her. But that knowledge, those thoughts were too private to disclose to anyone, and most especially to the man now standing watching her.

'He's been dead for over two years now and yet you still keep this place like a shrine for him,' he commented. 'Why?'

Were all Americans so forthright, so...so openly curious about other people's private lives? Claire wondered in exasperation. Wasn't there anything she could say to get it through to him that his questions were too personal and unwelcome?

'It was her home,' she told him evasively, hoping that he would drop the subject and tell her why he had returned.

Instead he pounced on what she had said with all the skill and speed of a mountain cougar, repeating softly, 'Was... Past tense; she's in the past, but so are you. This is the present and you should put the past behind you...'

Now what had he said? Brad wondered perceptively as he saw the way her face changed, her body tensing.

'The past isn't always that easy to forget,' Claire told him in a low voice. 'Even when we want to—' She stopped speaking abruptly and Brad guessed that she had said more than she had intended.

'Why did you come back?' she asked him, changing the subject. 'Have you changed your mind about wanting to stay here...?'

She didn't really want to have him lodging with her, Brad guessed, and had no doubt been pressured into it by her over-assertive sister-in-law. Why? Because Irene was anxious to protect her husband's job or because she was anxious to protect her marriage?

Under normal circumstances the situation would have been enough to have him backing off, making some excuse to let her off the hook, but he recognised that he didn't want to lose contact with her—not yet...not until...

Not until what? Not until he had pinned down what it was about her that provoked such a range of volatile and unfamiliar emotions and reactions within him. If you really need time to work that one out, you really are in a bad way, he derided himself inwardly. She intrigued him, angered him...incited him...excited him, and if the time ever came when she shared her bed with him he'd make pretty damn sure that there were no ghostly third parties there sharing it with them.

'No, I haven't changed my mind,' he told her, pausing deliberately before adding softly, 'Far from it.'

It was interesting the way she had coloured up as betrayingly and vividly as a sexually inexperienced girl.

'I...I'd like to check over the bedroom if I may,' he continued. 'Er...which door was it...?'

Claire couldn't help it; she could feel the hot colour flooding up under her skin. She was quite positive that he knew exactly which door it was—he was that kind of man—but to challenge him would be to unleash on herself all manner of emotional hazards that she doubted that she had the strength of mind to negotiate, not least the appalling, clear mental image that she had just had of Brad laughingly, lovingly, gently drawing the shadowy figure of a compliant, eager woman towards the protective shadows of an invitingly open bedroom door, the bed just visible within—the bed on which he would very shortly be making expert and intensely erotic love to the woman clinging so eagerly to him.

But that woman wasn't her... That woman could never be her.

As Brad saw the way she glanced towards the stairs and the shadow that crossed her face, he felt irritably angry with himself for tormenting her. It was so out of character for him—the kind of masculine behaviour he had often verbally checked in his brothers.

'It's all right,' he told Claire quietly. 'I think I can find the way after all. It's just that I suspect I may have dropped my wallet there earlier; that's why I came back...'

'Your wallet...? Oh. I...'

He had come back for his wallet... Then why pretend...? She didn't understand. Claire frowned as she watched him taking the stairs two at a time and heading straight for the master-bedroom door.

There were a lot of things about Brad that she didn't understand, she recognised uneasily as she waited for him to come back down. But what disturbed her most was the fact that she was actually acknowledging that lack of understanding, giving it a gravitas that it certainly did not merit.

CHAPTER FOUR

CLAIRE grimaced to herself as she emerged from the bright warmth of the school to discover that it was raining—hard.

It had been dry and fine when she had left home earlier in the evening, and with time in hand she had decided to walk to the school instead of taking her car.

She hesitated for a moment, wondering whether or not to go back inside and ring for a taxi, and then, realising that she was already wet, pulled up the collar of her jacket and started to walk quickly down the road.

Whilst she had hesitated about whether to walk home or not she had been conscious in a hazy sort of way of the car which had pulled up at the roadside, but had assumed simply that the driver was collecting someone.

Even when she heard the engine fire and saw the brilliant sweep of the headlights illuminating the roadway ahead of her, she still didn't realise what was happening. That recognition didn't come until her brain, subconsciously waiting for the car to pick up speed and go past her, warily relayed to her senses the fact that it had not done so and what potentially that could mean.

Instinctively Claire reacted to that awareness, quickening her speed, her head tucked protectively down, her body movements designed not to draw any unwanted attention to herself as she fought not to give in to the urge to stop and turn around. She could hear the car crawling along the road behind her in much the same menacing and terrifying way that panic was now beginning to crawl its way along her tense spine.

One heard about such things...read about them—men who preyed on vulnerable, unprotected women. Her mouth had started to go dry, her heart was pounding. The area of the town she was walking through was void of any private homes—just empty shops and public buildings with no other pedestrians in sight. Whilst the rest of the traffic sped past, either oblivious to or uncaring about the slow crawl of the car behind her, it continued its slow, deliberately menacing pursuit.

Not daring to risk turning round, Claire tried to walk even faster. Beneath her clothes she could feel the hot, nervous perspiration drenching her skin; her heart was beating so suffocatingly loudly that she could no longer hear the sound of the car engine.

Her body stiffened abruptly in terrified shock as she realised why. The car had stopped. She heard the sound of a car door being slammed, followed by determined male footsteps.

'Claire... Claire...'

Claire! Her pursuer knew her name.

Trembling from head to foot, Claire turned round, her eyes widening in disbelief as she recognised Brad coming towards her.

Brad... Brad had been following her. A combination of nausea and fury gripped her by the throat, rendering it impossible for her to speak or move as Brad came up to her.

'You're soaked,' she heard him saying to her. 'Come and get in the car...' He stretched out a hand, as though to guide her towards the waiting vehicle, but Claire shrank back from it, fury burning with fevered intensity in her eyes.

'What is it…? What's wrong?' she heard him demand, impatience edging up under his voice as she pushed his hand into his own now damp hair, grimacing in disgust as the heavy droplets of rain ran down the inside of his collar.

'"What's wrong?"' Claire stared at him in disbelief; her voice was cracked and harsh. 'I thought you were following me,' she told him.

She could see from his frown that he didn't understand.

'I was,' he agreed. 'I saw you coming out of the school. I was driving past on my way to the hotel…'

As he watched the way she backed off from him Brad was filled with guilty remorse. It had never occurred to him that she would mistake him for a stranger—the kind of pervert who preyed on solitary women.

'Hey, look…it's all right,' he tried to comfort her. 'I'm sorry; I—'

'You're sorry…?' Claire's voice was shaking as much as her body as she flung the words back at him.

'Claire!'

'No, don't touch me,' she demanded as she stepped back still further to avoid the hand that he was reaching out to her, only to be thrown heavily against him as a runner coming the other way whom she hadn't seen collided with her, knocking her so off balance that she knew that she would probably have fallen if Brad hadn't been there to prevent it.

The runner, obviously irritated by her and the fact that she had impeded his progress, muttered an ungracious curse before continuing on his way, leaving it to Brad to ask anxiously and quietly, 'Are you OK? That was some speed he was running at—quite some speed…'

'I'm fine,' Claire fibbed.

The physical shock of almost being knocked to the ground and the emotional trauma of fearing that she was being followed, stalked, by an unknown man were both taking their toll of her. Her head felt muzzy, her thought processes were slow and confused, her hip-bone ached where the runner had cannoned into her, her stomach was still churning nauseously and the trembling which had begun when Brad had first called out to her had now become an open shivering.

Add to all that the fact that she was also extremely wet and cold and 'fine' was just about as far from describing her condition as it was possible to get.

Brad obviously thought so too, because instead of accepting her polite disclaimer as his British counterpart would have done he immediately rejected it, exclaiming curtly, 'Like hell you are! You're soaking wet through and shivering fit to bust. Come on…let's get you into the car and home. What you need right now is a shower—a proper shower, good and hot and stinging, not these apologies for showers you have over here—followed by an equally hot, stinging drink… Are you OK?' he added. 'Can you walk as far as the car or would you like me to carry you?'

Would she like him to what?

Claire forgot for a moment that he still had both his arms around her, and her chin came shooting up proudly as she tipped her head back to look at him. Only it wasn't his eyes which her own were on a level with. It was his mouth.

Dizzily Claire stared at it, her tongue-tip hesitantly touching her own, suddenly dry lips; a swarm of confusing and unfamiliar emotions invaded her dazed senses.

The rain had soaked her hair, causing it to curl in soft ringlet tendrils around her face, making her, although she didn't know it, look closer to twenty-four than thirty-four. In the streetlight her skin had a luminous, transparent quality that made Brad want to reach out and touch it. British women had such delicate, pale skin, and Claire, with her fine-boned frame, had an added delicacy, a fragility almost, that aroused in him emotions...

The close contact with his body was warming her own, comforting it—an unfamiliar sensation to Claire and one that she instinctively responded to, luxuriated in on a level that was somehow beyond the jurisdiction of her normal strict self-control. Without realising what she was doing she nestled closer, exhaling her breath on a soft feminine sigh.

The hammer-blows of two different consecutive shocks had left her emotionally concussed, her senses and her emotions wandering blindly through an unfamiliar landscape where Brad was the only familiar landmark. Instinctively she clung to it...to him, her eyes huge and dazed in her pale face as she continued to focus on his mouth.

His mouth... It was strange to think that she had already been kissed by it. By him. Strange and dangerous and yet at the same time somehow headily exciting, alluring...with all the dark magic of something dangerous and forbidden.

She wanted to reach out and touch it, to trace its male shape, to...

The blare of a car horn on the opposite side of the road made her jump abruptly, bringing her back to reality, to normality.

Her face on fire with self-conscious anger and embarrassment, she tried to step back from Brad, shocked and confused by what she had been thinking—feeling.

'Come on; let's get you in the car,' he told her firmly, his voice as matter-of-fact as if it was not a very unfamiliar or shocking thing for him to have a woman staring up at his mouth...as though...as though... But then, perhaps it wasn't... She knew very little about him, after all, Claire reminded herself as she gave in and allowed him to walk her gently towards his car.

'I'm sorry I gave you such a bad shock,' she heard him apologising after he had helped her into her seat.

Claire couldn't bring herself to look at him and instead busied herself trying to fasten her seat belt. Her fingers felt numb and stiff, her actions slow and clumsy.

'It's just that I was on my way back from the office and I saw you coming out of the school and— Here, let me help you with that,' he offered, and without waiting for her agreement he gently pushed her hands away, leaning across her as he reached for the recalcitrant seat belt.

His hair was still damp and she could smell the cold, fresh scent of the rain on his hair and his skin. The nape of his neck, exposed as he leaned across her, was warmly tanned, unlike her own much paler skin. The rain had made his hair start to curl slightly.

A soft smile touched her mouth. She lifted her hand and then froze, her body stiffening in horror as she realised what she had been about to do. What on earth had come over her? The very idea… The mere thought of reaching out voluntarily to touch a man's skin…his hair…to stroke her fingers slowly through those almost boyish curls, to straighten them…was so alien to her, to everything that she was, that she could hardly believe she had actually been about to do it.

It took Brad's anxious, 'What's wrong? Is it your hip? I saw how hard he knocked you when he ran into you. It's bound to be bruised…' to bring her to her senses.

Claire felt the relief flooding through her as she realised that he thought her tension came from physical pain and hadn't understood…

'It's fine… I'm fine,' she told him brusquely.

'No, you're not,' Brad corrected her gently.

He was still leaning over her, looking directly into her

eyes, and her heart gave a fierce bound as she tried unsuccessfully to look into his.

'You're probably as sore as hell... You've had a pretty
nasty shock...a very nasty shock, I should say,' he
amended, 'if the way you reacted earlier is anything to
go by. Tell me, do you—?'

'I...I just don't like being touched,' Claire blurted out,
terrified of what he might be going to ask her, to force her
to reveal... 'Some people just don't...'

She was willing the betraying colour not to seep up
under her skin as she made herself meet his steady scrutiny
and willing herself as well not to remember the way she
had practically snuggled deeper into his arms such a very
short time ago, praying at the same time that he wouldn't
say anything about that either.

To her relief he didn't, saying only, 'No, some people
don't,' before giving her seat belt a small testing tug to
make sure that it was fastened and then turning away from
her to secure his own and start the car.

'I'll walk you to the door,' Brad announced after he had
completed the short journey to her house.

But Claire shook her head quickly, her voice slightly
huskier than normal as she said, 'No, no, it's all right...'

As he hesitated she added quickly, 'It's still raining
and there's no point in you getting wet again. I've got my
keys here and...'

For a moment Claire thought that he was going to insist on going with her; his body tensed and hers did too,
but then he seemed to change his mind, simply telling
her, 'Don't forget that hot shower or that drink. I'm not
sure what time I'll be through with the hotel in the morning but I'd like to bring my stuff over before lunch if that
fits in with your schedule. I've got an appointment with

our bankers in the afternoon and then in the evening we can talk terms.'

'Yes. Yes, morning will be fine,' Claire confirmed.

As he watched her run towards her door through the still heavy rain Brad wondered if he was doing the right thing. There was no denying that the feeling she aroused in him, his desire for her, was more than just a subliminal male impulse.

Earlier, holding her in his arms in the street, watching the way she had looked at him…at his mouth…

Come on, he warned himself; you haven't flown right the way across the Atlantic ocean to mess up your life with those kinda complications, to get hung up on a woman who may or may not be involved with another man.

And he wasn't the sort to want to indulge in some kind of casual, no commitment, no future type of sexual fling. Nor, he judged, was she. Which meant…which meant that he'd better put the thoughts and desires which had been running wild through his head virtually ever since he had met her way, way back in the darkest and most unreachable recesses of his mind, he told himself firmly as he saw the door close behind Claire's retreating figure.

After a brief pause he put his hire car into gear and backed out of the drive.

'No!'

The sound of her own voice uttering the sharp, high-pitched, frantic protest brought Claire abruptly awake, to sit upright in her bed, hugging her arms around her knees as she tried to control her body's frantic shivering.

Dry-eyed, she stared fiercely into the darkness, willing the nightmare to relinquish its hold on her.

It was not as though it was something she had never experienced before, even if over the years its frequency had decreased so that now it was something that occurred only when she was under some kind of stress.

No, the reason for the agitation that she was fighting so hard to banish now wasn't so much the fact that she'd had a nightmare—it was over now, after all, and she was awake—but that somehow it had developed a new plot—a new and extremely upsetting ending.

In the past it had always followed a familiar and recognisable pattern. The man...the darkened room, his hands reaching for her...his anger when she rejected him, her escape and his pursuit down narrow, dark, wet streets in which she was completely alone and unprotected, the only sounds those of her own terrified breathing and the pounding, ever closer footsteps of her pursuer.

In the past she had always managed to escape...to wake up before he caught up with her, but this time...this time...

Her teeth chattered together as her body gave a deep shudder.

This time she had not escaped; this time he had caught up with her, his hand...both his hands...reaching for her, holding her prisoner.

She had fought frantically against the horror of his re-membered and loathed touch, finally managing to turn round to face him, to plead with him for mercy.

Only when she had turned round the face she had seen had not been the one she had expected. Instead it had been Brad who had looked back at her, and inexplicably, as she'd recognised him, somehow the touch that had felt so terri-fying and so loathsome had become comforting and even more disturbing, actually welcome to her body.

Relief had filled her sleep-sedated body as her fear had turned to joy, and she'd actually stepped towards him, welcoming the firm warmth of his arms around her, the scent of his skin as he'd held her close, his jaw against her

hair as his arms had tightened around her and his voice
had soothed her.

'It's you,' she had said softly, breathlessly as she'd
pressed her trembling body against his, drawing support
from his proximity and strength, luxuriating almost in
the closeness of him, in the knowledge that with him she
was safe and protected, trembling between laughter at her
foolishness in ever having been afraid and tears because
of the memories that had caused that fear.

As he'd cupped her face in his hands and bent his head
to kiss her she had responded eagerly to that kiss, tightening her own arms around him, opening her mouth beneath
his, anticipating in her mind the sensual pleasure of feeling his naked body against her own—a pleasure which,
in her dream, both her body and her mind had recognised
as one with which it was already familiar. They had not
been new lovers unaccustomed to one another or unaware
of one another's needs; there had been a harmony between
them—an acceptance, a knowledge...

He had been so tender with her, so gentle, wiping away
her tears, sharing with her her emotional relief that he was
there holding her and that she had nothing, after all, to fear,
that with him she was safe...protected...loved...a woman
at last in every sense of the word...

A woman at last. Claire bit her lip now, balling her
hands into two tight fists of angry rejection. She was already a woman; she did not need a man—any man—to
reinforce that fact, and most especially she did not need
Brad to reinforce it.

She had no idea why on earth she had dreamed about
him like that and her face burned in the darkness as she
could feel the heat of desire, her dream of him affecting
her still...echoing through her body...

When Sally had talked about her marrying again it had

been easy for her to shake her head and say sedately that she was happy as she was.

No needs or desires had ever troubled her celibate sleep, and a comment made by another woman friend, when they had been having lunch together one day—that the young waiter serving them had a fantastic body—had left her feeling slightly shocked that her friend should have noticed and inwardly relieved that she herself had not.

Of course, there had been occasions over the years when she had felt uncomfortable with the knowledge that her own sexuality—or rather the lack of it—was so out of step with the times, but during the years of her marriage her life had been a very busy one. John had, in his own way, been a very quietly strong-willed man, and his confidence in the way their marriage worked had made it easy for her to ignore her own doubts about her lack of sexual desire.

Before now, at thirty-four and a widow, she had felt herself safe on the small plateau of security that she had thought she had found. There had, of course, been men who had shown signs of sexual interest in her, but she had gently and tactfully made it clear that she felt no corresponding interest, and the last thing she had ever expected to happen was that she should so unwontedly and inappropriately develop a personal sexual awareness of a man.

As she continued to stare into the darkness she felt as though a part of herself had suddenly betrayed her, become alien to her...and, because of that, somehow out of her control. Dangerously out of her control, she acknowledged, blushing as she fought to ignore certain memories of just how enthusiastically and passionately she had not just responded to Brad in her dream but actually initiated the sensuality between them.

Another shudder tormented her body, her skin now chilled by the cool night air, but her heartbeat was starting to return to its normal rhythm. Tiredly Claire lay down again, closing her eyes and willing herself to go back to sleep, but this time without dreaming about Brad.

Claire smiled ruefully as she reread Sally's postcard. It had arrived in the morning's post and showed an idyllic view of a soft white half-moon beach and an impossibly azure sea—'the view from the veranda of our beach-side bungalow', Sally had written.

They were honeymooning in the Seychelles and their hotel, according to Sally's ecstatic card, was every bit as wonderful as the brochure had promised.

Typically, though, as well as reassuring Claire that she was wonderfully, blissfully happy, Sally had added a cryptic postscript to her message, teasing Claire about the fact that she had helped to catch her wedding bouquet.

'Remember,' she urged her stepmother, 'you want a man you can have all to yourself, not one you've only got a share in.' A reference, Claire knew, to the fact that she had not been the only one to catch the wedding bouquet.

The arrival of Sally's card had helped distract her thoughts away from Brad and the disruption he was causing in her life. Nonetheless, when she heard a car pulling up outside her whole body tensed, and it was a relief to discover when she went to the door that her visitor was Irene.

'I'm just on my way to the supermarket and I thought I'd call to see if you needed anything,' her sister-in-law informed her as she came in. She gave a small sigh. 'Poor Tim; he hardly slept at all last night. Claire…if Brad should happen to mention anything about the company to you—'

'Oh, I'm sure he won't,' Claire interrupted her.

'Well, maybe not, but he is, after all, over here on his own and you do have a way of… Well, people do tend to confide in you…and the two of you will be spending quite a lot of time together…'

Claire stared at her.

'No, we won't,' she protested. 'We'll hardly see one another.'

'He'll be here at mealtimes…in the evening…you'll be having dinner together,' Irene pointed out. 'I mean, that was one of the reasons he wanted to live somewhere en famille, so to speak—because he didn't want the anonymity of dining alone in a hotel restaurant.'

Eating together… Claire swallowed nervously.

Later, as she walked across the kitchen, the American cookery book that Irene had given her caught her eye. Glaring irritably at it, she suffered an unfamiliar surge of rebellion.

If she had to feed Brad, then at least she could exercise some form of control over the situation by feeding him food of her own choice.

Determinedly she walked towards her freezer and removed the ingredients she wanted.

John had always praised her cooking. He had liked old-fashioned, simple home-made food, and over the years Claire had found ways of adapting recipes so that she was able to satisfy his taste for the food he remembered his mother making and also ensure that the meals she served were nutritious and healthy.

She had been particularly pleased with her version of his favourite beef-steak pie. That was as traditional a British dish as you could get, especially when served with her light-as-air dumplings and garden-fresh vegetables.

Pumpkin pie and pot-roast it wasn't, but it had been Brad's desire, his decision, to live 'en famille', as Irene had put it, and part of that, as far as she was concerned, meant eating the food she chose to serve.

She was too busy to be aware that it was gone eleven o'clock until she happened to look and see that it was almost twelve. Frowning, she lifted her hand to her face, depositing a smudge of flour on her cheekbone. The phone rang and she tensed. Somehow—she had no idea how— she knew that it was Brad who was ringing.

Reluctantly wiping her hands on her apron, she went to lift the receiver.

As she had known it would be, her caller was Brad.

'I'm just ringing to apologise for being late,' he told her. 'Unfortunately there was a slight problem here at the warehouse. Will it be all right if I come round now, or will that be inconvenient?'

'Now will be fine,' Claire confirmed, proud of the way she managed to keep the trembling in her body out of her voice.

Reaction set in after she had replaced the receiver, though. It was gone twelve now; would he expect her to provide him with lunch? All she had been intending to have was some left-over soup and fresh fruit. And what exactly, anyway, did he mean by saying that he wanted to live as part of a family? Hopefully, and if the hours that Tim worked were anything to go by, she wasn't going to have to see too much of him, and when she did...

Tonight, when they discussed the terms of his stay with her, she would just have to make it plain that as far as she was concerned the less contact there was between them the better.

CHAPTER FIVE

IT WAS almost one o'clock when Brad finally arrived. Opening the boot of his car, he removed a couple of suitcases and carried them into the house.

'Is it OK if I take these straight up?' he asked Claire tersely.

A little taken aback by his abrupt manner, Claire nodded.

Was he, like her, having second thoughts about the wisdom of moving in with her? she wondered as she waited downstairs for him to return.

'I'm sorry I didn't make our original time,' he apologised as he came back down again. 'There was a slight problem at the office. They had a break-in last night and although no stock was stolen we lost an extremely expensive piece of computer equipment.' His frown deepened.'It looks very much like whoever broke in knew exactly what they were going for...'

'But what about the on-site security guards?' Claire asked him. 'Surely they must—?'

'What security guards?' Brad queried with dry emphasis. 'It seems that for reasons of economy the security guards had been cut down from the original four to just one, and he was in another part of the site when the break-in took place. False economy, as it turned out...'

Claire winced as she heard the irritation in his voice, her mind going anxiously and immediately to Tim. She sincerely hoped that the blame for what had happened wouldn't fall onto his shoulders; technically he was not in charge of the site which housed the office and distribution centre...

'At least no one was hurt,' was the only comment Claire could think of to make.

'Somebody, no,' Brad agreed, 'but something, yes.' His voice had become a few degrees colder and very much harder as he told her, 'Ultimately our overall profits and, through them, the feasibility of the British side of our business are bound to be hurt by the cost of replacing the stolen equipment—even if our insurers pay out it will result in an increase in our premium, plus the business lost through the loss of the equipment...'

He shook his head, his frown lifting slightly as he added, 'However, none of this is your concern...'

'Tim is very conscientious,' Claire felt bound to point out to him in defence of her brother-in-law, her voice dropping huskily. 'Irene's concerned about him. We both are. He's been working such long hours recently and the stress—'

'You're obviously very fond of him,' Brad interrupted her.

'Yes, very,' Claire confirmed protectively, missing the quick, frowning glance he gave her.

Sally's postcard lay face down on the table next to him and he read it without meaning to. Who was the man in whom Claire only had a share? Was it Tim? Claire was certainly very close to him and very protective of him.

He liked Tim well enough—he was obviously a kind-hearted man although a little on the weak side—but the thought of him being Claire's lover filled him with such a surge of angry antagonism that he knew that if Tim had actually been there…

Hey…ease back, he warned himself. You're not here to get involved. Just because she's alone and vulnerable, just because it sounds like her marriage wasn't much of a marriage at all…just because she makes you feel as horny as hell and when you touch her all you can think of is taking her to bed, that doesn't mean…

'I…I'm not sure exactly what arrangements you want to come to as regards meals and so on,' he heard Claire saying. 'We haven't discussed… Irene did intimate that you wanted to live somewhere en famille…'

'Yes. Yes, I do,' Brad agreed, struggling to suppress an alluring vision of sharing breakfast with her, of watching her move about the kitchen, her hair still damp from her shower, her face free of make-up, her body tantalisingly naked beneath her robe.

When she stood next to him he would be able to smell the clean, fresh, feminine scent of her skin, the exposed V of the valley between her breasts headily close to him—so close that if he turned his head he would be able to reach up and pull her down onto his lap, burying his face…his mouth…in that deliciously fragranced, womanly secret place.

Was he experiencing some hormonal overload which resulted in thoughts more appropriate to one's teenage years than to one's present maturity? Brad wondered grimly.

'You'll want me to prepare dinner for you in the evening?' Claire was persisting.

'Ultimately, yes,' Brad agreed, 'but initially I'll probably be working into the evening so I'll grab something to eat myself…'

He was frowning again, remembering Tim's defensiveness over the problems he was having in meeting their high standards. It was Brad's view that Tim simply wasn't assertive enough, but he didn't want to make over-hasty judgements.

He had known all along that the task his uncles had forced on him wasn't going to be easy, but now... And getting involved with Claire, when she was Tim's family and when she obviously felt so strongly about him... One thing he did know, though, he recognised, was that if she and Tim were lovers then it couldn't be a very passionate relationship.

'Is that everything?' he heard Claire asking him. 'Have you anything else to bring in from the car?'

'Er...yes...as a matter of fact there is something. I'll just go and get it...'

He was only gone a few moments, returning with what looked like a very expensive balled-up cashmere sweater, which he was carrying very carefully.

'Er...we...I...we found this in the boiler room. Looks like it's been abandoned by its mother, and I...'

The cashmere bundle started to move, a surprisingly strong mewing sound emerging from it.

'It's a cat,' Claire protested.

'A kitten,' Brad corrected her, opening the cashmere to reveal its occupant. 'Not even six weeks old yet, I guess... Too young to survive on her own, anyway, that's for sure...'

'Her?' Claire questioned.

'Well, I don't know for certain, but she's so pretty I guess I thought she had to be female,' Brad confessed, both his face and his voice softening as he gently extracted the kitten from his sweater and showed her to Claire.

Her first thought was that the animal was so small that she was almost afraid to touch her; her second was that,

as Brad had said, she was extraordinarily pretty—a little
fluffy tabby with white socks and huge, brave eyes.

'John didn't like animals,' she heard herself saying uncertainly. 'He would never allow them in the house... He
thought—'

'He thought.' Brad stopped her. 'But what do you think,
Claire?'

Claire could see the anger in his eyes although she
couldn't understand the cause of it.

'This was John's home,' she reminded him with quiet
dignity, 'and I—'

'And you what? You were just a visitor here? But it's
your home now, isn't it? Your home, but perhaps not, after
all, a home—the home for this little one. What she needs
isn't just somewhere where she's permitted as a visitor;
what she needs is somewhere where she's wanted and
loved...'

For some reason his words hurt her, uncovering a wound
that she had not even acknowledged was there before,
Claire realised.

Without being aware of what she was doing she had
stretched out her hands and taken the kitten from him.
The creature felt as light as thistledown but surprisingly
warm, and as Claire held her she suddenly heard the most
extraordinary noise. It took her several seconds to realise
what it was and when she did she exclaimed, enchanted,
'She's purring!'

'She obviously likes you,' Brad told her.

'I'll have to keep her out of the drawing room,' Claire
heard herself saying crooningly as she held the kitten protectively.

'She probably can't lap properly yet,' Brad was warning her. 'You'll have to feed her with an eye-dropper for a
while. Cat formula will be best... We reared three of them

that way. The kids found them in an old barn. Skin and
bone, they were. I never thought they'd live...' He smiled
reminiscently to himself, remembering his sister Mary-
Beth's determination to save them.

He had been terrified that they weren't going to survive. It had been the first time since their parents' death
that she had taken an interest in anything.

Claire started to put the kitten down and immediately
she wailed in protest.

As he saw the soft, loving look in Claire's eyes Brad
mentally marvelled at the ability of the young of any spe-
cies to ensure their own survival.

'I've never had a cat before,' Claire told him uncertainly.
'I'm not sure what—'

'It's simple,' Brad told her. 'She'll need her own bed,
some food, plenty of love—oh, and a soil tray, and you'll
have to have her checked over by a good vet. Didn't you
ever have any pets as a child?' he questioned her curiously.

Claire shook her head.

'No...I...I was brought up by my great-aunt. My...my
parents were killed when I was very young...' She saw
his face and shook his head. 'It's all right... I can't even
remember them—at least, not clearly. Just...' She hesitated, not wanting to remember how often as a child she
had cried herself to sleep, clinging to the memory of her
mother's perfume, her father's voice...

'She...she didn't approve of pets and then John...'

Brought up by a great-aunt; that explained the air of
quiet attentiveness she had, that lack of modern restless-
ness that could be so wearying.

He wondered if she realised quite what an intriguing
person she was, and then reminded himself grimly that
the other man—whoever it was that she only had a part-
share in—had no doubt already told her so.

Did her relationship with him predate her husband's death? Somehow he doubted it. He could, however, well imagine her falling victim to someone in the aftermath of his death, needing someone to lean on and turn to... And who better, perhaps, than a man she already knew?

Surely she knew that it was a relationship that couldn't go anywhere, that she was demeaning herself by accepting such a meagre offering—a plastic and unsatisfying imitation of what love, commitment...sex between a man and woman should really be about?

It angered him that she could have allowed herself to be dragged into such an unfulfilling relationship. Angered him and saddened him as well.

And as for the man involved, whoever he was—Tim or someone else—he wasn't very much of a man, in Brad's opinion, if he could take advantage of someone so obviously vulnerable. Irritably Brad caught himself up. Take advantage of her! She was an adult woman, for God's sake, and just because she looked...and he felt...

She was still crooning softly to the cat and the thought crossed his mind that it was no wonder that her late husband had wanted her as a stepmother for his daughter. There was something about the soft, tender curve of her mouth as she held that impossibly small bundle of fluff and nothing that made his own guts ache and...

Hell, he didn't have space in his life for something like this, for someone like her. He had plans...dreams...that boat to build and sail.

'You'll have to find a name for her,' he told Claire gruffly. She flushed slightly as she acknowledged his comment. The kitten felt so soft and warm, its small body throbbing with purring pleasure as she held it.

'What about dinner this evening?' she remembered as Brad headed for the door. 'Will you—?'

'Yes, if that's convenient,' he confirmed.

He had a meeting with Tim at three and some paper-work to go through, but he guessed that he could do that later here, and he wanted to phone home, check that everything was OK, he admitted to himself. The fact that his siblings were all now adult didn't do an awful lot to lessen his feelings of responsibility towards them.

He frowned as he looked down at the postcard again. Mary-Beth had been going through a bit of a difficult time with her marriage recently. She was inclined to be very hot-headed and impulsive, with very clear and uncompromising views, outwardly strong-willed but inwardly still vulnerable.

There was a girl at work who had been making a bit of a play for her husband, and although nothing had actually happened Brad knew that she felt hurt and angry at the fact that her husband had obviously been slightly flattered by the girl's attention.

Brad could see both sides of the situation. His sister had been very wrapped up in the children recently, and her husband, Abe, whilst quite obviously loving her and their children, couldn't understand what she was so angry about, especially when he had been the one to tell her about the girl's interest in him.

Claire saw his frown deepen as he continued to stare down at the kitchen table and Sally's postcard but the kitten had started to cry, distracting her.

'Sounds like she's hungry,' Brad said. 'You could try her with a few drops of milk from an eye-dropper if you've got one.

'I'll pick up some formula and the other stuff for you on my way back to the office if you like.'

Claire stared at him. John would never have offered to do anything like that. He had been a little old-fashioned in that way, preferring to keep what he saw as their roles very clearly separate.

He had been the man of the house, the breadwinner, and financially he had made sure that Claire never had anything to worry about.

It would never have occurred to him, though, to offer to do any shopping for her and she knew that he would have been horrified if she had suggested it to him. That had been her responsibility.

The kitten had taken to the dropper eagerly and hungrily, her small stomach filling, much to Claire's relief.

She was going to be a real femme fatale, Claire decided, a natural flirt, and deserved to be named accordingly. As a temporary home for her, Claire had filled an old shoe-box with some soft cotton, and the kitten was now curled up asleep in it. As she watched her Claire tried not to think about how disapproving John would have been about her introduction to the household.

'Just remember,' she told the sleeping creature firmly, 'the drawing room is out of bounds.'

She could have sworn that in her sleep the kitten smiled a knowing, naughty feline smile.

John might not have approved of pets but she had always wanted one, Claire admitted to herself. Already just watching the small sleeping creature made her feel happy.

Happy...that was it. She was going to call her Felicity, she decided. Felicity. She said the name out loud, her smile turning into a small bubble of laughter as the kitten opened her eyes and stretched out her small body as though in approval of her new name.

A telephone call to a friend who had cats of her own had provided her with the name of a vet, and she now walked over to the calendar hanging on the wall to make a note of

the appointment she had made for Felicity, plus a note of
her follow-up appointment six weeks later, and as she did
her attention was caught by the red cross she had placed on
the calendar to mark her lunch-date with Poppy and Star.

Well, she certainly wasn't going to have any difficulty
in keeping to their agreement to resist the supposed power
of their contact with the bride's bouquet.

It would, of course, be different for the other two, or at
least she hoped it would be. Poppy would eventually get
over her teenage infatuation for her cousin and be able to
put it aside and recognise it for what it was, leaving her
free to give her adult love to a man who loved her in return.

Star's past history meant that it would not be easy for
her to allow herself to trust anyone enough to form a commitment to them... Difficult, but not impossible, and Claire
sincerely hoped that she would one day be able to do so.

Beneath that determined front of independence that
Star wore so challengingly and fiercely, Claire suspected
that there was still a part of her that was very much the
lonely, unhappy little girl who had seen her parents destroy one relationship after another and, with them, her
security and her belief in the capability of adults to genuinely love one another.

Claire had gone along with their vow to remain unmarried because she had sensed that they needed her support, but her sincerest hope for both of them was that there
would come a day when, out of the security of loving and
being loved, they could look back and laugh at the vulnerability and pain which had led them to be so afraid of love.

She was just on the point of returning Felicity to her temporary 'basket', having fed her again, when Brad returned.
He was earlier than she had expected and had obviously

not forgotten his promise to her—or rather to Felicity—because he came in carrying several packages.

'Found a name for her yet?' he asked as Claire went to let him in, still holding the kitten.

'Felicity,' she informed him, 'because her arrival in my home is most felicitous.'

Unlike mine, Brad reflected wryly. He was not oblivious to the fact that she was not entirely at ease with him and silently cursed Irene for having—he was sure—put pressure on her to have him to stay.

If the arrival in her life of something as small and waif-like as the kitten could make her mouth soften and her eyes warm with so much happiness, it didn't say much for the ability of the man in her life to make her happy, he decided critically. If he were in his shoes...

But he wasn't, he reminded himself, and the shoes he was in at the moment—his own shoes—were pinching just a mite too much for comfort.

His interview with Tim had been every bit as difficult as he had envisaged, with Tim being defensive and pessimistic. He preferred a situation where he could praise rather than blame; it got better results faster and, even more important, it helped to keep the sick-pay down. In his opinion, good self-esteem was the best incentive scheme that any workforce—any man—could have.

'Something smells good,' he commented to Claire as he put his packages down on the kitchen table and watched her replace the now sated kitten back in its box.

'It's beef-steak pie,' she told him, lifting her chin, the words almost a challenge. 'I suppose you'd have probably preferred a pot-roast or some pumpkin pie,' she added.

Ah... Brad thought; he now understood the reason for the challenge and the firm determination of that tilted chin.

Hiding a grin, he told her gravely, 'Well, now...that

would depend… The kinda pumpkin pie and pot-roast I'm used to, I guess it would be pretty hard for you to serve…'

Claire glared at him in indignation. What was he trying to say? That she wasn't a competent enough cook to make his precious national food?

She opened her mouth to refute his claim firmly and then saw the laughter warming his eyes and paused.

'Go on,' she invited him grimly, letting him know that she wanted to be let in on the joke.

The gleam of amusement became open, rueful laughter as he recongised that she had realised that he was teasing her. That was something he had missed when the kids had been growing up—someone to share his own more mature amusement…his laughter and sometimes his tears at their learning mistakes… Someone to share… Someone just to share his life, he acknowledged—someone like Claire who could recognise when he was deliberately baiting her… Someone like Claire…

Hastily he dragged his thoughts back under control.

'Well, you see, back home the girls kinda cut their milk teeth, in the cooking sense, on pot-roast and pumpkin pie, although, to be fair to my four sisters, mostly they've already had some experience of watching their moms cooking it before they're let loose on the real thing. Have you ever actually eaten charred pot-roast?' he asked her, adding feelingly, 'Four times…and that was just for starters…'

Claire started to laugh. She could well remember her own early attempts at cooking, and Sally's.

'Oh, no, poor you,' she said, her own mirth overcoming her instinctive sympathy as she started to laugh again.

'You can laugh,' Brad complained. 'I sure as hell feel I'm lucky to still have my own teeth… That's my side of the story,' he told her, and then asked softly, 'So, what's yours? What is it you've got against pot-roast?'

He had caught her off guard with no easy excuse at hand, and after an agitated hesitation she admitted reluctantly, 'Irene wanted me to cook it for you. She brought me this book of American recipes she had borrowed from someone. She thought it would make you feel...more at home...'

Aware of Claire's small, tell-tale pause before completing her explanation, Brad guessed that it was her husband's job which Irene had been concerned with rather than his stomach. But he couldn't blame her for that. There was nothing wrong in being a loyal wife.

Brad glanced round the kitchen. In every room of the house bar this one he had been immediately and intensely aware that this was another man's home, and if he felt conscious of that fact then how much more conscious must Claire be that this was, in reality, still another woman's home? How had she lived with that knowledge? he wondered. How had she managed to endure knowing that her husband was still in love with his first wife?

Was that why she had become involved with someone else...? If so, he could scarcely blame her, although...

'I...I thought we'd eat in here rather than in the dining room,' he heard Claire saying uncertainly. 'Sally and I always did and—'

'Sure. It's more homely in here,' he agreed calmly. 'But I'll need to shower first; is that OK? I'll only be about ten minutes, but if you give me a shout when you want me...'

Claire could hear him going upstairs as she started to lay the table. She and John had never really laughed together, never shared a sense of humour. John simply hadn't been that kind of man. He had taken life seriously, probably because of Paula's death, Claire acknowledged.

Laughter was supposed to be good for you but it had made her feel rather odd, she decided. She felt slightly dizzy, light-headed almost—'giddy', her great-aunt would have called it disapprovingly. Her mouth curled again and again into a reminiscent smile, an unfamiliar sense of pleasure and light-heartedness filling her.

'I wish Dad would lighten up a bit,' Sally had often complained during her teenage years, and Claire had sympathised with her because her stepdaughter had a wonderful sense of fun.

It must be nice to share that kind of intimacy with someone, Claire decided wistfully as she removed the pie from the oven and put the vegetables into the serving dishes. And they did say, didn't they, that laughter was the best aphrodisiac? Her heart gave a tiny little flutter, the heat from the oven making her face flush.

How much longer would Brad be...? It was over fifteen minutes since he had gone upstairs; perhaps she'd better go and give him that call.

As she walked along the landing she saw that the door to the master bedroom was open. Without thinking she stepped up to it and then paused. Brad's shirt lay on the bed, his shoes beside it on the floor, his trousers over the back of a chair, which meant that Brad, wherever he was, must be minus those articles.

She swallowed a small gulp of panic as the bathroom door opened and Brad walked into the bedroom before she had time to escape.

'Sorry. I'm running late, I know,' he apologised, apparently as oblivious to her flushed face as he was to the fact that all he was wearing was a short—a very short—towelling robe, secured so loosely around his waist that Claire was terrified when he lifted his hands to towel-dry his damp hair that it was going to come unfastened.

Unlike her, he was clearly no stranger to the intimacy of sharing his bedroom with a member of the opposite sex. She and John had very early in the days of their marriage established a routine which ensured that they went to bed at separate times, after allowing one another a decent amount of time and privacy in which to prepare for bed.

Claire suspected that it had been simply for the sake of convention and Sally that John had allowed her to share his room and his bed, and she had sensed his relief when, at the onset of his serious illness, she had suggested that she move into the spare room.

She was still standing just inside the door of Brad's room, transfixed, dizzied almost by the greedy fervour with which she was drinking in the sight of his barely clad body. A hot rush of shame flooded through her as she realised what she was doing. Quickly she turned away, stumbling back out on to the landing.

As a teenager, partially because of her upbringing and partially, she always assumed, because of her own nature, she had been rather naïve and slow to reach sexual awareness, but even when she had her daydreams had been more of the idealised, romantic variety—of meeting someone with whom she would fall in love and marry.

The actual physical details of her lover-to-be had never been something she had dwelt specially upon, and, unlike other girls she had known, she had certainly never drooled over bare male torsos or compared the rival attractions of a pair of well-muscled, strong male arms with an equally well-muscled and strong pair of male buttocks.

Nor had she ever thought about men—or even one specific man—in any sexual sense in the years since, so it was all the more of a shock now to realise that, when she had been standing there watching Brad as he moved lazily and easily around the room, in her mind's eye he had somehow or other disposed of his towelling robe and the

Brad she had been watching had been totally and magnificently—very magnificently, she blushed to recall—male.

'That was wonderful,' Brad said when he had finished eating. 'Irene mentioned that you'd be able to introduce me
as a temporary member at your local health club. I'm certainly going to need to go if you keep feeding me like this.'

He didn't look as though he needed to work out to her,
Claire reflected, but then she had no idea what kind of
lifestyle he normally lived; perhaps he exercised regularly at home.

'I must admit I've been a bit lax about developing a
proper exercise programme,' he told her, answering her
unspoken question. 'But when the kids were younger we
lived a pretty outdoors lifestyle, especially in the summer.
We'd be out on the lake most summer evenings and week-
ends, swimming or sailing...'

'The lake?' Claire asked him enviously. She had always
had a secret dream of living close to water. As a child it had
fascinated her, and a boating holiday—any kind of boating
holiday—was her idea of heaven, although the only time
she had persuaded John to hire a boat their holiday hadn't
been too successful. John had preferred luxury hotels but
she and Sally had had a wonderful time.

'Mmm...the town is close by the edge of a lake and most
folks locally spend a lot of their recreation time either in
it or on it. We had a sailing dinghy and—'

'I've always longed to be able to sail,' Claire told him
impulsively, and then flushed slightly. It was unlike her
to be so forthcoming with someone.

'Well, there's no reason why you shouldn't learn,' Brad
told her.

Claire shook her head. 'Not at my age,' she told him
quietly.

'Your age?' Brad scoffed. 'You can't be a day over twenty-seven, if that.'

'Well, I'm thirty-four in actual fact,' Claire informed him quietly, but inwardly she acknowledged that it was flattering that he had mistakenly thought her so much younger.

'Just because we're not under twenty-one any more, it doesn't mean that we can't still have dreams,' Brad told her softly. 'In fact sometimes the older we get, the more we need them.'

He paused, and Claire knew instinctively that he was thinking about a dream of his own. What was it? she wondered curiously.

'I've got this boat out on the lake; four years I've been working on her, stripping down the engines, making her seaworthy. I had this plan that once all the kids were off my hands I'd have some space in my life to do the things I want to do. I had this idea that I'd get the boat ready and that I'd then take off, sail wherever the tide and mood took me...'

'Why haven't you?' Claire asked him quietly.

'I got outsmarted by two wily old men—my uncles,' he told her drily. 'I was just on the point of telling them that I wanted out of the company when they beat me to it by announcing that they were both planning to retire— You don't want to hear all this,' he told Claire abruptly.

Yes, I do. I want to hear all about you...know all about you. Claire felt herself going rigid with shock as the words formed silently in her head but thankfully remained un-uttered.

'What about you? What are your plans for your future?' Brad asked her, obviously wanting to change the subject.

'I...I...don't really have any,' Claire admitted reluctantly. 'I've got my work at the school, although...'

'Although what?' Brad pressed her as she paused and frowned.

'There's a strong chance that it may have to close. Lack of funding,' Claire explained.

'Then what will you do?' Brad asked.

Claire shook her head. 'I'm not sure, although it is always possible to find some kind of voluntary work even if...'

'Even if it's not exactly what you might want to choose,' Brad supplied for her. 'What would you prefer to do?'

'I like working with children,' Claire confessed. 'There's something about their hope and optimism, even those...'

'You obviously love them,' Brad told her.

'Because they are easy to love,' Claire responded. 'And they have so much love to give...'

She should have had children of her own, Brad decided; she was that kind of woman—intensely loving and maternal in the very best sense of the word, and if he could recognise that then surely her late husband must have done too, so why...?

Their conversation was getting too intimate, too close to subjects that she didn't want to discuss, Claire recognised, quickly getting up from the table, saying that it was getting late, that they still hadn't discussed the terms of his stay with her.

Ruefully Brad took the hint and started to do so, outlining his requirements. They were less demanding than Claire had anticipated and the amount that he proposed paying her was so generous that it took her breath away. When she tried to tell him that it was too much he overruled her, pointing out things that she had overlooked, such as wear and tear, and reluctantly Claire found herself giving in.

In its box the kitten stirred and complained that it was

hungry; Claire laughed as she went to pick her up. Oh, yes, she had the mothering instinct—in full strength, Brad acknowledged as he studied the tender way she held the small animal.

The phone rang just as he was on the point of going up-stairs. Claire went to answer it and he could hear the won-dering joy in her voice as she exclaimed, 'Oh, darling... it's wonderful to hear your voice! I didn't know you were going to ring...'

Quietly he left her alone to enjoy her conversation with her lover, all his pleasure in the evening draining out of him. As he went upstairs he wondered savagely what the matter with him was. The last thing he wanted or needed was to get emotionally involved with any woman, but es-pecially with one who was not free to return his feelings.

'You've reached a very dangerous—a very vulnera-ble—age,' his sister Mary-Beth had teased him at Thanks-giving. He had laughed then, but now he wasn't so sure that she might not have had a point.

Downstairs Claire clung happily to the telephone receiver as she told her stepdaughter, 'I never imagined that you would ring. It must be costing you the earth...'

She could almost feel the warmth of Sally's laughter as it filled her ear.

'You're worth it,' Sally assured her, adding teasingly, 'Besides, I know I can always get you to sub me from my next allowance.'

John had left certain monies in trust for Sally, from which she received a small quarterly income and of which Claire was one of the trustees, and Sally's impulsive habit of spending this money before she actually received it was a standing joke between them.

'Don't be so sure,' Claire warned her, laughing. 'The FT index has fallen several points.'

'Look, I must go,' Sally told her. 'Chris is waiting for me.' She blew a string of kisses into the phone before hanging up, leaving Claire to replace her own receiver with a warm smile curling her mouth. Darling Sally. How empty and joyless her life would have been without her—her life and her marriage. A small finger of pain poked mercilessly at the secret sore place within her heart that she kept so carefully guarded.

Hurriedly she ignored it, going to attend to the increasingly noisy demands for food from Felicity, blocking out the emotional pain with physical activity. It was, after all, a tried and true formula and one she had perfected over the years.

CHAPTER SIX

BRAD was not in a very good mood. He had just spent the morning going over the books and checking through the order book and it was obvious to him that things were in an even worse financial mess than he had predicted.

The sensible thing to do would be simply to cancel the franchise, close it down as a loss-maker and cut their losses. But if he did that...

How would Claire react to the fact that he was putting Tim out of a job—and why should he care?

He leaned back in his borrowed chair in his borrowed office—Tim's office, in fact—and closed his eyes, considering his options.

If they made some improvements, tightened things up, developed a more aggressive selling stance and pulled in some more orders, there was a small—a very small—chance that they might be able to turn things around. But achieving that, meeting all those objectives—and they would have to meet them—would require some brutally demanding hard work and the kind of dedication that was synonymous with the term 'workaholic'. The kind of man that Tim just was not—at the moment!

It would mean recruiting a new agent, someone who could motivate the self-employed fitters who installed the units to adapt the same positive, speedy approach to their

work that the firm looked for in its American fitters. Mentally he reviewed the personnel on their home-base payroll.
There was someone who could take on such a challenge—
on a short-term basis—but how would Tim react to having
someone brought in over his head?

The company needed a very different kind of management approach from the one it presently had if it was to
survive and succeed.

Tim…Claire's brother-in-law…and her lover?

Brad closed his eyes again and expelled a weary sigh.

He had heard Claire coming upstairs last night shortly
after eleven; he had still been working and had, in fact,
gone on working until after midnight.

When she slept in her solitary bed in her solitary room
did she dream of her lover? Did she lie awake thinking of
him, aching for him, as he…?

He tensed and sat up as he heard the office door open.

'Ah, Tim. No, it's all right; come in. I wanted to have a
chat with you anyway.'

'But at least nothing's been said about any redundancy
yet,' Claire tried to console Tim.

'No, but it can only be a matter of time,' he predicted
gloomily.

Claire watched him sympathetically. He had arrived
half an hour earlier looking for Brad, who had apparently
left him just before lunch without giving any indication
of where he was going.

'I thought he might have come back here,' Tim had
told her when she had shaken her head in answer to his
initial query.

Much as Claire sympathised—and she did—there was
not a lot that she could say and even less that she could do

other than listen to him as he paced her kitchen and unburdened himself to her.

She sensed that Tim had been half hoping that Brad might have confided his plans for Tim's future to her and in a sense she was relieved that he had not; it spared her from either having to betray his confidence or withhold valuable information from Tim.

'Everything's changed so much,' Tim told her miserably. 'You've got to be so much more competitive, so much more aggressive, and I'm too old to learn those sorts of tricks. And God knows where I'm going to find another job at my age...'

He grimaced as the kitten started to wail. 'She'll scratch your furniture to ribbons,' he warned Claire.

'No, she won't,' Claire contradicted him serenely. 'I'm going to get her a scratching-post.'

'Mmm...' Tim eyed the kitten doubtfully. He knew how Irene would have reacted if he had turned up with it at home, but then Irene had never been as soft-hearted as Claire. In many ways Irene was very like her brother.

'Look, I'd better go,' he told Claire. 'Brad's probably back by now and wondering where on earth I am.'

'I'll see you out to your car,' Claire offered.

He looked tired and stressed, a bit like a slightly rumpled, unhappy teddy bear, Claire decided affectionately as they made their way outside.

'Thanks for listening to me,' he told her gruffly. 'I suppose if I'm honest I've known for a while that things can't go on the way they are, but one always hopes.'

Poor Tim.

'Try not to worry,' Claire advised him, reaching out to hug him affectionately.

* * *

As he drove down the road towards Claire's house Brad saw the two of them locked in a deep embrace, oblivious to his approach.

They broke apart, Tim turning to get into his car without looking behind him, and Claire remained on the footpath watching his car disappear, only aware of Brad's arrival when he slammed his car door. She turned to face him with a startled expression.

'Oh, Brad... You've just missed Tim,' she began. 'He—'

'Yes, I saw him,' Brad said tersely.

Claire tensed, searching Brad's averted profile anxiously as she recognised his curt withdrawal.

Was Tim right? Was Brad on the point of dismissing him? She knew that there was no way she could bring herself to ask him; all she could manage was a hesitant, 'Did you want to speak to Tim...?'

'Not right now,' he told her grimly, walking away from her and heading towards the house, leaving her to follow him—an act which in itself was so out of character for him that it caught her off guard. One of the first things she had noticed about him and reluctantly liked had been his quietly considerate good manners, his way of treating a woman with the kind of old-fashioned courtesy which seemed to have gone out of fashion.

'In fact, right now, I think it would be just as well if I didn't speak to him,' he threw at her over his shoulder as he reached the back door.

'You're...you're angry with him...' Claire guessed hesitantly.

'Angry with him! That's one way of putting it,' Brad agreed bitingly as he waited for her to precede him into the kitchen.

'I know...he is very anxious about his job...' Claire revealed, stumbling slightly over the words, wondering if she was doing the wrong thing in saying them. 'Tim may not be a particularly...ambitious or aggressive man,' Claire told him, feeling that she ought to do something to defend her brother-in-law and draw attention to his good points, 'but he is very conscientious, very—'

'You obviously hold him in high esteem,' Brad interrupted her.

The sarcasm in his voice made Claire feel uncomfortable.

'You obviously think I'm trying to interfere in something that is none of my business,' she felt bound to say, 'but—'

'But you'd like to know anyway what my plans are for the future of the British side of our distribution network and, of course, Tim's future with it. Is that it?' Brad asked her, and grimly continued before she could make any denial.

'Very well, I'll tell you. Some changes will very definitely have to be made. As you yourself have just said, Tim is not the most confident of men and his lack of assertiveness comes across to potential customers as a lack of confidence, not just in himself but in our product as well. Couple that with his apparent inability to recruit the kind of highly motivated and even more highly skilled technicians and fitters we pride ourselves on using back home and it's no wonder we're having the problems over here that we are having.'

'So, you do mean to cancel your contract with him and find a new distributor?' Claire challenged him.

To her surprise, instead of immediately conceding that she was right, Brad frowned slightly and then said slowly, 'No, not necessarily.'

When Claire looked questioningly at him, he explained, 'It occurs to me that Tim might benefit from an intensive course on self-assertion techniques plus some input from a more positive role model to show him—'

'How the job should be done,' Claire supplied wryly.

'No,' Brad corrected her quietly. 'To show him what can be achieved with a more positive approach...a different outlook if you like. We have someone working for us on the distribution side back home who would be perfect for the job, although it won't be easy persuading him to come over here. But that's my problem and you aren't interested in my problems, are you? Only Tim's. But then, after all, you are lovers.'

'Lovers?' Claire repeated in astonishment.

But before she could continue Brad was demanding angrily, 'When did it start? After your husband's death...? Before it?'

An affair! Brad thought she was having an affair with Tim.

'OK, I can understand that your...marriage may not have...satisfied you, but hell...surely a woman like you could have found a man who was free to have a relationship and not one...'

Claire stared at him in shocked disbelief. 'You have no right to make those kinds of assumptions about me,' she told him stiffly. 'You know nothing about me...or about my marriage.'

Even though she would rather have died than admit it to him, his comment about her marriage had hit a painful nerve, but not for the reason that he imagined.

'I would never have an affair,' she told him with passionate sincerity. 'Never... I couldn't.'

The vehemence in her voice fuelled Brad's fury. How could she deny it when he had seen the evidence with his own eyes, heard it with his own ears? And if she had to have an affair with someone, surely she could have found someone more…more worthy than her poor, downtrodden brother-in-law?

'"Couldn't"?' he challenged her contemptuously. 'Oh, come on. You're an adult, mature woman; you've been married… Your body knows how it feels to experience sexual desire, sexual fulfilment…sexual need; you must—'

'No,' Claire protested frantically. 'No, that's impossible; I could never… I have never…'

Something in her voice, in her face made Brad pause and look searchingly at her. She looked haunted, her eyes shadowed, her voice shamed…bruised.

'What is it?' he asked her. 'What is it you're trying to say?'

'Nothing,' Claire denied rigidly, starting to turn away from him.

But he reached out and caught hold of her arm, preventing her, telling her, 'No, you can't leave it like that. You could never…have never…what?' he pressed.

He could feel the slight tremor that she tried to suppress run down her arm as she refused to look at him.

It was no use, Claire acknowledged fatalistically. Brad wasn't going to give up until she had told him the truth. She closed her eyes, fighting back the engulfing wave of panic that threatened her. How on earth had this happened? How on earth had she got herself in such a situation, betrayed herself to such an extent?

As a child she had learned that the easiest way to deal with her aunt's displeasure whenever she provoked it was simply to take a deep breath and submit to it, rather like taking a nasty dose of medicine all in one big swallow, so that she could get the whole thing over and done with.

'I could never take a lover, have never had a lover,' she emphasised with quiet dignity, fiercely ignoring her voice's struggle not to wobble and the fact that she knew that her face, her whole body in fact, was burning with humiliated colour as she made herself admit the shameful truth to him—not that he had any right to demand it or any right to make her reveal it...

'John...our marriage... John married me because he wanted a stepmother for Sally. I knew...he told me...that he could never love anyone the way he had loved Paula, but that for Sally's sake he felt that he ought to provide her with a substitute mother.'

'And you were happy with that...you accepted that?' Brad persisted. There was something here that he didn't understand. Had she, perhaps, been so desperately in love with her husband that she had hoped that he would change his mind...that he would fall in love with her? His heart ached with pity for her, and anger as well.

'Yes,' Claire confirmed.

'But why?' Brad probed. 'Why? Why marry a man who you knew did not love you? A man who could never be a proper husband to you...never give you children... never share with you the pleasure of sexual fulfilment and commitment, the emotional...' He paused as he saw the way she shuddered at his mention of her lack of sexual fulfilment.

'What is it?' he asked her curiously. 'What's wrong?'

'I didn't mind the fact that John only wanted me as a stepmother for Sally because I didn't want to have a sexual relationship with him...or with anyone,' she told him doggedly.

For a long moment they looked at one another.

'You didn't want a sexual relationship...with anyone,' Brad repeated.

Something here was eluding him. There had been no sexual revulsion or rejection in her reaction to him when... Shock, yes...anger too. Shock, anger and arousal. He listed them carefully in his mind a second and then a third time just to be sure that he was not making a mistake and letting his own emotions and responses obscure hers.

He looked away from her and started to release her arm, too stunned by what she had said to know what to say or do, and then he looked briefly back at her and saw that her eyes were brimming with huge tears which she was struggling desperately to control.

'Oh, hell, come here,' he muttered roughly under his breath, reacting instinctively to her distress, reaching for her and wrapping her in his arms in a fiercely protective hug, rocking her against his body as he held her tight with one arm and smoothed the silky fineness of her hair with the other and tried to comfort her.

'It's OK… It's OK,' he told her gruffly. 'I'm sorry as hell that I upset you. I didn't… What I said was out of line.

'Talk to me, Claire,' he groaned as he felt her body tensing under her attempts to stifle her sobs. 'Talk to me… Let it all out… Tell me what it's all about.'

'I can't,' Claire sobbed. 'I can't…'

'Yes, you can… Of course you can… Whatever it is you can tell me…' Brad crooned the words in much the same way as he had once crooned similar reassurances to his brothers and sisters, comforting them through their childhood woes. Only Claire wasn't a child, and she certainly wasn't one of his siblings; his body was telling him that much.

Claire, thank the Lord, was too caught up in her own emotions to be aware of his arousal.

'Tell me,' he insisted, and then added with a smile, 'I shan't let you go until you do.'

'There was a man,' Claire told him reluctantly. 'Another graduate. Three of us were sharing a rented house. It was my first time away from home… I…I suppose I was very naïve… My great-aunt was very strict; I…I didn't have very much experience, didn't know…

'He…he came to my room. He said the gas in his own meter had run out and he had no money to replenish it. He asked if he could study with me… He offered to make our supper… I…I had just had a bath… Our rooms were very cold and I was wearing my…my nightdress and my dressing gown… I didn't know… I didn't think.

'I…I went over to my bookshelves to get a book I needed. He followed me over. He was standing behind me… He put his arms round me…' Claire moistened her upper lip, her eyes darkening as she relived what had happened.

'At first I was too surprised to realise… I thought…I asked him to let me go but he wouldn't; he just laughed. He started…he started…' She stopped and swallowed painfully.

'He started to kiss the side of my neck.' She gave a small shudder. 'I didn't want him to… I tried to move away but he wouldn't let me go. He started pulling at my dressing gown and…' Her voice faltered to a standstill.

Brad's arm tightened slightly around her. 'It's OK. Take your time,' he told her softly.

'I… Well, I'm sure you can guess the rest. He thought that by agreeing to him coming in I was…I was agreeing to have sex with him. He was furious with me when I refused—told me…called me…I…I thought he was going to force me…rape me…

'We struggled for a while and eventually I managed to get free. I ran out of the house and into the street. It was raining and I slipped on the wet pavement… John saw me…he was on his way home… He stopped his car and came to help me. When I felt him touch me, at first I thought… I was almost hysterical,' she admitted huskily, and Brad, remembering the night when he had un-wittingly pursued her down a wet street, winced inwardly and cursed himself.

'Eventually he managed to calm me down and make me explain. He took me home with him...made me stay the night.

'He was so kind to me, so...so caring... I felt so safe with him,' she told Brad quietly. 'So...it was easy being with him and Sally, who, coincidentally was a pupil at the school where I was placed for teaching practice. There was no pressure...no awful feeling that he was about to pounce on me...that I might somehow...that he might think...'

Claire gave a tiny, despairing shake of her head.

'You must think me very stupid, very naïve...to be so afraid of...of giving the wrong impression, of having some-one, some man think... But I'd never felt very comfortable with boys... My great-aunt... And sexually...'

She struggled to find the right words and could only say huskily, 'I didn't... Some people don't... The fact that John didn't want to consummate our marriage was never a problem for me, and before you make any more accu-sations,' she told him, a little more fiercely, 'I was never tempted to break the vow of...of fidelity which I'd made when we were married. You must find me very...very cow-ardly and...'

'No,' Brad denied. 'In actual fact I think you're very brave to have told me what you just have,' he elucidated gently when she looked uncertainly at him.

What he couldn't tell her was what he thought of her husband, a man whom she obviously still looked up to but who, as far as he was concerned, had cruelly and selfishly taken advantage of her by using her naïvety and insecurity to trap her into a marriage which had robbed her of any right to discover her own sexuality.

'How old were you when you and John married?' he asked her gently.

'Twenty-two,' Claire told him.

Twenty-two. His heart ached for her.

'Don't look at me like that,' she cried out fiercely when she saw his face. 'I don't want your pity. I wanted to marry John... I wanted...'

'To deny your sexuality. Yes, I know,' Brad said.

'Some people...some women just aren't very highly sexually motivated,' Claire protested defensively. 'They just don't feel...'

'Some women...some men are born with only a very low sex drive,' Brad agreed, 'but you aren't one of them,' he told her positively.

Claire stared at him, her eyes rounding, her face starting to flush slightly.

'How can you say that?' she protested. 'You don't know—'

'Oh, I know,' Brad interrupted. 'I know very well because of this...'

And then, before she could really grasp what was happening, he had tightened his hold around her, one hand behind her head, and fastened his mouth gently over hers in the lightest and most delicate of kisses until the tantalising brush of his mouth against her own made her reach up instinctively to pull him down closer so that her lips could touch his fully, her body melting in liquid pleasure into his as he started to kiss her properly.

How could she ever have believed that she didn't want this? Claire marvelled dizzily as her body threw off the shackles of self-restraint and fear and gloried unashamedly in its need to press even closer to Brad's.

It was like taking off dark sunglasses and suddenly being dazzled by the brilliance of the sun, Claire decided

in dazed euphoria as her senses revelled in their untram-
melled freedom to indulge themselves.

The sound of Brad's breathing, heavy and uneven, the
smell of his skin, the heat of his body... Greedily Claire's
senses absorbed each new, sensual discovery, each new,
sensual pleasure, whilst her mouth clung hungrily to his,
willingly obeying his tongue's urgent demand for her to
part her closed lips to allow it to dart inside with quick,
urgent strokes.

She could feel the harshness of Brad's chest against her
breasts as he started to breathe more deeply. The stiffness
of the cloth separating their bodies chaffed their unfamiliar tenderness.

She could feel the difference, the arousal in her breasts,
her nipples, her whole body, Claire realised.

And she could feel too the arousal in Brad's. But where
once the knowledge of a man's arousal had filled her with
revulsion and fear now her body shivered with heady, feminine triumph at her ability to cause such a reaction.

The discovery of her own sensuality and of Brad's reaction to it was like drinking a heady aphrodisiac. She almost
felt drunk on the effects of what she was experiencing,
Claire recognised in a daze of pleasure as, without even
knowing what she was doing, she rubbed her body provocatively against Brad's, opening her eyes to gaze drowsily
into his, her pupils so dilated that Brad caught his breath
in an instantaneous and intense surge of sexual urgency.

She didn't know what she was doing, he suspected as he
fought to control his own searingly intense desire. Not to
herself and certainly not to him. Oh, she knew that he was
aroused but she didn't know, had no way of knowing, just
how out of character it was for him to be so vulnerable to
sexual desire or just how fiercely intense that desire was.

She was still looking up at him, her mouth open over

his, her teeth tugging sensually at his bottom lip, and he
wondered what she would say if he told her how damned
close he was to making the most primitive and urgent sensual use of the table only inches behind them.

And somehow he knew that the way he was feeling right
now, the way she was unconsciously telling him what she
was feeling...satisfying each other once wasn't going to
be enough... No way was it going to be enough.

As he tried to stifle the groan of longing that her teasingly erotic movements against his body were causing,
he caught sight of the kitchen clock and cursed under his
breath as he saw the time.

The office was twenty minutes' drive away and he had
an appointment in exactly half an hour with a potential
customer.

'Claire...' He whispered her name into her mouth,
watching in aching regret as he saw her eyes start to cloud.
'Claire...I've got to go,' he murmured softly.

He'd got to go... But he couldn't go... She needed him,
wanted him.

'No...' Claire started to protest huskily, and then
abruptly she realised what she was doing, what she was
saying, the enormity of her own behaviour. Scarlet-faced
with mortification, she pulled away from him, unable even
to look at him, never mind actually meet his eyes as she
heard him explaining that he had an appointment but that
he would get back just as soon as he could.

'There was no need for you to...to do what you just
did,' she told him in a suffocated voice. 'I know you feel
sorry for me and that...'

Brad cursed silently, realising what she was thinking
and what she was probably feeling. She thought that he
had made love to her out of pity.

'Claire—'

'I suppose it must be quite a change for a man like you. I suppose I've got a certain curiosity value, if nothing else. After all, there can't be many women of thirty-four in this day and age who don't…who've never…'

'Claire, don't,' he begged her. 'You're wrong. It wasn't—'

'They used to be good music-hall fodder, didn't they—middle-aged virgins, repressed, dried up, fossilised…?'

He could hear in her voice the tears she wouldn't let fall and he ached to reach out and take hold of her, but she was already stepping back from him, her eyes wild and angry, warning him not to come any closer.

'This is all my own fault,' Claire told him bitterly. 'I should never have given in to Irene and agreed to let you stay here. I never wanted—' She stopped but Brad knew what she had been going to say.

'You never wanted me here in the first place,' he guessed wryly.

'Why can't you all leave me alone to live my life the way I want to?' she demanded fiercely. 'You… Irene… even Sally with that ridiculous trick to force us to catch her bouquet. As though anyone gives any credence to that ridiculous superstition these days…'

'What superstition?' Brad asked her curiously.

'The one that says the girl who catches the bride's bouquet will be the next to marry,' Claire told him angrily. 'Sally arranged it so that both of her bridesmaids and I were tricked into catching it. She even put something about it on her postcard.'

The postcard… Suddenly Brad understood. So that was what the reference to Claire having a part-share in a man had meant.

Claire glowered at him furiously as she saw the way he had started to grin.

'Look, I've got to go,' he reiterated, 'but I am coming back, and when I do don't even bother to think about running away, Claire,' he warned her firmly.

'This,' he told her softly, reaching out and touching her lips lightly with his fingertips before she could stop him, 'is just the beginning...'

Claire stared at him, transfixed by the sheer intensity of the jolt of sensation that had run through her at his touch.

She wanted to tell him that he was wrong, that she didn't want whatever it was that he thought they had started to continue, but somehow the words just wouldn't come and she had to watch in tongue-tied silence as he headed for the door.

The plaintive mewing of the kitten broke the heavy silence of the kitchen. Claire went automatically to pick her up, stroking the soft baby fur and marvelling at the little creature's capacity to trust and survive as she started to purr noisily.

She was still semi-dazed by disbelief at everything that had happened—not just the intimate physical sensuality she had shared with Brad and her unexpected response to him but, even more unbelievably, the fact that she had actually told him about her past, revealed to him the secret shame and shock she had felt and the way it had affected her whole life and her feelings about herself and her sexuality.

Not even to John had she confided her fear that she somehow had been responsible, had invited in some way that young man's assault on her, but somehow it had almost been as though Brad had known what she was thinking, what she was feeling...had known just how to encourage her to reveal that hidden fear to him.

And as for what had happened afterwards... Could it

have been the result of the release of all the emotions she had repressed by locking away her fears about what had happened and her dread that she had somehow been responsible for it?

It was a well-known fact that emotional trauma could have an extremely odd effect on human behaviour.

But what about the fact that the night before last she had been dreaming about Brad in the most erotic way?

The kitten gave a sharp howl of protest, making Claire realise that the eye-dropper was empty of milk.

Apologising to her, Claire refilled it, smiling at the way the little creature clung to the dropper with her front paws as she sucked on the teat.

Sally had already told her that she intended to wait until she was at least thirty before she and Chris started their family. She was twenty-five now, which meant that she was going to have a long wait before she became a grandmother, Claire acknowledged.

A grandmother... A rueful, slightly sad smile touched her mouth as she admitted to herself how much she would secretly have liked to have children, a family of which Sally would always have remained her eldest and most specially loved daughter.

It was not too late, of course. Women of her age and even older were having babies every day, many of them without the support of a husband or partner, but, having been brought up solely by her great-aunt, Claire had very ambivalent feelings about having a child on her own. Of course, if she were ever to find herself in a situation where for some reason she'd conceived accidentally, then there would be no question but that she would have her child and love him or her.

She bent her head protectively over the kitten as she realised the direction her thoughts were taking and just why the thought of an accidental pregnancy should have crossed her mind.

It wasn't going to happen, of course. She must make sure that it did not happen, she told herself sternly.

Outside it had started to rain, the wind gusting fiercely against the window.

The weather forecast had warned that they were in for a stormy evening with heavy rain and gale-force winds. As she returned Felicity to the new basket that Brad had bought for her and glanced out of the window at the lowering sky, Claire was thankful that she didn't have to go out.

CHAPTER SEVEN

BRAD grimaced in disgust as he realised that one of the tyres on his hire car had developed a slow puncture and was now flat. Cursing under his breath, he glanced from the car window to the bleak, empty landscape and the heavy rain. It was barely six o'clock in the evening but the sky was so overcast that it was already almost dark.

There was no one else around, the desolate area that the local council had designated as a new industrial complex as yet little more than a vast sea of mud, broken here and there by sets of footings.

It had been a chance remark during his interview with their potential new customer—an official from the head office of a locally based insurance broker which was thinking of installing air-conditioning in all its offices—that had led to his trip out here to look at the new industrial site.

He hadn't realised, until the other man had mentioned it, that the existing warehouse was built on a piece of potentially very valuable land. The town had expanded rapidly in the years after the warehouse had first been constructed—adjacent to the original owner's home—and although Brad had been aware that virtually all the property surrounding the warehouse was residential he hadn't appreciated the significance of this fact until the other man had brought it to his attention.

He had a client, he had told Brad, a well-known local builder, who he suspected would be very interested in acquiring the land for development if it ever came onto the market. After he had gone, a few brief enquiries by Brad had elicited the information that as prime residential building land the warehouse site was very good indeed, and, moreover, that if they were to move to a new purpose-built unit the savings they could make would more than offset the cost of such a move.

On impulse Brad had decided to drive out and look at the new industrial complex that the local council were building, but what he hadn't bargained for was the fact that his hire car was going to get a puncture.

It was still raining very heavily but there was no help for it—he was going to have to get out and change that tyre, Brad acknowledged, removing his suit jacket and opening the car door.

Ten minutes later, his hair plastered wetly to his scalp, his back soaked to the skin through the inadequate protection of his shirt, Brad had managed to remove the spare wheel from the trunk—the boot of the car, he amended grimly—and to locate the jack.

The unmade road along which he had driven to inspect the site was rapidly changing to a thick mush of sticky mud beneath the lashing downpour. Removing the rubber-backed lining from the boot floor to use as a kneeling pad, Brad started to jack up the car.

Half an hour later, so wet that he might just as well have been standing naked under a shower, and perspiring heavily from his efforts to release the wheel-nuts, Brad gave in. What he wouldn't give now for a can of lubricant, he thought, but the nuts, fitted by machine, were simply not going to budge.

He reached into his car for his phone and punched in the number of the car-hire firm.

It was over an hour and a half before he finally saw the headlights of the breakdown vehicle coming towards him through the heavy downpour of the continuing rain.

He had been reluctant to run the car engine for too long in case he ran out of petrol and his wet shirt, still clinging clammily and coldly to his skin, coupled with the sharp drop in temperature which had accompanied the driving rain made him shiver and sneeze as he stepped out of the car to greet the mechanic.

'Better watch it, mate,' the mechanic told him cheerfully as he sprayed the stubborn wheel-nuts and waited for the lubricant to take effect. 'Sounds like you've got yourself a nasty chill there.'

It was another half an hour before the wheel was finally changed, the wheel-nuts proving recalcitrantly stubborn but eventually coming free.

Thanking the mechanic, Brad climbed back in the car and restarted the engine.

Claire glanced uncertainly at the kitchen clock. Where was Brad? She had assumed, obviously erroneously, that he was going to be back in time for dinner but it was after nine now and she had long since disposed of the meal she had prepared for him.

When Brad hadn't returned when she had expected she had been tempted to phone the office, but she had reminded herself fiercely that he was simply her lodger and that was the only relationship between them—the only relationship she wanted there to be between them.

It hadn't been easy to ignore the mocking laughter of the inner voice that had taunted her, Liar, but somehow

she had made herself do so. If she'd wanted or needed any
confirmation that what had happened between them this
afternoon was something that Brad very definitely did not
want to take any further, she had surely had it in the very
fact that he had delayed his return for so long.

Don't run away, he had told her, but perhaps, like her,
he too had been caught up in the intensity of the moment,
suspending normal, rational judgement and reality.

Hannah had been round earlier to leave her a book that
she had promised to lend her on traditional Edwardian rose
gardens; she would make herself a hot drink and go and
sit down in the sitting room and look at it, Claire promised herself. She had just settled down when she saw the
headlights of Brad's car. Uncertainly she bit her lip, not
sure whether to stay where she was or go and greet him.

As his landlady, she ought perhaps at least to check to
see if he wanted anything to eat. She was not really sure
what the mode of behaviour should be between landlady
and lodger—where one drew the line between a presence
that was welcoming and one that was intrusive.

It was time to feed Felicity, she reminded herself, and
if she didn't appear Brad might think...might assume...

What? she asked herself grimly. That she was afraid...
embarrassed...self-conscious? Well, he would be right on
all those counts. She did feel all those things and more—
much more, she acknowledged, her body suddenly growing hot as she had an unnervingly vivid memory of the
way his mouth had felt on hers—his body, his...

Swallowing hard, she reminded herself that, no matter
what she felt, she did have a responsibility as his landlady
to make at least an attempt to behave in a businesslike
manner towards him.

Irene would certainly have something to say to her if
she learned that Claire had left him supperless. As she got

up and walked towards the door Claire heard Brad walk
into the hall and sneeze—once and then again.

Frowning now, she opened the door, her eyes widening
in shock as she saw his coatless, damply dishevelled state.

'Brad, what on earth…?'

'It's nothing,' he said. 'There was a problem with the
car and I had to wait for them to get a breakdown truck
out to me. I should have let you know, but I had no idea
how long they were going to be.'

A problem. Her heart thumped anxiously against her
chest wall. 'Not an accident?' she protested. 'You—'

'No, not an accident,' he assured her. 'I had a flat tyre,
that's all, but unfortunately—' he paused for another vol-
ley of sneezes, visibly shivering as Claire looked on in appalled consternation— 'I tried to change it myself and got
soaked,' he told her ruefully, his teeth suddenly chattering.

'You're soaked,' Claire told him. 'And frozen. You'd
better go upstairs and have a hot shower. I'll make you a
drink and something to eat.'

Had she got any cold or flu remedy in the house? Claire
wondered, listening anxiously as she heard Brad pause
halfway up the stairs for another fit of obviously feverish sneezing.

He was going to be lucky if all he got away with was a
bad chill, she recognised as she hurried into the kitchen
to fill the kettle and look through the drawers to try to un-
earth the old hot-water bottle she always kept handy for
cold sufferers. In these centrally heated days it probably
wasn't necessary but somehow it made one feel better,
Claire acknowledged. Sally certainly insisted on having
it whenever she went down with a cold.

A brief check on the high shelf where she kept her medi-
cines revealed the patent aspirin-based remedy which Sally
always swore worked for her. Expelling a small sigh of

relief, Claire picked it up. She had no doubt whom Irene would blame if Brad did become ill.

He was used to a much better regulated climate than theirs, she reminded herself as she added some brandy to the mug of coffee that she had made him. He would, perhaps, be better off going straight to bed and keeping warm there rather than coming down for something to eat. She could easily take him a tray of food upstairs.

His bedroom door was ajar when she went up with the coffee but, recalling what had happened the last time she had walked into his room, she paused, knocking and calling out uncertainly.

'Brad…?'

His husky 'Come in' confirmed her earlier suspicions about the state of his health.

'I've brought you some coffee,' she told him, and added, 'And I've put some brandy in it, so…'

'Wonderful,' Brad praised her. He was sitting on the edge of the bed, wearing the towelling robe she had seen him in before. As he reached out to take the coffee from her Claire saw to her concern that his face already looked hectically and feverishly flushed.

'I think you might be running a temperature,' she warned him gently.

'I think you're probably right,' Brad agreed. He was beginning to feel decidedly unwell. As a boy he had been very susceptible to frighteningly severe chest infections brought on by any kind of exposure to a cold or flu virus, but fortunately over the years he seemed to have developed a better immunity to them. Until now, he acknowledged, already recognising the signs of a return of his childhood symptoms.

'You ought to have something to eat,' Claire told him,

'but I don't think you should come back downstairs; you look—'

'I'll be all right,' Brad interrupted her stoically. 'A good night's sleep and a couple more of these...' he told her, pointing to the brandy-laced coffee she had brought him.

'I could make you an omelette,' Claire offered, but he was shaking his head.

'I don't think I could,' he told her ruefully. 'My throat...' He touched the tender area, wincing as he felt the tell-tale swelling of his glands.

'I've got some aspirin,' Claire said, but Brad shook his head again. 'I'm allergic to it,' he told her wryly. 'Look, I promise you, I'll be fine.'

The concern he could see in her eyes made him realise how tempting it would be to exaggerate his symptoms. If he hadn't been feeling so damn ill and weak there would have been a lot he could have done with that warm, womanly anxious look.

As he shivered involuntarily and started to sneeze again Claire made a soft sound of distress and urged him to get into bed.

'I can't,' he told her.

'You can't? But...'

Since he was already sitting on the side of the bed, Claire was puzzled by his refusal, until he informed her softly, 'In order to get into bed I've got to take this robe off first, and if I do that...' He paused deliberately, and as she unwittingly focused on the bare V of warm brown flesh in front of her, with its soft, tantalising tangle of silky dark hair, she suddenly realised what he meant: that he was naked beneath his robe.

Her soft, betraying 'Oh' and the quick flush of colour that stained her skin made Brad ache to reach out and take hold of her, to pull her down against his body and...

Stop that, he warned himself, stifling a low groan of
unexpected arousal. There were some things that even the
threat of a feverish chest infection couldn't keep down—
quite literally, he realised in wry self-mockery.

'I...I'd better go downstairs,' Claire mumbled awkwardly. 'I was wondering...if you'd like a hot-water bottle,' she added, and then wondered what on earth had made
her make such a patently silly offer. He was an adult, not
a child, and, unlike Sally, he—

'A hot-water bottle...' Brad closed his eyes and gave a
long, appreciative sigh. 'I can't think of anything I'd like
more...'

Oh, yes, he could, he corrected himself as he watched
Claire disappear. He could think of something he'd quite
definitely like very, very much more, and that was holding Claire's body next to his own...a real, live comforter.

Ten minutes later when Claire returned she was concerned to see how much more hectically flushed Brad
was, his breathing painfully rasping and laboured. As she
leaned across the bed to hand him the hot-water bottle she
could feel the feverish heat coming off his body. Concerned, she asked him, 'Would you like me to send for a
doctor? Your breathing... I'm—'

'No...I'll be OK,' Brad assured her. 'It sounds worse
than it is.'

'Are you sure?' Claire queried doubtfully. 'You—'

'I'm sure,' Brad told her firmly. 'A good night's sleep
and I'll be fine.'

It might not strictly speaking be the truth, Brad acknowledged ruefully as he watched Claire walking away
from him, waiting until she had closed the door behind her
to let his body relax into the racking fit of shivers he had
managed to suppress whilst she was there, but he knew

these feverish bronchial attacks of old and they always seemed worse to the onlooker than they actually were.

Claire made an irritated sound of self-criticism as she got out of the bath and remembered that she hadn't locked the back door. Reaching for her towelling robe, she pulled it on over her still damp body, acknowledging that she had better go and do so before she forgot—again.

The back door securely locked, she had almost reached her own bedroom when she heard a noise from Brad's room. She paused, and heard him cry out. Something was wrong.

Quickly she hurried into his room. The bedside lamp was switched on, a glass of water which Brad must have fetched from the bathroom earlier next to it. Brad was lying on his side, facing away from her, muttering something hoarsely under his breath. As Claire strained to hear what it was she automatically reached across the bed towards him, saying his name with anxious urgency.

When he didn't make any response her anxiety increased. She touched his bare shoulders lightly, wincing as she felt the heat coming off his skin, and listened to the harsh bark of his cough. This time he registered her presence, turning over to face her, saying something that she couldn't catch and then calling out sharply, 'No... No... It isn't true... Dad...'

Claire shivered as she heard the pain in his voice and realised that he was talking in his sleep—a very feverish and restless sleep, if the tumbled state of the bedclothes and the low, emotional sound of his voice were anything to go by, she recognised.

Did he dream of his dead parents often, she wondered compassionately as she heard him whisper his father's name a second time, or was this just a side effect of his fever?

As he'd turned over the duvet had slid down his body, exposing his torso, warmly tanned and firmly muscled, but it wasn't sensual feminine appreciation of his maleness that Claire felt most strongly as she looked at him but anxious concern as she saw the sweat-soaked dampness of his body hair and the hectic heat of his skin. She watched as, despite the heat, he started to shiver convulsively, another spasm of the harsh, dry cough she had heard earlier racking his chest so painfully that her own actually seemed to ache in sympathetic response.

Automatically she reached out to pull the duvet back up over him, instinctively soothing him with the kind of low-voiced, gentle comfort she had always given Sally as a child. The intensity of the fever worried her and she regretted not insisting on sending for a doctor earlier.

As she tried to tuck the duvet more securely around him her fingertips accidentally touched his skin. Its heat shocked her, fuelling her anxiety. She placed her hand against his forehead. His skin felt burning hot, his hair soaked with sweat.

He was talking in his sleep again, protesting about something or someone—she couldn't tell.

'It's all right, Brad,' she told him gently. 'Everything is all right.'

'Claire...'

Claire froze as the eyes she had thought closed in a deep, fever-fuelled sleep abruptly opened, their gaze focusing on and then fusing hypnotically with hers.

Claire found herself becoming slightly breathless and dizzy as she tried to wrench her eyes away from the hot, mesmerising glitter of Brad's and discovered that she could not do so.

'Claire,' he said again, his voice lower, huskier, the sound of her name something between a growl and a groan. Then he said huskily, 'You're here... I thought you were just a dream... Come closer.'

'No, Brad, you don't...' Claire started to protest, but with surprising strength Brad reached for her, one hand encircling her wrist, the other wrapping around her as he sat up and half lifted and half pulled her with firm insistence onto the bed next to him.

'I thought you were just a dream,' he whispered throatily as his hands framed her face. 'But you're not. You're actually here, and real...very, very real.'

Claire knew that she should say something, do something, but somehow she couldn't, didn't, her body shocked into immobility as Brad breathed the last three words against her lips before gently brushing his own against hers in a kiss that was so tenderly sweet with gentle promise that Claire felt her whole body ache with yearning for him.

This was no brutal, selfish assault on her body, fuelled by a male sexual desire that was completely without emotion or any recognition of her as a person, a woman with needs and emotions of her own.

This was the kiss of a man who knew, who understood, who even in what Claire could only suppose was some fever-induced physical desire for her was still carefully tender and mindful of her vulnerability.

Claire could feel her body start to tremble as Brad cupped her face in his hands and continued to caress her lips with his, brushing gently over them again and again until they felt softly moist, pliantly eager for a more lingering and intense caress.

Without knowing that she had done so Claire moved closer to him, her lips parting on a small breath of shocked

pleasure as she heard the low sound of hungry need that
Brad made deep in his throat.

She could feel the sensual stroke of his fingertips
against her skin as he massaged the delicate flesh behind
her ear, his mouth leaving hers briefly as he looked down
into her eyes, and then returning to it to kiss her with fierce
passion—once and then a second time and then a third,
until, unable to bear to be without the hungry contact of his
mouth on hers, Claire reached up and wrapped her arms
around him, holding him tightly, making small moaning
sounds of pleasure deep in her own throat, her whole body
on fire, trembling with the aching need she felt for him.

Like someone in a trance, Claire watched him as he released her and gently eased the robe back off her shoulders,
her skin as hot and flushed as his as she saw the look in
his eyes when his gaze caressed the slender nakedness of
her upper body—her slim, narrow shoulders, the creamy
smoothness of her skin, the round fullness of her breasts,
her nipples flushed and flauntingly erect.

No man had ever seen her naked body before. He
watched her with such obviously skin-tingling, erotic
thoughts and in such a way, with such an expression in his
eyes, that she instinctively responded to his subtle message
and to the full-blooded male approval and appreciation of
his lingering appraisal of her by arching her spine slightly,
her eyelids dropping to conceal her own expression as she
watched him back with parted lips and the sure, delicious
knowledge that he found her desirable—and, more, that
as a man he was just slightly enthralled, slightly and satisfyingly in awe of her womanhood.

It was a heady, aphrodisiac, potent mixture of new emotions for a woman whose only previous feelings towards
her sexuality had been a corrosive blend of shame and
self-judgement.

Nothing in the way Brad watched her made her feel ashamed. Nothing in the way he looked at her, nothing in the expression in his eyes, made her feel self-conscious or ill at ease, but her mind only absorbed these facts distantly, her senses, her emotions, her concentration focused instead on the way her body was responding to the subtle signs of sexual responsiveness to her in his.

Something about the way his chest rose and fell with increased urgency made her muscles tighten with delicious awareness.

Something about the hot, fiercely controlled smoulder in the way he looked at her mouth and then her breasts and tried not to flooded her body with feminine arousal and pride.

And, most especially, something about the way he moved the lower half of his body beneath the bedclothes, protectively and oh, so betrayingly trying discreetly to bundle the thickness of the duvet cover over the betraying, strong jut of flesh that it couldn't quite disguise made her smile a soft smile of secret pleasure and power to herself.

She deliberately leaned forward to kiss delicately first one and then the other corner of his mouth before teasingly circling the whole outline of his lips with her tongue-tip, her weight supported on the splayed hand she had oh, so accidentally placed provocatively between his open thighs.

Claire had never behaved with such sensual aggression before—had never dreamed that she could, never mind that she would actually want to and, even more mind-stretching, take actual pleasure in doing so.

The reason why she had come into Brad's bedroom was forgotten; the slow, hungry way he had kissed her had seen to that. It wasn't just her mouth that he had sensitised and aroused with his shatteringly erotic kisses, it was her mind, her emotions, her senses and her whole body.

She felt as though she was wrapped in a soft, sensual cloud of physical and emotional pleasure—a sensation both so elusive and so intense that it couldn't be examined or analysed, simply accepted and enjoyed.

The slow groan that built up in Brad's throat as she teased his mouth made her shiver with delicious pleasure, her eyes narrowing to soft, cat-like slits that made his darken to a fiery furnace of strong male desire as she focused on them.

His hand lifted to her throat, slowly stroking it, his thumb on the pulse, flooding her body with heat as her breathing deepened and quickened in response to his reaction to her.

Claire could feel her breasts swelling and tightening, and somewhere on the edge of her awareness she was conscious of a small sense of outraged shock from her real self that this new, sensual and very wanton part of her should take such obvious self-confident feminine delight in his reaction.

Her body tautened and arched with provocative sensuality, silently calling to Brad to absorb visually the effect that he was having on her and to respond to it by reaching out to stroke and caress the warm, taut flesh so tantalisingly within his reach and yet at the same time denied to him as Claire copied his own, earlier caress, cupping his face in both her hands, gently holding him slightly away from her body as she started to kiss him.

There was a wonderful sense of control and power in knowing how much he wanted her and yet knowing at the same time that he wouldn't break the gentle restriction that she had placed on him. A sense, too, of wanting to push him that little bit further, of wanting to test just how much he did want her, of wanting to prove to herself that his desire for her was just as fiercely intense as hers for him.

She heard the sound of frustrated protest that he made deep in his throat, a thrill of sensual excitement running down her spine as he suddenly turned the tables on her, taking control of the kiss from her, the swift thrust of his tongue between her open lips making her shudder in heated arousal, her body softening, swaying closer to his as though the flushed, hard tips of her breasts ached for the intimate contact of his body.

She wanted, Claire recognised dizzily, to press herself tightly against him, to rub her body against his as sinuously and sexily as a small cat; she wanted to feel the hard heat of his flesh against her own, the erotic rasp of his body hair against the nerve-shattering sensitivity of her desire-flooded breasts; she wanted...

She gave a small, shocked gasp of surprise as Brad suddenly bit her bottom lip erotically, his hands sliding down her arms to manacle her wrists as he lifted her arms gently above her head.

A thrill of pure, hot, womb-tightening sensation ran through her body in a powerful current as she sensed what he was going to do. The heat that flooded her lower body was at once fiercely and control-shatteringly new and yet somehow so familiar that she knew that it...that he was something her body and her emotions had secretly yearned for all her adult life.

She felt no sense of being constrained or afraid, no sense of discomfort or threat at the way he was holding her, only a hot, aching surge of sensual knowledge, an awareness of the deliberateness with which he moved. A tight, aching sensation of intense need made her eyes start to close in shivering appreciation of the way his mouth slowly caressed the sensitive flesh of her throat before moving downwards.

It seemed like an aeon before his mouth reached its

first destination, before she was able to expel her pent-up
breathing—a sharp, high cry of physical release as she
felt him slowly and gently lapping the hard, swollen flesh
of her nipple.

Unable to stop herself, Claire heard herself moan with
pleasure, her whole body shuddering as Brad dropped her
arms and gathered her close, her frantic response to him
destroying his own self-control as his mouth, which had
initially almost teased her with too gentle kisses, now suck-
led on her breasts with a fierce sensuality that made her
move urgently with rhythmic longing against him, her
body possessed of instincts and responses that she had
never, ever imagined it might know or exhibit.

Brad's mouth moved with fierce urgency over her mid-
riff and then her belly; his hands held her and stroked her
and finally lowered her onto the bed, where not even the
sight of him pushing away her robe as he knelt over her
and slowly, with sensual deliberateness, slid his hands ca-
ressingly up over her parted thighs had the effect of making her feel self-conscious or apprehensive.

She could feel the faint tremor in his hands as he
touched and held her, seeing the aching male hunger in
his eyes as he lifted his head and looked deeply into her
own before looking back at the soft, shadowed, exposed
triangle of silky hair that not so much concealed her sex,
Claire recognised as her heart started to race with feverish longing, but rather emphasised its feminine sensuality and allure.

She could see the way Brad's eyes darkened with open
desire as he placed one hand over her, his fingertips stroking the silky hair, parting the softly fleshed lips which were
already signalling their longing for his touch.

But as he knelt over her Claire's attention was suddenly
caught by something. 'No, wait,' she demanded huskily.

'What is it?' he asked her. 'I won't hurt you, Claire. I won't do anything you don't want... I won't...'

Quickly she shook her head. 'No,' she whispered fiercely. 'It isn't...' Her fingers touched his wrist, marvelling at the strength of bone and sinew that his flesh covered. 'I want to see you...' she whispered huskily. 'I want to look...to watch...'

For a moment she thought that he didn't understand what she meant, but then, as his eyes met hers, she saw that he did, and her breath caught on a small, fierce stab of pleasure as she saw, too, how much her whispered plea had aroused him.

Silently she watched as he pushed aside the duvet, aware not only of the tautly male eroticism of his body but of the way he was trembling slightly as well, of the way he paused, hesitated almost nervously, as he watched her watching him.

That he should exhibit such nervousness filled her with female tenderness. Gently she reached out and touched him, running her fingertips from his breastbone right down to where the fine line of body hair became a silky male tangle, openly, thickly sexual, that cushioned the power and promise of what lay over it.

This was her first self-chosen intimate contact with male arousal, but somehow to Claire, as she slowly looked at Brad and absorbed the physical reality of him, it was as though a part of her had known him and known this for always.

Even before her fingertips ran slowly and exploratively along the length of his taut arousal she knew exactly how his whole body would stiffen and shudder beneath her touch...how he would moan softly beneath his breath and close his eyes, arching his spine as he submitted to her exploration, only the fierce rigidity with which the flesh she was touching swelled just that little bit more against her touch betraying how much it craved the pleasure of her caress.

A man's body was at once both so sexually powerful and dangerous and so vulnerable, Claire marvelled, watching Brad's jaw clench as he tried to control his reaction to her. If just this, her lightest touch, had the power to affect him so intensely, how would he react if she were to bend her head and press her lips to his tautly sensitive skin—to kiss and caress it, to slide...?

She gave a tiny gasp of shock when she heard Brad saying something savagely fierce under his breath as he removed her hand and then lowered his head over her body, kissing her stomach and then her thighs with a frenetic urgency, touching her, stroking and caressing her, first with his fingers and then with his mouth until she was turning and twisting beneath the unbearable pleasure of what he was doing to her, alternately shuddering with the seismic convulsions that engulfed her and pleading with him to stop, crying out to him that she couldn't endure such sensual ecstasy.

Only Brad wouldn't stop, and it wasn't until he was finally buried deep inside her, his body moving with rhythmic urgency within hers, his voice thick and guttural with praise and pleasure as he finally succumbed to his own desire, that she recognised that physical ecstasy and female fulfilment could be even more intense a second time than it had been the first.

Half an hour later, still feeling blissfully euphoric from the intensity of their lovemaking and emotionally dizzy from the unexpectedness of what had happened, Claire struggled to fight off the waves of sleep washing over her, murmuring a soft sound of appreciation as Brad drew her closer to his body and kept her there, unable, it seemed, to relinquish her, his lips feathering gently against her hair as Claire drifted off to sleep.

When she came awake abruptly later in the night, at first she had no idea where she was, but the physical sensation of Brad's hot body next to hers and the sound of his voice as he cried out something unintelligible in his sleep froze her into shocked awareness as she realised what she had done.

Her body shaking with reaction, she started to ease herself free of Brad's still constraining arm.

At some stage Brad must have switched off the lamp because the room was now almost in darkness. However, there was still enough light for Claire to be able to see that the fever which had originally brought her into Brad's room, anxious for his health, had disappeared. Still trembling, she eased herself out of his bed, her eyes widening as she caught sight of her discarded robe lying on the floor.

As she shrugged herself into it, her hands were trembling so much that she couldn't fasten the tie-belt.

Hot shame scorched her skin as she remembered how eagerly, how unbelievably provocatively she had silently encouraged Brad to remove it... As her mind relayed flickering, unwanted images of what had happened to her she shrank inwardly from what they were revealing to her. She didn't recognise the image of herself they were giving her, the message about herself that they were giving her. She didn't want to recognise them.

In her anxiety to get out of Brad's room she almost stumbled, holding her breath as he moved in his sleep, his forehead furrowing as he reached out an arm across the bed as though searching for her. For her...or merely for a woman...any woman...?

Had he known it was her when...when he had behaved in that incredibly sensual way, or had he simply been in the

grip of some fevered state of semi-consciousness? Claire
fervently prayed that it was the latter as she hurried back
to her own bedroom.

But then, as she climbed into her cold bed, she stiffened. Brad had called her by her name… He had opened
his eyes and looked at her, recognised her. He had whispered to her, made it clear that he wanted her.

How on earth was she ever going to be able to face him
again? she wondered miserably. For a man to make love to
a woman without being committed to her, without loving
her, was still, in the eyes of a too cynical world, socially
acceptable. For a woman to do the same thing…

But she had not done the same thing, had she? She…

Claire sat up in bed, hugging her arms around her
knees, forcing herself to confront the truth.

She was not permitted the merciful excuse of being able
to blame her behaviour on male hormones or a deep fever,
and she knew that underneath the sheer sensuality of what
she had done, the fierce intensity of a physical desire so
strong that it had caught her off guard like an unexpectedly strong current in a previously placid stretch of calm
water, she was emotionally drawn to Brad—emotionally
responsive to him.

Emotionally drawn… A bitter sound of smothered hysterical laughter rasped at the back of her throat.

Be honest with yourself, she jeered inwardly; you're
in love with him. You, a woman of your age, are making
a fool of yourself with emotions more suited to a girl in
her teens.

A woman of her age maybe, but she did not have the experience, the knowledge of herself as a sexual being, that
other women of her age enjoyed, Claire admitted painfully. In that regard she was as naïve and unknowing as
a girl in the throes of her first adolescent love affair. And

her age made those feelings more painful, more hard to bear, not less.

'Admit it,' she whispered as she bent her aching head to her raised knees; 'you were attracted to him right from the start but you pretended not to know it, and tonight when he touched you...' She swallowed painfully.

She hadn't tried very hard to resist, to stop him, had she? On the contrary...

Why was it so hard for her to face the truth about her feelings for Brad?

Did she really need to ask herself that question?

Claire's mouth curled into a small, bitter expression of pain. No, of course she didn't. It was hard because she knew already the pain that loving Brad was going to cause her.

To love a man who didn't love you back when you were seventeen was bad enough, but at seventeen life still had the power to heal the hurts it inflicted. There would inevitably be another man, another love. But at thirty-four it was for ever, for life—a once-and-for-all love.

As Claire closed her eyes, willing the tears she could feel gathering at the back of her eyes not to fall, she reflected on how very little she actually seemed to have known about herself. All those years of believing that it would be impossible for her ever to share true physical intimacy with a man, all those years of believing that the trauma of her youth and the inhibitions, the doubts about her own sexuality...about herself...

Tonight had shown her just how wrong she had been. In Brad's arms, beneath Brad's touch, her body had flowered into the full bloom of its sensuality...of its sexuality.

What was going to happen when he woke up and remembered...? As Claire fought to suppress the pain that she could feel seeping relentlessly through her body she

reflected that Irene was not going to be pleased when she
learned that Brad had moved out, which she knew already
was what was going to happen.

CHAPTER EIGHT

CLAIRE woke up with a start. She could hear the front door-bell ringing and the sun was streaming in through her un-curtained bedroom window. Groggily she lifted her head from her pillow and was appalled to discover that it was gone ten o'clock.

Throwing back the bedcovers, she reached for her robe, pulling it on over her naked body, avoiding looking at her reflection in the dressing-table mirror, her skin flushing slightly as the slow, almost voluptuous movements of her body silently betrayed the events of the previous evening.

As she hurried along the landing she saw that the door to Brad's bedroom stood open. The bed was empty and neatly made up. No need to ask herself why Brad had not woken her before he had left, she thought grimly.

Whoever was outside the front door was obviously getting impatient; a finger pressed the bell in a long, imperious ring.

As Claire went to open the door she could see through the glass panes a woman she didn't recognise standing outside with two small children—a young girl at her side and a baby in one arm.

When she pulled open the door to her she could see that the young woman was frowning anxiously and that she looked tired and drawn. The baby had started to cry and the girl joined in, the young mother closing her eyes in exasperation as she tried to calm them.

'Is Brad here?' she asked Claire anxiously, her frown returning as she appealed urgently, 'This is where he's staying, isn't it? He did give me the address but I wasn't sure I'd written it down properly.

'Yes…it's all right,' she soothed the baby, her soft, transatlantic accent so very similar to Brad's that just to hear it made Claire's susceptible heart turn over.

'Yes. You've got the right address,' she reassured the young woman, standing back to usher her inside and at the same time automatically offering to take the baby from her.

'Oh, yes… Thanks… He's very damp,' she informed Claire ruefully, 'and pretty hungry too…'

Claire wasn't really listening; her heart was turning over painfully inside her too tight chest as she looked into the baby's now fully opened eyes and saw just how like Brad's they were.

A spasm of deep, wrenching pain like nothing she had ever known seared through her, her eyes too dry for the tears she ached to cry, the small sound of protest she could feel rising in her throat luckily suppressed.

'I'm Brad's sister, by the way—Mary-Beth,' the young woman introduced herself as she ushered the little girl inside and then reached for their luggage.

His sister. As Claire focused on the other woman's back she could feel herself starting to tremble with relief. Just for a moment, looking at the baby and seeing Brad's eyes in his small and as yet not really fully formed face, she had thought…assumed…

'He is here, isn't he? I had to come. I had to see him,' she told Claire emotionally, her eyes suddenly filling with tears.

'No, I'm afraid he isn't,' Claire informed her. 'He'll

probably be back soon, though,' she added comfortingly.
'I can give you the office number and you can ring him
there,' she offered helpfully, but the other woman shook
her head.

'No...no, I'd better wait until he gets back... You see,
he...he doesn't...he isn't exactly expecting us...' She paced
the hall edgily, avoiding Claire's eyes.

Something was very obviously wrong, Claire guessed.
No one, however impetuous, came rushing across the Atlantic with two small children, one of them still too young
to walk, just on a mere whim.

'You must be hungry and tired,' she said quietly. 'Let's
go into the kitchen and see if we can find you something
to eat, shall we?' she suggested softly to the baby, who had
stopped crying but was gnawing hungrily on his fingers
as he focused wonderingly on her unfamiliar face.

'I guess we are,' her unexpected visitor agreed, but
Claire sensed that food was the last thing on her mind,
and now that she had had the opportunity to study her a
little more closely she could see the tell-tale signs of strain
and unhappiness etched into her face and eyes. The little
girl too, clinging so closely to her mother's side, had an
expression in her eyes that had been caused by something
more than the confusion of a long transatlantic journey.

Mary-Beth had said that she would wait for Brad to
return, but Claire suspected that whatever had brought
her rushing to find him meant that she needed to see her
brother more urgently than that.

Her heart started to thud a little too fast at the thought
of telephoning him. What would he think when he heard
her voice? That because of last night she was making un-
founded assumptions about him...about them...?

His sister's obvious need was more important than her
own pride, Claire told herself firmly as she led the way

to the kitchen, settling Mary-Beth in one of the comfortable Windsor chairs and then going to retrieve from the
laundry room the high chair she kept for emergencies, still
holding the baby, who was now quite contentedly gur-
gling up at her.

'You're obviously very good with children,' Mary-Beth
told her ruefully, watching her. 'He's screamed practically
the whole way here.'

'And he was sick three times,' a small voice piped up
from Mary-Beth's side, the little girl's face stern with big-
sisterly disapproval.

'This is Tara.' Mary-Beth introduced her daughter. 'And
that smelly, damp bundle you're carrying is Abe junior...'

'Abe senior is my daddy,' Tara piped up. 'But he hasn't
come with us. He's—'

'Hush now, Tara,' Mary-Beth interrupted quickly. 'I'm
sorry,' she apologised to Claire. 'We're putting you to an
awful lot of trouble. I should have rung Brad before we
left but...'

Tears suddenly filled her eyes, and as she looked away
Claire felt her own throat closing up in sympathy for her.

Half an hour later, when the children had both been fed
and were soundly asleep upstairs in one of the bedrooms,
Claire poured her unexpected visitor a fresh cup of coffee
and tried again to persuade her to let her telephone Brad.

'No, no... Oh, where is he? I need to see him to talk to
him. He's the only one...'

Fresh tears filled her eyes.

'When everything you thought you could rely on—everyone you thought you could rely on—lets you down and
it seems that there's only one person left for you to turn to,
you don't always think things through properly... Brad's
always been more than just a brother to us. He's the one

we always automatically turn to when things go wrong for us…and I guess that's why…'

She bit her lip and looked directly at Claire as she went on huskily, 'You've probably already worked out why I'm here… I found out three days ago that Abe, my husband, has been having an affair with a girl at work.

'He tried to deny it, of course, but they were seen downtown in a bar by a close friend of mine. He told me that he had to work late…and I believed him, even though I knew she'd been making a play for him. I thought he loved me, you see,' she said sadly.

'Look, you've had a long flight. Why don't you go upstairs and lie down?' Claire suggested gently. She could see from the deep unhappiness in the other woman's eyes just how much her husband's infidelity had hurt her.

'Abe kept insisting that it wasn't true—that he was simply trying to help the girl sort out her personal problems. He said he hadn't told me because he knew the way I'd react… He said that I never had time to listen to him any more anyway, because the children were more important to me than he was. He even said that Brad mattered more to me than him…that I paid more attention to what Brad had to say…that it was Brad I always turned to for help…'

As her emotions caught up with her she swallowed painfully and then said huskily, 'I think I will go up and have a rest, if you don't mind. I'm beginning to feel that so much has happened that I can't even think straight any more… Abe doesn't even know I'm here,' she added tiredly. 'I just wanted to see Brad so much… I needed him so much… I just kinda grabbed the kids and some stuff and phoned the airline and the next thing I knew we were all on our way…'

As she stood up she stifled a yawn, her eyes dark with exhaustion.

* * *

Claire waited until she was sure that Mary-Beth was asleep before telephoning the office.

Brad, she discovered, wasn't there and so she spoke to Tim instead, who informed her that Brad was expected back within the hour.

'Could you ask him to give me a ring as soon as he comes back?' Claire asked her brother-in-law, without explaining why she needed to speak to him. Brad's family was his private affair and she didn't think it right to discuss what had happened with anyone else.

A quick check upstairs confirmed that her visitors were all still asleep.

As she put fresh towels in the bathroom she wondered how long they were likely to stay, and also wondered, half-enviously, what it must be like to have someone like Brad to turn to—someone you could rely on so completely that you could simply walk out of your home with two children and a couple of suitcases, knowing that if you could get to him he would solve your problems for you.

She was being a little unfair, Claire reproved herself. No amount of brotherly concern could surely compensate for an unfaithful husband and a broken marriage. And she had seen the apprehension and confusion in little Tara's eyes. An uncle, no matter how loving and concerned, could not replace a father.

Not that she blamed Mary-Beth for feeling as she did. To discover that your husband—the man you love and to whom you had committed yourself and who you believed had committed himself to you, the father of your children—had been seeing another woman…had been making love with her…must be one of the most painful experiences that life could hold.

As she went back downstairs Claire checked her fridge. From the way Mary-Beth had toyed with the food she had

had earlier Claire doubted that she would have much appetite, but the children were a different matter, especially the baby.

She had plenty of fresh vegetables and fruit that she could cook for him and put through the blender, Claire decided, and as for Tara—well, with a bit of luck the little girl might be enticed into helping her, which would give her mother the chance to have some private conversation with Brad.

Claire suspected from the anxious looks that Tara had given her mother when her father had been mentioned that the little girl was already aware that something was wrong between her parents.

Children, even very young ones, were dismayingly quick to pick up on things like that and to suffer through it, Claire knew, often blaming themselves for the problems between their mothers and fathers.

A small sound from upstairs checked her and she paused to listen to it... Was it the baby crying?

As she went towards the door she heard the sound of a car pulling up outside.

Brad? She had expected him to telephone her, not to come straight back. A small flutter of apprehension gripped her stomach.

This would be the first time they had seen one another since last night—the first time since... But this was not the time for her to become involved in her own feelings; she...

She tensed as the kitchen door opened and Brad came striding in. When he saw her anxious expression his forehead creased in a frown and he hurried towards her.

'Claire, what is it? What's wrong?' he asked, starting to reach for her as though he was going to take her in his arms, Claire recognised, her throat tight with emotion, her colour starting to rise self-consciously as she fought the

temptation to move closer to him, her body already reacting to his presence, his proximity, to its need to recreate
the intimacy they had shared last night, its need to encourage the physical bond it wanted to establish between them.

Claire acknowledged how easy it would be simply to
close the distance between them, to walk into his arms as
though it was her right to do so.

Against her will she found herself looking at his mouth,
her glance lingering on it betrayingly as she felt her own
lips start to tremble slightly. Last night's intimacy had left
her so sensually, so sensitively attuned to him that she
could almost feel the warm pleasure of his mouth on hers.

'Claire...'

The hoarse urgency with which he said her name
brought her back to reality, her body tensing as she heard
sounds from the hall.

'Brad—' she began warningly, but the door was already
opening and Mary-Beth was rushing into her brother's
arms, crying emotionally,

'Oh, Brad, thank the Lord you're here...'

'Mary-Beth...?' Claire could hear the surprise in Brad's
voice as he held his sister and looked questioningly at
Claire over her head. 'What...?'

Quietly Claire left the room and closed the door behind
her. They would have things to say to one another that
needed to be said in private, without her.

She could hear the baby starting to cry and moved instinctively towards the stairs to go and comfort him.

When she went into the bedroom Tara had obviously
just woken up.

'Where's my mommy?' she asked Claire uncertainly.

'She's downstairs talking to your uncle Brad,' Claire
told her, and then asked, 'Do you know where the spare
nappies are? I think your brother needs changing.'

'Nappies?' The little girl's face creased in confusion whilst Claire quickly tried to recall the American word for what she wanted.

'Diapers,' she remembered with relief, then gently but firmly involved Tara in the job of cleaning and changing her small brother, deliberately drawing it out as long as she could to give Mary-Beth a chance to talk to Brad. Claire suspected that she would not want Tara to overhear what she had to say to Brad about her husband's infidelity. The little girl was obviously already distressed enough by what was happening.

As Claire picked up the now dry and cooing little boy to give him a cuddle she saw the way Tara kept glancing anxiously towards the door and guessed that she wouldn't be able to keep her distracted for very much longer.

To her relief she heard the kitchen door opening and Mary-Beth's and Brad's voices on the stairs.

'Mommy,' Tara demanded as soon as her mother came into the bedroom, 'when are we going home? I want my daddy...'

Mary-Beth had obviously been crying and Tara's mouth started to tremble ominously as she looked at her mother. It was Brad who saved the situation, following his sister into the room and swinging the little girl up into his arms, saying cheerfully, 'Hello, pumpkin...'

'Uncle Brad... Uncle Brad...' Tara squealed in obvious pleasure, hugging him tightly round the neck.

'I'll get on to the airport and see how quickly they can get you a return flight,' Brad was saying to Mary-Beth over Tara's head.

'I'm not going back—not on my own, not without you,' Mary-Beth insisted.

'Mary-Beth, I've already explained why I can't come with you,' Brad told her firmly. 'I have commitments here.'

'Maybe, but they aren't as important as your commitment to your family; they can't be, Brad,' Mary-Beth told
him quickly. 'You know the uncles will understand. I need
you.'

Claire could see that Brad was frowning.

'Mary-Beth, I can't.'

'Then I'm not going back,' she told him determinedly.
'Not on my own.'

'Abe—' Brad began, but Mary-Beth refused to listen.

'I don't want to talk about him, or to him.'

'You have to talk,' Brad told her quietly. 'For the kids'
sake, if nothing else. He is still their father and he does
have certain rights—'

'He has no rights. He lost those the day he started fool-
ing around with that—that…' Mary-Beth had started to
protest bitterly but Brad shook his head warningly as Tara
looked at her mother in anxious concern. 'If you want me
to talk to him then you're going to have to be there too,'
Mary-Beth insisted.

Claire could see that Brad wasn't too pleased about his
sister's demands.

'There's no way I want to so much as see him again
after what he's done…' she announced.

It was plain to Claire that Brad's sister's temperament
was as tempestuous and fiery as her dark red hair suggested, and there was no doubt also that she was deeply
hurt by her husband's infidelity. Beneath her very obvious
anger Claire could see the misery and pain in her eyes.

'You said Abe denied being involved with anyone else,'
Brad was reminding her. 'He said—'

'He would say that, wouldn't he?' Mary-Beth derided
bitterly. 'He knows what he stands to lose. Oh, Brad, how
could he… I thought he loved me…us…'

Tears welled up in her eyes and Tara, seeing her mother's distress, started to cry noisily in sympathy.

'Would you like me to take the children?' Claire offered quickly. 'You must both still have things you need to discuss...'

'I've said everything I want to say,' Mary-Beth said fiercely. 'I don't care what you say, Brad; there's no way I'm going back to him and I didn't come all the way over here to have you make me...or to listen to you defending what he's done. I thought you'd be more understanding... more sympathetic...'

She was crying in earnest now. Quietly Claire held out her arms to Tara, trying not to let the revealing flush of pleasure she could feel heating the pit of her stomach flood betrayingly into her face when Brad smiled at her with appreciative relief as he handed his niece over to her.

'I want to stay with my mommy...' Tara started to protest as Claire took hold of her, but Claire had enough experience from her work at the school to know how to deal with her apprehensive need to remain with her mother.

'Do you?' she said calmly. 'Oh, dear. I was hoping you'd come downstairs with me and help me make some special bis...er...cookies. I expect you're very good at baking, aren't you?' she asked.

'Yes. I'm very good,' Tara agreed, and then asked, 'What kind of cookies?'

'What kind would you like to make?' Claire asked her. The baby had gone peacefully back to sleep, she noticed as she gently shepherded Tara out of the room.

She and Tara had almost finished their cookie-baking exercise before Mary-Beth and Brad reappeared, and during the half-hour or so that they had been together Claire had learned a good deal about her Mommy and Daddy and

how much she loved them both from Tara, who had chattered happily to her as they worked together.

'It looks like I'm going to have to go back to the States
with Mary-Beth. I've managed to get us seats on a flight
this evening,' Brad told Claire tersely as he obeyed Tara's
demand that he come and see what she had been making.

'I'm sorry about all this...' he added grimly, making a
small gesture that included his sister and Tara.

'It's all right,' Claire assured him. 'I'm just glad that you
were able to respond so quickly to my message. I hadn't
expected you to come straight back—'

'What message?' Brad asked her, frowning.

Claire stared at him.

'I rang the office to tell you about Mary-Beth, and when
you weren't there I left a message with Tim for you to
ring me.'

If he hadn't got her message then how had he known
to come back? Claire wondered. But before she could say
anything Mary-Beth was demanding his attention, wanting to know exactly what time their flight was and worrying about the fact that she had neglected to bring enough
baby food for Abe junior with her.

'You should have thought about that before you left,'
Brad told her sharply.

Whilst he was obviously making every attempt to
sort out his sister's problems for her, he did not appear
to be as sympathetic to her plight as Claire had expected
him to be, and was certainly nothing like as partisan, refusing to join Mary-Beth in condemning her husband and
rather to the contrary suggesting to her that she should
have discussed the situation more fully with Abe before
walking out and subjecting her two small children to all
the stress and bewilderment of a transatlantic flight.

Sensing that Mary-Beth was unhappy with her brother's

response, Claire quickly offered to take her to the local supermarket where she would be able to buy some branded
baby food for her little boy.

'Brad, could you take me?' Mary-Beth appealed. 'I just
can't think straight at the moment.'

It was only natural that Mary-Beth should want her
brother with her rather than a stranger, Claire told herself
firmly, and it was no doubt illogical of her to feel, on the
strength of what little they had actually shared, so emotionally bereft and excluded from what was going on.

Several times since he had returned to the house Brad
had looked as if he wanted to say something to her, Claire
acknowledged, and it was obvious that he was none too
pleased with his sister's disruption of his life. But, in reality, what else could he do other than agree to her demands
that he return home with her? Claire acknowledged.

It was plain to her, even without knowing Mary-Beth
or having met her husband, that it would need all of Brad's
skilled counsel and wisdom to heal the rift in his sister's
marriage.

'Claire,' she heard him saying quietly, his hand touching her arm lightly, as though he wanted to draw her
away from Mary-Beth and the children. As though...as
though...what? Claire asked herself ruefully. As though he
wanted to isolate both of them from his family, as though
he wanted to have her to himself. That's some imagination you've got there, she warned herself.

'I really am sorry,' he told her in a low voice. 'If I
thought there was any way I could persuade Mary-Beth
to go home on her own—'

'She needs you, Brad,' Claire interrupted him gently.
And so do I, her heart cried silently, but of course she
couldn't allow herself to voice such words and wouldn't
have done no matter what the circumstances; to have done

so would have been immature and selfish. 'She's obviously very upset about…about her husband,' Claire felt bound to add.

'Yes.' Brad looked rather grim. 'She always has a tendency to flare up over nothing and I doubt that this will be any exception. Abe's just not the type to stray from his marriage.'

'Mary-Beth obviously doesn't share that view,' Claire pointed out wryly.

'No,' Brad agreed heavily, glancing at his sister, who was trying to soothe the children's fretting. 'This couldn't have happened at a worse time…' he began to say; his hand was still resting on her arm but now the light grip of his fingers had somehow or other become a gentle stroke.

An automatic reflex action to the feel of her skin beneath them or the tender, soundless reassurance of a lover? Claire wasn't sure.

'Brad,' Mary-Beth called out impatiently, 'you're going to have to get to that supermarket.'

Was she imagining the regret she could see in Brad's eyes as he released her arm and moved away from her? Claire wondered.

'And so Brad's gone back to America with his sister?' Hannah asked as Claire started to unload her dishwasher.

'Yes, that's right,' Claire agreed woodenly.

Hannah had come round half an hour ago, two hours after Brad and Mary-Beth had left with the children. By now, no doubt, they would be airborne and on their way back home.

'I'm not sure when I'll be coming back but it should be within the week,' Brad had told her before he'd left. They had been standing in the hall, Brad frowning down at her, his expression grimly sombre—because he was con-

cerned about his sister or because he was regretting what
had happened between them the previous night? Claire
had wondered.

She flinched now as she recalled her own brief moment
of weakness when she had almost reached out to him and
begged him to…

To what? To tell her that their lovemaking had been as
earth-shaking, as cataclysmically, emotionally and physically intense for him as it had been for her? That, like her,
he had been confronted by a revelation of emotions for
her—love for her so strong that he knew his life would
never be the same again?

Fortunately, she had been able to stop herself before
she had done anything more than stretch out her hand towards him.

Mary-Beth had hugged her warmly before she'd left,
thanking her appreciatively for all that she had done, but
Brad hadn't made any move to touch her, Claire had noticed.

'How long will he be gone for?' Hannah pressed.
'You're going to miss him. There's something about having a man about the house…'

'He's only been here a couple of days, Hannah,' Claire
reminded her neighbour tersely, and was instantly ashamed
of herself when she saw the hurt expression in Hannah's
eyes. The trouble was that Hannah was right—or almost…

It wasn't just a matter of her going to miss Brad, she was
already doing so—missing him, aching for him, yearning
for him, filled with all manner of insecurities and doubts,
wondering if as far as he was concerned his sister's marital
difficulties had occurred most opportunely—contrary to
what he had said before he'd left. It was a galling thought
and an extremely painful one.

So you went to bed with him and had sex, Claire taunted

herself later when Hannah was gone. So what? Why should that have had any deep meaning for him?

Did Brad even remember what had happened between them? she pondered starkly. He had, after all, been in the grip of an extremely strong fever earlier in the evening.

Which was the worst scenario for her? she wondered painfully. For him not to have remembered a single thing about them being together, or for him to have remembered but to have decided that it was something that he simply felt had no real meaning for him?

And, given the choice, which would she have preferred—to have experienced all that she had in his arms, to have discovered her capacity for emotional and physical love and endure all the pain that must surely now follow, or to have remained in celibate obliviousness?

It was a question she didn't feel she could answer, not with all the long, empty nights ahead of her without Brad beside her.

CHAPTER NINE

A WEEK went by without Claire hearing anything from Brad, and then another, and then halfway through the third she received a telephone call from Tim advising her that Brad had been in touch with him.

'He did try to ring you but he said there was no reply. His uncle—the one who runs the business—has had a heart attack and is in Intensive Care and Brad has had to step in and take over from him, so obviously there's no question of him returning here in the immediate future.'

'But what about his things? They're still here,' Claire protested. Her body felt numb with shock; until she'd heard Tim telling her that Brad wouldn't be coming back she hadn't realised how much she had been depending on him returning...how strongly she had been clinging to that frail link between them.

Now Tim had severed it, leaving her feeling that she was crashing through space, tumbling helplessly from a great height, her stomach seized with fear and nausea as her whole world dissolved around her.

'I expect he'll want us to make arrangements to ship whatever he's left behind out to him,' Tim told her. 'Just let me know what there is and we can sort all that out for you.'

After she had replaced the receiver Claire went upstairs, moving like a sleepwalker as she went into the room that

Brad had occupied. Was she imagining it or did the very
air in there still carry a faint scent of him—of his soap,
his skin, himself? Her whole body bowed with misery
and loss.

She went across to the bed, smoothing her fingertips
over the pillow, hot tears filling her eyes.

It was ridiculous for her to be behaving in this fashion, she derided herself. She was a grown woman. Grown
women didn't fall intensely and passionately in love in the
space of a handful of days—or at least they weren't supposed to. Their hearts weren't supposed to ache with all
the intensity and anguish with which hers was aching right
now, and nor were their bodies.

Their bodies...her body... Her body. Oh, how it had
deceived her, led her into a trap of false security, letting
her believe that it was impossible for it to feel, to want, to
need the way it was doing right now.

Brad had said that he'd tried to ring her, Tim had told
her. Her head dipped defensively as she remembered those
last, frantic hours before he had left, his sister's resentment
at what she had seen as Brad's support of her husband in
his insistence that she needed to return home to talk to
him and that it wasn't fair on her children—on their children—simply to walk out, no matter what provocation she
might think she personally had had to do so.

Brad had tried to talk privately to her then and foolishly she had hoped that he had wanted to reassure her, to
offer her if not his love then at least the reassurance that
there was something between them worth pursuing. But
now she wondered if she might have been wrong, if what
he had wanted to say to her was more along the lines of
Thank you, it was very nice, but now it's over.

Over... Her throat constricted on a small half-sob, a
painful spasm of emotion. It had never really properly

begun. What was there, in reality, to be over? All they had had, all there had been was simply a...a one-night stand... a bit of a sexual adventure, and she had been a fool to believe that it was anything more.

And, that being the case, there was precious little point in compounding her folly by thinking about what might have been, tormenting herself with implausible, unrealistic daydreams. No, she would be better off simply forgetting about the whole incident...about Brad himself—forgetting it and firmly locking the door on it and throwing away the key.

It was an easy enough resolve to make, but a much harder one to keep, Claire discovered in the weeks that followed.

Irene commented in a slightly miffed manner on her lacklustre response to life in general and to her own good news in particular that Tim had responded so positively to Brad's suggestions, including his recommendation that Tim should consider going on a self-assertion training course.

'Of course it will mean that someone will have to come over from America to take charge of things for a while,' Irene had confided. 'But Brad says he has someone in mind for that—their top distributor over there. Tim is already in contact with him and they seem to be getting on very well.'

But even her sister-in-law's plans for the future failed to move Claire to anything more than dull indifference—a reaction which she herself felt barely registered as a meagre one out of ten on the scale of her emotionally misery, but which apparently Irene had seen fit to accord a much higher anxiety-rating, as Claire discovered when she received an unscheduled visit from her stepdaughter in the middle of what had so far been a particularly harrowing day.

She had discovered earlier in the morning that the school where she worked was to be closed, its pupils amalgamated with those at another school on the other side of town.

It wasn't so much the fact that her voluntary services would no longer be required that upset her but the knowledge of how difficult some of their children would find it to adapt to new and, to them, potentially threatening surroundings and routines, and she was still worrying about the fate of the children when Sally arrived unexpectedly.

'Is something wrong?' Claire asked her stepdaughter anxiously, knowing that she should have been at work.

'According to Aunt Irene I'm the one who should be asking you that question,' Sally told her forthrightly, adding more gently, 'I haven't wanted to pry, but it's been obvious ever since we got back from honeymoon that something is wrong. Every time I've spoken to you it's been almost as though you're not really… You've been so…so distant almost that I had begun…' Sally paused and bit her lip, her face flushing slightly.

'It isn't anything to do with the wedding, is it…and with that trick Chris and I played on the three of you with the wedding bouquet? Only when I rang Star the other day she was very curt with me and said she was too busy to speak to me, and as for Poppy—well, I know how she's always felt about Chris, but she was so young when she first developed her crush on him.

'I never meant to hurt any of you,' Sally told her urgently, coming over to kneel down beside Claire and to lay her head on her lap as she had done when she was a little girl in need either of a confessional for some minor crime or some extra cosseting and reassurance.

Automatically Claire reached out to stroke the shin-

ing head of hair just as she had done so many times when
Sally had been growing up.

'If you're cross with me about the bouquet, please believe me, we…I only did it because—well, because Chris
and I… Well, I'm so happy myself, I just wanted all of
you—but most especially you…'

Sally bit her lip, her voice slightly strained as she continued emotionally, 'You've been…you are such a wonderful mother to me, much better than…a much better parent
to me than Dad ever was. I've always known that and,
well…I've always loved you…more…best…but it wasn't
until Chris pointed it out to me that I realised that your
marriage, that my father…'

She raised her head and looked at Claire. 'It must have
been very difficult for you. After all, he never made any
secret of the fact that Paula…that…'

'He still loved your mother,' Claire supplied for her.
'She was your mother, Sally,' she reminded her stepdaughter gently, 'and I honestly don't mind you referring to her
as that… You see, I know I have my own place in your
love and in your life, and if anything it isn't jealousy or
envy I feel for her, but sadness and pity because she was
deprived of so much pleasure in not being here to watch
you growing up.

'When you have children of your own they're going to
want to know about her and you're going to want to tell
them, but I shall be the one who cuddles them and tells
them stories and gives them forbidden treats…'

'You'll always be Mum to me,' Sally told her tearfully.
'Always… I know there's been a bit of gossip about the
bouquet and the pact the three of you made not to get married because of it—Hannah told me and I've heard it from
someone else as well—but I honestly never meant to cause
any of you any embarrassment or to hurt you…

'I know that, Sally,' Claire reassured her.

'Well, if that's not what's wrong, then what is it?' Sally persisted. 'And don't tell me "nothing", because it's obvious that something is wrong.'

'I heard this morning that they're going to close the school,' Claire told her.

'Oh, no. I am sorry… I know how much you've enjoyed working there.' She stood up, her face and voice lightening with relief as she added, 'Irene was convinced that the reason you've been so withdrawn has something to do with that American you had staying with you. Bart—'

'Brad,' Claire corrected her quietly, getting up to go and fill the kettle to make them both a hot drink and keeping her face carefully averted just in case something in her expression should betray her.

Just saying Brad's name had made her heart somersault violently and it was now thudding so heavily against her chest wall that it was practically making her dizzy and slightly faint.

For the first time ever Claire actually felt glad when her stepdaughter had gone. Right now Sally was still living in a cloud of post-honeymoon euphoric bliss, but once that started to fade and she was back to being her normal sharp-eyed self Claire doubted that she would be able to keep the truth from her for very long. If Irene had already guessed that something was wrong—and, even worse, why—what chance did she have of concealing the truth from Sally?

The answer lay in her own hands, Claire told herself firmly. If she didn't want the pain and humiliation of her nearest and dearest discovering how stupid she had been, then she was going to have to make much more of an effort to force herself to forget Brad and her love for him.

More of an effort. She gave a small, twisted smile. Right

now simply getting through the day without him was just about as much effort as she was capable of making, which was pathetic and ridiculous given the fact that she had only known him a matter of days.

Maybe in that short space of time she had developed an emotional rapport with him, an emotional intimacy which had led to her telling him things about herself that she had never dreamed of confiding to anyone else. Maybe during that time she had developed an emotional need for him, an emotional hunger and intensity...which he quite plainly had not reciprocated, she reminded herself flatly. If he had...

As she cleared away her and Sally's dirty coffee-mugs she paused to stare blindly out of her kitchen window. Next week it would be three months since the wedding. She had put a red cross by the date on her kitchen wall-calendar.

As she glanced desolately at it she reflected grimly that at least she of the trio who had fallen into Sally's carefully orchestrated trap would be able to keep their rendezvous knowing that there was no chance of her breaking the light-hearted vow they had all made to remain single.

Quietly Brad watched from the sidelines as his family busied themselves with their self-appointed tasks.

Today they were holding their annual barbecue—an event that Brad himself had instituted the year after their parents' death, when, instead of grieving and mourning their loss in the traditional way, for the sake of the younger siblings and to ensure that their parents were never forgotten he had decided to hold a small barbecue to celebrate the fact that they were still together, that their parents had loved them and still loved them, even if they could not be there with them to show it.

Over the years the original small, homely event had

expanded until it was now almost a local institution, with
virtually the whole town seeming to attend, its venue having moved from the backyard of their home to a site on
the lake shore.

Spring was just beginning to give way to summer and
the days were longer and warmer. Later in the year this
tree-sheltered site would be enervatingly stifling, but right
now it was just protectively warm enough for the younger
members of the group to beg pleadingly to be allowed into
the water.

Brad smiled ruefully to himself, witnessing the clumsy,
unpractised flirtation that one of his nephews was attempting with a disdainful redhead who one day was going
to be stunningly attractive but who right now still wore
her hair in braids and had a sexually pre-adolescent, thin,
leggy body.

Once it had hurt him almost unbearably, knowing that
his parents had died at this time of the year when nature
was so full of promise and vigour, when everything was
green and fresh and growing, but over the years that pain
had softened into acceptance.

'You look very pensive.'

Brad smiled as Mary-Beth came over to him, slipping
her arm through his and resting her head on his shoulder.

'I still haven't thanked you properly for insisting that
I come back and talk properly to Abe. If I hadn't done...'
She gave a small, rueful shake of her head. 'That temper
of mine; you'd have thought by now I'd have learnt not to
trust it.'

'I'd have thought by now you would have learnt to trust
Abe,' Brad told her dryly.

'Well, you know how it is... Somehow, losing Mom and
Dad... I guess I'm always going to feel a bit insecure...
like thinking that Abe was having an affair when he was

doing no such thing. But you're not much better,' she accused her brother. 'Look at the way you've stayed single... avoided any emotional commitment.'

Avoided emotional commitment. Brad frowned as he looked back at her. 'And how the hell do you work that one out?' he demanded grimly. 'Look around you, Mary-Beth, and tell me that again.'

'Oh, I don't mean you've avoided any emotional commitment to us,' Mary-Beth protested. 'You've been the best brother...the very best there could ever be. But...haven't you ever wanted anyone of your own, Brad? I mean we've all married... Don't you feel lonely sometimes, wish that you'd...?' She bit her lip as she saw the way that he was looking at her.

'Now don't you go putting that stern elder-brother look on your face with me. We all know how much you've sacrificed for us, how much you must curse us all to perdition at times, especially the uncles...'

She paused, drawing an abstract pattern in the sandy earth with the toe of her shoe. 'We all know you didn't want to go to Britain...nor to come back and take over the business. And I know, even if the others don't, that the old boat you've got down at the jetty is your equivalent of what us kids used to call our "running-away money". But if you really left here to sail around the world on your own, Brad, you'd hate it. You're a family man...a patriarch—'

'Don't bet money on it,' Brad advised her harshly, preparing to walk away, but Mary-Beth tugged on his arms, restraining him.

'Don't go yet; there's something else I wanted to say. We all know that Uncle Joe wouldn't have survived his heart attack if you hadn't come back...if you hadn't been in there pitching for him, but he's never going to be strong enough to go back to running the business, Brad, and we—'

'You what?' he asked her grimly. 'You've been depu-
tised to soften me up and make sure I won't get any ideas
about wanting to lead my own life, is that it?'

'Brad…'

Brad knew how much he'd upset her and cursed himself
under his breath as he saw the tears in her eyes.

'You've changed so much recently,' Mary-Beth accused
him. 'Become so withdrawn…so…so angry. All we want
is for you to be happy.'

Later on, after they'd hugged and made up, Brad
watched as she walked to join her husband and children.

Everyone here bar him had someone of their own, he
reflected bleakly. Once that would not have bothered him;
once he would not even have had such a thought, because
they were all his family—a part of him, as he was of them;
once he would never have spent an event like this standing on the sidelines wishing with all his heart that he were
somewhere else, and with someone else.

Why hadn't Claire returned his phone call? He had tried
so hard to make time to talk properly, privately with her
before he and Mary-Beth had left, but the opportunity had
just not been there. And then arriving home to be greeted
by the news that his uncle Joe was seriously ill and was
not expected to survive had meant that his own personal
emotional needs and desires had had to be pushed to one
side whilst he dealt with the practical problems that his
uncle's heart attack had caused.

When he had finally got the time to himself to ring her
she hadn't been there and he had had to speak to Tim instead to explain what had happened. All week he had expected Claire to ring, rushing home whenever he could to
check his answering machine.

But when one week had gone by and then another without her getting in touch he had told himself that he already

had the answer to the question that he had secretly wanted to ask her, and that there was no point in going over and over in his mind...in his body those precious, gut-wrenching hours that they had spent together as lovers, that special, heart-aching time when he had hoped...believed... when he had finally recognised that he had at last found the thing—the person—that he had subconsciously been looking for all his adult life, and that without her in it his life would go on being incomplete.

He would go on being incomplete. This...she was the reason for all the dissatisfaction he had felt with his life over the years; she was the reason she had never felt able to reach out to any other woman in a way that would make her a permanent part of his life.

Was it his fault that she did not feel the same way? Had he rushed her...frightened her...put her off with his inability to control his sexual desire for her? Knowing what he did about her past, shouldn't he have been able to take things more slowly, to let her set the pace for any physical intimacy between them?

But it hadn't been any chauvinistic male need to prove either to her or himself that he possessed some magical ability to restore her sexuality to her, to reactivate it, that had motivated him; he knew that. He had simply wanted her so much...been so overwhelmed by his love for her that the sad, pathetic truth was that he had been totally unable to stop himself.

What kind of admission was that from a grown man...a mature man to have to make? he wondered in dry self-disgust. And he was surprised because Claire didn't want anything more to do with him?

On the other side of the clearing his uncle Joe, still restricted to a wheelchair but very much back in control of his life, beckoned to him. Warily Brad crossed the clearing and crouched down beside his uncle's wheelchair, asking him with a cheerfulness he didn't feel, 'How do you think it's going, Joe? Seems like everyone is having a good time.'

'Everyone but you,' his uncle told him forthrightly. 'No, don't bother denying it,' he added before Brad could speak. 'I've been watching you this past half-hour and it seems to me...' He paused and then said shrewdly, 'Seems to me you haven't been the same since you came back from England.'

'Much you would know,' Brad scoffed banteringly. 'When I came back from England you were in Intensive Care, giving us all the fright of our lives.'

'Well, I've made my three score and ten—and some besides,' Joe reminded him virtuously, but Brad wasn't deceived. He knew his uncle and his soft-spoken deter- mination to live to celebrate his one hundredth birthday.

'You're an old fraud,' he told Joe ruefully now.

'And you're a fool,' the older man came back, watch- ing him with fierce fondness. 'None can deny that you've done a good job standing in for your parents, Brad, nor that you've always put others before yourself, but they're all grown and gone now and unless you want to end up lonesome and alone...

'Who is she?' he asked craftily. 'Someone you met in England...? I was stationed over there during the war, you know; nearly married an English girl myself... My, but they're pretty. Would have married her, too, if she hadn't decided she preferred a fighter pilot to me. Worse mis- take I ever made.'

Brad gave his uncle a frowning look. Joe, as he knew from wide experience, was a shameless manipulator of the truth when it suited him and this was certainly the first that he had ever heard of a wartime romance. His uncle's shrewdness in guessing about Claire had thrown him off guard, though.

'I've never heard about any English girl before,' he told his uncle.

'That's because I don't mention her. Don't like to admit to having made a mistake. That's a trait we both share… Should have married her when I had the chance, only I thought I'd kinda make her wait a little. I was young and I dare say a little swelled-headed at times. She didn't want to wait, though, and I lost her…

'Oh, I got over it…kinda… I came home after the war, met your aunt Grace and we got married, but I never forgot my English girl. Margaret, her name was. Peggy, they called her. Pretty as a rose, she was, with the softest skin.' He gave a sentimental sigh.

'Oh, Grace and I got on well enough together. She'd lost a fiancé during the war herself and so we both knew the score. Kinda makes you think, though. When I look around me now, see all of you together… If I'd married Peggy perhaps my grandchildren would be here now. There's nothing like having a family of your own, Brad.'

'I have a family,' Brad pointed out brusquely to him. And besides, she…my English girl…doesn't want me, he wanted to say, but the habit of keeping his own problems to himself, which had begun with his parents' death, was too deeply ingrained now to be overcome.

'A man belongs where his heart is, Brad; that's his true home,' his uncle told him quietly.

His uncle was right, Brad acknowledged later as the first of the early-evening shadows started to fall and the family gathered around the fire, the little ones snuggling up to their parents, the older ones—the soon-to-be teenagers—hanging together in their own small, private group, too old now to want to mimic those they saw as the babies of the family by staying with their parents and still too young to be allowed to separate themselves from the family group.

Abe picked up his guitar; he was a good musician, with a tuneful voice. When Mary-Beth had first met him he had been the lead singer in a local group; Brad smiled to himself, remembering how he had come the stern, heavy older brother, warning her about getting involved with a boy who played in a band.

Abe started to sing an old folk tune familiar to all of them; the other adults joined in, their voices gradually swelled by those of the youngsters, the unlikely mingling of all their voices producing a surprisingly harmonious sound—rather like the mingling of the family itself, Brad reflected. But for him a vitally important note was missing—a vitally needed sweetness, a vitally important person.

Quietly he turned away from the fire.

On the other side of the lake his boat still waited for those all-important repairs, but his dream of sailing her had lost its savour. His life felt empty...he felt empty, he recognised.

His uncle had been right. His heart wasn't here any longer; it was thousands of miles away across the Atlantic with a woman whose soft cries of love still returned at night, every night, to haunt and torment him.

Claire... Claire...

CHAPTER TEN

SHE was obviously the first to arrive for their lunch rendezvous, Claire recognised as the head waiter escorted her through the almost empty restaurant and into the conservatory, seating her at a central table with a wonderful view of the hotel gardens with such a flourish that she felt it was a shame that there was no one else there to witness it.

Giving him a warm smile as a reward for his professionalism and a compensation for his lack of a worthy audience for it, she refused his offer of an aperitif.

If she hadn't spoken to the other two earlier in the week to confirm their arrangement she would have been tempted to think that they weren't coming.

Her heart had gone out to Poppy when she had telephoned her and heard her subdued voice.

'The most peculiar thing has happened,' Sally had told her importantly the day prior to her telephone call. 'Chris has forbidden me, on pain of total withdrawal of my chocolate-bar allowance, to talk about it, but...'

'But...?' Claire had pressed, but Sally had shaken her head regretfully.

'I can't tell you, but if it is true I just can't believe... Although Chris says he always thought that...'

'Poppy's fallen in love with someone else?' Claire had suggested helpfully.

'Well…no…no…' Sally had shaken her head firmly. 'I promised Chris I wouldn't say anything. It's all a bit delicate, you see…a bit…well, a bit difficult…and, to be honest, I'm still not sure I believe…' She had given Claire an apologetic look. 'I want to tell you but…'

'It's all right,' Claire had comforted her. 'Poppy is in a very vulnerable position at the moment,' she had added gently, inwardly reflecting on how much she would hate it if she thought that people were gossiping, speculating about her relationship with Brad, especially since the semi-public knowledge of their jokingly made vow of celibacy seemed to have added a certain piquancy to any gossip about their love lives. 'Obviously Chris wants to protect her from any additional hurt; that's only natural.'

'Yes, it is,' Sally had agreed, giving her a grateful hug. 'You will let me know if there are any signs of cracks appearing in the walls of female single solidarity, though, won't you?' she had added more light-heartedly.

'Certainly not,' Claire had told her roundly. 'It's one for all and all for one and you're the last person I would tell,' she had added teasingly.

'Mmm…well, I haven't heard anything from Star,' Sally had continued, 'in simply ages. I know she's been away a lot. Did you know, by the way, that Uncle Tim has consulted her about a new PR image for the company? Aunt Irene told me.'

Claire had made a noncommittal response, only too well aware of the fact that she had been avoiding Irene and all too well aware of how easily her sharp-eyed and even sharper-tongued sister-in-law could destroy the fragile barrier of self-protection that she was trying to erect around herself.

It was no use deluding herself, she admitted wearily now; there was no real protection, no real escape from the heartache of loving Brad. She might be able to banish him from her thoughts during the day but she had no control over her subconscious at night, and she had lost count of the number of times she had woken up, her face wet with tears, aching with loneliness and longing for him…

'Good, I'm not the last, then.'

Claire smiled as Star came hurrying towards her.

'Poppy not here yet?'

Claire shook her head as she smiled at the younger woman. 'She will be coming, though,' she told her. 'I spoke to her the other day.'

'Mmm…she may be coming, but if the gossip I've heard is true she won't—' Star broke off as Poppy herself came into the conservatory.

If the gossip was that Poppy had fallen in love with someone new, then her appearance certainly didn't bear it out, Claire reflected compassionately as she smiled at the new arrival. If anything, Poppy looked thinner and more unhappy than she had done the last time Claire had seen her.

As she patted the empty chair next to her own in a motherly fashion she studied her discreetly.

Poppy had definitely lost weight and she was very much on edge, glancing nervously over her shoulder as she sat down and lowering her voice as she greeted them, even though they were the only people in the conservatory.

'Well, I don't know about you two,' Star announced, reaching for the menu that the head waiter had left on the table, 'but I am hungry and fully intend to celebrate our first three marriage-free months. At least mine have been—marriage- and indeed man-free,' she added archly, looking questioningly from Claire to Poppy. 'Have you two…?'

'I don't have any plans to marry,' Claire told her hastily, mentally crossing her fingers as she acknowledged her inability to claim the true spirit of their pact.

'Nor do I,' Poppy echoed, but her face was slightly flushed and Claire could have sworn that she saw the sheen of tears in her eyes before she blinked them away.

Poor girl; was it her love for Chris that was the cause of them or was there someone else? If so…

As she made a pretence of studying the menu Claire sent up a small, heartfelt prayer that whatever unhappiness was presently clouding Poppy's life would soon be lifted and that she would enjoy the happiness and fulfilment that a girl of her age should have.

And as she made her private wish it struck Claire how much she had changed…how much knowing Brad had caused her to change. Three months ago her prayer would not have been as heartfelt simply because she would not have known what the three of them were missing…what true emotional and sexual fulfilment was.

Now that she had known fulfilment, if only fleetingly and briefly, she hated to think of the two younger women seated at the table going through their lives without knowing it.

Women, her sex, she was convinced, no matter how strong or successful they might appear in public—in the eyes of the world—had a need to focus their lives at an emotional, personal level that was so deep-seated, so intrinsically a part of their nature that it could never be totally ignored.

That, she suspected, was her sex's greatest weakness… and its great strength?

'To us—to single, unfettered emotional freedom and to celibacy,' Star toasted when they had all been served with their main course and the waiter had left.

Dutifully Claire raised her glass to join in the toast,

but as the glass touched her lips she discovered that they were trembling slightly, her mind filled by an achingly clear image of Brad.

If she closed her eyes now she knew that she would almost be able to taste his mouth…his kiss…him on her lips in place of the suddenly too bitter sharpness of the wine. Now it was her turn to blink away unwanted, betraying, emotional tears.

Brad! If she could wipe away her memories, expunge the knowledge of how it felt to love him, of how it had felt to be physically loved by him—if she could forget for ever the sound of his voice as he'd gently coaxed her to confide in him…would she do so?

Claire was jolted back to reality as Poppy suddenly jumped up from the table, pushing back her chair, her face a sickly shade of grey-white, perspiration beading her upper lip.

'I'd better go and see if she's all right,' Claire told Star, getting up. 'You don't think she's suffering from some kind of eating disorder, do you?' she asked anxiously, conscious of how very thin the younger girl looked and the way she had been toying with her food without really eating anything.

'I don't know,' Star told her, 'but if the gossip I've heard is true it's…' She paused as the head waiter came hurrying to the table to announce that there was a telephone call for her.

'I'd better take it,' she told Claire. 'Will you excuse me?'

Nodding, Claire hurried across the conservatory. To her relief, when she walked into the cloakroom Poppy was standing in front of the mirror brushing her hair, a little more colour in her face than there had been when she had rushed away from the table.

'I'm sorry about that,' she apologised wanly to Claire.

'It must have been something I've eaten. But...er...not here...' she added hastily as Claire looked concerned. 'I—'

'Of course; you've been away on business, haven't you?' Claire remembered. 'Your mother mentioned it when I rang to check if you were going to be able to make it for lunch. A conference, wasn't it? In Italy?'

To Claire's astonishment a dark tide of colour had swept over Poppy's previously too pale skin, leaving it a bright scarlet.

Why on earth should her mentioning her business trip to Italy have provoked such a self-conscious response? Claire wondered as they both made their way back to their table, but she was too kind to draw attention to Poppy's embarrassment or to make any comment about it when Star joined them.

'So, same place, same time...same rules in three months' time?' Star said when Claire had settled the bill. 'Unless, of course, either of you have been withholding anything...?'

'Three months,' Claire confirmed, quickly getting out her diary and flicking through the pages. 'That's fine by me...' Did her voice sound as hollow to the other two as it did to her? she wondered.

Outside the restaurant, Star announced that she had an afternoon appointment with Tim. 'That was him on the phone just now. He wanted to tell me that head office are considering the outline PR plan I put forward, but it seems that I might have to fly over to America to discuss things in more detail. Not that I mind, just so long as they're pay-ing the bills.

'You've met this Brad who heads the business, haven't you?' she asked Claire. 'What's he like?'

'He's...he's very...very pleasant,' Claire managed to stammer, and ignored the way Star's eyebrows lifted interrogatively as she waited for her to expand on her admittedly unenlightening comment.

'I...I didn't... I hardly knew him, really,' she told her bleakly, telling herself that it was, after all, the truth; the man she had thought she had known could not really have existed, otherwise he would not have walked out of her life in the way he had. The man she'd thought Brad was had been created by her own imagination, her own need, she told herself bitterly. She had created him and, in doing so, had also created her own heartache and misery.

'Mmm...well, it seems that he's now taken over the running of the company and that he intends to realign the working of the British side of things so that it runs efficiently and generates more sales; hence the new PR programme.'

Claire gave her a painful smile. It seemed that Star knew more about what was going on in Brad's life than she did, but why should that surprise her? She had purposely not mentioned Brad to Tim or Irene, not given in to the temptation to ask any questions about him and what he might be doing, but it hurt almost unbearably nonetheless to hear someone else discussing his plans...his life... his future... A future that did not, could not include her.

As Star drove off Claire turned to Poppy and was just about to ask her if she felt well enough to drive or if she would prefer a lift when a Jaguar suddenly came to an abrupt halt in front of them.

Claire heard the swift indrawn hiss of Poppy's breath as the driver got out. She almost seemed to shrink back as he strode towards her, grimly taking hold of her arm and pushing her unceremoniously in the direction of his car.

Claire watched them thoughtfully. She didn't envy Poppy her ride home with him, she decided ruefully as he

slammed the door on the young woman and then walked
round to the driver's side of the car.

Claire had virtually driven all the way home when, on a
sudden impulse, she turned the car round and, parking at
the side of the road, climbed out and walked towards the
entrance to the small park where she had first seen Brad.

There weren't many children in the park today. Claire
paused to watch a duck with her now half-grown babies
paddling purposefully across the small pond towards her.
A slight smile touched her lips as she shook her head and
told her, 'Sorry, Mama Duck, but I don't have any bread.'

'I do,' a warmly rough male voice said in her ear, trans-
fixing her with disbelieving shock. 'Or, at least, I have an
airline sandwich.'

Claire couldn't move, couldn't speak…couldn't so much
as look over her shoulder just in case the unthinkable had
finally happened and she had begun to suffer daytime de-
lusions that Brad was with her as well as night-time long-
ings for him.

'Claire…speak to me…say something, please, even if
it's only "Get the hell out of here"…'

All at once Claire felt her self-control snap. She started
to tremble—physically violent shudders that made her
whole body shake—tears blinding her as she struggled
to focus on Brad's face, seeing only his blurred outline
through the humiliating self-betrayal of her uncheckable
tears.

'Claire, Claire, please don't,' she heard Brad groan. 'I
never meant to give you such a shock. I came here on
impulse to try and find the courage to call you and…
Claire…'

Claire tensed as he suddenly reached for her, wrapping

her fiercely in his arms, holding her so tightly that she could feel the heavy thud of his heartbeat.

The familiar, ached-for scent of him enveloped her, dizzying and deluding her senses into the belief that he wanted her, and, of course, her body reacted immediately and passionately to that belief—so much so that she was scarlet-faced with embarrassment as she felt him check slightly when he saw and, she suspected, felt the betraying thrust of her nipples against the soft silkiness of her shirt.

It was a thoroughly modest and proper shirt, buttoned well past her cleavage, with a neat, small V-neck and made of a sensible mixture of man-made fibre and natural silk— not the kind of blouse that could ever be described as either deliberately alluring or provocative—and yet suddenly, humiliatingly, she was uncomfortably aware of the way her breasts were pushing openly against it and the way...

'Oh, God, Claire, have you had any idea what you're doing to me?' she heard Brad protesting thickly, but he didn't remove his gaze from her body, and having lifted his hand to shield her body from the stare of a passer-by he didn't immediately let it drop to his side again, and Claire knew with suffocating certainty that one deep breath, one small movement was all it would take to have the warmth of his palm pressed against her and...

'Claire.'

She wasn't going to move, wouldn't have moved at all if the shock of the anguish in Brad's voice hadn't jolted her...unbalanced her.

And, of course, it was only natural that Brad should reach out to save her. And just as natural that his gaze should fix avidly and hungrily on her mouth as it half opened in a small, startled gasp when his palm moved with quick, half-rough and totally male intensity over the fabric-covered curve of her breast, again and again, as though he couldn't believe that he was actually touching her, as though his skin, his hand, his body was greedily hungry for the physical feel of her.

This couldn't possibly be happening to her, Claire decided weakly as his other arm curved round her, binding her to him, and his mouth finally covered hers.

She could not possibly be standing here, in her local park, in full view of anyone who happened to be passing, being kissed by Brad with such passionate intensity that if he hadn't been holding her up she doubted that she would have had the strength left in her body to stay upright.

And, since it couldn't possibly be happening, there was nothing to stop her throwing herself heartily into her small, private fantasy, was there? No reason why she shouldn't abandon all the restraints she had once thought such an intrinsic part of her personality and respond to Brad as she had once responded to him in the privacy of his bedroom—as she responded to him every night when she dreamed that she lay naked in his arms, his body hard with longing against hers...just the way it felt now...

It took the amateurish wolf-whistle of a passing schoolboy to bring them both back to reality. Scarlet-faced, Claire looked uncertainly into Brad's eyes as he reluctantly released her.

'Did you walk here?' he asked gruffly. He was still holding onto her hand and still looking at her as though... as though...

Silently Claire shook her head, not trusting her voice.

'We'd better take our time driving back to your place,' Brad told her. 'Because once we are there it's going to be one hell of a long time before we do any sensible talking... a hell of a long time before I can do anything other than make love with you. God, Claire, do you know how much

I ache for you right now? If that damned bush over there was just a little bigger...'

Claire couldn't, even though she knew she was playing with fire, just couldn't help glancing wistfully towards the bush in question, an unremarkable rhododendron which would certainly not afford two full-grown adults enough privacy to make love.

'Claire,' Brad growled teasingly.

'I've missed you so much...' Claire's voice wobbled slightly. She swallowed hard and then admitted, 'I've wanted you so much...'

'Not half as much as I've wanted you,' Brad told her fiercely. 'If you had, you'd have returned my phone call instead of letting me think—'

'Returned your phone call?' Claire stared at him.

'Yes, I left a message with Tim when I couldn't get hold of you, asking you to call me.'

'I never got it,' Claire told him blankly. 'Tim just said that you'd rung. He was under an awful lot of pressure,' she defended her brother-in-law when she saw Brad's face. 'I expect it just slipped his mind. After all, he didn't know... he probably just thought you wanted to ask me to forward your things on or something.'

'Or something,' Brad agreed ruefully. 'When you didn't ring, I thought you were trying to tell me that you'd had second thoughts...that you didn't, after all, feel as I felt... that you didn't... There's only so much a man can do without feeling that he's pressuring a woman...harassing her. I told myself that if that was what you wanted then I owed it to you to keep out of your life, keep away from you...'

'But you are here,' Claire pointed out, holding her breath. Was he going to tell her that seeing her was accidental, that he was simply here on business...?

It wouldn't alter anything, of course—wouldn't change

the fact that he obviously still wanted her. He had apparently never stopped wanting her, but her sore, tender heart yearned to know that she was the cause, the reason for him being here…even if she was being unrealistic and even a tiny little bit unfair…

'Mmm…' Brad agreed, his mouth quirking into a wry smile as he admitted, 'OK, maybe I'm not such a good modern new man as I like to think… Maybe I did think it was worth giving it one more shot, or maybe I missed you, wanted you such a hell of a lot that I just couldn't help myself,' he told her sombrely.

'Three days ago my uncle Joe told me that a man's real home, his real family…his real life lies where his heart is…with the woman his heart is with—and I knew that he was right. I came over on the first flight I could book. I've been sitting in this park for close on an hour, trying to work out what I was going to say to you and what I was going to do if you rejected me.'

'And if I didn't…if I don't reject you?' Claire asked him, hardly daring to breath. 'You are my life now, Brad,' she continued. 'I loved John—he was strong when I needed a father-figure—but I realise now that there are different forms of love and what I feel for you—as a man, as a lover—is difficult for me to express here, in public. My car is parked close by,' she added breathlessly. 'We could be home in five minutes, and—'

'Oh, no,' Brad told her, catching hold of her free arm and holding onto her. 'Oh, no, ma'am, that's not the way it's going to be… Not this time; no way… This time there's no way you're going to get me into bed, not unless you promise me first that you're going to make an honest man of me.

'Have you any idea what it was like for me,' he demanded mock-indignantly, 'having to be there with my family, knowing that sexually you'd used me and then walked away from me, rejected me? How do you think I'd have felt if they'd known that? If you'd got me pregnant?' he added outrageously, his face perfectly straight whilst Claire's mouth fell open in feminine indignation at his taking over of what was surely her role.

'Not that I would have minded sharing the making of our child with you,' Brad added huskily. 'I've always wanted kids of my own... Having them around kinda gets to be a habit, you know, and I kinda miss all the little ones...'

'You told me you were going to mend your boat and sail it round the world—on your own,' Claire reminded him severely, entering into the game, her heart suddenly so light...her whole body so light that she felt almost as though she could actually physically float through the air instead of walking.

'Ah, yes. Well, I was, but that was before...'

'Before what?' Claire demanded.

'Before you seduced me, beguiled me, stole my heart and my desire for independence, made me want to spend my every waking minute and all of my sleeping ones with you,' Brad told her throatily. 'Oh, yes, most definitely all my sleeping ones...'

'I thought you didn't want to go to bed with me,' Claire said provocatively as he leaned forward and started to nibble the side of her neck. Sensations so delicious that she felt positively sure that she had lost her ability to reason filled her all the way down her body, right down to her toes, which she curled up inside her shoes as a soft tremor of exquisite pleasure shivered tantalisingly through her—a warning...a reminder of that so much more intense pleasure Brad had...

'I didn't say I didn't want to,' Brad mumbled, still nibbling at her skin. 'I just said I wasn't going to, not unless you had promised to marry me first.'

'Marry you...?' Claire looked at him in bemused shock. 'You want to marry me? But...'

'No buts,' Brad told her firmly. 'I'm not having these five children we're going to have growing up thinking you didn't love me enough to commit yourself to me. Besides, it would give them a bad example. I'm a firm believer in marriage. Just ask my family—'

'Five children!' Claire repeated, weakly protesting. 'Brad, I'm thirty-four years old.'

'So what? These days a modern woman can put off starting a family until she's forty if she chooses to do so. Of course, maybe I am being a little restrictive in just saying five,' he mused. 'There are twins in my family and it's a known fact that women in their thirties are more prone to producing twins, so who's to say...? I do like round numbers, though, don't you? So we'd have to go for six...'

'Six,' Claire murmured faintly, round-eyed with disbelief.

'Six,' Brad promised, apparently misreading her expression. 'But only if you promise right here and now that you are going to marry me... Wait a minute,' he told her, reaching for the case he had placed on the floor beside the bench which he had obviously been sitting on when she had walked towards the ducks.

He opened it and produced a small pocket recorder, switched it on and held it towards her.

'Now promise me you're going to marry me,' he instructed her. 'I want some verbal evidence to make sure you don't go back on your word... And besides,' he added in a very different and far more serious and emotional voice, 'I just want to hear you say it, Claire. God, you can't know how often, how much I've ached to hear you say you want me over these past damned weeks.'

'Oh, yes, I can,' Claire corrected him softly. 'Because I've wanted you in just the same way and just as much... I thought when you didn't get in touch that you were trying to tell me that you didn't want any...that it was just... that I was just... Brad,' she protested huskily as he took her back in his arms, her protest silenced by the fierce, possessive and totally male hunger of his kiss.

'I know why you're doing this,' she told him breathlessly when he had eventually let her go, deciding on a little light-hearted teasing of her own. 'You just want to make me want you so much that I'll agree to anything just to get you into bed...'

'Mmm...has it worked?' Brad asked her softly, giving her a wholly male and very dangerous look that made her whole body shake with excited desire.

'Er...yes...I think so,' she admitted.

'You're going to marry me,' Brad stressed.

'I'm going to marry you,' Claire agreed.

Several hours later, still shamelessly snuggled up next to him in bed, her body deliciously, sensuously satiated by the intensity of their lovemaking, Claire marvelled that she could ever have believed that he didn't love her.

'And you're sure that you won't mind making your home in the States?'

'My home is with you,' Claire told him huskily, meaning it. 'Of course I'll miss Sally and my friends, but Sally has Chris now and, after all, she's only going to be a plane journey away... And Felicity will come with us, of course.'

'Of course,' Brad agreed, leaning over to stroke the kitten who had come upstairs to see what they were doing.

'Mmm...I wonder if the company can afford to charter its own jet?' Brad mused, adding with a teasing smile, 'After all, with all these kids we're going to have, it's common sense—'

'Brad,' Claire protested, 'we don't even know if I can conceive yet.'

'Wanna bet?' Brad challenged her, drawing her even closer to his body as he leaned across her to whisper in her ear. 'I reckon that he or she…or even they,' he added with a wicked smile as his hand caressed the warm curve of her stomach, 'is tucked up safe and sound in here right now.'

Claire laughed and accused him teasingly of wanting to ensure that she married him, but she had a sneaking feeling that he was probably right. When they had made love earlier there had been a distinct sensation within her body—a secret female sense of somehow being so totally and primitively open to him and the intense thrust of his body within hers that she had actually felt as though her womb itself was extra responsive to him. A ridiculous and nonsensical feeling, she knew, but still…

'I'd like us to be married here,' he told her softly. 'If we wait until I take you home the family will take over and then—'

'You're not worried that they won't approve of me, are you?' Claire queried, suddenly a little apprehensive.

'No way,' Brad laughed. 'They'll approve of you all right. No, I just want to have you to myself for a little while before they swoop down on us. The way I feel about you, the way I want to be with you, is still all very new and precious to me,' he told her huskily, linking his fingers with hers and then lifting her hand to his mouth, tenderly kissing each digit before lowering his mouth to her lips.

'And to me as well,' Claire whispered back against his kiss.

* * *

They were married very quietly in a small, private church ceremony just short of a month later. Just in time to prevent too much gossip about the arrival of their eight-month baby, Claire told Brad ruefully.

Her pregnancy had been confirmed the previous morning and Brad hadn't stopped saying, 'I told you so.'

'It might not have been then,' Claire had protested, but, of course, she knew that it had, and didn't really begrudge Brad his small victory—or at least only first thing in the morning when she felt horrendously queasy.

At the end of the week they would be flying out to America—first to New York and from there to Brad's home town. Claire had slightly mixed feelings about meeting Brad's family; she felt both excited and apprehensive. Brad had telephoned them to tell them that they were married and Claire had spoken to his sisters and brothers and to his uncles, all of whom had welcome her warmly into the family.

'Just so long as we're together I don't care where we live,' she had told Brad only that morning, and had meant it.

Now a smile curled her mouth as she snuggled up against Brad's side. It was mid-morning, but they had had a late night having dinner with Sally and Chris.

'I can hear the doorbell ringing,' she told Brad sleepily.

'You stay where you are; I'll go and get it,' he told her.

Claire smiled as she watched him shrug on his robe. He had the most beautiful, sexy body... Just looking at him made her catch her breath and want to reach out and touch him. He was gone about five minutes and then she heard him coming back upstairs.

'It's for you,' he told her slightly grimly, holding a beautifully arranged bouquet of flowers with a sealed note attached to it.

'Is there something or someone I ought to know about?' he asked her semi-jealously as he handed it to her.

As she took it from him Claire frowned slightly.

'I don't think so,' she responded. 'This is a wedding bouquet. It must…' Suddenly her frown melted and she broke into warm laughter as she realised why the bouquet of flowers was so familiar. It was an exact replica of the one that Sally had had—the one she had 'dropped' as she'd 'fallen' down the stairs at the reception, the one which Claire, Poppy and Star had so misguidedly caught.

As Claire explained why she was laughing to Brad she tore open the sealed note, a rueful smile curling her mouth as she read what Sally had written.

'One down, two to go!'

* * * * *

Best Man to Wed?

PENNY JORDAN

PROLOGUE

Poppy Carlton stared mournfully across the now empty garden, furiously trying to blink away her tears.

It seemed only yesterday that she and Chris used to play here. She had been happy then, never thinking that there might come a day when she and her cousin would not be so close, a day when someone else, another woman, would become the main focus of his life, his time, his future, his love.

Fresh tears brimmed and welled over. Poppy dashed them away with the back of her hand.

She had known for months, of course, that Chris and Sally were going to marry, but somehow, until the actual day of the wedding, she had gone on... What? Hoping that he would change his mind, that he would look at her, love her as a woman and not just as a cousin?

'Your turn next,' Chris had laughed affectionately at her as she had leapt forward with Claire, Sally's step-mother, and Star, her closest friend, to catch the bouquet which Sally had dropped as she'd slipped on the stairs.

Her turn next. Impossible. She would *never* marry now. How could she when the man she loved, the only man she had ever loved or ever would love, was lost to her?

And of course her other cousin, James, Chris's elder

brother and best man, would have to have witnessed the whole thing—the falling bouquet, her instinctive attempt to save it along with Claire and Star, and, worst of all, the compassion and, humiliatingly, the relief as well in Chris's eyes as he had made some cumbersome joke about her at least waiting until he and Sally had returned from their honeymoon before fulfilling the traditional prophecy that went with the catching of the bride's bouquet.

Oh, yes, James had seen all of that and predictably had made no attempt to spare her the full force of his cynical denunciation of her feelings as he had told her, 'Grow up, Poppy; grow up and *wise* up. It would never have worked; the pair of you would have been in the divorce courts within a year if Chris had ever been fool enough to take you up on what you're so pathetically desperate to give him.'

'You don't *know* that,' Poppy had spat back angrily. '*You* don't anything.'

'Oh, no,' James had mocked her softly. 'You don't know *what* I know.' He had added, 'And if you did...' He had paused, smiling nastily at her before challenging her with, 'Of course, if you ever feel like finding out...'

'I hate you, James,' Poppy had retaliated passionately.

No, she would never marry now, and all Sally's determined attempt to engineer it so that she was one of the trio to catch the bridal bouquet had done was reinforce that fact.

CHAPTER ONE

SLOWLY, gravely, Poppy knelt in front of the bonfire that she had just constructed, oblivious to the damp seeping into the knees of her jeans, the dying rays of the evening sunlight turning her silky brown hair a dark, rich red and illuminating her in a beam of light as, head bowed, she carefully struck a match with such seriousness that she might have been igniting a funeral pyre.

Which in effect she was, Poppy acknowledged tiredly as she watched the kindling that she had carefully arranged start to burn, flames crackling as they ran from twig to twig, racing towards the wooden trinket box at their heart.

As she stood up Poppy had to dig her hands deep into the pockets of her jeans to prevent herself pulling the kindling aside and snatching the box to safety.

It was over, she told herself mercilessly, closing her eyes, unable to look, unable to watch almost a whole decade of ceaseless devotion and love being eaten up by flames. A sharp breeze sprang up out of nowhere, ruffling the silky curtain of her hair, scattering sparks from the fire, whirling-dervish-like, amongst its flames, teasing them, snatching from them a handful of photographs, most of them charred beyond recognition, only one of them still recognisable, the pale pink lipstick shape of her own mouth imprinted brightly across its surface.

Tears stung Poppy's eyes, her heart twisting and aching with anguish as her emotions overcame her will-power and she stretched out helplessly to clasp the photograph which fate, it seemed, had decreed that she should not destroy.

As Chris's beloved features swam before her, tears filled her eyes and she missed the photograph, the wind whirling it out of reach. With a small cry, Poppy tried to pursue it, but someone else reached it before her, taking it from the breeze's playful grasp with mocking ease, a taunting expression crossing his saturnine face as he looked at it and then back at her.

'James!' Poppy said his name with loathing as he came down the garden towards her, still holding her photograph.

James might be her beloved, darling Chris's elder brother and her cousin but no two men could have been more unalike, Poppy reflected bitterly as James stopped walking and studied her bonfire.

Whereas Chris was all sunny smiles, warmth and laughter, good natured, easygoing, an open, uncomplicated individual whom it had all been too heart-breakingly easy for her to fall in love with, James was just the opposite.

James rarely smiled, or at least not at her, and James was most certainly not good-natured, nor easygoing and certainly not uncomplicated; even those who liked and approved of him, such as her mother, were forced to admit that he was not always the easiest person in the world to deal with.

'It's because he had to step into his father's shoes

whilst he was still so young,' her mother always said in his defence.

'He was only twenty when Howard died, after all, and he had to take full responsibility for looking after his mother and Chris, as well as the business.'

Her mother had to defend James because he was her nephew. Poppy knew that but she hated him, loathed him, and she knew that he reciprocated those feelings even if he cloaked his in a more urbane and taunting mockery towards her than she could ever achieve towards him. It shocked her that people who didn't really know them always claimed that of the two brothers James was by far the better looking...

'He's very, very dangerously sexy,' one of the girls who worked for the small family company which James had taken over on his father's death had told her.

According to her mother, by hard work and dedication he had built the company into something far more impressive than it had ever been during his father's day.

'I'll just bet he's a real once-in-a-lifetime experience in bed,' the girl had added forthrightly.

Poppy had shuddered to listen to her, thinking that if she *really* knew what James was like, how cruel and hard he could be, she wouldn't think that. Personally Poppy couldn't think of any man she'd want less as a lover, but then there was only one man that Poppy wanted to fulfil that role in her life...in her heart...in her bed, and there always had been.

She had been twelve years old, a girl just on the brink of womanhood, when she had looked across the table at her first semi-grown-up birthday party and fallen head over heels in love with Chris. And she had gone on loving him and hoping, praying, longing for him to love

her in return, not just as his cousin but as a woman...
the woman. Only he hadn't done so.

Instead he had fallen in love with someone else. Instead he had fallen in love with pretty, funny Sally.
Sally, who was now his wife... Sally, whom Poppy
couldn't hate even though she had tried very hard to
do so.

Chris and James didn't even look very much like
brothers, if you discounted the fact that they shared
the same impressive height and breadth of shoulder,
Poppy decided now, watching James in angry resentment. Whereas Chris had the warm good looks of a
young sun-god, his floppy brown hair golden at the
ends, his eyes the same blue as a warm summer sky,
his skin a mouth-watering gold, James looked more
demoniac than godlike...

Like Chris, he too had inherited his Italian grandmother's warm skin colouring, but in James it was
somehow harder, more aggressively masculine, bronzer
than Chris's softer gold, just as his eyes were a far
harder and colder nerve-freezing light aqua— the kind
of eyes that could chill your blood to ice from three
metres away if they chose. His hair, too, was much
darker than Chris's—not black but certainly very dark
brown, with dark flecks of burnt gold that gleamed like
amber in the sunlight.

Poppy was not a complete fool; she could see that
physically some women might be drawn to a man of
James's type, and that of his type, perhaps, as the girl
at work had said, he was an outstanding example, but
she could never find him attractive. There was his temper, an ice-cold, rapier-sharp, humiliatingly effective
weapon of destruction onto which she had run in furious, blind hotheadedness more times than she could

bear to remember, and his sarcasm, which could rip your pride to shreds like the mountain cougar's velvet-sheathed claws.

'What the hell is going on?' he demanded now as he walked towards her.

Mutinously Poppy glowered at him. He hadn't looked at the photograph as yet and she itched to demand its return, her stomach muscles cramping with tension.

'Mum and Dad are out,' she told him ungraciously. 'There's only me here...'

'It's you I wanted to see,' James told her urbanely, walking past her to squat down on his heels and study her bonfire.

Why was it, Poppy thought, watching warily, that such an action by any other man dressed as James was now—in an expensive, immaculately tailored business suit, highly polished shoes and a pristine white shirt—would have immediately rendered him ridiculous, but made James look completely the opposite? And why, she demanded irritably of life, should the bonfire—*her* bonfire—deposit its unwanted windborne detritus of smoke and sooty smudges in her direction and not his?

Life just wasn't fair...

Fresh tears smarted in her eyes. Hastily she blinked them away just as she heard James commenting sardonically, 'What exactly is the purpose of all this self-sacrifice Poppy? Not, one trusts, some immature and ignoble hope that out of the ashes of this maudlin act a new and stronger love for Chris will rise, like a phoenix, only this time one that he shares, because if so—'

'Of course not,' Poppy denied swiftly, too shocked by his contemptuous accusation to pretend not to understand what he meant—or to deny the purpose of the bonfire.

It was typical, of course; only James could make
that kind of assumption about her motivation for doing
something; only James would accuse her so unfairly.

'If you must know,' she told him bitterly, 'I was trying to do what you've been telling me I should do for
years, and that is to accept that Chris doesn't…that he
never—' She broke off, swallowing hard as her emotions threatened to overwhelm her.

'Damn you to hell, James,' she swore shakily. 'This
has nothing to do with you…and you have no right—'

'I *am* Chris's brother,' he reminded her crisply, 'and
as such it's my brotherly duty to protect him and his
marriage from—'

'From what?' Poppy demanded shakily. 'From
me…?' Bitterly she started to laugh. 'From me,' she
repeated. 'From my love—'

'Your *love*!' James interrupted her, his mouth twisting. 'You don't even begin to know the meaning of the
word. In the eyes of the world you might be a mature
woman of twenty-two, but inside you're still an adolescent,' he told her crushingly, 'with all the danger to
yourself and to others that that implies.'

'I am not an adolescent,' Poppy denied furiously,
angry flags of temper burning in her cheeks.

'The way you can't control your emotions says that
you are,' James corrected her coldly. 'And, like an adolescent,' he continued bitingly, 'you positively enjoy
wallowing in your self-induced misery, the self-aggran-
dised "love" you claim you feel for Chris. But you, of
course, being you, have to drag everyone else into the
plot as well.'

'That's not true,' Poppy gasped furiously. 'You—'

'It is true,' James told her grimly. 'Look at the way
you behaved at the wedding… Do you think that a sin-

gle person there didn't know what you were doing, or how you felt?'

'I wasn't *do*ing anything,' Poppy protested, her face as white now as it had been red before.

'Yes, you were,' James told her. 'You were trying to make Chris feel guilty and to make everyone else feel sorry for you. Well, it isn't people's pity you deserve, Poppy…it's their contempt. If you really loved Chris—*really* loved him—you'd put his happiness before your own selfish, self-induced misery.

'You claim that you're not an adolescent any longer, that you're an adult. Well, try behaving like one,' James told her witheringly.

'You have no right to speak to me like that,' Poppy told him chokingly. 'You have no idea how I feel or what—'

She froze as James burst out laughing—a harsh, contemptuous sound that splintered the early evening air.

'No idea…? My dear Poppy, the whole town knows how *you* feel.'

Poppy stared at him.

'Nothing to say?' he jeered.

Poppy swallowed painfully. People did know how she felt about Chris. She couldn't deny that, but not because she had deliberately flaunted her feelings to make Chris feel guilty, as James had so unfairly claimed.

It was simply that she had been so young when she had first fallen in love with Chris that it had been impossible for her to keep her feelings hidden, and she had loved him so long that people were bound to have noticed. But she had never, ever, as James was claiming, used her feelings to try to manipulate Chris, or, indeed, anyone else, into feeling sorry for her.

Of course, she deplored the fact that people *were*

aware of her love for Chris—why else on the evening
when he and Sally had broken the news of their engagement to the family had she made a silent vow that somehow she had to find a way to stop loving him?

All right, so far she might not have been successful,
but at least she had tried—and was still trying.

It should have helped, she knew, knowing that Sally
was so right for Chris and that they were so very, very
much in love; with any other girl but Sally she might
have suspected that that gesture of hers in ensuring that
Poppy was one of the trio who was tricked into catching Sally's wedding bouquet had been, at best, a clear
warning to her that it was time for her to find a man of
her own and, at worst, a tauntingly vindictive underlining of the fact that she had lost Chris. But Sally was far
too genuinely nice and warm-hearted to do anything
like that and her motives, Poppy knew, had been completely altruistic.

That hadn't stopped it hurting, though. And now
here was James deliberately making that hurting worse.

'How I feel…what I do is none of your business,' was
the only response she could manage to James's taunt.

'No?' James gave her an ironic look. 'Well, what *is*
my business is the fact that you are employed by the
company as a linguist and interpreter and, as such, I
see that you're down to fly out to Italy for the international conference next Wednesday.'

'Yes,' Poppy agreed listlessly. The previous year,
when the conference had been arranged, she had believed that Chris would be representing the company
at the conference, and when he had asked her if she
would like to go too she had walked on air for days afterwards, her imagination fuelling wildly romantic and,

she realised, looking back, totally impossible fantasies featuring the two of them.

The reality, she knew now, would be rather different. Even if Chris had still been going, the four days of the conference would be filled with meetings, whilst she would be called upon to use her language skills, both in verbal translations and paperwork, which from previous experience she knew would keep her tied to her hotel bedroom when she wasn't actually attending the conference with the company's small sales team.

'The flight time's been changed,' James informed her. 'I'll pick you up here at six-thirty. I've got to drive past on my way to the airport, so—'

'*You'll* pick me up?' Poppy interrupted him, shocked. 'But you aren't going. Chris…'

'*Chris* is on honeymoon, as you very well know, and won't be back for another week,' James reminded her grimly, giving her a tauntingly sardonic look as he added unkindly, 'Surely even you aren't self-deluding enough to believe that he'd cut short his honeymoon to go to Italy with you? Or was that what you were secretly hoping, Poppy…secretly wishing he would do? My God, just when the hell are you going to grow up and realise that—'

'That what?' Poppy interrupted him furiously, fighting to control the way her mouth had started to tremble as she goaded James wildly. 'Go on, then, say it. Say what we both know you're just dying to say, James. Or shall I say it for you…?'

Her chin tilted proudly as she forced herself to look straight into his eyes without flinching. 'When am I going to realise that Chris doesn't love me, that he will never love me…that he loves Sally…?' she said bravely.

She knew that her eyes were over-bright with betray-

ing tears, but she couldn't help it; her emotions were
too strong for her, too overpowering.

'Of course I know that Chris won't be going to Italy,'
she told James tiredly, turning away from him as the
box at the heart of her small bonfire suddenly crackled
fiercely and was engulfed by flames.

The pain inside her heart as she watched it burn was
so sharp and driving that she had to force herself not
to reach into the fire and retrieve the box, shaking it
from the flames. Inside it were all her precious, cherished memories and souvenirs of her years of loving
Chris: the present he had given her for that momentous
twelfth birthday when she had first fallen in love with
him...the card he had sent her...the other gifts he had
given her over the years.

Quite mundane, perhaps, in many ways, and certainly not the gifts of a lover; no doubt in James, for instance, the small, precious hoard that she had guarded
so tenderly would only provoke derision and contempt,
but to her...

Yes, she had known that Chris wouldn't be going to
Italy, but it had never occurred to her that James would
be attending the conference in his place. She had assumed that someone else from the sales team would go
instead. She frowned suddenly, something striking her.

'If you're going to Italy, you won't need me there,'
she announced as she turned back to look at him. 'You
speak Italian fluently.'

As well he might, Poppy reflected ungenerously.
After all, his grandmother on his mother's side was
Italian and both he and Chris had frequently spent sum-
mer holidays with their Italian relations. But whereas
James had always been very fluent in the language,
Chris had not absorbed it quite so well.

'Italian, yes,' James agreed coolly, 'but this is an international conference, remember, and your knowledge of Japanese is required. So, if you were entertaining any ideas about spending your time mooning around daydreaming about Chris, I warn you that we're going to Italy to work...'

'You don't have any right to warn *me* about anything,' Poppy challenged him dangerously, inwardly seething with resentment at the fact that he had called her professionalism into question.

She was well aware how strenuously he had opposed her appointment to the post of interpreter and translator within the company, sneering that it was nepotism and that it would be cheaper to send such work out to tender.

She shouldn't have been listening outside the office door when he and her mother had argued about her appointment, Poppy knew, and she really hadn't intended to do so but had simply been on her way to see her mother.

However, what she had heard him say about her had made her all the more determined to prove just how wrong he was and just how valuable she could be to the company, and she had immediately put aside her own initial doubts about the wisdom of going to work for the family electronics business.

When her mother had first suggested that she did so, Poppy had been reluctant to agree, wanting instead to establish her independence, but the knowledge of how difficult it was proving for her to find a job by herself, coupled with the fact that she'd known she would be working closely with Chris, had overcome her scruples and she now firmly believed that in the short time she had been with the company she had proved her worth.

'I *know* I'm going to Italy to work,' Poppy added pointedly now. 'After all, I'm not the one who…'

She paused, alarmed by the look in James's eyes which told her that she had gone too far.

'Go on,' he invited silkily, his voice suddenly softly dangerous.

'Well, I'm not the one with the family in Italy,' Poppy blustered, shrugging.

'Are you trying to say that I'm using the company to finance my own personal plans?' James suggested ominously.

'Well, you aren't exactly involved in the sales side of things, are you?' Poppy demanded aggressively. 'The sales team—'

'As managing director and chairman of the company, I am involved in everything,' James told her softly. 'Everything… Not so much as a paper-clip disappears without my knowing about it, Poppy, you may be sure of that,' he told her with a wintry look that made her colour up hotly as she remembered the occasions on which she had 'borrowed' company stationery.

'And as for the sales team… On this occasion,' he told her smoothly, 'they won't be coming with us.'

'With *us*?' Poppy stared at him in disbelief. 'You mean it will be just you and me…?' She couldn't keep the horror out of her voice.

'Just you and me,' James confirmed.

'I'm not… I won't…' Poppy began, and then stopped as James suddenly smiled at her gently…too gently, her instincts warned her as she wondered edgily if refusing to accompany him would be grounds for dismissal from her job. James was clever like that…sneaky enough too, and she knew how much he had always resented the fact that she was working for the company.

'You're the boss,' she told him, attempting a careless shrug but suspecting from the narrow-eyed, glinting look of mockery that he was giving her that she hadn't really deceived him.

Four days in Italy with James... She tried not to shudder. She couldn't think of anything that came closer to her idea of purgatory.

She winced as a cloud of acrid smoke from her bonfire was suddenly blown into her face, making her cough and choke. As she stumbled clear of it, she saw that James was studying the photograph that he had snatched from the wind, and she could feel the hot tide of embarrassed colour starting to burn her face.

It was not the fact that the photograph was of Chris that bothered her; it was an old one taken when she had been fourteen and he seventeen. She had taken it herself, snatching it with her new camera at a family party, and had later, with great daring, had the original print blown up.

No, what was causing her whole body to burn with humiliated embarrassment was the fact that virtually the whole of Chris's face, but most especially his mouth, was covered in tell-tale lipstick kisses where she had deliberately—oh, shaming to remember now—pressed her open lips with passionate intensity against Chris's.

A wave of toe-curling, excruciatingly horrible embarrassment, more intense than any self-consciousness she had ever suffered before, poured through her with scalding heat. Her body tensed in readiness for James's taunting laughter as she resisted the desire to compound her humiliation by reaching out to try to snatch the betraying photograph from him.

But, instead of laughing, James was simply looking

from the photograph to her…to her mouth, she recognised with searing misery…and then back again…

Unable to bear the nerve-stretching silence of
James's clinical study of her any longer, Poppy gave
in to temptation and did what she had promised herself she was now mature enough not to do—she darted
quickly towards him, reaching out her hand to snatch
the photograph from him. But as she reached him he
realised what she was trying to do and grabbed hold of
her with one hand, whilst retaining possession of her
photograph with the other.

'Let me go,' Poppy demanded, all sense of restraint
and dignity overwhelmed by the humiliation-fuelled
anger that gripped her, her hands pummelling furiously
against James's chest as she writhed impotently against
him, struggling to break free.

She had no chance of doing so, of course; her brain
knew that even if her emotions and her body refused
to accept it.

James was a good six feet two to her five-four and
at least five stone heavier; add to that the fact that she
knew perfectly well that he swam and ran regularly as
well as practising the art of aikido and it was no wonder that her furious attempts to break free were doing
more to exhaust her strength than his.

Even so, she still persisted, demanding through gritted teeth, 'Let go of me…James…and give me back my
photograph…'

'Your photograph.' Now he did laugh—a harsh, contemptuous sound that made her long to clap her hands
over her ears to protect herself. 'I suppose this is the
nearest you've ever come to kissing a man with passion, isn't it, Poppy? After all—'

'No, of course it isn't,' Poppy denied untruthfully.

She was damned if she was going to let James make her feel even worse than she already did.

'No?' James queried silkily, his eyes narrowing cynically as Poppy inadvertently looked up at him. 'So who was he, then? It certainly wasn't Chris, and yet, according to you, he's the only man you've ever loved…the only man you could ever love…'

Poppy's face flushed scarlet with fury as she realised that James was quoting back at her the impassioned words that her sixteen-year-old self had declared to him when he had asked her tauntingly if she had grown out of her crush on his younger brother yet.

'No one you know,' Poppy shot back at him furiously. 'In fact…'

'No one anyone knows, including you, is more like it,' James contradicted her drily.

'That's not true,' Poppy lied hotly.

'No?' James taunted her. 'Well, let's just put it to the test, shall we…?'

Before she knew what he intended to do, somehow he had shifted his weight and hers, so that she was momentarily off balance and forced instinctively to reach out and cling to him for support, whilst he took advantage of her vulnerability to tighten his hold on her, using not just one but both arms this time to imprison her against him, holding her so close that she could actually feel the hard, firmly muscled length of his thigh against her and the equally firm thud of his heart.

'James,' she began, automatically tilting her head back so that she could look at him and show him how angry she was, but her complaint died away in her throat as she saw the way he was looking at her…at her mouth…and her own heart began to trip frantically in a series of far too fast, shallow little beats that made her breathing quicken and her muscles tense, her lips parting as she tried to draw extra air into her suddenly oxygen-deprived lungs.

A small sound—a protest, a soft moan; even she wasn't quite sure which—gasped its way past the locked muscles of her throat and was lost, stifled by the slow, deliberate pressure of James's mouth against hers.

This couldn't be happening, Poppy thought, her mind reeling with shock and disbelief. James's mouth against hers, covering it, caressing it, possessing it...

Frantically, she tried to turn her head out of the way, panic flooding her body with a trembling agitation and a desperate need to break free, but James forestalled her, one hand still binding her firmly against his body whilst the other grasped a handful of her hair, twisting it through his fingers, and then cupped her jaw, imprisoning her beneath the growing pressure of a kiss that was making her feel increasingly vulnerable.

She could feel the strength in his fingers where they rested against her skin, their touch cool in marked contrast to the burning heat of her own flushed face, just as the steady thud of his heartbeat underlined the wretchedly fast race of her own.

She knew, shamingly, that she was trembling from head to foot, and she knew, even more humiliatingly, that James must know it too. She could feel his fingers sliding along her throat, stroking her skin gently...*gently*...James.

Tears blurred her vision, burning behind the eyelids she refused to close as she glared her enmity into the cool, clear aqua of James's unreadable eyes.

All these years of dreaming of Chris kissing her, Chris holding her, Chris's mouth caressing and possessing hers, and now it had to be *James* who was turning what should have been one of the most treasured moments of her life into a mocking parody of everything that her first kiss of real passion should have been.

Was it really for this that she had refused dates and explorative teenage snogging sessions? Was it for this that she had held aloof from the sexual freedom that university could have afforded her? Was it for this that she had spent her nights and some of her days dreaming and yearning…? So that James could mock her and destroy her cherished fantasies with a cruel kiss that could only be designed to taunt her—a kiss that…?

Poppy stiffened as her brain belatedly recognised something that her traitorous senses had shamingly already seemed to acknowledge—namely that if it hadn't actually been James, her loathed elder cousin, whose mouth was caressing hers she might almost…could almost…

Poppy gave an outraged gasp as she realised just why her lips, her mouth, seemed to be softening, yielding, almost enjoying the sensual contact with James's, her eyes snapping fire when she registered the sudden, heart-stopping gleam darkening James's as he finally lifted his mouth from hers.

Her legs felt oddly weak as she stepped back from him, Poppy recognised dizzily—and not just her legs either.

'Well, whoever he was, if indeed he did actually exist,' she heard James saying derisively to her, 'he wasn't a very good teacher. Either that or…'

'Or what?' Poppy recovered just enough to challenge him. 'I wasn't a very good pupil…?'

'Oh, I wouldn't say that.'

Poppy stared at him, caught between disbelief and suspicion, waiting for the taunting barb that she was sure was to come, but instead he simply stood there whilst her gaze dropped helplessly from his eyes to his mouth—in fact it might have been jerked there on strings which he controlled, so little ability did she have to stop its betraying movement.

'Yes?' she heard James murmur invitingly.

'Give me back my photograph,' Poppy demanded huskily, determinedly forcing her gaze back to his eyes, hoping that he would put the hot colour burning her face down to the heat of her bonfire.

But, instead of acceding to her demand, to her disbelief James tore the photograph—*her* precious photograph—into small pieces and then casually walked over to the now dying bonfire and dropped them into its burning embers.

'You had no right to do that,' Poppy protested chokily. 'That...'

'What else did you intend to do with it?' James asked her. 'It's over, Poppy. Chris is married now. Accept it; he never loved you and he never will,' he told her cruelly.

'How dare you—' she began.

But he stopped her, continuing bluntly, 'And it's time you grew up and accepted the truth instead of living in an adolescent fantasy world.'

He had started to walk away from her, to Poppy's relief. Seeing him tear up her precious photograph and consign it to the bonfire had brought back all her earlier misery and despair and she knew that tears weren't very far away. She had humiliated herself enough without James seeing her cry.

He paused and she tensed as he turned round to look at her.

'Don't forget,' he warned her, 'I'll pick you up at six-thirty on Wednesday morning. Don't be late...'

CHAPTER TWO

POPPY woke up abruptly and stared anxiously at the illuminated face of her alarm clock, her heart thumping in dread at the thought that she might have overslept.

Five o'clock. She let her breath out in a sigh of relief and switched off the alarm, which she had set for five-thirty, as she swung her legs out of her bed. She hadn't slept well at all—and not just last night, but every night since the wedding, and, if she was honest with herself, for a long time before that too.

Yesterday she had come home to find her mother and her aunt poring over the proofs of the wedding photographs.

It had hurt her to see the way both of them had looked slightly uncomfortable at her arrival. It had been exactly the same at the wedding, she acknowledged: people treating her with the kind of well-intentioned caution and sympathy which was meant to be compassionate but which had the effect of somehow making her feel just the opposite. An outsider...a spectre at the feast.

The only person who had treated her anything like normally had been the other bridesmaid—and Sally's oldest and closest friend—who Poppy had quickly learned held a very cynical and wryly funny view of relationships and commitment.

'Love may not last, but, believe me, enmity does,' Star had told Poppy grimly during one of their brides-maid-dress fittings, 'and I've got the parents to prove it. I swear that mine pour more energy and emotion into loathing one another and fighting with one another than they ever did into their marriage, their supposed love.'

She had seen the way her aunt had surreptitiously slid out of sight the photographs of the bride and groom in happy, loving close-ups as they kissed for the camera, and as she'd walked out of the kitchen she had heard her aunt telling her mother how much she liked Sally, and how very, very much in love with her Chris was.

'I never thought he would fall so deeply in love,' Poppy heard her adding as she paused on the stairs, not wanting to listen and yet somehow unable to stop herself. She was a masochist addicted to the source of her pain, she told herself bitterly as the older woman continued.

'Of the two of them James has always been the more passionate and intense one. Chris has always had a much sunnier, more resilient nature. I just wish… How is Poppy? She…'

Quickly Poppy moved out of earshot, her body trembling inwardly with a mixture of pain and indignation.

She knew how James would have reacted if he had been privy to that conversation, how he would have taunted her for allowing herself to become the object of other people's pity—something *he* would never allow to happen to him. Poppy's mouth twisted into a small, bitter smile as she tried to imagine James being involved in any situation, any relationship which might cast him in such a role. Impossible.

It was all very well for her aunt to describe James as the more intense of her two sons—maybe he was,

Poppy allowed, though she thought it more a case of his being intent on having his own way and steamrollering anyone who stood in opposition to him. But more passionate? And because of that passion, as her aunt had somehow implied, more vulnerable than his more easygoing younger brother? No way.

The only intense passion she had ever seen James exhibit was that of anger—the kind of anger that she had felt when he had given her that unwanted, hateful kiss of contempt.

Poppy shivered now as she hurried into the bathroom, the chill invading her body—that tiny, betraying sensation—nothing at all to do with the coolness of the early morning air.

In fact, as she glanced through the window she could see that the pre-dawn sky was clear and that it promised to be a fine, warm day.

No, the reason for the almost electric shock of sensitivity raising goose bumps on her skin lay not outside her body but within it. Its cause was her own fiercely denied and totally shocked awareness of the fact that something within her, some alien, unknown, unwanted part of her, had been physically responsive to the practised skill of James's kiss.

It wasn't a subject that she had any desire to explore and in order to dismiss it she spent her brief time under the shower running through the list of Japanese technical terms that she had committed to memory the previous evening.

The conference they were attending was a new one and it promised to be a highly prestigious event. Until James had announced that he would be going, taking the place not just of Chris but also of the sales team, Poppy had been looking forward to it.

The venue was not Milan, where she had been on previous occasions, but a newly opened, exclusive spa resort in the mountains, and the brochure that Chris had shown her had made the event read more like an exclusive holiday than a work event.

Not that she would have any time to enjoy the facilities of the spa, Poppy reflected as she stepped out of the shower and reached for a towel. James, she suspected, would see to that.

As she reached for her underclothes she caught sight of her naked body in the bathroom mirror. She had always been slim but during the weeks leading up to the wedding she had lost weight and now, she acknowledged, she was getting close to looking almost thin. Mentally comparing her fragile, slender body with Sally's almost voluptuously feminine shape, she admitted that it was no wonder that Chris should prefer the open sensuality of Sally's body to the fine-boned thinness of hers.

James had commented derisively on her lack of feminine curves only the previous Christmas, when they'd had their obligatory dance together at the firm's Christmas party. His hands had spanned her waist completely and he'd taunted her with the fact that her body was more that of a girl than of a woman.

'Just another indication of your reluctance to grow up and accept life as it really is,' had been his sardonic comment.

'I am adult; I'm twenty-two years old,' Poppy had countered angrily.

'On the outside,' James had agreed, 'but inside you're still an adolescent clinging to a self-created fantasy. You don't have an inkling of what real life is all about, Poppy…real emotions…real men.'

She had denied his comments, of course, but it hadn't made any difference.

It hadn't always been like this between them; they hadn't always shared an enmity which seemed to deepen and harden with the years instead of relaxing and easing.

As a child she had adored James. *He* had then been the one who had rescued her from *Chris's* teasing, the one who had patiently taught her to ride her first bike, fly her first kite, the one who had mopped up her tears when she'd fallen off the former and over the strings of the latter.

But all that had changed when she was twelve and had fallen in love with Chris. James's good-humoured, elder-cousin indulgence of her had turned to contemptuous hostility once he had recognised her feelings for Chris, and she had reciprocated with a fury and dislike which had grown over the years instead of abating.

The last thing she wanted to do, she admitted to herself as she dressed quickly in her working 'uniform' of cream silk shirt and straight skirt of her taupe suit, was to spend the next four days exposed to James's contempt and hostility, but it was not in her nature to take the cowardly way out of refusing to go; she took her job too seriously for that.

The actual translation work she did might not be enough to keep her busy eight hours a day, five days a week, Poppy acknowledged, but a look around at the kind of job her peers had been forced to take—some of them with much better degrees than her own—had made her determined to prove her worth to the business; an evening course in computer technology had turned out to be a wise investment of her time, as had her determination to involve herself in the administrative side of the business.

To some, such work might have seemed mundane, but Poppy felt it had given her a working knowledge and an insight into the running of the company which would be just as valuable on any future CV she needed to prepare as her language skills and her degree.

The overnight bag which she had packed the night before was downstairs in the hall. Picking up her suit jacket she studied her reflection in her bedroom mirror critically.

Her hair, soft and straight, made her look younger than she actually was, she knew, but she was loath to have it cut. Chris had once told her that he thought long hair on a woman was incredibly feminine. Sally, though, oddly enough, had a short, almost boyish crop of blonde curls.

Her features didn't lend themselves well to exaggerated make-up and her skin was too pale, she decided critically. Her eyes, her best feature, were large and almond-shaped and fringed with thick dark lashes which looked ridiculous when loaded down with mascara. Her nose was short and straight, and her mouth, in her view, was an odd mismatch, her top lip well shaped and moderately curved whilst her bottom lip was wider and fuller, somehow giving her mouth a sensuality which she personally found distressing and which she always tried to play down with a softly coloured matt lipstick.

So far the early spring weather had been unseasonably fine and warm and her skin had begun to lose its winter pallor, but she had still slipped on stockings beneath her skirt. Bare legs, no matter how blissfully cool, did not, in her opinion, look properly businesslike.

Downstairs she made herself a cup of coffee and

a slice of toast which she knew she wouldn't eat. Her stomach was already churning nervously. She had never particularly liked flying.

James and Chris's father, her uncle, had been a keen amateur pilot who had been killed with a friend when they had flown into a freak electric storm. She remembered how devastated Chris had been at his father's death. They had cried over it together, sharing their grief. James, on the other hand, had retreated into grim, white-faced silence—a remote stranger, or so it had seemed to Poppy, who'd looked contemptuously upon her and Chris's shared emotional grief.

She heard James's car just as she was swallowing her last mouthful of coffee. Quickly putting down her cup she hurried out into the hall, pulling on her jacket and picking up her handbag and case as she went to open the door. Like her, James was dressed formally in a business suit, not navy for once but a lightweight pale grey which somehow emphasised his height and the breadth of his shoulders.

As he took her case from her, Poppy saw the brief, assessing glance he gave her and her chin started to tilt challengingly as she waited for him to make some critical or derogatory comment, but instead, disconcertingly, she suddenly became aware that his original scrutiny had turned into something a little more thorough and startlingly more male as his eyes lingered on the soft curves of her breasts.

It was the kind of inspection that Poppy was used to from other men; that telling but, generally speaking, acceptably discreet male awareness of her as a woman. But to be subjected to it by *James*… James who'd sternly reprimanded his younger brother when Chris had teasingly commented on her new shape the first day she had self-consciously worn the pretty, flower-sprigged cotton bra that her mother had gravely agreed that her eleven-year-old's barely thirty-inch chest demanded.

Seeing James focus on that same chest in such a very male and sensual way when for years Poppy could have sworn that he was totally oblivious to the fact that she had grown from a child to a woman was a very disconcerting experience.

Somehow just managing to resist the temptation to tug the edges of her jacket protectively together, Poppy gave him an angry glare. How would he like it if she focused on…a certain part of his body in that way.

'Have you got everything?' she heard him ask her before her brain could come up with an answer to her own question. 'Tickets, passport, money…?'

'Of course,' Poppy responded, grittily withholding the angry comment she wanted to make. This was a business trip to Italy, she reminded herself grimly, and she intended to preserve a businesslike distance between them, if only to prove to James that she was not the adolescent child he constantly taunted her as being.

Outside, his Jaguar gleamed richly in the early morning sunshine. As he opened the passenger door for her, Poppy could smell the rich, expensive scent of the car's leather seats. Chris and her mother, who, like James, were directors and shareholders in the company, drove cars with far less status and the urge to remind James of this fact was irresistible as he slid into the driver's seat next to her and started the car.

'Very nice,' she commented, smoothing the cream leather with her fingertips. 'A perk of the job, I presume…?'

'No, as a matter of fact, it isn't,' James shocked her by denying as he swung the car into the traffic. 'It's time you brought yourself up to date with current tax laws, Poppy,' he told her acidly. 'Even if I wanted to make use of my...connection with the company to my own financial advantage, the current tax penalties involved in owning an expensive company car would prohibit me from doing so.'

Poppy could feel her face start to burn as she interpreted the message in the first part of his statement. Unlike her, *he* did not have to benefit from his connection with the company, he was implying.

Resentment burned angrily in Poppy's chest. Was she *never* going to be judged on her own merits, instead of being condemned because of her mother's position as a shareholder? How would James like it if she pointed out to him that the only reason he was the company's chairman was because of his father?

Poppy moved irritably against the restriction of her seat belt, all too aware of how easily James could refute such an accusation. Although he had the reputation within the company of being a demanding employer, noone disputed the fact that the company's present success was due to his hard work. And no matter how much he might demand of those who worked for him it was never any more than he demanded of himself.

The traffic was starting to build up as they got closer to the airport and already Poppy's stomach was beginning to clench nervously as she anticipated what lay ahead. It was the moment of take-off she dreaded most; once that was over it was easier for her to relax.

The spot in Italy where the conference was being held was three hours' drive from the airport, which meant, Poppy suspected, that they would be spending the better part of the day travelling. She had brought some work with her to keep her occupied during the flight—and to ensure that she didn't have to talk to James—but she couldn't help wistfully reflecting how different things would have been if her travelling companion had been Chris…a Chris who was not married to Sally or anyone else, a Chris who—

Stop it, she warned herself sternly. He *is* married to Sally and you've got to stop thinking about him…stop loving him…

As she quickly blinked away the weak tears she could feel threatening her, she heard James say sardonically, 'Poor Poppy, still hopelessly in love with a man who doesn't want her. Why do I get the impression it's a role you actively enjoy playing?' he asked her savagely, the harshness in his voice shocking her almost as much as the cruelty of his accusation.

'That's not true,' she denied chokily.

'That's not the impression I get,' James said to her as he negotiated the maze of slip-roads that led to the car park. 'In fact I'd say the role of self-pitying lover is one you've embraced with far more enthusiasm than you appear to have had for embracing *real* love.'

Poppy's face burned hotly as he parked the car and opened his door. She wasn't going to dignify his comments by responding to them…or defending herself, she told herself fiercely. Nor was she going to let James see how much they had hurt her.

'It's no wonder that Chris prefers to take a real woman to bed,' James told her cruelly as he opened her door for her and waited like a gaoler for her to get out.

I *am* a real woman, Poppy wanted to protest. Just as real as Sally, just as capable of giving love, of inciting passion and desire. But was she? Was there something inherently feminine and desirable in Sally that was missing from her? Was she somehow lacking in

that vital ingredient that made a woman lovable and
desirable?

All the doubts about herself and her sexuality which
had sprung into life with the news of Chris's engagement to Sally and which she had rigorously and fiercely
ignored and denied suddenly rose up inside her, a fully
armed enemy force which James's words had carelessly
set free from the prison in which she had concealed
them.

Did he know about the fears, the insecurities about
her sexuality that these last months had brought? Poppy
wondered numbly as she waited for him to remove their
cases from the boot of his car.

How could he? It was impossible. He was simply trying to goad her, to hurt her, to provoke a reaction from
her which would enable him to reinforce his condemnation of her as immature and foolish.

Quite what his purpose was in doing this Poppy
didn't really know, had never really questioned. The
enmity which had developed between them had grown
alongside her love for Chris until she'd accepted it in
the same way that she had accepted that love. But, despite the fact that Chris's marriage had now forced her
to accept that she had to find a way of severing herself
from the past and finding another focus for her life,
of accepting that Chris could never be a part of that
life in the way she had so much hoped, it seemed that
since the wedding James's antagonism to her had simply increased.

Why? Was he perhaps trying to force her into leaving the company? Was his desire to hurt her, to undermine her...to destroy her...to do with the business, or
something more personal?

James had locked the car and was waiting impatiently for her to join him.

These next four days were going to be the longest of her life, Poppy reflected.

'You can relax now; we're airborne...'

The sound of James's voice in her ear made Poppy open her tightly closed eyes, her pent-up breath leaking in a relieved sigh from her lungs as she recognised the truth of what he was saying.

Having shudderingly refused the window-seat that James had offered her, she had fastened her seat belt and willed herself not to give in to her childhood need to have a familiar hand to cling to as the plane had taxied down the runway and started to lift off.

At least she had managed not to do that, although... Surreptitiously she slowly released the tense fingers she had not been able to stop herself from curling into the immaculate smoothness of James's suit jacket—and not just James's suit jacket, she acknowledged uncomfortably, but James's very solidly muscled arm as well.

His dry 'Thank you, Poppy' as she tried to remove her hand from his arm without him noticing what she had done made her flush guiltily and avoid looking at him.

Did he never feel afraid? she wondered bitterly. Did nothing ever dent that iron self-control of his? Had no one ever made him ache...hurt...yearn for her so much that nothing else...noone else mattered?

If anyone had, she had certainly never been aware of it, Poppy thought, but then she had been too involved in her own feelings to pay much attention to anyone else.

As always, now that they were actually airborne, her fear left her, her body starting to relax...

She refused the drink that the stewardess offered her and reached for her case and the work she had brought with her. James, she noticed, was already engrossed in some papers which he had removed from his brief-case. Well, at least whilst his attention was on them he wouldn't be able to pick on her, she decided with relief.

'Oh, James, just look at that view,' Poppy breathed, unable to keep the awed delight from her voice as she stared through their hire-car window at the panorama spread before them.

Transport had been arranged from the airport to the conference centre, but James had opted to make his own arrangements and independently hire a car, and Poppy had felt no trepidation at the thought of travelling with him, since she knew that not only was he a very safe driver but that he was also familiar with Italian roads.

The thought of spending three hours shut up in a car with only him for company had been a different mat-ter and until they had started to climb into the moun-tains she had resolutely occupied herself with her own thoughts rather than try to engage him in any conver-sation. Conversations with James, she had decided bit-terly, always seemed to lead to the same place—to them arguing.

Pride and her awareness of how unsympathetic and antagonistic towards her he was had prevented her from trying to defend herself by telling him that loving Chris had become a burden she desperately wanted to remove from her life.

Had they had a different relationship, had they been closer, had she felt able to trust him, to turn to him for help, she might have been able to admit to him how much she longed to have someone to confide in, some-

one to whom she could talk about her feelings and her
guilt at her own inability to leave behind a love she
knew could only cause her pain. If things had been different…if *he* had been different…if he had still been the
same James he had been when she had been a child…
But he wasn't, and somewhere, somehow, the cousinly
love that he had once felt for her had gone.

Her determination not to give him any opportunity
to criticise or condemn her whilst they were alone by
keeping silent and aloof from him had disintegrated,
though, as the road had started to wind through the ancient chain of mountains, taking them through small
villages and dusty towns in whose Renaissance squares
Poppy could very easily visualise the richly liveried
men-at-arms who, along with the princes who had once
commanded them, had fought over the prizes of the fer-
tile plains below them.

Today, the towns were tranquil, only their architecture a reminder of the past turbulence and turmoil, the
scenery around them so spectacular that it bewitched
Poppy into forgetting her vow of silence to exclaim
over its beauty.

James, of course, was bound to be less impressed,
Poppy recognised; he had relatives in Tuscany and
Rome and was no stranger to the beauty of Italy's countryside, nor her architecture. And Poppy told herself that
she ought not to feel rather like a child told off for a
crime it hadn't committed when James turned his head
to look at her in response to her impulsive comment
and said tautly, 'But no doubt a view which you would
enjoy far more if it was my brother you were seeing it
with. Too bad that Chris doesn't share your enthusiasm. He's a modern city man, Poppy—something else

he and Sally share, something else you and he don't,' he told her unkindly.

Poppy said nothing, turning her head away so that James couldn't see the quick, betraying sheen of tears filming her eyes.

She knew, of course, that Chris did not share her love of history…of the past…of the awesomeness of nature, as James had just said, and as Chris himself was the first to cheerfully admit.

Nor did she intend to defend herself by contradicting James's comment or by telling him that he was wrong and that, oddly enough, she had not actually been wishing that Chris were in the car beside her.

She hadn't…but now she did, and with such heart-aching intensity that she was almost swamped by her misery.

Thank heavens it couldn't be much further to the hotel, she thought. She closed her eyes and leaned back in her seat, keeping her face turned towards the window and averted from James.

Four days, four times twenty-four hours… She gave an involuntary shudder. Please God, let them pass quickly, she prayed.

'Poppy.'

Sleepily Poppy opened her eyes and eased her aching body into a more comfortable position when she realised that the car had come to a halt and that they had reached their destination.

The hotel, as she had read in the brochure, had originally been a medieval fortress built by an Italian prince, set high up in the mountains to guard his territories, but reading about it had not prepared her for the raw magnificence of a structure which seemed to be carved out of the rock itself, rising up steeply from the walled courtyard in which they were now parked.

Even though she knew that the original fortress was now just a shell which had been used to house a far more modern and luxurious centre, Poppy felt awestruck and faintly intimidated by the sheer, stark rise of the stone edifice in front of her, which was softened only slightly by its mantle of ivy and roses.

The *palazzo* had been used as a private home for several centuries, abandoned only when it had been commandeered by the German army during the Second World War, and Poppy knew that in addition to the luxurious state rooms which had now been adapted to form the hotel's reception rooms the original Italian water garden had been restored to working order and restocked with the varieties of roses and other plants with which it would originally have been adorned.

And yet, despite knowing just how luxurious the spa promised to be and being hit by the heat of the sunshine when she stepped out of the car, unable to remove her gaze from the sheer sweep of rock from which the outer wall of the fortress had been cut, Poppy couldn't quite repress a small shiver.

'Not the kind of place you'd want to be incarcerated in as a prisoner,' she heard James saying behind her, his comment so exactly mirroring her own thoughts that she turned towards him in surprise as he added drily, 'I wouldn't give much for anyone's chance of escaping from here.'

'No.' Poppy agreed bleakly. A prisoner would probably have about as much chance of escaping from such a place as she had of escaping James over the next few days.

The car park was starting to fill up rapidly with other

arrivals. Picking up their cases, James touched Poppy briefly on the shoulder.

'Reception seems to be that way. Let's go and get booked in before it develops into too much of a scrum.'

Once inside the hotel, the austere, almost forbidding impression of the fortress as a prison was totally banished by the breathtaking luxury of the reception area, a huge, vaulted room illuminated by crystal chandeliers, the walls decorated with glowingly rich frescos. Only a room this vast could take such an abundance of gold, crimson and blue, Poppy acknowledged dizzily as she followed James towards the central reception desk.

Immaculately groomed girls, in suits as understated as their surroundings were ornate, busied themselves dealing with the rapid influx of guests, and Poppy was cynically amused to see that James, who was in fact behind three other men trying to claim one girl's attention, received the full wattage of her very alluring smile whilst they were totally ignored.

Poppy had always known that other women found her elder cousin attractive. She could even remember how, in the days before she had fallen in love with Chris, she had actually felt angry and jealous herself if he paid her schoolfriends more attention than he did her, but those days were gone now, and even though she registered the assessing look the receptionist gave her as James leant over the desk to speak to the girl and handed her their passports she was not affected by it. The receptionist was welcome to him. She gave a small shudder. She could think of nothing more loathsome... noone more...

She tensed as she suddenly realised what the receptionist was saying to James, and hurried towards him, demanding angrily, 'What does she mean, *our* room?'

The girl was already reaching behind her to hand James a pass-key. *A* key, Poppy noticed in disbelief.

'James...' she urged, but James had already anticipated her and was turning back to the receptionist, telling her in swift, fluent Italian that there appeared to have been a mistake, and that they required two separate rooms.

'No,' the girl denied, shaking her head, picking up their passports and a list she had in front of her. She read out carefully, 'Mr and Mrs Carlton,' and then said, first to Poppy, 'You are Mrs Carlton,' and then to James, 'and you Mr Carlton.'

'I am Poppy Carlton,' Poppy confirmed, 'but I am *not* his wife. We are not married... I am not...his wife,' she emphasised.

When the receptionist continued to gaze blankly at her, she turned angrily to James, appealing, 'You tell her, James. Explain...make her understand.'

How could such a mistake have been made? Poppy fumed as she stood back whilst James quickly explained to the receptionist the misunderstanding which seemed to have occurred and asked her to change their booking from one double room to two singles.

Chris's secretary had made the original bookings. She was comfortably middle-aged and extremely efficient and Poppy couldn't believe that she could have made such a mistake. The receptionist had summoned the duty manager at James's request and James was now explaining the situation to him and reiterating the fact that they required two separate rooms.

The duty manager shrugged and shook his head. 'That, I am afraid, is not possible,' he told James. 'The hotel is fully booked for the conference, every room already taken...'

'But they must have somewhere...some room,' Poppy gasped as she heard what he was saying.

'None; there is nowhere,' the duty manager repeated firmly.

'Then we'll just have to find somewhere else to stay,' Poppy burst out.

Her face flushed beneath the withering look that James gave her as he asked her sardonically, 'Where exactly did you have in mind? The nearest town is forty miles away.'

'Then...then I'll just have to...to sleep in the car,' Poppy asserted wildly. 'I—'

'For four days?' James gave her a derisive look. 'Don't be so ridiculous...'

'James, you can't let them do this,' Poppy protested as the duty manager turned away from them to deal with the harassed-looking courier in charge of a party of Japanese businessmen who, from what Poppy could hear of their agitated conversation, had lost not just some luggage *en route* but one member of their party as well. 'Do something.'

'Such as?' James asked, gesturing to the now packed reception area and the press of people demanding attention from the receptionists.

'You've attended conferences before; you know what they're like,' he pointed out. 'The rule is if it can go wrong it will...'

'Maybe, but it's never *gone* wrong before,' Poppy seethed. 'How can they make a mistake like that...? There must be something you can do... Offer to pay them extra...to...'

'Poppy,' James told her, speaking slowly and patiently as though she were a child too young to grasp what he was saying. 'There *are* no empty rooms. Believe me. I just heard one of the receptionists telling another that she's already been forced to give up her staff room and share with someone else on another shift because of overbooking. Believe me, it's either this room or nothing.'

It was on the tip of Poppy's tongue to tell him that if that was the case then there was no way she was staying. But then she remembered how much James would relish her giving him an opportunity to prove how unprofessional she really was and she forced the impulsive words back.

James, taking her acceptance for granted, was already signing the register and taking possession of their pass-cards.

'We might as well find our own way,' he told Poppy. 'God knows how long we'd have to wait for a porter.'

Like her, James was only carrying a briefcase and an overnight bag. She just hoped that the hotel's laundry facilities were better organised and more reliable than its booking system, she reflected angrily as she followed James towards the nearest bank of lifts.

The modern part of the complex had been built around an atrium and as the lift took them upwards they could look down past the open balconies to the greenery and splashing fountains below them.

Although the complex had been given the title of spa it did not actually possess any natural hot springs or spa waters of its own, the term, Poppy suspected, being used in a slightly looser sense to embrace the fact that it offered a wide range of self-indulgent treatments and dietary regimes and holistic alternative therapies.

Their room was on one of the upper floors, the silence as they stepped out of the lift onto the polished marble floor broken only by the hum of the air-conditioning.

'This way,' James instructed her. Their room was halfway down the corridor and Poppy waited whilst James opened the door, and then froze with shock as she followed him inside and stared in white-faced disbelief at the room's one, single, solitary double bed.

A double bed...

She looked at James, then back at the bed, announced flatly, 'I don't believe this...'

'Correct me if I'm wrong, Poppy,' James told her smoothly, 'but, as the company's official translator, wouldn't it normally fall within your field of operations to provide correct foreign translations for those departments which might need them?'

'You know it would,' Poppy agreed irritably. 'But—'

'In that case you would then be the person responsible for providing a correctly worded translation for this booking.'

'If I had been asked for one, yes,' Poppy agreed. 'But—'

'And I think I am also right in saying,' James continued grimly, 'that when this particular booking was made you believed that you would be attending this conference with Chris...'

Poppy stared at him in shocked disbelief as she realised what he was implying.

'Yes, I did think I would be coming here with Chris,' she agreed furiously, 'but that does not mean that I deliberately altered the booking so that Chris and I would be forced to share a room. I had nothing to do with this booking. It was made by fax whilst I was away on holiday, and if you think for one moment that, no matter what...my feelings for...for *anyone*, I would ever stoop to doing something like this…that I would ever try to force…or manipulate a man…any man, but most especially one I…I cared about to—'

She couldn't go on, her words abruptly suspended by the force of her emotions.

'I can't stay here in this room with you,' she protested huskily when she could trust herself to speak again. 'I can't…and I—'

'Stop being so hysterical,' James told her coldly. 'You don't have any choice. Neither of us does. This conference is very important. I've spent months making contact with various international companies who'll be attending it…potential customers, and I don't have time to waste dealing with a hysterical, manipulative idiot who—'

'I did *not* arrange this. It has nothing to do with me,' Poppy protested furiously. 'The last thing I want…I would ever want…is to share a be—a room with you…'

'I believe you,' James told her, adding cuttingly, 'But then you didn't think you would be here with *me*, did you? And, I promise you, Poppy, you're not exactly my ideal choice of bed-mate either. What the hell was that conniving little mind of yours planning? Some kind of emotional blackmail…? A threat to tell Sally that Chris had been sleeping with you if he didn't come across and—'

'*No!*'

Her denial had been as explosive as a blow, Poppy acknowledged as she stared at James in sick disbelief. Did he really think she could…would stoop to something so underhanded as that?

Her mouth twisted bitterly as she made herself look straight into the wintry contempt of his eyes and told him quietly, 'I love Chris, James, and in my book that

means putting him first…not wanting to hurt him…
Despite what you seem to think, I don't need you to
tell me that Chris doesn't feel the same way about me.
Do you really think I'd want him on those kinds of
terms…? That I'd want any man who…?' She swallowed, unable to go on.

'What I think is that you've become so obsessed
with your so-called love for Chris that you don't know
what's reasonable or rational any more…'

'You're wrong,' Poppy told him, but she could see
from the look on his face that he didn't believe her.

CHAPTER THREE

POPPY exhaled her pent-up breath in an angry hiss of despair, turning away from the panoramic view through the bedroom window in front of her and quickly averting her eyes from the bed.

James was downstairs in the conference hall where he had gone to check that their display stand, which had been shipped out via their Italian agents, had been assembled correctly, and she knew that sooner or later she was going to have to join him. After all, that was why she was here.

Officially, the conference didn't open until the morning but she knew from previous experience that the conference hall would be teeming with people getting ready for the opening.

How had it happened? she wondered miserably. How could such a mistake have occurred and, even worse, how could...how dared James imply that she had had anything to do with it, that she had deliberately manipulated things so that she and Chris would be sharing a room?

She had already contemplated refusing to share the bed with him, but the room's furnishings, although elegant, were not particularly comfortable and the marble floor would certainly not make a comfortable bed.

The saving grace was that at least the bed was a good size and there should be no danger of the two of them actually having to sleep close together. If she lay on her side and faced away from him, she might even be able to pretend that James wasn't there at all.

And at least there was one thing she most definitely did not have to worry about. There was no way that James would try to take advantage of the situation or of her. She almost laughed aloud at the very thought.

Years ago, when they had all been children, there had been occasions when they had all holidayed together, and whilst they had never actually shared a bedroom there had been the kind of family intimacy between the cousins which had been natural under such circumstances.

That had been when they were children, though, Poppy acknowledged, and there was a vast difference between a five-year-old and a thirteen-year-old running, dressing gown-clad, between their separate bedrooms and two adults of twenty-two and thirty sharing the intimacy of a bed as well as a bathroom.

The flimsy cotton robe that she had brought with her was hardly as protective or concealing as the thick, fleecy dressing gown that she had worn as a child and… Poppy froze and closed her eyes, cursing herself under her breath as she remembered that the one thing she had decided there was no need for her to bring with her was any kind of nightdress.

Remembering the golden rule of easy travelling— only take what you can carry on and off the plane in your hand luggage—she had kept her packing to the bare minimum… 'Bare' being the operative word, she reflected grimly now.

Normally she was quite happy to sleep in her skin…

she preferred it, in fact…but under these circumstances…

Tiredly she ran her hand through her hair. Her skin
felt grubby and gritty from travelling and the one thing
the room did have, which had impressed her, was a huge
walk-in shower.

James wouldn't be in any hurry to return—after all,
he would have as little desire to spend any time in her
company as she did to spend time in his—and it made
sense to take advantage of his absence to have a shower
now rather than to wait until he had returned and then
suffer the embarrassment of using the bathroom whilst
he was there.

Poppy had already unpacked the clothes that she had
brought with her and, quickly selecting clean underwear, a fresh shirt and a pair of simple, well-cut silk and
linen trousers in her favourite shade of warm cream,
she hurried into the bathroom, where she hesitated before leaving the door slightly ajar and then checking to
make sure it couldn't swing closed.

As a child she had once been locked in the bathroom
at the house of friends of her parents and the small incident had left her with what she knew to be an irrational
fear of the same thing ever happening again. Irrational,
but strong enough to ensure that she could never actually bring herself to lock herself in any kind of room.

She showered the stickiness of their journey off her
skin first before lathering it generously with her favourite shower gel. Poppy rarely wore full-strength
perfume, preferring the more subtly fragrant effect of
shower gels and body lotions, so that the only way other
people could tell that she was wearing any would be if
they actually touched her or…

She closed her eyes, clenching them against the hot

sting of tears which she told herself were stupidly self-pitying as she recognised the direction her thoughts were taking and the deliberate self-infliction of pain in acknowledging that the only person who could share her awareness of her body's delicate fragrance would have to be someone who was very physically intimate with her...a lover. But she had no lover...no one to love her... He loved someone else...

She knew that she was crying silent, anguished tears as she turned off the shower and soaped her body, too lost in the misery of her own despair to hear the bedroom door opening, so that it wasn't until he thrust open the unlocked bathroom door that she realised that James was back.

For a second neither of them said anything, the only sounds to break the silence being the noise of the dripping shower and her shocked, indrawn breath as the lather that covered her body in creamy ribbons of foam slid off her skin, leaving her sleek and silky and completely naked.

For once Poppy's reactions were the faster, her breath squeezing out of her lungs, her arms lifting to cross over her bare breasts in a gesture that was as instinctively feminine as it was hopelessly inadequate as a means of concealing her, her eyes brilliant with shock as she looked helplessly towards the towel airing on the rail, which was closer to James than it was to her. To reach it she would have to step out of the shower and walk right past him and...

Gritting her teeth and giving him a look of pure, vitriolic loathing, she prepared to do so. He had seen just about all there was to see of her now, after all, she decided grimly, and if he thought that she was going to stand there cowering whilst he enjoyed her embarrassment…

But, to her amazement, as she took a step forward he suddenly reached for the towel, his expression difficult to read, his eyes darkening, his mouth hardening in a way that made her tense and watch him.

Being the recipient of James's anger and contempt was nothing new to her, but on this occasion, she decided indignantly as he suddenly reached for the towel and almost threw it at her, she had no idea what on earth she was supposed to have done to merit the glittering fury she could see in his eyes.

'Cover yourself up, for God's sake, will you, Poppy?' he instructed her harshly. 'You aren't a child any more, even if emotionally you do still behave like one.'

'You should have knocked,' she told him fiercely as she wrapped the towel around her body.

'You should have locked the door,' James countered, 'or are we still playing at make-believe and fantasising that somehow I'm going to turn into Chris…?'

'I don't *have* that much imagination,' Poppy told him bitterly, and added for good measure, 'No one could have…'

'Be careful, Poppy,' James warned her coldly, 'otherwise I might just forget that you are still, after all, my cousin and that as such—'

'I might be your cousin,' Poppy interrupted him recklessly, 'but that still doesn't give you the right to come barging in here, nor to treat me as though…as though I'm some kind of child you—'

'No?' James stopped her. 'Then how would you like me to treat you…?'

There was a note in his voice that made Poppy stiffen and turn her head to look over her shoulder at him, at first in query and then in shocked disbelief as she saw the way he was looking at her.

She had always known that James was a man with an extremely high-voltage sexual charisma—she had heard other women telling her so often enough after all—but to be suddenly and unexpectedly subjected to a thorough sexual scrutiny of such blistering heat and savagery that it virtually stripped the thick fluffy towel from her body and left her feeling far more naked and vulnerable than she had felt when she had actually been naked was unexpectedly shocking.

As she followed the way he was slowly and oh, so deliberately studying every line of her body, every curve, every hollow, in some satanic way, it was almost as though she could see herself through his eyes, see what he was seeing as he visually stripped her and examined her as cruelly and callously and dehumanisingly as though her body were a piece of merchandise that he had every right to assess and value and reject.

When he had finally finished his assessment and his eyes met hers, she had no defence left against the shock of what he had done, no barriers strong enough to put up.

She couldn't make a sound…couldn't shed a tear, couldn't express in any way her sense of outrage and humiliation, her feeling of shocked pain at the way he had assessed her as a woman and then dismissed her. No, not a woman, she decided as she tried to swallow past the hard lump blocking her throat. Not a woman but just a piece of flesh, a body…a thing without any right to emotions or needs of her own, without any right to self-respect or…

As she finally managed to break eye contact with him and find her voice, she told him croakily, her voice creaking under the weight of her fury, 'I've often wondered why you've never settled down, James…married…had a family…but now I know. If that's how you see women…if that's how you treat your women—'

'You know nothing about *my* women,' James interrupted her harshly, and then added contemptuously as he moved closer to her and took hold of her chin in a grip that she couldn't manage to break, 'Let's face it, Poppy, you know nothing about *being* a woman…what it means…how it feels…'

'In your opinion,' Poppy spat at him, finally managing to wrench herself out of his grip. 'But I'll tell you one thing I do know, James, and that's that you're the last man I'd want to show me…the last man I'd *let* show me,' she added emphatically.

'Don't tempt me,' James responded grimly as he turned towards the door, pausing only to warn her, 'Don't challenge me, Poppy; you can't win and you won't like the consequences… I came to warn you that we're likely to be in for a chaotic few days. The hotel seems to have overestimated its ability to handle the mechanics of the conference and so they've had to suspend room service.

'This evening's dinner is due to be served at eight-thirty and if you want something to eat I'd advise you to make sure you're downstairs early. I've got a strong suspicion that we aren't the only ones with problems.

'I overheard someone else's conversation whilst I was talking to our agent and it seems that some of the rooms which should have been ready for occupation aren't.

'I've still got a few things I need to iron out—' he glanced at his watch '—so I'll meet you downstairs at eight.' He paused for a moment before adding silkily,

'Unless, of course, you feel you're going to want another shower...'

Giving him an angry glare, Poppy started to step past him, but he stopped her, reaching out and picking up the clean underwear that she had forgotten and handing it to her.

'Don't forget these, will you...?'

Snatching them out of his hand, flushing as she saw the way he was looking at her perfectly respectable but admittedly rather plain, no-nonsense bra and briefs, she couldn't resist saying contemptuously, 'I suppose a man like you prefers something...something in scarlet satin.'

For a moment she thought that he wasn't going to bother replying, but as she turned towards the door she saw his mouth starting to curl slightly at the corners and his eyes glint with the same dangerous, glittering mockery which she had learned long ago presaged his more razor-sharp attacks on her pride.

'Satin, yes,' he drawled tauntingly. 'Scarlet...no, never. But you're way out of date with your ideas of what a man finds sexy in a woman these days, Poppy, or of what a woman might do in that department to turn him on. No wonder you couldn't get Chris interested.

'Next time—if there ever *is* a next time...or a next man—try baiting your trap a little more cleverly. A seductive little whisper in a very public place that underneath the very respectable skirt you've got on you're wearing...nothing...works wonders, or so I've been told...'

'You're disgusting,' Poppy told him furiously, her cheeks burning as she realised what he meant. 'And, for your information, I would never—'

'Oh, no, Poppy,' James corrected her mock-gently,

'I'm not disgusting, but you most certainly are naïve…
very naïve.

'Now, didn't you say something about coming here
to work? I want you to send a fax for me, please. I hope
that your Japanese is as good as your mother claims.
I've just been talking to one of the German groups; their
linguist spent two years in Tokyo…'

'Probably as a geisha,' Poppy muttered disrespect-
fully under her breath as James finally walked out of
the bathroom and left her in peace to get dressed.

It didn't matter that she was his cousin and that there
had been countless occasions in their shared childhood
when he had seen her naked. She could even remember
once suffering the indignity of having her seven-year-
old self stripped of her torn and filthy clothes, summar-
ily dumped into the bath and virtually scrubbed clean
by him at the same time as he delivered a lecture to her
on what was likely to happen to her if her mother found
out that she had deliberately ignored her instructions
that she was not to play in the stream at the foot of their
shared holiday-cottage garden.

Then she had foolishly actually been grateful to
James…and, even more ridiculously, seen him as her
saviour… Now she knew better, she decided.

James had been right about the chaos, was Poppy's first
thought as she waited for him to join her in the crowded
foyer as they had arranged. She had already talked to
several other people whom she had recognised from
other conferences and they had confirmed what James
had already told her.

It seemed that the hotel manager had overestimated
their ability to cope with something as complex as organising such a large-scale event.

'They say that two of the chefs have already left and that they've had to bribe the others to stay,' a German sales manager whom Poppy had met at Frankfurt the previous year had confided to her.

At the time, Chris had teased her gently that Gunther Weiner was obviously attracted to her, and as she'd listened to him she had wished achingly that it were Chris's attraction for her that they were discussing and not another man's…

She heard Gunther asking her if she had again attended the conference with her cousin.

'Yes,' she told him absently, her attention on James, whom she could see making his way towards them.

Excusing herself to Gunther, she went to meet him.

'Who was that?' James demanded curtly, looking over her shoulder at Gunther.

When she told him he demanded, 'What did he want?'

The aggression in his voice surprised her. 'Well, not our company secrets, James,' she told him, enjoying mocking him as he constantly did her, adding with relish, 'Hard though you may find it to believe, *he* is more interested in me.'

She looked at him, waiting for him to come back at her with some typically derogatory response, and then looked curiously across the room to see what was occupying his attention and causing anger to tighten his mouth to a hairline, but he still seemed to be watching Gunther walking away from them.

Dinner, predictably, was a chaotic and hurried affair, although the food was surprisingly good—not that she had very much of an appetite.

Once they had finished eating James announced that he had some business he wanted to attend to and left her to her own devices. Poppy decided that she might as well explore the rest of the hotel.

The brochure had stressed the benefits of the spa, highlighting the various treatments available, but upon enquiry Poppy discovered that the delay in completion of the building work had meant that most of these facilities were not yet up and running.

There was the Jacuzzi, the sauna and steam room, the gym and the swimming pool, the receptionist informed her, although no one was allowed to use them after ten o'clock in the evening.

It was already gone ten but, nevertheless, Poppy decided that she might as well take a look. The brochure had shown photographs of the swimming pool and Jacuzzi area which had included views through the floor-to-ceiling glass wall on one whole side, looking straight out across the sheer rock-face to the spectacular view beyond it. And, even though it was now dark, the moon was almost full, and should shed enough light to illuminate at least some of the view.

Poppy found her way to the sports centre quite easily. The swimming pool was clearly marked, set in a circular, enclosed area with a raised platform overlooking the now covered pool on one side and allowing a view through the huge expanse of glass she recognised from the brochure on the other.

The remaining two walls, from what she could see in the dim lighting, had been painted with frescos, and a columned walkway led from the pool towards the Jacuzzi and, beyond it, to what she presumed to be another entrance.

As she paused to study the frescos with interest, she heard a sudden sound from the Jacuzzi. Lifting her head, Poppy stared curiously towards it. There appeared to be two people in the water. As she watched, she heard a feminine giggle followed by a soft shushing sound and then male laughter, accompanied by the rhythmic sound of the water moving, as if...as if...

Poppy could feel her face starting to flush as she suddenly realised what was happening...what she had interrupted. They were not, as she had originally thought, two people simply illicitly using the Jacuzzi after hours but a pair of lovers who had obviously decided to try out for themselves the pool's aphrodisiac effect, and then, having discovered that it was not in operation, had patently decided that they might as well make use of... make love in it, after all.

Even though she knew that there was no way they could see her, Poppy felt her face burning an even deeper red as she heard one of them—the woman, she suspected—giving a small, soft moan.

Quickly turning on her heel, she started to walk away. Her face was still burning by the time she reached her room...their room, she acknowledged as she took off her jacket and saw thankfully that there was no sign of James. And she decided that she might as well prepare for bed whilst she had the place to herself.

Seeing that couple making love, hearing them, knowing what they were doing hadn't just embarrassed her, it had also brought back all the pain of knowing that Chris was lost to her... Her throat and eyes ached with the weight of the tears that she refused to allow herself to cry. The last thing she needed now was for James to come back and find her in tears, and yet, as she prepared for bed, her heart ached with the pain of her loss, her mind filled with feverish, tormented thoughts and mental images.

What was it like to have your love...your need...

your desire for a man reciprocated? To know that he wanted you? To feel his desire for you? To know that you had the freedom to reach out and touch him, to share every sensual and emotional intimacy with him? To love him and be loved by him?

Her hands trembling, Poppy pulled on the robe she had unpacked earlier. Used to sleeping naked, as she climbed into the large bed she grimaced at the unfamiliar drag of the fabric against her skin, already disliking the cumbersome restriction of the cloth. As she reached out to switch off the bedside light she was already yawning.

Poppy was having the most wonderful dream. In it all her heartache and loneliness had gone, melted away by the loving warmth of the man whose arms held her so tightly, the man whose body shielded and protected her own, the man who whispered to her that he loved her and that he had always loved her, that he would always love her...

A delicious thrill of pleasure ran through her as she moved even closer to him, pressing her body against his, enjoying the satin warmth of his skin against her own, her senses glorying in the nearness of him, in her freedom to share such intimacy with him, to show him her love.

She had known him for a long, long time...loved him for a long time, but this familiarity, instead of lessening the intensity of the pleasure that lapped at her body in soft, warm waves, only increased it. It gave her a sense of security, an ability to shed her inhibitions and to show her feelings, her desire for him freely and openly, to reach out and touch him, to smooth her fingertips over his skin.

In her sleep Poppy made a soft, contented sound of pleasure as she snuggled closer to James, burrowing against his body, unaware of what she was doing and of the fact that the robe that she had so carefully and resentfully put on earlier was now lying on the floor where she had thrown it, having finally, in her sleep, given in to the irritation of its unaccustomed feel against her skin and pulled it off.

James, disturbed by the sensual movement of her body against his, woke up, cursing silently as he reached out to push her away and put some distance between them.

In her sleep Poppy protested about the removal of the warmth which had been giving her so much pleasure, the body which had felt so good against her own, the man who had made her feel so protected and loved, and she protested both verbally and physically, muttering a husky plea for him to come back and, at the same time, resisting his attempts to put some distance between them, wriggling her body back against his and curling her fingers possessively around his wrist.

'Poppy…' James warned her savagely under his breath.

He had always prided himself on his self-control. The need to conceal his own feelings had been something he had learned young—he had had no other option when his father had died or when… But there came a point when no amount of self-control was enough, when no man…

He took hold of Poppy's shoulder, shaking her, but her eyes remained tightly closed, her body locked in sleep. In the moonlit room he could see the rich tumble of her hair, silk against silk where it lay against her skin; he reached out and touched it, smoothing the tangled tendrils.

Poppy smiled sensuously as she breathed in the familiar scent of his skin. She moved her head and touched her lips to his shoulder, sighing blissfully as she absorbed the taste of him, opening her mouth so that she could touch him with her tongue.

James went completely still and then slowly lifted his hand from her hair, but it was too late—had been too late, he suspected, since he had walked into the bedroom and seen her discarded robe lying on the floor and known that she was sleeping naked.

'Poppy.'

As he said her name he gathered up his strength to push her away and instead discovered that he was actually gathering her closer—so close that they were lying body to body—and that the hands which should have been holding her away from him were actually moving urgently over her skin, following the narrow contours of her back, the feminine curve of her waist and hips, the smooth roundness of her buttocks.

Her lips were still touching his skin, and against his body he could feel the excited thud of her heartbeat.

If she woke up now she would feel the equally aroused pounding of his, and the even more betraying arousal of another part of him. If he had any sense, any thought of self-preservation he would...

James bent his head and slid one hand into Poppy's hair, tilting her face up to meet his, covering her mouth with his.

When Poppy woke up she discovered that she was being kissed in the most sensual, demanding and exciting way that she had ever known, her whole body responding to the hungry male pressure of the mouth caressing hers, the male hand that held her locked against him so that their bodies fitted together as exactly and perfectly as two separate pieces of one complete whole.

As she breathed in dizzily, she felt her breasts swell and press against his chest, his body moving to accommodate the movement of hers, the sensation of his skin dragging slightly against hers so shockingly erotic that she trembled and moved more urgently against him, wanting to repeat it, wanting to feel him against her—

She wanted to feel *all* of him against her, she recognised longingly as she moved her body pleadingly against his, trying to seek even closer contact with him, needing to feel the sensual roughness of his body hair against her, wanting more, much, much more than the tormenting male heat and hardness of his aroused body, which, for some reason, he was allowing merely to rest lightly against hers when she wanted…

Poppy tried to show him exactly what it was she wanted by opening her mouth under his and kissing him passionately at the same time as she moved her hips against him, pressed her breasts against him, arched her spine and made soft keening sounds of need as she opened her legs and rubbed her body hungrily against his.

It was unfair of him to withhold himself from her like this when he knew how much she wanted him, how much she needed him, how much she loved him.

Poppy's soft moans of protest turned to sharper sounds of delight when he suddenly responded to the urgent little movements of her body, thrusting his thigh between hers and making her shiver from head to foot with pleasure at the sensation of his hair-roughened flesh moving against the silky softness of hers.

It must feel good to him as well, she realized, because now he kissed her much more passionately, thrilling her with the husky growl of her name as he held her face in his hands and circled her lips with his tongue-tip, using the weight of his body and the pressure of his hands to make her lie completely still while he teased her with the movement of his tongue and an even more erotic movement of his hips to the point where she couldn't be still any more and her body physically and very visibly shuddered in uncontrollable response to what he was doing to her.

For how many years had she longed for him like this, dreamed of him holding her like this, wanting her like this, loving her like this…? All the feelings and needs she had suppressed surged up inside her in a flood-tide that swept her with it, drowning out everything but her need and her desire.

'No,' she protested in a husky whisper when his mouth left hers and he lifted her wrist to kiss the delicate, blue-veined skin. 'Not there, not there,' she urged; her body burned, ached, hurt almost with her need for him.

The memory of the couple that she had discovered in the Jacuzzi made her shudder, the blood burning up under her skin as he lifted his mouth from her wrist and asked her thickly, 'Not there… Where, then, Poppy? Where…?'

His voice sounded different, deeper, rougher, much more raw and masculine somehow, and she shivered again as she recognised why. It was the voice of a man who was aroused…who wanted her…

'Here,' she told him, placing his hand against her breast, holding her breath almost as she looked first into his eyes and then at his mouth. His mouth…

'Here,' she heard him repeat softly, and the feel of his mouth against her, slowly caressing her nipple, was almost more than she could bear. Her body, her senses weren't equipped to handle so much pleasure, and yet not to have it would have been a loss she could not bear to contemplate.

'And this one?' she heard him asking her hoarsely as he slowly released one breast to turn to the other, lingering over a delicate exploration of it whilst he waited for her response.

Did he really need to ask? Poppy wondered feverishly, but she still said the words, whispering them jerkily as she told him, 'Yes…oh, yes…yes…'

This time the sensation of his suckling on her nipple actually made her cry out in exquisite, sharp pleasure—a high, bitter-sweet sound that made him take hold of her so tightly that she could feel the bite of his fingers against the flesh of her waist, his mouth moving on her so demandingly that she wasn't sure if she could endure such intense pleasure.

She could feel the sexual tension that he was creating within her coiling and stretching like a tautly drawn cord from her breasts right the way down her body so that her womb ached as hotly as her breasts and her need for him drenched her skin in a moist heat.

And somehow, as though he knew how and where that cord ran and why, he started to trace its pathway along her body until the sensation of his mouth moving over her made her tremble wildly and cry out to him that she couldn't bear any more, that the intensity of what she was feeling was too much for her to endure, that she felt as though the terrible pressure of her desire for him was somehow going to tear her apart, destroy her self-control, make her…

Her eyes wet with tears, she tried to tell him how not even all the years of wanting this, of aching for him had prepared her for the intensity of what she was experiencing...how she had never known that just looking at his body, so strongly and powerfully male, would fill her with a need that she couldn't control and that touching him and being touched by him would quicken her pulse and her heartbeat until her whole body shook with the violence of their excitement.

'I never knew it would be like this,' she told him helplessly. 'All these years and I never knew it could be...it would be...'

She felt his own hand tremble as he cupped her face and kissed her gently, his mouth absorbing the dampness of her emotional tears.

'No,' he told her thickly, 'but I did.' And then he was kissing her as Poppy had never known that it was possible to be kissed, so that the pressure of his mouth and the thrust of his tongue was an act of possession as intimate and shockingly intense as the final act of possession itself.

His hands swept down over her body, his thigh nudging hers apart, his body so fully aroused that her hot flood of eager response was shot through with small, bright sparks of apprehensive female awe and female pride at knowing that she was the one who had aroused him so intensely, that she was the one he wanted, the one...

The touch of his hand against her sex as he stroked her swamped her with hot forked-lightning darts of pleasure, making her move her body closer to him, making her...

She reached down for his hand, her voice unsteady with emotion as she told him, 'No...not that...it's you

I want…you.' And then, as her control broke when he moved over her then into her, she cried out, 'Oh, yes… yes. Oh, Chris, I want you so much—'

'Chris!'

The name was snarled at her, hurled back at her, the exquisite, unbearable, unimaginable pleasure of the slow penetration of her body by his ceasing in mid-thrust as she felt him grasp her shoulders and then lift one hand to her face as he demanded savagely, 'Open your eyes, Poppy. I am *not* Chris.'

No, of course he wasn't Chris. How could she ever have imagined that he was, deceived herself that he was, believed that he was? Poppy agonised in shocked self-awareness as she looked up into the icy, furious glare of James's eyes.

Her teeth started to chatter, her brain seized by a nausea so intense that it paralysed any logical thought.

Like someone in a trance she stared up at James. James, who had touched her more intimately than any other man had ever done. James, who had made her body feel…want. James, who…

He had started to withdraw from her but her body had no intention of giving up on the pleasure that his had promised it; her body had no conscience, no aware-ness, no knowledge, after all, of Chris as its lover; her *body* only knew the pleasure that *James* had given it and as it tightened and clung to his and she heard herself uttering a surprisingly fierce and strong, 'No,' Poppy's eyes registered her own confusion and disbelief.

It was Chris she loved, Chris she wanted, she pro-tested inwardly to her wayward flesh, but it didn't want to listen to her; it knew no Chris, it only knew that it wanted…must have what it had been promised, and as James started again to withdraw from her Poppy found that somehow, without knowing how, she was actually moving against him, reaching out to hold onto him, imploring him with words which she would once have denied that she could ever bring herself to say to any man, no matter how much she loved him—much less this man.

'No, please don't… I want you… I want you… Oh, please…I want you so much…'

The words became a husky, rhythmic accompaniment to the increasingly urgent movements of her body as it tried frantically to draw him deeper within itself, tried and, unbelievably, it seemed, succeeded, Poppy realised in dizzy, trembling relief. She was too caught up in the intensity of her body's drive towards its sensual goal to be able to concentrate on anything other than the pleasure of that deepening sense of fullness within her; she was so caught up in it that nothing, nothing could be allowed to bring an end to that sensation of heady, addictive pleasure.

She wanted him, needed him, ached for him too much to care about what he was actually saying as his body began to move within hers again.

'No, you don't, Poppy; you want my brother. But I'm the one you've got. I'm the one who's touched you, caressed you, aroused you, shown you…taught you what it is to feel real physical desire, instead of dreaming some idealised dream; and I'm the one—'

When he heard her cry out he stopped speaking abruptly, his hand tangling in her hair so that he could look into her eyes before she could defend herself from him and close them.

The pain, so sharp that it had been responsible for her high-pitched, shocked cry, had gone as quickly as it had come, but the ache which had preceded it had not, nor the need and the slight trembling of her body. And the quickened pace of her breathing had nothing to do with any fear or desire for him to stop.

He was doing it deliberately, Poppy guessed. Having deliberately aroused her, he now wanted to humiliate and punish her by stopping and...

Angry tears filled her eyes as she glared back at him. 'You can't do this to me,' she protested frantically. 'You can't leave me now, without... You can't...'

She didn't see his expression before, without warning, his lids dropped, his lashes veiling it from her.

He wasn't looking at her face any more, Poppy recognised, but he was looking at her body, at her breasts in point of fact, and as he looked he lifted one hand and cupped one of them, stroking the taut nipple whilst he asked her softly, 'I can't what, Poppy?'

She couldn't answer him; the way he was touching her had galvanised her whole body into a shuddering shock of hot, fluid reaction.

'James... James...' she heard herself pleading achingly.

'Say it... Say it... Say my name,' she heard him telling her softly. 'Tell me again how much you want me, Poppy; tell me again what it is you want, Poppy...*who* it is you want. My God, if you knew...'

Poppy knew that she should stop him, tell him that she hated him, loathed him, detested him, but she also knew that she wouldn't, couldn't; she was blind, deaf and dumb to everything but the urgency he had generated within her. If he stopped making love to her now, without...before...she thought that she would die.

'I want you... I want you...' she whispered obediently, her breath catching in her throat as she re-sponded to the deep rhythm that he was slowly imposing on her—felt it, clung to it, ached for it and finally, as she heard herself cry out his name, abandoned herself totally to it, letting him drive her beyond the safe, known edge of her universe and out into the void that lay beyond it, carried along by wave after wave of pleasure and the hot pulsing of his own release within her.

Her body was still trembling with the aftershock of it many minutes later when she fell into an exhausted sleep.

James watched her for several seconds, his mouth bitter, before turning his back on her and putting as much distance between them as he could.

CHAPTER FOUR

POPPY woke up reluctantly, an ingrained sense of self-preservation warning her that it was safer to cling to the protective blanket of sleep, that she wouldn't like what she was going to have to face when she opened her eyes and remembered what had happened.

She didn't. The shock of the appalling flashbacks that poured over her in an icy deluge of self-knowledge made her sit bolt upright in bed and exclaim out aloud, 'No! I couldn't have... I didn't...'

But she knew, all too well, that she had. The space in the bed next to her where James must have slept was now, thankfully, empty.

Where was he? He must have gone down to the conference hall, she decided.

'And you'd just better get yourself up and dressed and ready to face him when he comes back,' she warned herself grimly.

Face him! The mere thought of doing so was enough to make her stomach churn wildly and her body burn with shamed heat.

Quickly she scrambled out of bed; her body ached slightly in a way that was new and unfamiliar, the self-conscious heat scorching her skin becoming searingly intense as all too vivid and detailed unwanted memories of the way she had behaved, the things she had said the previous night returned.

As she stood in the shower she could see where James's passion was already beginning to bruise her skin—the passion *she* had urged him, *begged* him to show her.

'No. I didn't... I couldn't have...' Poppy moaned, but she knew that she had, and, worse, she knew that he must know it too.

'I thought he was Chris,' she whispered helplessly in defence of her body's physical treachery, its undeniable and inescapable, illogical and unbearable sexual response to him.

By the time she was showered and dressed it was almost eight o'clock. She ought to go downstairs and have some breakfast, Poppy acknowledged, but the last thing she felt like doing was eating. No, not the last thing, she admitted mercilessly; that was having to see James, having to look at him and know what had happened between them, having to...

She tensed as she heard the bedroom door open and saw James walk in.

Despite her determination not to do so, she could feel herself starting to flush, her eyes looking everywhere but at him.

'I...I was just on my way down to breakfast,' she told him untruthfully, hurrying towards the door.

'Not yet. There's something I want to say to you—'

'No!' The speed and vehemence with which she blurted out her panicky denial betrayed her all too clearly, Poppy knew, as James reached out and took hold of her wrist, swinging her round so that he was standing between her and the door.

'Let me go,' she demanded fiercely. 'I want you—'

'So you told me—last night,' James interrupted her, watching her mercilessly as the colour came and went in her face and her body stiffened as though he had struck her.

'No,' she whispered in denial. 'That...that wasn't you. I...'

Her whole body trembled as she fought for something to say, some reasonable and logical explanation of what she had done, what she had said, what she had felt. But, finally acknowledging that there was none, she reached desperately and dangerously for the only thing she had left, picking it up and hurling it at him with all the force of her pent-up, tangled emotions.

'What happened last night wasn't... It didn't... I didn't... I thought you were Chris... I was dreaming about him and when... You must have known that I thought you were him,' she cried out defensively. 'You must have known that I would never... That...'

She stopped abruptly as she saw the dangerous warning expression on James's face, her stomach dropping sickeningly as she realised how angry he was.

'Go on,' he invited her softly. 'You were saying that you thought I was Chris, that you were dreaming about Chris, but you weren't asleep when we made love, were you, Poppy? You knew very well who it was, who was holding you...touching you, pleasuring you,' he told her tauntingly, 'even if you do claim now that you wanted it to be my brother...'

'I...I believed that you were your brother,' Poppy lied doggedly, driven into a corner by his refusal to allow her the secure defence she so desperately needed. 'I wanted—'

'You wanted me,' James told her bluntly. 'Even if you do prefer to lie to yourself now. You can deceive your-

self all you like, Poppy, but you won't deceive me… I
was the one who—'

'I was pretending that you were Chris,' Poppy told
him frantically, unable to listen to any more. 'I—'

She stopped abruptly as she saw the ominous white
line of fury deepen around James's mouth, her stomach
knotting into tight cords of anxious dread.

'I see… You *pretended* I was Chris… You *pretended*
I was my brother, did you, my cheating little virgin…?'
His eyes dropped to her mouth and then lower, caressing the whole of her body in a hatefully knowing way
that made her skin burn as though all the flames of hell
were consuming it.

Her body trembled as he drawled, 'But then, of
course, you aren't a virgin any longer, are you, Poppy?'
And he took her by surprise by roughly jerking her towards him, holding her by her upper arms, his body so
close to her own that she could feel its angry heat, and
she was shaken, driven into a state of shockingly unexpected, aching weakness.

Fighting to deny what her body was frantically trying
to tell her, desperate to ignore the tormenting clamour
of the need it refused to understand that it couldn't be
allowed even to *feel*, never mind acknowledge or openly
demonstrate, she was barely aware of the furious tension in James's voice and eyes as he told her savagely,
'And I can tell you this much—no matter how much
you might want to deny it now, it was *me* you wanted
last night, Poppy, *me* you begged to hold you and touch
you…to take you and fill you with my body, to—'

'No…' Poppy protested shrilly. 'No, that's not true…
I thought you were someone else… It was Chris I
wanted, not you…' she told him piteously.

'That wasn't what you were saying last night,' James

reminded her brutally. '"I want you… I want you…"'
he mimicked her breathlessly, making her cringe as he
caught so devastatingly the note of aching hunger and
need she clearly recognised as being her own.

'You knew I thought you were Chris,' she told him.
'You must have done. You know how much I love him.
You should have stopped… Why didn't you?'

'Why? Because I'm a man,' he told her callously.
'And when a woman makes herself available sexually to
a man, comes on to him, urges him, pleads with him and
begs him the way you were doing with me last night…'

He paused and looked at her, then told her grimly, 'If
you're looking for an apology, Poppy, or even a defence,
I'm afraid you're not going to get one. I gave you what
you asked for. What happened between us last night
happened because—'

'Because I believed you were your brother,' Poppy
interrupted him passionately.

'No,' James corrected her mercilessly. 'You may have
wanted me to be Chris…needed me to be him…but you
certainly knew that I wasn't. You knew—'

'Stop it, stop it…' Poppy demanded. 'I don't want
to talk about it any more. I just want to forget that the
whole thing happened,' she told him sickly.

'And you think I don't?' James challenged her brutally. 'You think I *like* knowing that you used *me* as
a substitute for my brother, that you vented on me all
your pent-up, virginal frustration at not being able to
have him?'

The way he was speaking to her shocked Poppy into
white-faced silence. James might, in the past, have been
unkind to her, might have been angry with her, but he
had never, ever been so sexually explicit with her, nor
so…so…

'What, nothing to say for yourself?' he demanded
bitingly.

'I… It wasn't like that,' Poppy protested, ashen-
faced. 'You're making it sound as though…as though I
was the one…as though it was me who…'

'Well, wasn't it?' James asked her. 'You say you want
to forget the whole thing happened. Well, let's just hope
that we'll both be allowed to do just that…'

The note of warning in his voice made Poppy raise
her head and look at him directly for the first time since
he had entered the room.

His eyes were as cold as the Arctic Ocean and just
as cruelly destructive.

'What…what do you mean?' she asked him nervously.

'Use your head, Poppy,' James advised her grimly.
'Last night, at your insistence, we made…had sex, and
surely even you aren't naïve enough to have forgotten
that there could be…consequences of our…intimacy?'

'Consequences…' Poppy faltered in a stricken voice
as she realised what he meant. 'No,' she protested in
panic. 'There couldn't… We couldn't…'

'Oh yes, there could,' James corrected her roughly,
'and we most certainly did, if my memory serves me
right. And, whilst I've never had occasion to put them
to the test, I have no reason to doubt the efficiency of
my reproductive organs and last night they—'

'Stop it…stop it…' Poppy begged torturedly, covering her face with her hands as she sobbed. 'You're just
trying to frighten me. I can't be… You can't have…'

She heard James laughing savagely at her as she un-
covered her face to look at him, his mouth twisted in
contempt.

'How modest,' he jeered. 'You can't even bring

yourself to say the words, can you? How modest…
how proper…and, my God, how inappropriate… Shall
I tell you what you said to me last night, what you asked
me for?' he demanded mercilessly. 'Shall I repeat for
you the words you said to me…the way you urged me,
begged me to fill you with—?'

'No…no…' Poppy moaned. 'I keep telling you it was
a mistake…'

'A mistake?' James shook his head. 'Oh, no…it
wasn't *a* mistake,' he told her, 'it was *your* mistake,
Poppy. Your mistake.'

He released her so unexpectedly that she staggered
slightly, her legs shockingly weak, but when James
would have reached out to steady her she pushed him
away angrily, fighting to suppress the tears she desperately needed to cry.

'I don't know how I could ever have believed that
you were Chris,' Poppy cried out in anguish. 'You are
nothing like him—nothing. Chris is kind and gentle;
he's…he would never—'

'Never what?' James interrupted her savagely. 'Never
arouse you the way I did, never make you want him the
way you wanted me, never make you feel, experience,
know what it really is to be a woman? Is that what you
were going to say, Poppy?'

'No,' she denied vehemently.

'No,' James agreed crushingly. 'You aren't capable
of being that honest with yourself, are you? *You* prefer
the delusion of your cosy, pretty, girlish dream. Well,
try being even more honest with yourself, Poppy. Try
telling yourself that if you had been in bed with Chris
the reason you would have woken up this morning still
in your virginally intact state would have been, quite
simply, because he didn't want you.'

'And *you* did,' Poppy challenged him shakily, desperately trying to use her anger to protect herself from the pain of acknowledging the truth of his words.

'*I* wanted *a* woman,' James told her cruelly, 'and you made yourself available. I'm not the man to look a gift-horse in the mouth...'

'You do surprise me,' Poppy flashed back with heavy sarcasm. 'I never thought of you as a man who'd be satisfied with a woman who really wanted another man...'

'Who says I was satisfied?' James taunted her. 'If you really think that your immature, adolescent fumblings came anywhere near to giving *me* satisfaction, you've got a hell of a lot to learn—only next time don't expect me to do the teaching.'

'Don't worry, I shan't,' Poppy told him furiously, but inside her anger was already draining away, leaving her feeling sick and empty and not just shamed by her inexplicable behaviour in bed with James, but also vulnerably conscious of the sexual inexperience he had mocked her for.

She longed for the ability to make some witty, crushing remark—the kind of remark she could imagine her friend Star making, which would leave her the victor of their verbal confrontation—but Poppy knew that she simply didn't have either the strength or the energy to find one.

From now on, for the rest of her life, no matter what else might happen to her, each and every time she looked at James she was going to remember just what had happened between them and how she...

'I don't care what it takes or where I have to sleep tonight—I am not going to share that bed with you again,' she told him shakily.

The smile he gave her was as cruel as a hunting

wolf's—a baring of his teeth almost that made her feel
that he would like nothing more than to savage and
destroy her.

'What's wrong?' he asked her silkily. 'Afraid that
you might discover that it isn't really Chris you want
after all and that your body—?'

'No...' Poppy denied quickly—too quickly? she wondered miserably as she saw the look in James's eyes.
That wasn't the reason why she didn't want to share that
bed with him for a second night, she reassured herself
as she made her way down to the conference hall. Of
course it wasn't. How could it be?

She knew that it was another man she had really
wanted, another body she had really yearned and ached
for even if...even though...

She swallowed painfully, unable to deny the unwanted and tormentingly vivid memory she had of looking into James's eyes, of knowing who he was and still
wanting, still saying...

'Hey, are you all right?'

Poppy realised that she had actually closed her eyes
and walked right into Gunther as she heard the concern
in the young German's voice and opened them to see
him looking anxiously at her.

'I'm sorry,' she apologised huskily. 'I was just thinking about...something...'

'There is no need to apologise,' he told her with a
charming smile. 'I was indeed hoping that I might have
the chance to talk with you today—'

'Don't tell me you want my services as a linguist?'
Poppy teased, responding to the warmth in his smile
and only too glad to have something, some*one* to take
her mind off James and the appalling events of the pre-

vious night. 'If you do, I certainly shan't believe you,' she added. 'Your English is very good.'

'No...not that,' he assured her. 'What I wanted to ask was if you would have dinner with me this evening...'

Have dinner with him. Poppy gave him a bewitchingly dazzling smile.

'I'd love to,' she told him fervently and honestly. *Anything*, she felt; right now she would be grateful for anything and *anyone* who kept her away from James.

'Poppy, if you've quite finished socialising...'

James's voice cracked between them like a whip, making Poppy spin round guiltily, her nervous, 'James,' causing Gunther to look slightly puzzled as he watched her.

'We are here to work,' James reminded her curtly. 'I've got a meeting with a consortium of Japanese buyers in fifteen minutes and I'll need you there to translate, and there are several points I need to run through with you first.'

'I'll be with you in a moment, James,' Poppy told him, trying to stand her ground instead of tamely giving in to the command she had heard in his voice.

She might be his cousin and an employee of the company but she was still her own person, still had her rights. Tilting her chin, she looked away from him and back to Gunther and told him clearly, 'I'd love to have dinner with you tonight, Gunther. Would eight o'clock be all right...?'

Instead of walking away and giving her the privacy to complete her conversation with the young German, James had waited for her like a jailer, determined not to let her get away, she decided angrily as she fell into step beside him and they made their way through the crush towards their own stand.

'If it's his bed you're thinking of sharing tonight, Poppy,' James warned her cynically as he took hold of her arm and guided her through the surging throng, 'I should warn you that you won't get much privacy, nor much bed space. The hotel management have already had to put an extra bed in the room he's booked into as a result of their overbooking!'

'How dare you say that?' Poppy hissed furiously at him, her face burning. She couldn't bear the way he was making her feel so...so cheap...so... 'Just because... just because I... Just because of what happened last night,' she told him in a breathless rush, 'that doesn't mean that I'm now going to go to...to have sex with... with anyone...'

'Really? You do surprise me...' James told her sardonically. 'After all, if you haven't got the scruples not to use one man in place of another, I shouldn't have thought—'

Smack!

Through the tears clouding her eyes, Poppy could see the hazy dark red outline of her open-handed slap against the lean tautness of James's face. She stared at it in shocked, silent horror, unable to believe what she had done, unable to believe the anger, the lack of self-control, the sheer weight of misery and self-disgust which had driven her to overreact in such a way.

As the crowd pressed and surged around them, she was conscious only of James and the frightening stillness of his body, the icy coldness of his eyes, the tension of the coiled strength within him that menaced and held her in paralysed thrall.

'How very predictable and old-fashioned of you,' he told her softly, at last. 'But I've got news for you, Poppy. As an innocent and appallingly inexperienced virgin you might just...*just* have been able to get away with such outdated and sexually stereotyped behaviour, but since you can't any longer lay claim to your mummified virginal state it's time you learned that physical violence from a woman to a man can do a lot more than just get his adrenalin pumping...and that, in the language of sex, it can be a big come-on, as much an indication of desire as verbally saying to a man that you want him...'

'No!' Poppy asserted. Her face felt stiff, wooden, numb, so that it was almost impossible for her lips to frame the small, vehement denial.

'Yes,' James insisted softly. 'Oh, yes, Poppy—and before you start making any more denials you might also think about this. Even in the days when it was acceptable for a woman to slap a man's face, it was a weapon she used knowing that it was a two-edged sword—that the man in question might take it as the rebuke she intended but that he might retaliate by assuaging the blow to his pride by inflicting one to hers...'

When he saw the way she was looking at him, James's mouth twisted contemptuously. 'Oh, come on, Poppy,' he derided her. 'Don't tell me you've never read a book or seen a film where the hero retaliates to the heroine's slap by taking hold of her and kissing the breath out of her...'

'That's just fiction,' Poppy protested shakily. 'And besides, you...you aren't a hero...and...'

'And you certainly aren't a heroine?' James supplied for her. 'Maybe you're not, but just try remembering, the next time you feel like venting that nasty temper of yours on me, that I'm fully capable of retaliating and that I know just how to make you wish to hell that you'd had second thoughts...'

'By kissing me!' Poppy scorned, outwardly defiant

but inwardly shaking with the tension and shock of the intense anger she could feel emanating from him. There had been anger between them before, but never anything like this, never anything as dangerous or out of control as the heaviness in the air she could feel vibrating between them now.

'No,' James told her quietly, shaking his head. But just as the breath was starting to leak in luxurious relief from her lungs he threw her into an ice-cold yet furnace-hot seizure of sick disbelief as he told her slowly and with obvious relish, 'No, Poppy, not by kissing you but by taking you upstairs and spreading you out beneath me on the bed and—'

'What?' Poppy dared to demand hoarsely as she tried to mask her fear. 'By raping me?'

The smile he gave her made a violent spasm of tension engulf her body, visibly shaking it whilst he watched her knowingly.

'Oh, no,' he told her silkily, 'it wouldn't be rape, Poppy, not with you crying out to me that you wanted me, begging me to touch you, to take you, to...'

She was going to faint, Poppy decided. She could already feel the coldness invading her body.

Closing her eyes, she willed the betraying symptoms to subside and not to shame her even more than she had already been shamed.

'I hate you, James,' she told her cousin through gritted teeth. 'I hate you more than I have ever hated anyone else in my life...'

She was desperately tempted to turn and walk away from him, to lose herself in the crowd. It would be easy to do...easy to escape him...but for how long? Ultimately she would have to face him and, with him, the additional taunt not just of what had happened last night but of her lack of professionalism in her work as well.

No, the best way to treat him was to behave with indifference, simply to ignore him, to distance herself completely from him and from what had happened. To close off within her mind the entire episode, to seal it up and bury it somewhere where she would never, ever have to look at it again.

'And so how are you enjoying the conference?'

Poppy made a wry face as Gunther smiled at her across the dinner table.

'I too am feeling the same,' he told her ruefully, 'and wondering if I am really in the right job. At university I had plans, dreams of being a writer, but in Germany these days it is not so easy to find a good job. My parents—my father—urged me to think of the future...' He gave a small shrug and Poppy another smile.

'But it is boring of me to talk of myself... I wish to learn more about you.'

'There isn't very much to learn,' Poppy confessed, whilst her conscience prodded her, reminding her that there was a good deal more to know than there had been twenty-four hours ago, even if it was not exactly the kind of knowledge she could ever envisage herself passing on to anyone—sharing with anyone.

It was fortunate that the Japanese businessmen whom James was dining with this evening had their own interpreter with them, even if it had galled Poppy slightly to see the way that James had watched the diminutive and very attractive Japanese woman and listened to her as she'd translated his comments to her colleagues.

He patently had a good deal more respect for her and

her professional skills than he did for her own, Poppy reflected, and that knowledge rankled.

'You are looking angry,' Gunther told her. 'Have I...?'

'I was thinking about something else—someone else,' Poppy admitted.

'It is a pity that there has been so much confusion and lack of organisation over the conference,' he commented.

'Mmm,' Poppy agreed. 'Although I doubt that we would have had much time to enjoy the hotel's facilities even if they had been finished.'

'This is true,' said Gunther, and then added hesitantly, 'I had thought of hiring a car and exploring a little of the region tomorrow; I was wondering if you would care to join me...?'

Poppy was sorely tempted to agree, just for the relief of getting away from James, but, despite what James seemed to think, she did take her work seriously and she knew that if she had been here with Chris or, indeed, with any other members of the company's sales team she would never even have considered using Gunther as a means of escaping from them, and so she shook her head, gently refusing his invitation.

'Remember, if you should change your mind about joining me on my tour of the region,' Gunther told her later in the evening when they had finished their dinner, 'you only have to say.'

'You're very kind,' Poppy told him truthfully.

They had lingered in the dining room longer than most of the other diners, but Poppy was nervously aware that she couldn't put off saying goodnight to Gunther and returning to her room for much longer.

His room was in a different part of the building from

hers and when they parted in the foyer Poppy felt her heart start to thud in anxious dread. Would James be in the room already? And if he was...?

By the time she had reached their floor, her hands were shaking so much that she could hardly insert the pass-card into the lock, but to her relief, when the door swung open and she stepped inside the room, there was no sign of James.

She undressed and showered quickly, unable to bring herself to look properly at her body, so that she didn't have to see those small but oh, so betraying tell-tale marks.

Once dried and wrapped in her robe she stood for several minutes on the threshold of the bedroom, staring at the pristine smoothness of the large bed, her heart pounding so heavily and painfully that she automatically put one hand over it to ease the pain it was causing her.

She couldn't sleep in that bed again, she acknowledged, licking her dry lips. She simply couldn't.

Her legs trembled as she walked quickly towards it, her glance drawn repeatedly to the door as she pulled frantically at the heavy duvet, dragging it off the bed and onto the floor, her body drenched in nervous perspiration as she prayed that James wouldn't come in before she had finished.

Even doubled over underneath her, the quilt wasn't thick enough to mask fully the hardness of the marble floor, but at least this way she was signalling unequivocally and loudly to James that, despite his goading remarks, she had no desire to endure a repetition of the previous night's events.

But as she lay tensely in the darkness Poppy knew that not all of his cruel taunts could be rejected. She *had* begged him to make love to her, she *had* responded to him, wanted him…she *had* been the one to insist, to demand that what was happening between them be brought to its ultimate conclusion.

'Because I wanted him to be Chris,' she whispered painfully to herself. 'I needed him to be Chris…'

But she had known that he wasn't. She had known that he was James—had known and had not stopped, had not ceased wanting…needing…aching…

The tears that burned the backs of her eyes felt like acid, raw and painful, bringing her no real relief, but then what relief could there be from the thoughts, the emotions that tormented *her*? she acknowledged miserably.

It might be impossible for her to deny or escape the taunts that James had thrown at her but it was equally impossible for her to understand why it had happened, why she had turned to James, responded to James, wanted James to such an extent that she had knowingly, wantonly and, yes, deliberately encouraged him to…

To what? she asked herself as the tears rolled down her face. To have sex with her, to make love to her, to transport her to a place she had not previously known existed; to take her there, and once there to…?

No, no, no, Poppy denied, rolling herself even more tightly in her duvet as she tried to stem both her tears and the hot, raw ache burning inside her.

It was close to dawn when Poppy woke up, her body stiff and aching, one of the pillows she had wrenched from the bed still beneath her head, the other… Hot scarlet colour flooded her skin betrayingly as she realised that she had her arms wrapped round the pillow as though…

Quickly she thrust it away from her, at the same time lifting her head to look anxiously towards the bed, praying that James was asleep and that he hadn't seen the pathetic way she had cuddled up to the pillow, her tension changing to surprise and then bewilderment as she realised that the bed was completely empty and that James wasn't there.

If he hadn't returned to their room then where had he spent the night—where was he spending the night? Poppy wondered, for some reason instantly picturing the pretty Japanese woman and the way her silvery laughter had caused James to smile in a way he had never smiled at her.

Had they spent the night together? Neither of them had made any effort to conceal the fact that they found one another attractive, Poppy acknowledged sourly. She hadn't missed the subtle message in the way that she had gently touched James's arm to underline some comment she had been making, and she certainly hadn't misinterpreted the sudden gleam in James's eyes as he'd looked back at her, nor the way in which he had moved closer to her.

Well, *she* was welcome to him, Poppy told herself fiercely. All she herself wished was that she had known what he was going to do. That way, she could have slept on the bed instead of on the floor and, instead of waking up with her body aching and her neck stiff, she would have enjoyed a decent night's sleep.

Yes, the Japanese woman was welcome to James. Poppy gave a small shudder. Did he make a habit of sleeping with two different women on consecutive nights? It seemed so out of character; she would have thought that he would have more concern for his health, more...more self-control, she decided bitterly.

It gave her a very odd and very unwanted feeling inside to think of James with another woman. Odd because that specific feeling was one she was more used to feeling in relation to Chris, and unwanted because... because...

Of course it wasn't jealousy she was feeling, Poppy comforted herself as she dragged her aching body onto the bed, hauling the duvet with her. How could it be...? She was just thankful that James wasn't here with her.

And yet, as she closed her eyes and tried to go back to sleep, no matter how hard she tried to summon up the comforting mental image of Chris's beloved features, it was James she kept on visualising. James, his eyes darkening as he leant over her.

'No,' Poppy denied aloud in growing panic. 'No, no, no...'

CHAPTER FIVE

'AH, JAMES. I am glad to see you again. It was good last night, wasn't it?'

Poppy tried not to gape as the Japanese translator came over to their stand where James had just been informing Poppy that he had some documents he wanted her to translate; the woman's eyes were eloquent with feminine emotion as she reached out and touched James's hand.

She might just as well not have been there, Poppy decided as she saw the way James turned towards the other woman, the way he smiled at her and bent his head protectively towards her.

Poppy had been midway through her breakfast when James had slid into his seat opposite her, calmly ordering his coffee without giving her any explanation of his overnight absence.

'Very good,' Poppy heard James agreeing throatily now.

Poppy could have sworn that his glance rested just a fraction too long on the other woman's body as she smiled coquettishly at him then announced that she must return to her colleagues—but not before she had leant forward and murmured provocatively to James,

'I have some free time this afternoon; you did mention that you have a car...'

Poppy waited, expecting to hear James declare in the curt way she was familiar with that he was too busy to take any time off, but, to her indignation, instead she heard him responding, 'I do indeed. What time exactly will you be free?'

As soon as the woman was out of earshot, Poppy couldn't resist reminding him, 'I thought you said we had come here to work; in fact I—'

'What's wrong?' James interrupted her, not allowing her to finish. 'Not jealous, are you?'

'Why should I be? She's welcome to you. I suppose you were with her last night, were you?'

'And if I was,' James countered urbanely, 'is that really any business of yours?'

For some reason that she could not quite define, Poppy found his relaxed and indeed almost amused attitude not only infuriating but humiliating as well.

'Yes, as a matter of fact, it is,' she told him furiously. '*You* may think nothing of going from bed to bed, woman to woman, of being... I suppose you might even have quite a high opinion of yourself for being some sort of sexual stud...' she added for good measure. 'But I am not promiscuous and I have my health to think about and—'

'Oh, do you indeed?' James interrupted her with ominous calm. 'Odd that I didn't get the impression that your health was one of your primary concerns the other night,' he goaded her bitingly.

Poppy shot him a bright-eyed look of defiant fury.

'That was because—' She started to defend herself, but James would not let her finish.

'Because you wanted to pretend I was Chris,' he fin-

ished for her, knowing well by now the way her answer
would come out. 'Well, I have news for you, Poppy.
When it comes down to it, far from being the untar-
nished, fantasy figure you seem to think he is, of the
two of us I suspect that Chris would toll up the greater
number if we had to list our previous bed-mates. So, in
reality, the chances of you endangering your "health",
as you so coyly put it, would be rather greater with him
than with me.'

Poppy told him hotly, 'I don't believe what you're
saying. Chris has never...he would never... He's not
like you,' she told him flatly. 'He would never sleep
with someone just for...just for sex.'

'I never suggested that he might,' James corrected
her. 'I simply said that of the two of us he has probably had the greater number of partners, and for your
information, Poppy, I do not sleep with women "just
for sex"...'

The look in his eyes warned Poppy not to try to take
the argument any further, but she was too wound up,
too angry to pay it any attention.

'You did with me,' she pointed out recklessly.

For a moment she thought she had won and that he
wasn't going to reply. After all, what was there that he
could honestly say?

She soon found out.

'I...had...sex...with...you,' he told her with cold
emphasis, carefully spacing out each word, so that
there was no way she could avoid their impact—like
so many carefully aimed and deliberately fired bullets,
she decided as she tried sickly to absorb their spreading
pain—'because you wouldn't let me do anything else...'

'You're just saying that to...to punish me,' Poppy

protested, her mouth trembling as she tried to blink away her shamed tears.

'No, Poppy, I am not,' James denied grimly. 'There comes a point where a man—any man—simply cannot stop. That's a known fact and I can hardly deny it, but way before *I* had reached that point you were the one who was... You were the one who wanted—'

'Not you,' Poppy cut in swiftly. 'I didn't want you. I could *never* want you.' She moved away from the stand abruptly—so abruptly that for a moment the hall spun dizzily around her—refusing to listen to James as he told her to come and sit down, turning on her heel and hurrying, almost running away from him.

How dared he say those things to her, make her feel so cheap, when he knew...? Well, let him go and spend all day with his new Japanese woman-friend; let him spend all night with her as well... She only wished he would.

'Poppy, what is it? What's wrong?'

As Poppy looked up into the kind, concerned face of Gunther, she came to a sudden decision.

'Gunther,' she told him quickly, 'if that offer you made of showing me something of the region is still on, I've changed my mind. I would like to come with you...'

'It will be my pleasure,' he told her with a beaming smile. 'I will not be free until two o'clock, though...'

'That will be fine,' Poppy assured him. She should have James's translations done by then so at least he wouldn't be able to accuse her of not doing her job. He could not accuse her of anything, she decided fiercely, ignoring the tiny inner voice that warned her that what she was doing was not just extremely dangerous but potentially very irresponsible as well.

If James could take time off to enjoy himself with

his new Japanese friend, then he was hardly in a position to take her to task for doing something similar, was he? And as for the fact that she would officially be on company time, she would make up the hours she spent with Gunther somehow or other, she told herself grimly; that was one accusation at least that she would make sure James could not throw at her.

It was almost twelve o'clock when James came into the bedroom, where Poppy was hard at work on the translations which had proved more complex than she had originally thought. He demanded peremptorily, 'Have you finished yet, Poppy?'

'Almost,' she told him, mentally crossing her fingers that when she gave the documents a final read through she wouldn't come across anything she had missed. She didn't miss the way James's frown deepened as he looked over her shoulder at what she was doing, and she immediately challenged him defensively, 'If you're not satisfied, James, or if you think that you could have done any better...'

'If I could, the company wouldn't be employing you as a translator,' James told her crisply, picking up the work she had completed, adding as he started to read it, 'You know, Poppy, there has to be a division between our role as cousins and that of employer and employee. You're very fond of insisting that you got your job with the company on merit and not by trading on your relationship with your mother, but you don't seem to mind trading on our cousinship in our roles of employer and employee...'

'You're the one who's doing that, not me,' Poppy defended herself immediately. 'After all, if we weren't cousins, there's no way you'd have been able to force me to share a bedroom with you...'

She could see from his expression that he didn't like what she was saying. Well, tough, she decided. He was the one who had brought the subject up, not her.

'You know your problem, don't you, James?' she challenged, swinging round to glower at him. 'You're a control freak, but you can't control *me*. No one controls me...'

'No,' James agreed drily. 'No one does, not even you.'

As he looked at her Poppy had a vivid memory of the most recent occasion on which she had betrayed her lack of self-control, and as she felt the hot tide of colour start to flood up in a give-away rush under her skin she turned quickly away from him.

'I thought you were supposed to be taking your Japanese friend out today,' she muttered as she gathered her papers together.

'I am,' James agreed, glancing at his watch as he took the papers from her. 'Have you finished now? Is everything here?'

'Yes,' Poppy confirmed tersely, noting that he was eager to be away.

'More wine?'

Poppy smiled as she shook her head, covering her almost empty glass with her hand.

'No, I suppose I hadn't better either,' Gunther agreed regretfully. 'Not as I'm driving.'

They had driven through the warm Italian countryside for almost two hours before finally stopping in a small, dusty town so pretty that it might have come straight out of a film or operetta.

They had explored it like two schoolchildren set free from their lessons, buying and eating delicious home-made ice cream the taste of which had made Poppy close her eyes in disbelieving bliss.

It had been Gunther's suggestion that, instead of heading straight back, they equip themselves with food and wine and have an impromptu picnic on the banks of the river they had seen earlier.

'Have we got time?' Poppy had asked him doubtfully. She wasn't wearing her watch and she hadn't been sure how long they had spent wandering around the town.

'We'll make time,' Gunther had told her grandly, and because she was enjoying the relaxation of being away from James and of putting to one side all the anger and anxiety that her constant confrontations with him were causing her Poppy had laughingly given in and agreed.

She had no idea now how long they had lingered over their alfresco meal, but she guessed from the lengthen-ing shadows that it was growing late.

'We really ought to go,' she told Gunther reluctantly.

'What if I refuse?' Gunther teased her. 'What if I say that I want to keep you here for ever and never take you back?'

Even whilst she laughed, Poppy was unable to stop the sadness shadowing her eyes.

Their afternoon had given her a brief respite, but she knew that there was no real escape from her un-happiness, especially not with someone like Gunther, who, nice though he was, was no match for a man like James...

James... Poppy froze. Why should she be connect-ing her inability to respond to the more intimate over-tures that she knew Gunther wanted to make to James?

Surely it was her love for Chris that stood between her
and any other man who might show an interest in her?

'Poppy, what is it?' Gunther asked her hesitantly.
'You look so...so sad... If you have a worry...a problem...if there is something I can do to help...'

'No. It's... There is nothing...' Poppy denied quickly.

What would Gunther say, what would he think if
he knew the truth? What would he think of her then?
What would her friends, her family...Chris...think of
her, if they knew what had happened with James...?
But they would never know, she comforted herself. No
one must ever know.

As she stood up and helped Gunther to clear away
the remnants of their picnic, anxiety like so many sharp
knives caused her darting, stabbing flickers of pain that
seemed to pierce her heart and she was filled with a
sense of shame, bewilderment and confusion.

How could she have been like that with James...
wanted him, urged him? Her hands were trembling as
she picked up her jacket.

If only there were some way she could wipe the
events of that night from her memory and her conscience...from hers and from James's.

It *was* late, Poppy realised once they were back in
the car and heading back to the hotel. Later than she
had thought, and already growing dark.

It was just as well that she had already eaten, she
decided as she glanced at the clock on the car's dash-
board, because they were certainly going to be too late
to have dinner.

In the end it was gone ten o'clock before Gunther
finally pulled into the hotel car park; a wrong turning
had added several extra miles and almost a full hour to
their return journey and Poppy just hoped that James

was too preoccupied with his Japanese lady-friend to be aware that she had been playing truant.

'Thank you, it's been a lovely afternoon,' she told Gunther quickly, pulling away from him as he made to put his arm around her.

She could see the disappointment in his eyes but to her relief he didn't try to force the issue, simply falling into step beside her as he escorted her inside the hotel.

Once inside the foyer, Poppy searched it anxiously, but fortunately there was no sign of James.

'I'm afraid my wrong turning has caused you to miss dinner,' Gunther apologised, 'but perhaps—'

'It's all right, Gunther,' Poppy assured him, forestalling him. 'I couldn't really eat anything else anyway, not after that delicious picnic…'

If she went straight up to the room now, showered and prepared for bed, she could, with luck, be fast asleep before James came in—if indeed he was planning to spend the night with her and not with…

With her? Poppy could feel the angry, self-betraying heat burning her skin as she hurried, head defensively down, towards the lifts. Of course, she had not meant that James would be spending the night *with* her, merely that he would be spending it in their room. What had he done to her, she wondered resentfully, that she was now having to monitor even her own private thoughts?

She walked out of the lift and along the corridor, inserted her pass-card into the lock and pushed open the door.

'Where the hell have you been?'

The shock of James's unexpected presence in the bedroom caused Poppy to stare at him in speechless silence.

'Where have you been, Poppy?' he repeated.

'I...I... Out,' Poppy told him unsteadily, alarmed by his fury.

'Out. Out where?' James demanded.

'I... Gunther... I went out with Gunther,' she admitted huskily. 'He...he had hired a car for the afternoon and he wanted—'

'Spare me the details, I can well imagine exactly what it was he wanted,' James told her savagely. 'And, to judge from the look of you and the length of time you've been gone, he got it.

'Did you enjoy it, Poppy?' he demanded acidly. 'Did you beg him...plead with him—?'

Before she knew what she was doing Poppy had flown at James, raising her hand to bring it down hard against his face, goaded beyond endurance by the hateful things he was saying to her, desperate to make him stop.

But instead of retreating from her, instead of reacting as she had imagined and recognising how offensive, how unbearable, how unwarranted and undeserved his accusations were, he took hold of her with such speed that she had no time to do anything other than give a small gasp of startled shock as his fingers manacled her wrists and he swung her round in front of him, using his weight and her vulnerability to tip her over onto the bed.

As he leaned over her, imprisoning her, Poppy could see the dark flecks in the topaz brilliance of his eyes, which, when she focused on them, seemed to mesmerise her into a state of shocked numbness. Then she heard him say, 'I warned you what would happen if you did that again, Poppy.'

And then he was raising her hands above her head, holding them, shackling them there, his body poised powerfully over hers.

'I know why you're doing this,' Poppy protested wildly. 'You're doing it to punish me because your pride can't bear knowing that I don't want you.'

'Is that what you told your German friend?' James snarled at her.

'Gunther and I just spent the afternoon together. We didn't...he's not...'

Poppy tensed as she realised that her efforts to break free of James's constraining hold had caused the soft, full skirt she was wearing to ride up, exposing her thighs.

'Let me go, James,' she begged shakily when she saw the way he was looking at her body. 'You don't really want me,' she added huskily, 'You can't, and—'

'Who says I can't?' James taunted her softly. 'I'm a man, Poppy, and, as any man will tell you, there's nothing quite so erotically stimulating as having a woman tell you she wants you, as having her beg you to fulfil her and satisfy her, as having her cry out to you that she needs you, aches for you...'

'No,' Poppy denied in panic. 'I didn't mean it... I... You can't do this, James. I don't want you...'

'Liar,' he told her softly, and as though to prove her self-deceit he reached out his free hand and ran it slowly up over her trembling body.

The hard, warm feel of his palm against the tense sensitivity of her bare thigh made her quiver from head to foot in what Poppy told herself despairingly was outrage and rejection, but long before James's hand had smoothed its way over her waist to lie mockingly just below the full curve of her breast she knew that she was lying to herself.

'But I *can't* want you...'

She hadn't realised she had whispered the shocked

words out loud until she heard James warning her through gritted teeth, 'Take care I don't make you eat those words, Poppy, or endure the sexual equivalent, because, I promise you, if I do…once I do…'

Poppy's whole body shuddered as she realised what he meant, realised and, to her appalled anguish, visibly reacted to that knowledge not with shock and rejection but instead with something—some need—she couldn't bear to acknowledge.

'I don't want this, James,' she told him defiantly, but she knew as he lifted his hand and slowly started to un-fasten her top that she was lying, and, what was worse, she knew that he knew it too.

Why, why was her body responding to him like this? she wondered helplessly as he peeled away her top to reveal the warm curves of her breasts.

She tried to will her body not to react to the warmth of James's breath as he bent his head towards her.

'No!'

Even as she made the thick, guttural denial and twisted her body desperately from side to side, Poppy knew shamingly that, far from making her want to be released from the sensual bondage of James's mouth's possession of her breast, the deepening and intensifying sensation of that possession as he subdued her attempts to break free of him somehow only increased the erotic effect of his mouth against her body.

Lost in the sensation caused by James's mouth slowly savaging the sensitive flesh of her breasts, Poppy was unaware of the fact that he had unfastened and removed her skirt until she felt the sudden coolness of the air-conditioning against her bare skin, her only covering the small white triangle of her cotton briefs.

James still had her hands pinned above her head, and

as he released her breast and started to unfasten his shirt
Poppy turned her head to avoid looking at him, knowing already what just the thought of the satin heat of his
naked skin against her own was doing to her, and as she
did so she inadvertently caught sight of her reflection in
the mirror on the wall, her body tensing as she stared
transfixed at her image, unable to withdraw her gaze.

Was that really her, that creature with the dark,
tangled mane of hair, the full, swollen mouth whose
colour echoed that of her erotically pouting nipples, her
skin so creamily pale, so silky and glistening as she lay
against the coverlet of the bed, her spine arched, her
body stretched out like some wanton, sensual offering?

Even to her own eyes there was something about
her almost voluptuous dishevelment, the disarrange-
ment of her limbs that positively flaunted her sensuality, her sexuality, she recognised in wide eyed shock,
the white triangle of her briefs somehow more of an
enticement than a barrier, her thighs slightly parted as
though...as though...

'What are you looking at?' she heard James ask as he
pulled off his shirt and stepped out of his trousers and
leaned towards her, his image joining hers in the mirror, his mouth curling in a smile that made her stomach
muscles lock in protest against the wave of shocked excitement it caused her.

'Ah,' he said softly, 'so you like looking at yourself,
do you, Poppy? You like watching whilst—?'

'No,' Poppy protested, her face burning as she heard
him laugh and saw the way he stretched out his hand
and slowly ran his fingertips along her skin, making
her shiver and tremble in helpless response.

'Well, remember what I said about making you eat
your words,' he reminded her softly. 'Would you like

that, Poppy?' he added, so gently that the words slipped up under her guard. 'Would you like to know what it feels like to have a man's mouth against your body whilst he…?'

His hand was covering her sex now, not touching or caressing her, simply lying there, but the weight and heat of it, the knowledge of it, was enough to accelerate the pulse which had been slowly throbbing there ever since he had first taken hold of her—throbbing in a deep, fierce ache so intense that she felt sure that he must be able to feel the vibrations as they shook her helpless body.

He was naked now, his body darkly powerful in contrast to hers, his skin like the taut, warm pelt of a jungle killer.

The urge within her to reach out and touch it, to touch him was so compelling that Poppy couldn't withstand it, her fingertips trembling as they finally came into contact with his body.

The fierce shudder that ripped through him made her stare at him in confused surprise, her eyes staring straight up into the dark heat of his, her breath coming faster between her half-parted lips as her body responded instinctively in its recognition of the arousal of his.

For some reason his arousal shocked her. Shocked her and excited her, she acknowledged, unaware that her eyes were betraying her emotions to him, unaware of anything other than the heat and power of him as he lowered his body against hers and took hold of her, smothering any protest she might have wanted to make.

Whilst her body shivered its pleasure in his arms, her lips responded to the pressure of his, parting, opening, her mouth drinking in the taste and feel of him.

In the distance Poppy could hear a sound—a soft, keening cry of desire and urgency that she didn't recognise as hers until James lifted his mouth from hers and demanded roughly, 'Now tell me that you don't want *me*...that you want my brother.

'Look, Poppy,' he commanded, one hand cupping the side of her face, turning it so that she was forced to look at her reflection in the mirror—at *their* reflections in the mirror—at the way that, without knowing she had done so, she had arched herself against him, opened her thighs to accept the weight of one of his between them, to accept it and...

Poppy shivered as she saw the way her flesh clung longingly to his, the way her whole body silently betrayed its yearning need.

'No... No, this isn't what I want,' she protested in a panicky whisper. 'This can't be what I want. *You* aren't what I want...'

As she tried to push James away, to reassert her independence, her determination to reject everything that both he and her body were telling her, she saw anger and another emotion she couldn't define flash like warning darts of fire through the brilliance of his eyes.

'Why are you doing this?' she protested huskily. 'You don't want me. You don't even like me. You must want... What happened?' she asked him bitterly. 'Did your Japanese lady-friend turn you down after all? Well, that's not my fault, so don't try to...to...take out your frustration on me.'

'Why not?' James challenged her brutally. 'Why shouldn't I use you the way you used me? Exactly the way you used me!'

Poppy gasped in shock at the ugliness of his accusation. 'That's not fair... It's not...it's not true,' she defended herself. 'What happened the other night was a...a mistake,' she told him shakily.

'Was it? Well, there won't be any mistakes this time,' James responded mirthlessly. 'Look into the mirror, Poppy,' he instructed her again, adding forcefully when she tried to turn her head away, 'Look...and tell me what you see.'

Poppy's whole body trembled beneath the weight of her emotions. How could she tell him what she saw? How could she shame herself by putting into words what her body was so obviously experiencing—the desire, the need...the sensuality she could see in every taut line of her flesh, every aching curve, every inch of the body she could barely recognise as her own as she was forced to look, witness its open hunger for the man holding it?

The man holding it... And that man was James. *Not* Chris but James. James, whom she could not possibly cerebrally want or desire, whom she did not even like, never mind love.

What had happened to her? she wondered helplessly as she caught back a panicky sob. And why had it happened to her? Why had her own flesh so blatantly turned traitor on her? Why was it...she...so out of control, so...so...

'The other night you told me you wanted me... begged me to make love to you. This time, when you say those words again, there'll be no taking them back, Poppy, no pretence that you think I am Chris. This time both of us know just who exactly it is you're crying out for.'

Was that why he was doing this to her? Poppy wondered achingly. Because his pride couldn't stomach the thought that a woman—any woman, but most especially a woman whom, after all, he had made it clear he despised so absolutely and completely—should dare to prefer another man? Was this, then, male pride, male anger, male desire, male power generated and fed by some testosterone-fuelled need to be first, to be the best?

'Say it again, Poppy,' she heard James demanding softly as his mouth started to caress her throat in what she knew was a slow and deliberate assault on her defences. 'Tell me you want me...'

'No,' Poppy refused stubbornly, panicked by the thought of losing control, by the knowledge that what he was doing could all too easily *make* her lose control.

She felt her whole body shudder as his mouth burned paths of fire down over it. In the mirror she could see her tortured twisting and turning as she tried to evade his lips and hands, but already her denials and her movements possessed a slow, drugged quality that made them sound and look more like some subtle form of enticement than genuine rejection.

There was something about the sight of James leaning over her, half straddling her, something about the sheer, naked power of his body that sent waves of heat blistering through her, that made the hands she knew she had reached out to fend him off somehow seek to draw him closer instead.

When she felt the warmth of his mouth caressing her stomach, she cried out to him to stop, but his hands were already sliding her briefs free of her body, and although she fought desperately not to look the sight of his dark head against the pale silkiness of her thighs caused such a fierce spasm of sensation within her that her whole body jerked visibly.

'No, don't—please don't,' she whispered protest-ingly, but his hands were already holding her, lifting her, his lips stroking the soft, vulnerable flesh on the inside of her thighs, his palm resting against her sex, touching it, making it…her…tremble in a paroxysm of combined anxiety and pleasure.

Even though she had known what was going to happen, *how* he was going to punish her and exact full payment for her defiance, her denial, and, even though she had thought she had prepared her body so that she could defend herself from it, the shock of his mouth actually moving against the most intimate part of her— and her reaction to it—caused her to cry out helplessly to him that she couldn't bear such pleasure, that she was afraid of what he was going to do to her, of what she was feeling.

'James… James…'

She heard herself call his name as her body exploded in violent spasms of intense pleasure and knew she was babbling incoherently to him as he moved over her and took her in his arms, kissing her breasts and then her mouth with the taste of her body still on his lips.

'James… James…'

Her body was still quivering, still empty…still aching for him, she recognised in breathless wonder.

'Say it,' he demanded against her mouth. 'Say the words, Poppy…'

'I want you,' she told him helplessly. 'I want you… I want you…'

The words became a dizzy cry reinforcing each thrust of his body within hers—a meaningless litany to accompany the waves of pleasure and need that were building higher and higher.

Poppy heard herself cry out his name again as the pleasure finally crested, her body damp and weak…

drained of life and energy as she clung to him in the aftermath of her passion.

In the mirror she could still see their reflection, their bodies entwined. She could feel the tears sliding helplessly down her face. What had she done...? What had she become...? She no longer recognised herself in the person she now seemed to be and that made her feel more desperately afraid than she had ever felt in the whole of her life.

It was only as she finally slid into an exhausted sleep that she realised that she had barely thought of Chris since she had walked into the bedroom and seen James.

Because she couldn't bear to think of Chris and the purity of her love for him after what she had done—after what James had made her do, she told herself numbly as sleep finally claimed her.

CHAPTER SIX

'POPPY, can you come down to my office, please? There's something we need to discuss.'

Poppy could feel the palms of her hands growing clammy with nervous perspiration as she clung tightly to the telephone receiver.

'Does it have to be now, James?' she asked tersely. 'Only I'm just in the middle of working on those Japanese documents you want and—'

'Now, Poppy,' James interrupted her curtly.

As Poppy replaced the receiver she stared unseeingly through her office window, oblivious to the neat trimness of the grass borders broken up by colourful patches of shrubs which decorated the company's car park.

They had been back from Italy almost ten weeks— long enough, surely, for her to have at least begun to get over the shock of what had happened when they were there. But instead she had taken to avoiding James as much as she possibly could and suspected that he was doing exactly the same thing with her.

Pushing her chair away from her desk, she stood up, gritting her teeth against the nervous dizziness making her head swim and her heart pound with sick tension.

Unlike most heads of businesses, James preferred to have his office on the ground floor. It helped to keep

his feet on the ground, he had once told Poppy sternly
when she had questioned such unusual behaviour. A
successful business was like a pyramid, he had added
obliquely, and whoever stood at its peak was in a very
vulnerable position unless he or she knew that the base
on which it was constructed was stable and able to support the rest of the structure.

Then, as a teenager, Poppy hadn't truly understood
what he meant; now she did and, albeit rather begrudg-
ingly, had to respect him for it.

As she hurried down the two flights of stairs to
the ground floor she wondered nervously why James
wanted to see her. It couldn't be anything to do with
the documents she was working on, they hadn't reached
the deadline for those yet.

Walking along the corridor to James's office, she
saw that the door to Chris's office was open, but, true
to the vow she had made herself on the day of his and
Sally's wedding, she refused to give in to the temptation to look to see if he was there.

There was no sign of James's secretary as Poppy
hovered outside his closed office door. She knocked
reluctantly and then went in.

James was seated behind the desk which, like all
the other furniture in the room, was strictly utilitarian.
He did not believe in wasting company money on non-
productive luxuries, and yet, disconcertingly, the lack
of normal, status-symbol fittings seemed to emphasise
the aura of leadership and power that emanated from
him rather than diminish it.

He was her cousin as well as her boss and it was ridiculous that she should feel like a child summoned
before a disapproving teacher, Poppy decided as she
waited to hear why he had sent for her.

There were some papers on the desk in front of him and her heart missed a beat as she saw the familiar letterhead of the Italian spa.

'Stewart Thomas asked to see me this morning,' he told Poppy, referring to the company's accountant.

Poppy's heart started to thump even more heavily. She had submitted her quarterly expenses to the accounts department the previous week. She was always painstakingly careful with them, but ever since James had hauled her over the coals for inadvertently putting a private petrol bill through her expenses she had lived in nervous dread of accidentally repeating her error.

'If it's about my expenses,' she began quickly, 'I—'

'No, Poppy, it's not about your expenses,' James told her. 'It's about this.' He picked up the letter in front of him as he spoke and pushed it across the desk towards her.

Uneasily Poppy picked it up.

'It's the bill from the Italian hotel,' she acknowledged. 'I...I understood I didn't have any expenses for that. You—'

'This isn't about your expenses, Poppy,' James repeated grimly. 'At least not in the way you mean. Take another look at the bill and this time read it properly, or would you prefer me to do it for you? Perhaps I should; that way we might at least save some time,' he told her curtly, flicking the paper away from her and reading out the words. 'Mr and Mrs Carlton: one double room.'

Poppy stared at him, the colour leaving her face, driven out as much by the acid note she could hear in his voice as by what he had actually said.

'But...but it was a mistake... They made a mistake,' she told him huskily. 'You said so yourself... You said...'

'It doesn't matter *what* I said,' James told her. 'What matters is the interpretation that Stewart Thomas and no doubt anyone else who happens to have seen this is going to put on it. The mere fact that he felt he ought to bring it straight to me says it all...don't you agree?'

Poppy felt sick.

'But you paid the bill before we left. They gave you a receipt, and—'

'And now they've sent a copy of it here,' James told her. 'God knows how many people had already seen it before it reached Stewart's desk.'

'But...but you explained to him what happened...? That the hotel had made a mistake, that they were over-booked.'

'Oh, yes, I told him,' James agreed, 'but—' He stopped speaking as his office door was unceremoniously pushed open and Chris hurried in, looking uncertain and confused.

'James, I don't know what's going on, but I've just overheard—' He broke off when he saw Poppy, looking frowningly from her stricken white face to James's grimly angry one.

'Yes, Chris, what have you overheard?' James probed.

'Well, I don't suppose it means anything, but as I walked past the general office I heard one of the girls talking about the fact that you and Poppy had...were... They're saying that the two of you are lovers,' he finished awkwardly. 'The whole place is buzzing with it,' he added. 'What on earth's going on?'

Whilst Chris had been talking James had stepped out from behind his desk and was now, Poppy realised, standing next to her.

As Chris looked at them both, to Poppy's shock

James reached out and took hold of her hand, linking fingers with hers and then squeezing hers warningly as he said, 'We had hoped to keep it to ourselves for a little while longer but...yes, it's true; Poppy and I—'

'But this is wonderful,' Chris interrupted him enthusiastically. 'Just wait until I tell Sally. When did all this happen and why haven't you said anything? Too preoccupied with other things, I suppose,' he chuckled. 'I know how it was with me and Sally when we first fell in love and I've no need to ask if you are in love, you must be, James, if you were idiotic enough to think the pair of you could get away with booking into a double room without anyone finding out. Have you told the family yet or—?'

'We didn't—' Poppy began quickly, anxious to make him understand that he had got it wrong, that there was nothing between her and James, that it was all a horrible mistake, that...

But James stopped her, the pressure of his grip on her fingers silencing her denial in her throat, his voice overriding hers as he told Chris smoothly, 'We didn't want to say anything to anyone yet. It's all so new to us that we wanted to keep our...feelings to ourselves.'

'Well, you can hardly do that now,' Chris laughed. 'Not with the whole place knowing that the two of you have spent four nights in bed together.'

Poppy had to bite down hard on her bottom lip to prevent herself crying out with pain as she heard the amusement in his voice. Didn't he *know*, didn't he *care* that *he* was the one she loved, not James?

'Just wait until I tell Sally,' he repeated.

Poppy burst out frantically, 'No...'

'No,' James concurred, giving Poppy's tender fingers another warning squeeze as Chris gave her a surprised look. 'Not yet. We still need a little more time to ourselves.'

'Well, you're going to have to go public with the family soon,' Chris warned him. 'They're bound to hear the gossip that's going round. I know that Ma and Aunt Fee only come in once a month or so, but—'

'Thanks, Chris,' James interrupted his brother. 'I hear what you are saying but...'

'But it isn't anything to do with me,' Chris finished cheerfully for him. 'Well, I doubt you'll get either Ma or Aunt Fee to agree with that, and you know that it's Aunt Fee's annual birthday lunch on Sunday. You're not going to find it easy to keep them from guessing the truth; after all, the family is used to seeing the pair of you either quarrelling or ignoring one another, not holding hands and...'

Immediately Poppy tried to pull her hand away but James refused to let her go.

If he wasn't going to tell Chris the truth then she would just have to, Poppy decided, turning away from James to reach out imploringly to Chris with her other hand as she began, 'Chris, please, there's—'

'Chris, that call has come through for you from Bensons,' Chris's secretary interrupted, putting her head round the door to give him the message.

'Thanks...I'm on my way,' he responded, pausing only to say ruefully to Poppy and James, 'You might as well tell them, you know; there's no way you're going to be able to keep it a secret now...'

Poppy could hardly contain herself long enough for Chris to close the door behind him before she turned on James and demanded furiously, 'Why didn't you tell him the truth? Why—?'

'What truth?' James interrupted her. 'Is that re-

ally what you want me to do, Poppy?' he asked curtly.
'Do you really want me to tell Chris what happened—
exactly what happened, *everything* that happened?' he
emphasised cruelly.

Humiliated, Poppy looked away from him.

'No, you know that's not what I meant,' she admitted, white-faced, adding in a choked whisper, 'But you
had no need to let him think, to let him believe that…'

'That what—that you and I are lovers? What would
you have preferred me to do? Tell him it was just sex…
just a four-night stand.'

'You could have said it was a mistake,' Poppy burst
out. 'You could have told him that the hotel was confused by the fact that we share the same surname…'

'I could, yes,' James agreed. 'And then what…?'

'What do you mean?' Poppy asked him in confusion.

'If I had told him that, Chris would have been bound
to ask what had happened, how we had resolved the
mistake. In other words, Poppy, he would have expected
me to say that the mistake was put right and that we
were given separate rooms if not separate bills.'

'And whose fault was it that we weren't?' Poppy demanded frantically. 'We can't let people think that…that
we are lovers,' she told him miserably.

'We can't let people, or we can't let Chris?' James
demanded. 'Face it, Poppy, he couldn't care less. In fact
he's probably relieved to have you off his back. It's time
you started living in the real world, Poppy. You and I—'

'There is no *you and I*,' Poppy denied fiercely. 'I hate
knowing what happened between us,' she told him passionately. 'I feel sick every time I think about it. I know
you've always hated and despised me, James; well, now
you've made me hate and despise myself even more

than you do.' She headed for his office door. 'No more, James. I just can't take any more.'

'Poppy, are you sure you're all right?'

Poppy gave her mother a lacklustre smile and fibbed, 'Yes, I'm fine.'

'She's probably missing James,' Chris teased her. He and Sally had arrived minutes earlier, the first guests to arrive for her mother's annual birthday lunch, and the four of them were standing in her parents' conservatory whilst her father poured the drinks.

Poppy shot her mother an anxious look, but she appeared to have missed Chris's comment.

'Don't worry, he'll be here,' Chris told Poppy. 'He rang me last night to say he'd be bringing Ma with him.'

For the first time since she had fallen in love with him Poppy found that she actively didn't want to be with Chris. She could tell from the looks he and Sally were exchanging that he *had* told his wife about her supposed relationship with James.

How many of the other guests her mother had invited also knew about it? Poppy wondered, her face burning. Where *was* James? What was she going to do if he didn't arrive...if she was left to face people's questions and curiosity on her own? A dizzy panicky feeling gripped her as she looked anxiously through the drawing-room window, searching for some sign of James's arrival.

'Poppy, what is it? Who are you looking for?' her mother asked her.

'N-nothing...no one,' Poppy stammered, but she knew that her face was flushing guiltily and she could see that her mother was puzzled by her behaviour.

'Poppy, my dear...and how was Italy?' a friend and

neighbour of her parents enquired heartily after he'd greeted her mother. 'A beautiful country and, of course, you went with James who is part-Italian himself...'

'Oh, have you and James been on holiday together?' a slightly deaf great-aunt asked with interest, picking up on the conversation. 'How nice; I always thought that the two of you would be well suited.'

'James and Poppy went away together to Italy on business,' Poppy's mother explained hastily.

Nearly all the guests had arrived now and Poppy's heart missed a beat as she saw Stewart Thomas and his wife on the opposite side of the room. She had had no idea that her mother had asked him and his wife to come. What was she going to do if Stewart said something to her mother about the hotel bill?

Panic seized her. Had James done this deliberately— left her on her own to face the consequences of what she had done? She started to shiver as her panic turned to a cold sweat of sick fear. How was she going to face everyone—her parents, her family?

James had to come, she reassured herself. He was bringing his mother. Chris had told her so. She could see Stewart Thomas and his wife talking together and she was sure that she was the subject of their discussion from the way they kept looking across at her.

A car drew up outside and James and Chris's mother got out, but James wasn't with her, Poppy realised in dismay as she recognised her aunt's companion as a long-standing male friend.

'Oh, dear, are we the last to arrive?' Poppy heard her aunt saying as her parents welcomed them in. 'I'm so sorry. There was a last-minute change of plan; James was supposed to be bringing us.'

'Don't worry, it's a cold lunch,' Poppy's mother responded. 'Come in and have a drink.'

Why wasn't her mother asking where James was? Poppy worried frantically. Why hadn't her aunt *said* why he wasn't with them?

'Poppy, you're looking awfully pale; I hope that son of mine isn't working you too hard. How was Italy, by the way? The countryside in that area is just so magnificent. I haven't seen you since you got back…'

Poppy glanced nervously over her shoulder before responding to her. Stewart was standing within earshot of their conversation, talking now to her own father.

'I…'

'Oh, I don't think Poppy got an awful lot of time to look at the scenery,' Chris informed his mother, giving Poppy a wicked look. 'Although I do believe she has become a devout admirer of a certain aspect of Italian—'

'James!'

Poppy couldn't contain her relief as she saw the tall, familiar figure striding into the room. The agonised, reproachful look she had been about to give Chris was forgotten as she hurried across to James's side, her brain not registering the surprise on some people's faces and the more worrying knowledge and amusement on others' until it was too late—until she had reached James's side, until she had clutched anxiously at his arm, until she had by her own actions and in full view of everyone there confirmed all that she had told James so fiercely *he* had to deny.

'Poppy?' she heard her mother saying uncertainly, her face registering her disbelief that Poppy should even acknowledge James's presence, never mind rush across the room to virtually throw herself into his arms, to clutch at him as though he were her only life raft in a life-threatening sea.

'You'll have to tell them now,' Poppy heard Chris chuckling. He and Sally, as well as her own father and mother and aunt, had followed her to James's side and all were now looking at them.

'Tell us what?' Poppy's mother asked, puzzled.

Helplessly Poppy looked at James.

'Poppy and I—' James began quietly.

But Chris beat him to it, informing them happily, 'Poppy and James are in love; in fact—'

'At last. Oh, Poppy I can't tell you how happy this makes me!' her aunt exclaimed. 'The two of you have always been so right for one another. I can still remember the way you used to follow James around when you were a child. Virtually as soon as you could walk you used to toddle after him, and now—'

'And now she's finally caught up with him,' Chris teased, interrupting his mother who was dabbing the emotional tears from her eyes as she hugged Poppy.

'How long have you known?'

'When did all this happen?'

'Have you made any plans yet?'

Poppy stood like someone in a trance as her family's happy congratulations fell on her like blows, whilst at her side James was as still and cold as stone.

'I told you you'd never be able to keep this to yourselves,' Chris reminded them gleefully when Poppy's father had gone to open some champagne.

'*Now* I know why you looked so disappointed when I arrived without James.' James's mother smiled as she hugged Poppy a second time. 'Oh, Poppy, I can't tell you how pleased I am... I thought that James—' She broke off and shook her head, smiling at Poppy through her tears.

What was wrong with them all? Poppy wondered dizzily as her father started to hand round glasses of champagne. They all knew that she loved Chris and yet they were behaving as though…as though her relationship with James was somehow expected…a foregone conclusion.

She heard her father proposing a toast whilst someone else congratulated James and asked him when they were to be married.

'Well, you won't want to wait long, will you?' interrupted Sally. 'And, after all, it isn't as though you need to look for a house or anything; you can move straight into James's…'

Could she see just the tiniest hint of relief in Sally's eyes? Poppy wondered achingly as Chris turned to hug her. He didn't kiss her, she noticed. Did he suspect the truth…? Did he know that *he* was still the one she loved?

'So when did all this happen?' Poppy's mother asked her when the excitement had finally started to die down a little.

In Italy, Poppy was about to say, but James got in before her, saying firmly, 'Last Christmas.'

Poppy turned her head to stare at him. Last Christmas they had had one of the worst quarrels they had ever had, when he'd accused her of trying to make Sally uncomfortable at the family's Christmas party by 'mooning about', as he'd put it, over Chris.

She waited for her mother to laugh and accuse James of lying but instead she simply smiled and said that they had done very well to keep it to themselves for so long.

'We didn't want to steal Chris and Sally's glory,' James fibbed smoothly.

'So now we've got another wedding to plan; when do you…?'

A wedding… Poppy gave James an appalled look and told her mother quickly, 'Oh, no, we can't—'

'We can't quite make up our minds when,' James overrode her smoothly.

'Well, at least you won't have to look for a house,' her mother continued, repeating what Sally had said earlier, giving James a rueful look as she added, 'I thought at the time that it was rather odd for a single man to be buying what was obviously a family home. I suppose I should have guessed then; Poppy has always had a weakness for those Victorian houses down by the river.'

Whilst Poppy bit back her shocked response—that she had had nothing to do with the choice of James's present home—James himself responded with a calm, 'Yes, I know; I remember how as a little girl she used to insist on taking the long way home from school so that she could walk past them.'

It was true, she *did* love the magnificent terrace of large Victorian houses whose long gardens backed onto the river, and had even fantasised about living in one, but with Chris, not James.

She had been angry when James had bought one of them, resentful almost, refusing to go to the small house-warming party he had given.

All through lunch Poppy was conscious of the interest they were causing. She herself didn't have any appetite, she had lost weight since her return from Italy but then she was so stressed, so on edge that it was no wonder she didn't want to eat.

'I want to talk to you.' Poppy tensed as she heard James speaking quietly in her ear.

'We can't…not now. Not here.'

'I'm leaving in half an hour,' James told her, glancing at his watch, 'and when I do you're coming with me.'

'No,' Poppy protested. 'I can't… What will people think?'

'They'll think that we're in love and that we want to be on our own to—'

'Stop it,' Poppy hissed, her face starting to burn. 'Why did you have to say…to let them think…?'

'Why the hell do you think?' James demanded grimly.

Poppy's flush deepened as she remembered that all too betraying 'James!' and the way she had virtually flung herself into his arms.

'Where are we going?' Poppy asked James after she had fastened her seat belt. She had tried to get out of leaving with him, using the excuse that her mother would need her to help clear up, but James had refused to listen and now here she was, seated next to him in his car, wondering why on earth she had been so stupid as to allow the curious glances of a few people to drive her into seeing James as an ally…a refuge.

'Where do you think?' James asked her drily as he turned the car in the direction of his own home.

'Not there,' Poppy protested as she realised where they were going.

'Why not? Where else is there where we can talk without being overheard?'

'We don't have to go to your house. You could just park the car and…say…'

'Oh, yes, and have anyone who saw us—and certainly someone would—put it about that the pair of us are so hot for each other that you'll let me have you in the back of the car?'

'Stop it,' Poppy demanded, hot-cheeked. 'Don't talk about me like that. I would never...' She stopped, the words of denial choking in her throat. How could she tell James that what he was saying made her feel cheap? It was too late to argue with him any more. He was already turning into the road to his house, which was right at the end of the terrace and had a large expanse of garden to the side of it as well as to the rear.

The houses, three storeys high, possessed cellars as well as attics, most of which had been converted into garages and storage spaces respectively. As James parked his car in his garage, she shivered a little, dreading the interview ahead.

'This way,' James instructed her, opening the car door for her.

As she followed him up stone steps and through a door into the main hallway she tried not to betray any interest in the house which she had so far refused to visit, even though her eye was immediately taken by the elegance of the plasterwork ceiling and the generous proportions of the hall and stairs.

The rich mahogany of the panelled doors gleamed softly in the early evening sunlight and Poppy had to suppress an urge to reach out and touch them to see if the wood felt as warmly alive as it looked. Disconcertingly, she remembered that the last time she had felt such an urge to touch something that something had been James—the sleek warmth of James's body.

A fierce shudder galvanised her body, causing James to frown as he watched her. The stairs and hallway had been carpeted in a natural cord matting which provided the perfect background for the richness of the rugs laid over it. If this had been her home she would have added some feminine touches such as a huge bowl of flowers on the circular table, Poppy decided, but otherwise she couldn't fault James's taste.

'In here,' he told her, opening one of the doors.

Poppy blinked as she stepped through it and was momentarily blinded by sunlight. The room was huge, running the whole length and half the width of the ground floor, with windows overlooking both the front and the back, and James had furnished it with a mixture of antique and modern furniture which somehow melded magically together to make it look both elegant and welcoming.

'Now,' James began as he followed her into the room and closed the door behind him, 'do you mind telling me exactly what you're playing at?'

'I...I don't know what you mean,' Poppy said.

'Oh, come on, Poppy, don't give me that. What the hell were you doing coming up to me like that and making it obvious that—?'

'That what?' Poppy defended herself, tears stinging her eyes. 'That we'd been to bed together? They already knew that—or they would soon have known,' she amended more honestly.

James was frowning. 'What do you mean? Surely Chris—?'

'Not Chris,' Poppy interrupted. 'No one had said anything, but Mum had invited Stewart Thomas and I could tell from the way he and Diana were looking at me...' She bit her lip, unwilling to tell him how vulnerable she had felt, how afraid and alone it had made her realise she was when she had seen the way Stewart and his wife were looking at her and had known what they must be saying.

'It's all right for you,' she told James fiercely. 'No one would think any the less of you for…for what happened…but it's different for me.

'Why did all this have to happen?' she demanded passionately, tears clogging her voice.

'Do you *really* have to ask?' she heard James saying roughly. 'It had to happen because of this, Poppy. Because of this…' And then he was holding her, kissing her, his mouth almost brutal as it devoured hers, but even more shocking than the raw sensuality of his kiss was her own response to it—her *body's* response to it: avid, eager, hungry, shamelessly accepting, urging, inciting him to…

Poppy gave a small moan of panic as she felt his hand move towards her breast. Once he touched her there she would have no hope of stopping the frightening, out-of-control rush of sensation that she could feel building inside her, threatening her. As she panicked and started to pull away from James, she was engulfed by the return of the dizzy sensation she had felt earlier on, only this time it was accompanied by a surge of nausea and weakness.

Helpless to escape it, she closed her eyes and gave a small moan.

'Poppy—Poppy, what is it?' she heard James demanding forcefully as she fell forward against him. When his arms locked round her to support her, she felt the dizziness start to recede and, mercifully, with it her nausea.

'How long has this been going on?' James asked her curtly. He was still holding her, still supporting her, and inexplicably it was somehow easier simply to stay where she was, leaning against him, than to make herself move away; her legs still felt oddly weak and she couldn't get out of her mind how afraid and vulnerable she had felt when he hadn't been there, how relieved she had been to see him standing there in her parents' drawing room.

'How long has *what* been going on?' she asked him weakly.

'You know what I mean, Poppy,' James warned her harshly. 'Are you pregnant? Are you carrying my child?' he asked her grimly.

Carrying his child. The colour came and went in Poppy's face as the importance of what he was saying struck her.

'No, no, of course I'm not,' she denied. How…? 'I can't be pregnant, James,' she told him piteously. 'I can't be…'

'You may not *want* to be,' James corrected her bitingly.

Pregnant, with James's child… Poppy swayed shakily. Of course she couldn't be…could she? As she mentally counted the weeks and then slowly recounted them since their return from Italy and acknowledged what she had previously ignored—namely that her period was now months overdue—she went cold with shock.

'Poppy?' James demanded gratingly.

'I…I don't know,' she whispered through numb lips, and then as the panic exploded inside her she told him frantically, 'James, I can't be pregnant… We can't…'

'It's perhaps just as well that we've already warned everyone that we intend to get married,' James told her curtly, ignoring her shocked denial and coolly interpreting the reason for her panic.

'We can't get married,' Poppy protested, her eyes glazed with shock.

'We can't not,' James corrected her. 'Not now.'

'But I may *not* be pregnant,' Poppy told him. 'And even if I am...'

'If you are, what?' James asked her harshly. 'If you are, you'd rather destroy my child than—?'

'No,' Poppy told him vehemently. 'No, I could never do that...never.'

'Then we don't really have any other option, do we?' James told her. 'If you *are* carrying my child, we *have* to get married...'

'Yes,' Poppy whispered, knowing that it was true. Had they been strangers and not cousins maybe then she could have contemplated bringing her child up alone, but under the circumstances...

'I may not be pregnant,' she repeated, but she could hear the lack of conviction in her voice and knew that James could hear it too.

As she closed her eyes she had a vivid memory of feeling James deep within her body, of experiencing that fierce, female surge of triumph at knowing that he was there, without realising then just what that feeling meant. Now she suspected that she did. She'd have to get one of those test things from the chemist's, she decided bleakly; either that or visit their family doctor.

'I never wanted this to happen,' she told James bleakly. 'I never wanted—'

'Either me or my child?' he suggested. 'No, I know that... I... No doubt you'd far rather fantasise that it's Chris's child you're carrying, just as you wanted to fantasise that he was the one making love to you. Unfortunately—for both of us—it wasn't him. It was me!'

CHAPTER SEVEN

'Poppy, I need to talk to you.' Poppy shivered as she listened to the curt tones of James's voice relaying the terse message to her over her answering machine.

Mercifully, at least as far as she was concerned, he had been away on business for the past three days and today she wasn't going into the office since she was taking three days' holiday. Later in the day she was due to have lunch with Sally's stepmother and her fellow bridesmaid—an arrangement which had been made at Star's suggestion three months ago, on the day of Chris and Sally's wedding.

As she remembered the certainty and vehemence with which she had insisted then that there was no way she would ever marry, Poppy could feel her stomach starting to churn nauseously with a now familiar mixture of panic and misery.

She supposed if she were a different sort of person, a braver sort of person, she could defy James, refuse to marry him and bring up her child—their child—on her own; there had certainly been times since her visit to the doctor had confirmed what she had already secretly known in her heart—that she was carrying James's child—when she had toyed unrealistically with the idea of simply running away...disappearing...avoid-

ing all the misery and anguish that she knew lay ahead
of her.

But how could she? How could she hurt her parents
by doing something like that? And besides, no matter
where she ran to she could never escape from herself
or from the knowledge of what she had done.

However, she could not face James yet, even though
she was acutely conscious of the thoughtful looks
her mother had been giving her and suspected that it
wouldn't be long before she questioned her increasingly hard-to-conceal bouts of sickness and put two
and two together.

There were alternatives, of course, she acknowledged tiredly as she prepared for her lunch date, but
they were simply not options she could ever choose to
take. Little though she had wanted or planned to have
a baby—*any* baby, never mind James's—now that she
knew that she actually *had* conceived... Poppy placed
her hand protectively over her stomach. No, she couldn't
do that, couldn't take away the life that she and James
had created.

She knew why James had left that message on her
private line, of course; she knew perfectly well what it
was he wanted to ask her... The unexpected business
commitment which had taken him abroad had meant
that he had had to leave before he could question her
about the outcome of her visit to the doctor and she
knew she would have little alternative but to tell him.

The last thing she felt like doing today was going
to lunch. What would the other two think if they knew
that soon she would be breaking the vow that they had
all made to remain unmarried? Would *they*, like her
parents and her family, assume that she was actually in
love with James? That all the years she had spent lov-

ing Chris had simply been a youthful infatuation which
had really meant nothing?

It had shocked Poppy to discover that her parents,
and especially her mother, seemed to think that James
was so right for her—that they were so right for one another. Even Chris had told her how pleased he was for
both of them. It seemed to Poppy that the only people
who weren't pleased or happy about the fact that she
and James had supposedly fallen deeply in love with
one another were she and James themselves.

Oddly enough, instead of feeling hurt by Chris's
comment, by his inability to see the truth, what Poppy
had experienced had been a totally unexpected and disconcerting sense of irritation and exasperation...

The restaurant was quite quiet, the conservatory where
they were lunching pleasantly cool, but Poppy still felt
queasy and uncomfortably warm as she sat down.

She could see the faintly concerned looks that Claire,
Sally's stepmother, was giving her as she toyed with
her food and made monosyllabic responses to her conversation, but the smell of food was making her head
swim and her stomach churn—or was it the fact that
just being there was bringing home to her the enormity
of what she had done and the way her life was bound
to change?

Panic filled her as she realised how unprepared for
change she really was. Unable to face another mouthful of food, she pushed away her plate and stood up.

Once she reached the sanctuary of the ladies' cloakroom she discovered that her nausea had subsided, and
by the time Claire came in search of her she felt sufficiently in control of herself to apologise for her sud-

den exit, even if her voice did shake a little as she said the words.

What would they think once they discovered the truth, these two women with whom she had sworn a vow to remain unmarried and so disprove the myth of the potency of catching the bride's bouquet?

And, no matter how quickly she and James got married, once the baby arrived people were *bound* to guess the truth. Her face burned hotly. There was no onus on couples these days to marry before having children, and had she and James genuinely been in love she knew that her prime emotion on learning that she had conceived his child would have been one of intense joy and delight.

But they were *not* in love and she had conceived his child whilst believing…whilst wanting another man, and that was the source of her shame and anguish, of her dread at the prospect of marriage to him.

She was relieved when the lunch was finally over. Having said goodbye to Star outside the restaurant, she and Claire were left alone together. As Claire turned to her, clearly about to say something, Poppy saw James's familiar Jaguar driving towards them, James himself at the wheel, and she froze, torn between her need to turn and flee and her knowledge that physically she felt incapable of moving so much as a muscle. The Jaguar stopped abruptly in front of them and James got out and strode towards them.

Poppy winced, and she felt James's fingers curl round her arm, locking on it in a grip that she couldn't break. 'James, what are you doing here? How did you know where to find me?'

'I looked in your diary,' he told her witheringly. 'Get in the car.'

'James… I…'

I don't want to go with you, she had been about to say, but he shook his head, telling her grimly, 'Not now, Poppy; I'm not in the mood for it. Where the hell have you been?' he demanded as he propelled her towards the Jaguar. 'Why the hell haven't you been in touch with me?'

As she turned towards him he warned her, 'No games, Poppy; you know what I mean, you know what it is I want to know...'

Just for a heartbeat Poppy contemplated lying to him, telling him that she wasn't pregnant after all, but the impulse soon died, shrivelled by the hot, dry blast of his anger.

'I was right, wasn't I?' James continued mercilessly, after he had bundled her into the car, slid into the driver's seat and set the car in motion. 'You *have* conceived my child.'

'Yes,' Poppy admitted tonelessly. Why, when she knew how little emotion there was between them, how lacking in tender, loving feelings their relationship was, did she have this urge to cry, to turn to James and beg him to stop the car and put his arms round her, hold her, make her feel safe...make her feel protected...make her feel loved?

She tensed her body, expecting his anger to accelerate at her confirmation of her pregnancy with the same velocity with which the car had increased speed, but instead he remained oddly quiet—so quiet in fact that Poppy felt impelled to turn her head and look at him—the first time she had looked at him since he had stopped the car and come striding so angrily towards her.

James wasn't paying any attention to her; his gaze,

his concentration appeared to be fixed on the empty road ahead of them.

'I...I won't... I can't not have my baby,' she told him doggedly, realising only as she gave voice to the shaky words just how strongly she already felt about her child, how protective of it, how determined always to keep it from hurt and from harm.

Now James did look at her, and the look in his eyes made her wince slightly as he told her starkly, 'If I thought for one moment that you might... This baby is *mine* as well as yours, Poppy, and if I thought that you'd do anything—and I do mean *anything* to harm it...'

Poppy's body shook as she listened to him. That he would insist on them both 'doing the right thing' she had never doubted—he was that sort of man—but the emotion she had heard in his voice as he'd told her that the baby—her baby—was his child as well had left her lost for words, grappling with the shock of suddenly discovering a side to him that she had never imagined existed.

She knew, of course, how protective he could be towards his close family, but it had never occurred to her that those feelings might extend to a child he had never even intended should be conceived.

'We'll need to talk to your parents,' she heard him warning her, 'and then my mother...'

'Do we...are we...? They'll have to know the truth,' she told him, unaware of how haunted and unhappy she looked as she whispered rather than stated the words.

'Yes,' he agreed quietly. 'Or at least part of it. I warn you, Poppy, that not just for your own sake but for the baby's sake as well there is *one* truth that it is advisable that no one should ever know.'

Poppy's heart started to thump heavily as he turned his head to look at her.

'What…what do you mean?' she asked him, her mouth dry with foreboding.

'They must *never*—no one must *ever* have any reason to think that our child…our relationship…is the result of anything other than love.'

'Love?' Poppy swallowed hard as she stared at him aghast. 'But no one will really believe that. They all know the way I feel about Chris…'

'They all know that you had an adolescent crush on my brother,' James corrected her coldly.

'I can't pretend that I've fallen in love with you,' Poppy told him. 'No one would ever believe me.'

'No? Then you'll just have to find a way of *making* them believe you,' James informed her. 'Unless, of course, you actually want people to guess the truth.'

'No,' Poppy denied sharply, her face burning with hot colour.

'No,' James said sardonically. 'You're caught between two equally unpalatable choices, I'm afraid, Poppy. You either pretend you love me or you take the risk of people questioning why, if you don't, you and I conceived a child. It's a question of the lesser of two evils.'

'Chris will never believe that I've fallen in love with you,' Poppy protested feverishly.

'He is far too busy with his own life and his new wife to have any time to spare questioning what's going on in yours. Face it, Poppy, what you choose to do or not to do with your life isn't of much interest to Chris, other than as a cousin, and if anything—'

'He'll be only too relieved not to have the embarrassment of me loving him any more,' Poppy broke in shakily. 'Yes, so you've already told me.'

'Are both your parents at home this evening?'

'Yes—yes, I think so,' Poppy confirmed as she tried to grapple with the confusion of her thoughts. Part of her ached and longed to turn the clock back and to have things as they were, but if that were possible that would mean... Her hand moved automatically towards her stomach. The discovery of how emotionally attached she had become to the thought of her child in such a short space of time shocked her.

'Good. We'll need to talk to them as quickly as possible. I think so far as the general public is concerned the fact that the family has barely got over one big wedding should serve as a reasonable excuse for the haste of ours...'

'But people are bound to guess, especially once the baby—'

'So let them guess,' James shrugged as he shot back his cuff to glance at his watch. 'I'll come round about eight,' he told her as he brought the car to a halt outside her parents' house.

Poppy reached numbly for the doorhandle. She felt tired and drained, alone, and even afraid. This wasn't how she had imagined things would be...how her life, her marriage would be. And never, ever in her darkest nightmares had she envisaged a scenario so starkly devoid of love and emotion.

James had got out and was now standing on the pavement beside her. As the panic flared inside her she turned towards him.

'We can't marry one another, James,' she protested. 'We don't love each other. We have nothing in common, nothing to keep us together, nothing to make our marriage real.'

All her fears and her pent-up sense of loss and anguish were contained in her voice and her expression as she turned pleadingly towards him, but James ignored them, taking hold of her right there in her parents' drive, his hands firm and compelling as he gripped her upper arms and told her savagely, 'No! We've got this much, Poppy.'

And then he was kissing her, his mouth hard and warm on hers, burning the numb immobility of her lips into fierce, painful life as they softened and then clung to his, his touch conjuring up inside her a sharp, whirlwind sensation and taut, aching need.

Their surroundings, their situation, everything else faded into insignificance as Poppy clung helplessly to him whilst her body responded to his touch, his kiss.

When he finally released her, it took her several seconds to realise where they were and why. Tears glittered brightly in her eyes as she started to turn away from him, her face hot with shame. *Why* was it that she responded so immediately and so physically to him? *Why...?*

'Poppy,' she heard him saying when she made to walk away. The sound of his voice halted her and she turned automatically to face him. 'We've also got this,' he reminded her, one hand on her arm, the other, fingers spread, placed against her stomach.

She could feel the warmth of his touch through her clothes—male and somehow oddly possessive—and even though she knew it was impossible Poppy could have sworn that the new life within her responded somehow to his touch, knew it almost.

Head bowed, she stood there unresisting as the tears again filled her eyes like liquid crystals. She could feel James moving towards her, closing the gap between them. She could feel the warmth of his breath as he bent his head towards her, and the fear that he might kiss her again, might bring back the wretched, treacherous surge of desire that he seemed to summon up within her so effortlessly lent her the impetus to push away from him and half run towards the sanctuary of the house.

'I'm afraid that I'm really the one to blame.' James's hand reached out and took hold of Poppy's. His grip felt oddly comforting, warming the icy chill of her own nervously tense fingers.

James had just finished telling her parents that they intended to marry as soon as they could—and why. The silence which had followed his announcement had caused Poppy to hang her head in shame as she'd waited for the blow to fall and for her parents to demand to know how she came to be carrying James's child when they both knew how much she loved Chris, but to her astonishment neither of them made any such comment. Instead, they hugged her lovingly whilst her father cleared his throat.

'Oh, darling, I always knew that eventually you and James would sort out your differences, although I must admit, I didn't expect it to happen quite so—'

'It's my fault,' James repeated, gently tugging Poppy towards him so that she had no alternative but to allow him to draw her into the protection of his body.

And he told her parents with an apparent sincerity that had Poppy holding her breath and staring up at him in wide-eyed disbelief, 'Having waited for so long, having loved and wanted her for so long, once Poppy... Well, let's just say that I let my feelings get the better of me without fully thinking through the potential consequences. And, wrongly or not, I can't pretend that the end result isn't one that fills me with great joy, even though for the sake of conformity I should have taken steps...

'My main concern in all of this is that Poppy isn't upset and that you'll forgive me for depriving you of the opportunity to spend the next twelve months organising our wedding,' he told Poppy's mother wryly.

'Well, I must admit that you have rather surprised us,' Poppy's mother confessed, 'although... Don't look like that, darling,' she reassured Poppy. 'I do remember how it feels to be so very much in love, you know,' she said gently. 'Your father and I...'

Poppy's father coughed again, making her mother laugh.

'It will have to be a quiet family wedding, of course; have you made any plans? Poppy will need a dress, of course, and then there'll be the wedding breakfast...'

'No,' Poppy protested. 'I...' She flushed as both her parents looked at her. 'I won't need a dress,' she told them huskily. 'Not for a register office wedding. I—'

'It won't *be* a register office wedding,' James interrupted her curtly. 'We'll be getting married in church,' he told her mother, to Poppy's shock.

And then, before Poppy could say anything, he cupped her face in one hand and there, in full view of her parents, turned it up towards his own, kissing her lightly on the tip of her nose and then far more lingeringly on her mouth before saying softly, 'I don't want anyone thinking that either of us regrets what's happened or that our child isn't welcome and a wanted addition to our lives. And I certainly don't want them thinking that our marriage is anything other than a celebration of the love we feel for one another and for him or her.'

It wasn't until he kissed the moisture from the corners of her eyes that Poppy realised she was crying. As James released her she saw that her mother's eyes looked suspiciously damp as well.

'I can't wear a white dress,' she told her mother shakily. 'It will have to be—'

'Ivory or cream,' her mother agreed, apparently totally misunderstanding her. 'White has never been a good colour for you. I remember when I was buying your christening robe...

'If it's just going to be a family affair, James, I think we should have the wedding breakfast here. We'll have it catered, of course. Have you told your own mother yet?'

'No, Poppy and I are going to see her later.'

This was news to Poppy but she had no energy left to argue. She was still shaken by James's ability to lie so convincingly. If she hadn't known better, even *she* would have been taken in by the little performance he had just put on for her parents.

And she couldn't help thinking how much, if she had genuinely loved James, those words, that confirmation of his commitment to her and to their child would have meant to her. It struck Poppy all at once how little she actually thought about Chris these days, but then she had hardly had the luxury of having the *time* to think about him, had she? Before, when there had been no James in her life, no plans to make for the future, no other matters to concern her, she had had the leisure to indulge in as many daydreams about Chris and how it would be if he loved her as she wished.

And besides, it seemed wrong somehow, unfair to her unborn child to indulge in the immaturity of daydreaming about a man she could never have—a man who was not that child's father.

It shocked her a little bit that her parents should so easily accept the supposed transfer of her love from Chris to James.

She *had* loved Chris.

Had loved him?

For some reason Poppy felt as though she was suddenly standing on the edge of a very deep and dangerous chasm which had totally unexpectedly opened virtually beneath her unsuspecting feet.

'Ready?' she heard James asking her.

She swallowed nervously. Ready for what? For the future—their future? How *could* she be when it wasn't a future she would have chosen for herself?

Six weeks after, they were married in church with her wearing an ivory lace and silk wedding dress which had originally been made for James's Italian great-grandmother. The dress had been a gift from James's aunt, who had travelled from her home in Rome especially to bring it and, Poppy suspected, to congratulate her on her good taste and good fortune in marrying her favourite relative.

It had only had to be let out a little bit at the waist. Her pregnancy might not be showing physically in her body as yet, Poppy acknowledged as she stood mutely at James's side after the ceremony, his wife now and no longer just his cousin, but she suspected that the time she had had off work with the debilitating bouts of sickness which had accompanied the early weeks of pregnancy had alerted most people to the reality of the situation.

However, no one had actually said anything, apart from Sally, who had commented rather enviously earlier in the day as she'd helped Poppy to dress for her wedding, 'Chris and I said that we would wait a few years before we started a family. I thought that was what I wanted but now... I suppose there's something about conceiving a child by the man you love that adds a special depth to your relationship...a special closeness. You only have to look at how happy Claire and Brad are,' she said wistfully, 'now that they're married and expecting a baby...'

Poppy hadn't known what to say. How *could* she tell Sally of all people the truth? And now it was too late to tell anyone anything. Now she and James were married, husband and wife, a couple, a pair...parents-in-waiting.

Poppy shivered, closing her eyes as she remembered the moment when James had lifted the heavy antique veil from her face to look at her in absolute silence, before raising his hands to cup her face.

Her whole body had trembled so much that it had even felt as though his hands were trembling as he'd bent his head and then slowly kissed her, not with sensual passion, not with any emotion she could put a name to or recognise, but with something else—something in the way he'd looked at her, something in the solemnity of the vows they had just taken that had brought a lump to her throat and made her lips quiver beneath his.

Had anyone other than she noticed the way his fingers had gently brushed her stomach as he'd released her face, his touch as much a wordless, secret promise to their child as his vows had been a public one to her?

Poppy doubted it; *that* gesture had not been for public view; that gesture, that vow had been something private between James and his son...or daughter— something which she'd felt at that moment had actually excluded her. It had also made her acutely conscious of the reason why they were marrying and of the fiction of James's public display of love for her.

Chris came up to them now, to envelop his brother in a bear-hug of emotion and to give Poppy a wide, beaming grin. His hair needed cutting and the way it flopped into his eyes made him look both boyish and slightly bashful.

As she listened to Sally scolding him lovingly for unfastening the top button of his shirt and removing his tie, Poppy wondered what would have happened if it *had* been Chris's child she was carrying and not James's; how *would* Chris have reacted in such circumstances? She tried to envisage him calmly taking control as James had done, seeing her parents, explaining what had happened to them, taking the blame and the responsibility, and she was forced to acknowledge that if Chris had been the father it would have been more likely that *she* would have been the one to take charge, to do the explaining…to take the blame.

'Stop it,' she heard James telling her warningly. Then he said, 'It's me you're married to, Poppy, not Chris. My child you're carrying—mine!'

'Don't you think I *know* that?' she returned bitterly. Her dress suddenly felt uncomfortably tight round her waist, her head ached and she felt hot and tired.

'I hate all this hypocrisy,' she told James angrily. 'All this pretence.'

'Really? You didn't seem to mind the pretence the night you convinced yourself you were in bed with Chris and not with me,' James reminded her bluntly.

Shocked by the unexpectedness of his attack, coming so soon after his convincing act of love in church, Poppy could only stare at him in silence until she was rescued by the welcome sound of her mother's voice exclaiming, 'Darling, are you all right? You look rather pale. Come and sit down. Everyone's here now and the caterers are ready to serve lunch.'

CHAPTER EIGHT

'IT WON'T be long now.'

Poppy had balked at the idea of a honeymoon but James had insisted, pointing out that it would look odd if they didn't go away, and in the end she had had to give in, although she had wished she hadn't when he had told her where they were going.

'Italy!' she had protested. 'No, I can't, not Italy; it will remind me of your Japanese friend—the one you spent the night with at the hotel,' she had begun, childishly driven into the panicky reaction by her own misery.

But James had stopped her, telling her firmly, 'The only person I spent the night with at the hotel was you.'

'One night you didn't come back to the room,' Poppy had accused him challengingly.

'Yes, but not because I was with someone else. If you must know, I stayed up all night working.'

Poppy hadn't quite been able to bring herself to look at him. 'I still don't want to go back to Italy.'

'We don't have much choice,' James had told her coolly. 'My mother is insisting on giving us the villa as a wedding gift and it would look churlish to refuse.'

Poppy had known he was right. James's mother had not used the villa since James's father's death, preferring, she said, to keep her happy memories of the holidays they had spent there intact.

Now she had told James and Poppy it was time that other members of the family enjoyed it, and since James had always been far more in touch with his Italian heritage than Chris she had decided that James and Poppy should have it.

Poppy had been there once with her parents, as a child, and she remembered how awed she had been by the Tuscan countryside, by the richness of its colours and the warm vibrancy of its people and its life.

One unexpected side effect of her pregnancy had been that her body temperature seemed to have risen by several degrees, and the air-conditioning in the car that James had hired for them was a welcome antidote to the heat of the Italian summer, beneath which the Tuscan countryside drowsed.

Whenever Poppy thought of the area she always thought of it in terms of its colours—amber, saffron, warm browns and rich terracotta—the colours of the earth, colours which, for her, echoed its richness and warmth, its bounty, their depth leavened and lightened by the cerulean sky.

The villa—their villa now—was small and relatively isolated and had originally been a wedding gift from James's father to his mother.

'James was conceived there,' she had told Poppy several days ago, 'and I've often wondered if that is why he is so much more in tune with his Italian heritage than Chris.

'You do love him, don't you, Poppy?' she had asked quietly. 'Because I know how much he loves you, how much he has always loved you.' And Poppy had bowed her head.

She had no idea why, when James could so obviously
and easily lie to his mother, she seemed unable to do
the same, but perhaps her aunt had taken the tears in
her eyes as a sign of her love for James rather than the
reverse, Poppy decided, because she had not pressed
the matter, simply touching Poppy's bent head gently.

The small town several miles away from the villa
was just as Poppy remembered it. A couple of dark-eyed
children watched them from an open doorway as they
drove past and Poppy's heart turned over, seized by the
quick, melting surge of emotions she had become familiar with in these last weeks.

'What is it? What's wrong?' James asked her, but
she did not feel able to tell him, to explain.

Did all women feel like this when they knew they
were carrying a child? she wondered. Did they all experience this—this emotional awareness of the vulnerability of all young things, this need to protect and cherish?
The strength of her love for a child she had never intended to conceive, the bond she felt with it already,
constantly amazed her. She might not love *James* or he
her, but she would—she did even now—love their child.

And so did James, she acknowledged, moving her
head to look at him as he turned off the main road and
onto the narrow dirt track that led to the villa.

Time and the hot Tuscan sun had turned the original deep terracotta of the building into a soft, faded
colour somewhere between pink and brown. The shutters, closed now against the afternoon sun, were painted
white. The local farmer whom James's mother paid to
maintain the property for her had obviously repainted
them recently, Poppy decided as she noted their dazzling brilliance.

James stopped the car and got out. Uncertainly Poppy went to join him.

'Paolo should have been down with some supplies for us,' he told her, referring to the farmer. 'If not, I'll leave you to get settled in and drive back to the village to get some. Is there anything in particular that you would like?'

'Only water,' Poppy told him, grimacing a little. Her mouth, like her body, felt dry and dusty from the journey. The heat, coupled with her own inner tension, had also made her feel slightly light-headed. As she blinked dizzily in the sun, she saw that James was frowning.

'You'd better get inside out of the heat,' he told her.

'I'm pregnant, James, that's all,' she responded irritably. 'There's no need to fuss. Not that you *are* fussing—fussing on *my* account,' she added bitterly. 'You don't give a damn what happens to me.'

'Would you want me to?'

Poppy stiffened as she heard the challenge in his voice.

'We both know what's really bugging you, Poppy,' James added grimly, 'and it isn't my so-called "fussing", is it? For God's sake!' he exclaimed, 'I know I'm not Chris but just when the hell are you going to grow up and realise—?' He stopped, rubbing the back of his neck with his hand and frowning as he narrowed his eyes against the sun.

'Let's get inside,' he told her, turning towards the front door to the villa.

Silently Poppy followed him, deliberately keeping her distance as he unlocked the weathered wooden door. Inside the villa it felt blissfully cool. Whilst James opened the shutters Poppy made her way to the kitchen. Paolo had obviously been, because there was a box of groceries on the kitchen table. As she looked through it Poppy sniffed appreciatively at the locally cured ham and the freshly picked tomatoes, suddenly feeling unexpectedly hungry.

'Aha, you like that, do you?' she teased the baby, speaking her thoughts out loud as her mouth watered at the sight and smell of the fresh, locally baked bread.

'You're going to be like your *papà*, are you, and favour your Italian heritage?' she laughed as her tiredness melted away, her body relaxing now that it was released from the tension of James's constant presence. It was something new that she had only started very recently, this verbal communication with her child.

'Well, don't expect me to be a doting Italian *mamma* and spoil you,' she warned with very obvious untruth. Then spinning round, her face flushing, she realised that James was standing in the doorway. How long had he been there? Long enough to overhear her silliness, she guessed, and quickly defended herself.

'All the books say that it's important to communicate with the baby even before it's born, to let it know that you're there, that you care, that you love it.'

'And do you love it…him or her?'

'He or she is my child… How could I not do?' Poppy demanded huskily.

'Your child is also mine,' James reminded her. '*Mine*, Poppy,' he reiterated. 'And, let me warn you now, if you ever, *ever* attempt to pretend that my child has my brother for its father, in the same way you pretended that he was your lover—'

'Paolo doesn't seem to have brought us any milk,' Poppy told him, quickly turning away, not wanting him to see the flush burning her face.

'Poppy,' James warned.

'No...no, I shall never try to pretend Chris is my... our baby's father,' she said. 'Not to myself or to anyone else.

'James, how are we going to endure this?' she demanded starkly, turning back to face him, her eyes betraying her misery. 'We don't love each other.' Her voice quickened with panic. 'We don't even like one another.'

'We'll endure it because we have to, because of him or her,' James told her grimly, his glance resting tellingly on her stomach before he picked up the car keys which he had dropped on the table. 'I'll take the cases upstairs and then I'll go down to the village for some water. I'll put your luggage in the main bedroom—I'll sleep in the other one...'

The villa only had two bedrooms, both of them very spacious, and one bathroom, which was off the larger of the two rooms so that whoever was using the smaller had to walk through the main bedroom to get to it. James's mother had always said that one day she would add a second bathroom, but she had never got round to it.

Without waiting for her to answer, James walked towards the door.

The rear of the villa was shaded by a vine-covered patio. The summer that Poppy had stayed here with her parents they had eaten most of their meals on it. How on earth was she going to endure two weeks cooped up alone here with James? And if she couldn't bear the thought of spending *two weeks* alone with him, then how was she going to get through all the years that lay ahead of them? Tiredly she went upstairs.

Paolo's wife had made up both beds on James's instructions. How had he explained the fact that a honeymooning couple required two double beds? Poppy wondered dully as she stripped off her clothes and showered off the dirt of their drive before pulling on clean underwear and crawling beneath the lavender-scented linen sheets.

Poppy smiled contentedly to herself as she slipped on her soft lawn cotton dress and glanced out of the bedroom window. The sky was a perfect, clear blue, promising another sunny day.

It was just as she let the loose folds of her dress fall round her hips and started to straighten up that she felt it—no more than the briefest flutter of sensation—a movement as delicate as the touch of a flower petal falling against her skin. She recognised it straight away, instinctively, calling out automatically, without thinking, 'James…quick…'

'What is it? What's wrong?' he demanded as he responded to her summons, pushing open her bedroom door and standing watching her.

She had dreaded this time—being isolated from everyone else, being alone with James, knowing that it was bound to reveal all the flaws in their relationship, all the reasons why they should not have married, and yet astonishingly the days had actually passed very quickly.

Her body, perhaps exhausted by the trauma of the weeks leading up to the wedding, had wanted only to relax and absorb the heat of the sun. Her instincts had caused her to focus not on the antipathy which existed between her and James but on her need to protect the life growing within her, and, yes, there had been times, moments when she had been heart-wrenchingly conscious of all that she had forfeited, all that she would never have—all that both of them had forfeited, she acknowledged, in committing themselves to a marriage without love—and then she had ached with pain and an intense but nebulous sense of loss and despair.

And yet, oddly, it had not been Chris whom she'd thought of at such times—his image, the memories of him cherished all through the years of her adolescence seemed to have lost their old power to give her succour.

'What is it?' James repeated, frowning.

As she looked back at him, noticing how very masculine he looked in a pair of soft, natural-coloured linen shorts and white T-shirt, his legs bare and very brown, his forearms surprisingly strongly muscled for a man who spent so much of his time seated at a desk, Poppy felt a sharp pang of unexpected emotion, an unexpected and devastating awareness of how intensely male James actually was.

It was, she felt, as though suddenly she was seeing him in a different way, as though she had walked into a room in which all the familiar objects had been moved around so that she saw them with fresh eyes—saw them and found that she had allowed habit to conceal the true depth of their appeal from her.

Her heart suddenly seemed to beat a little bit faster and she knew that she had flushed slightly.

'Don't you feel very well?' James was asking her. For the first few days of their stay he had insisted that she remain in bed in the morning until he had brought her a cup of tea and some plain biscuits.

Initially she had been irritated by such coddling, telling him curtly that she knew it was for the baby's sake and not hers, but these last couple of mornings she had actually found that she was quite enjoying being spoiled—a feeling which had sneaked up on her, catching her unawares.

'No. No, I feel fine...'

Now that he was here, frowning at her, obviously irritated at being interrupted, she was beginning to regret the impulse which had led to her calling him, and besides...

'It was nothing,' she told him, starting to turn away from him. 'I was just wondering if you still intended to go into town later on.'

'Yes, we need petrol and food and—'

He broke off as Poppy suddenly gave a small, startled gasp, hurrying to her side, his frown deepening as he touched her on one slim brown arm and said, 'Poppy, if you're not feeling well...'

'No, it isn't that,' she denied, her flush deepening to a happy glow of pleasure as she told him breathlessly, 'It's the baby; it's moving... Feel,' she added impetuously, taking hold of his hand and placing it on her body.

When she felt his resistance she immediately let go of him, snatching her fingers away from his as though the contact had burned her, quick, emotional tears she couldn't conceal filling her eyes as she tried to move back from him. Only James wouldn't let her, and, despite his initial withdrawal, his hand was now lying against her body, firm and warm and somehow oddly comforting and reassuring.

The baby must have thought so too, she decided hazily, because it suddenly shifted much more vigorously than it had before, causing Poppy to laugh out loud in maternal pride as she saw the look of mingled disbelief and awe in James's eyes.

An unfamiliar tinge of colour was darkening his face, making him look somehow different and vulnerable. He had lowered his head slightly, his gaze fixed on where his hand lay against her, and Poppy had an odd and devastating urge to reach out and hold him.

As she tried to absorb the full implications of what she was experiencing it seemed to Poppy that somehow or other the foundations of her whole world had shifted dangerously beneath her, leaving her very afraid and alone.

'Feels like she's going to inherit your talent for making her presence felt,' was James's only comment as he removed his hand and stepped back from her, but although his voice was steady Poppy could see how moved he was by what he had experienced.

'She?' she queried, her own voice husky. 'You want it to be a girl, then?'

'Yes,' James confirmed, his voice becoming familiarly harsh. He added, 'At least that way...' He shook his head, his mouth clamping shut on what he had been about to say.

It surprised Poppy that he should want a daughter; she had imagined that a man like James would only value sons. Despite the fact that they were cousins, she knew surprisingly little about him as a man, she recognised, but she was learning.

Oh, yes, she was learning, she acknowledged later in the day, lying in a chair in the garden, waiting for James to return from his trip into town. And not just about James.

The odd feelings that she had experienced this morning—that shaft of pure, liquid desire that had shot through her when she'd seen him standing in the bedroom doorway, that flood of heart-rocking emotion that had swamped her as she'd watched him reaching out to make contact with their child...

Frantically she tried to control and dismiss them by comparing them with the love she had always felt for

Chris, but somehow it was impossible for her to summon up anything more than a faint echo of the emotion which had dominated her entire life for so many years.

Even picturing Chris was an effort, and when she did the face that looked back at her through her imagination was simply that of her cousin and not her adored, longed-for lover. Her body and her heart were empty of the intensity of yearning that she had expected to feel.

Was it her pregnancy that was responsible for her lack of physical and emotional desire for Chris? She had desired James only a few hours earlier, she admitted, and she desired him now.

She moved her body uncomfortably on the sun-lounger but the torrent of heat engulfing her had nothing to do with the strength of the sun. She sat up, her face burning with the shock of her discovery. She couldn't want James. It was impossible.

But she wasn't an innocent girl any more; she was a woman—a woman who knew perfectly well how her body reacted when it was aroused, when it wanted and desired. There was no mistaking such signals, no confusing them with something else.

But James, of all men. Was it something to do with the fact that they had already been lovers?

Instinctively Poppy looked towards the front of the villa, searching for some sign of his return, her heart racing. She wanted James to come back, Poppy acknowledged; she felt vulnerable without him, afraid of her own feelings and what they might mean, alienated from her past and apprehensive about her future.

It might be the baby who was responsible for her see-sawing emotions, she tried to reassure herself; it had to be… And for her physical desire…?

* * *

'We'd better make a move if you want to eat out tonight,' James warned Poppy.

She was still sitting outside, watching the sun set, or so she told herself. In truth, since James had returned from town, she had actually been surreptitiously watching him, frantically trying to mask her avid need to keep him within sight as she desperately tried to understand what was happening to her.

Why, why should the most mundane of normal human attributes, such as the way he walked, the sheen of his skin, the fluid ease of his movements, even the warm brown curve of his throat, suddenly evoke such intense feelings and needs within her? Why, when she had known him all her life, should she suddenly have become so suffocatingly aware of him that he had only to come within five yards of her for her heart to beat frantically fast?

And why, when she had never, ever even thought such a thing before, should the mere idea of him touching her bring the tiny hairs up all over her body whilst her skin itself tingled in a silent agony of aching demand?

She had no answer to such questions, Poppy acknowledged soberly, there was no answer...

'I'll go and get changed,' she said now in response to James's comment and went indoors.

The sun had turned her skin a soft, warm peach-gold; her tan was much lighter and more delicate than James's. It must surely be her pregnancy that had given her flesh such a rounded feel and such a healthy glow, she thought as she caught sight of herself in the bedroom mirror.

Although the baby had barely started to show as much more than a slight swell, she was already beginning to feel more comfortable in softer clothes, and was glad now that she had let Sally persuade her into a pre-wedding shopping spree.

The fluid ice-cream-coloured dresses that Sally had chosen were not her normal style but oddly they seemed to suit her, although she had never thought of herself as being feminine enough to wear thin muslins that drifted over her body, sleeveless and scoop-necked so that they showed her tanned arms and clung subtly to the slightly fuller curves of her breasts.

'These will be wonderfully cool,' Sally had enthused. 'All you'll need to wear under them is a pair of briefs. Try this one,' she had insisted, rummaging along the rail and producing a fine, soft mint-green cotton dress with a drop waist and inverted pleats, which buttoned down the front.

'Oh, yes!' Sally had exclaimed when Poppy had reluctantly put it on. 'James will enjoy that...all those buttons. Men love buttons...'

Poppy remembered how her hands had trembled as she'd wrenched it off. She had decided not to buy it but somehow or other Sally had managed to get it included in her purchases, a fact which she had not discovered until it was too late and she had got it home.

Now, having showered, her hands trembled again as she put it on, but this time for a different reason.

'James will enjoy that...' Sally had said, and the sheer intensity of the surge of sensation that hit her as she closed her eyes and pictured him reaching for those small buttons, unfastening them to reveal the curves of her naked body, made Poppy shudder from head to foot and cry out against its torment.

'Poppy...?'

As she opened her eyes, her face flushing, she re-alised that James must have heard her.

'What is it? Is it the baby? Is something wrong?'

He walked towards her, his own torso bare, the cream linen trousers that he had pulled on so softly shaped that they revealed the taut hardness of his thighs as he moved.

Poppy watched him, mesmerised, her lips slightly parted as she absorbed every movement.

'James.'

He had come close enough for her to touch him now and dizzily she did so, lifting her hand to his arm and her glance to meet his, her eyes already darkening with need and desire.

'I want you,' she told him unsteadily. 'I want you, James. I...'

'Poppy...' he began, but she didn't want to hear what she knew he was going to say, her body trembling as her fingers tightened on his arm.

'No, no...I don't want you to say anything. I just want... James, I'm so afraid,' she told him shakily. 'I don't understand what's happening to me...why I should...'

She could feel him starting to pull away from her, his body tense.

She began to tremble, afraid both of being close to him, because of her desire for him, and of being apart from him, because he was the only stable, familiar thing in a world which had suddenly become alien and out of control.

As he leaned towards her, her lips inadvertently touched his skin, igniting her desire into a fireball of wrenching need. She moaned his name and started to press desperate, hungry kisses against his chest and throat, her control swamped by the scent and taste of him, by the feel of his skin beneath her mouth, the way he swallowed as her lips feverishly caressed his throat, the way his hands tightened on her shoulders as he reached out for her—not to push her away but to draw her nearer.

The thud of his heartbeat beneath her palm suddenly accelerated and his hand curved round the back of her neck, moving her slowly, guiding the clinging moistness of her mouth over his skin whilst his fingers tightened in her hair and he said something roughly under his breath.

And then suddenly he was the one kissing her, cupping her face and holding her immobile whilst his mouth covered hers. What was it about a certain man's kiss that was so sensually arousing, so impossible to resist? Poppy wondered dizzily as her mouth clung passionately to his, opened hotly beneath his, inviting the swift, fierce invasion of his tongue, her whole body shuddering in response to the effect that he was having on her.

Aching, she pressed herself closer to him, aware of his own arousal through the barriers of their clothes, wanting to be even closer to him, wanting…

'James, my dress…' As she whispered the words against his mouth, she opened her eyes and looked up into the brilliance of his. It felt as if she was looking right into the sun, she acknowledged dizzily, only even more dangerous.

She could feel the heat of her reaction to him flooding her body, filling it, making her ache for a different kind of fullness, a different fulfilment that could only come from him, from his touch, from his body. She could see him frowning as he started to look down her body at her dress, as though not understanding what she wanted.

'Take it off,' she whispered. 'I want to feel you next to me, James… All of you,' she insisted huskily.

Without knowing she had done so, she had already lifted his hand to the front of her dress, to its buttons, and now she watched, her body still, taut with aching anticipation, as he slowly reached out and started to unfasten them, his gaze never leaving hers as they slowly slid free.

When he reached the buttons that secured the dress across her breasts Poppy started to tremble. She was wearing nothing underneath.

'What is it you want from me, Poppy?' James asked her rawly, stopping what he was doing whilst he waited for her answer.

'You know what I want,' Poppy whispered back.

'Show me,' he demanded.

Boldly Poppy did so, taking his hand and placing it on her bare breast. The feel of his hand against her body, cupping the smooth warmth of her, his thumb-tip slowly caressing her already hard nipple, made her shiver with aching pleasure, her eyes closing as she leaned yearningly towards him, her spine arching.

'What is it you want, Poppy?' she heard him mutter hoarsely as his mouth caressed her throat and then started to move lower.

'Is it this…? This…?'

'Yes. Oh, yes… Yes. Yes, James…' Poppy responded, the words subsiding into a moan of relief as his lips finally covered a nipple, playing delicately with it at first, as though he was holding back, afraid of being too passionate with her and hurting her. But the increased sensitivity of the fullness of her breasts only made her ache more for the hot suckle of his mouth that her body could still remember.

She moved urgently against him, showing him without words what she wanted, clasping her hands behind his head as she held him against her body, unable to keep the spasms of pleasure from rippling betrayingly through her as she cried out to him that she couldn't bear any more, that she was afraid of the pleasure he was giving her, afraid of the intensity of what she was experiencing.

But James didn't appear to be listening to her. Instead his mouth was caressing her body, kissing every inch of the flesh he exposed as he continued unfastening her buttons, pausing only when he reached the small swell of her belly, his hand covering the place where the child rested. He lifted his face to look at her and then, without a word, picked her up and carried her over to the bed, pushing her dress off her shoulders so that it slid to the floor before he laid her gently down.

For a long time he simply looked at her, and to Poppy, who had never once in her whole life imagined any man looking at her like that, never mind James, it came as a shocking revelation to recognise that instead of wanting to cover herself from him, instead of feeling self-conscious about her nakedness, she felt a sense of pride and joy in knowing that he was looking at her, in knowing just why his glance kept on returning to her gently rounded belly, in knowing just by looking at him that the sight of her aroused him.

She had never guessed that it was possible for a woman to feel so sexually strong, so sexually powerful and yet, at the same time, so vulnerable, so much in need, achingly soft and ready inside.

'James…'

She released his name on a soft, yearning sigh, reaching out her arms to him and then stopping, her face flushing tellingly as she whispered to him, 'Take off your clothes. I…I want to see you.'

For a moment she thought he might refuse, but then, as she saw the expression in his eyes, she realised that something in what she had said had touched him, reached him on some deeply personal level, almost as though her words had pleased him emotionally as well as physically.

Unblinkingly she watched as he unfastened his belt and then removed his clothes, her eyes wide, her face hot as she absorbed every detail of him.

It shocked her to feel an unmistakable frisson of female pride and smugness in knowing that, powerful and male though his body was, it could still be contained within hers, aroused by hers…as it was now.

She wanted to reach out and touch him but he was already leaning over her, bending his head as he gently kissed the small dome of her stomach.

The sensation of his mouth circling her navel was so unexpectedly erotic that her eyes widened still further at the shock of it, her body starting to tremble as she felt him removing her briefs.

How was it that whereas such a very short space of time ago she could not possibly have envisaged him touching her this kind of intimacy between them now— just the accidental touch of his hands against her skin— was enough to arouse her to the point where she was shamefully aware of just how ready her body was for him?

So ready that there was no point in dissembling, in acting out some kind of coy mock reluctance, in doing anything other than reaching out helplessly towards

him and closing her eyes with a shuddering sigh of ecstasy as he took hold of her and slowly fitted his body
to hers, his actions, his movements controlled and gentle and yet, at the same time, so strongly powerful that
her body was convulsing with light spasms of pleasure
just at the feel of him within her.

James made love to her again later, this time with his
mouth and not with his body, easily disproving her assertion that she was already satisfied.

And then, before he could stop her, she, with great
daring, did the same for him, shocked by the intensity
of her own pleasure when he cried out beneath the un-
tutored caress of her hands and mouth, trying to stop
her before being overpowered by her gentle insistence
and his own flooding desire.

For the first time Poppy slept within the curve of his
arm, her sleepy mind knowing that such intimacy felt
good and yet warning her at the same time that such
feelings made her very vulnerable. But Poppy was too
relaxed, too sleepy to heed that warning.

CHAPTER NINE

'WHEN I look at you, I'm not so sure that Chris and I made the right decision in opting not to start our family for a few years,' Sally commented enviously to Poppy as they shopped together one Saturday afternoon, re-iterating the sentiment she'd expressed on the day of Poppy and James's wedding.

She stopped to draw Poppy's attention to the window of a small, exclusive babywear boutique before continuing hesitantly, 'It's different for you and James, I know. For one thing, James is so much more...so much more ready to be a father than Chris. You can tell how pleased he is about the baby.'

'Yes,' Poppy agreed quietly.

And it was true. There was no doubt that James wanted and already loved his child, but he certainly didn't feel the same way about its mother. Ever since that time in Italy when she had begged him to make love to her, he had held her at a distance, becoming so remote from her that now, six weeks later, it was virtually impossible for Poppy to imagine that they had ever been lovers; but these were things she couldn't say to Sally, who believed that they were deeply in love, or to anyone else.

The reality of her marriage was a secret she had to

keep from everyone, the reality of her feelings for James a secret she had to keep from him—a secret she had had to keep from him ever since they had last been together, last made love!

She could still remember how it had felt to wake up in the morning with James beside her, to experience that extraordinary, purifying rush of love and self-knowledge, to reach out to touch him with it shining in her eyes and then to have *him* wake up and turn away from her, rebuff her, reject her.

And she had thought back to the evening before and been filled with mortification at the way she had behaved, the things she had done, the things she had said, and, even more painful to endure, the way she had felt.

She suspected now that she must have known the truth then, even though she had refused to acknowledge it. Certainly now when she looked back there seemed to be no other reason for what she had done, but in mitigation she had to admit that it would have been hard for the girl she had been—the girl who had stubbornly and publicly insisted that she could only love one man and that that man was Chris—to confess that she had been wrong and that everyone else had been right, that she had confused infatuation with love and that when she had finally discovered the difference it had been too late to turn back the clock.

If only she could. The pain of her infatuation for Chris was nothing when compared with the agony of heart and soul that she was enduring now, knowing that she loved James and knowing equally well that he did not love her.

She knew quite well why James had suddenly decided that he needed to spend so much more time away, take so many overnight business trips, and it had nothing to do with the fact, as everyone else seemed to suppose, that he wanted to clear some time to be with her and their baby, to be with her for his or her birth and in the weeks afterwards.

She supposed that it was another indication that she had finally, if somewhat belatedly, joined the real, adult world that she had not even tried to question James about his actions, about his withdrawal and his silence; that she had simply bowed her head and accepted the fact that he did not love her.

She was too aware now to attempt to deceive herself into believing that he might somehow, implausibly, fall in love with her as she had done with Chris. He wouldn't. And knowing that she loved him, knowing just why her body ached so much with wanting him, had also made it impossible for her to try to reach out to him physically through sex. It would be like drinking contaminated water—initially thirst-quenching but also potentially harmful, destructive, carrying with it the power to destroy her.

Having sex with James might temporarily ease the physical ache within her body, but it wouldn't satisfy her emotional need for him, and could, in fact, only underline it. And so she had rigidly enforced a strict control over herself, keeping as much physical distance between her and James as she could, in public as well as in private. And only on the nights when he wasn't there did she allow herself the luxury of tears, of crying herself to sleep. But then there were plenty of those.

She wondered tiredly what excuses he would make for being away so much once the baby was born. No doubt he would think of something and she would smile and concentrate her love on their baby, knowing that for as long as their marriage lasted he or she would be her only outlet for it.

James was due to go away again this evening and she had deliberately delayed returning from her shopping trip with Sally so that he would have left before she got home.

Automatically she found herself driving more slowly as she approached the house, dreading seeing his car. Thankfully it wasn't there. Relieved, Poppy parked her own car and hurried into the house. Despite the fact that she hadn't wanted him to be there, the house felt achingly empty without him, like her heart...like her life.

She had just finished making herself a cup of tea when she heard the doorbell ring. Frowning, she went to answer it, and was surprised to see Chris standing outside.

'Come in,' she invited. 'James isn't here but...'

'It's you I've come to see,' he told her, looking slightly awkward.

Poppy frowned again. Since her marriage to James she and Chris had not really been alone together. She winced, remembering how, on her return from honeymoon, she had not even noticed that Chris was away from the office until James had commented on the fact.

'It's...it's about Sally,' Chris told her after he had followed her into the kitchen and she had poured him a cup of tea.

'Sally?' Poppy queried.

'Yes...yes, it's this baby thing. She's got it into her head that she wants a baby,' he blurted out. 'She knew when we got married that... I'm not like James. Of course I want a family, but not yet... I want to have Sally to myself for a while but she won't listen to me.'

'Oh, Chris, I'm so sorry,' Poppy sympathised. 'But

it's Sally you should really be talking to about this,' she advised him gently, 'not me...'

It was odd how the boyish look which had once caught so painfully at her heart now just made her feel cousinly—motherly almost.

'Yes, I suppose you are right,' Chris agreed ruefully, adding warmly, 'It's good to see you and James so happy together, Poppy... You've always been special to me,' he added in a muffled voice, leaning forward to give her a fierce hug that took her breath away as well as her balance.

Neither of them heard the door open or saw James come in until he rasped, 'What the hell's going on here?'

It was Chris who answered him, apparently oblivious to his fury and Poppy's anxiety as he responded cheerfully, 'Sorry, James; I just came round to have a chat with Poppy. I shan't forget what you said,' he told her, before glancing at his watch and announcing, 'I'd better get back; Sally will be wondering where I am.'

Poppy trembled as she saw the way James watched her as Chris closed the door and left.

'And what exactly was it that you said, that he won't forget?' he demanded menacingly. 'Or can I guess? Were you telling him how much you still love him, Poppy? How much you still want him?'

'No,' Poppy cried out in shocked protest. 'No, James, you've got it all wrong. It wasn't anything like that... Chris—'

'Don't lie to me, Poppy,' James interrupted her harshly. 'There isn't any point. We both know how you feel about Chris. How did you get him to come here? What did you tell him? That you wished he'd been the one you'd married, that he was the one you wanted when you lay in my arms—is that what you told him?'

'No,' Poppy denied, alarmed by the violence in his voice. 'No, of course not. James, you've—'

'No! What did you tell him? Did you tell him, perhaps, about the way you begged me to make love to you...about the way you pleaded with me to satisfy you?'

Poppy stared at him in shock. She had never seen him so angry, so out of control.

'My God, you couldn't wait long enough to make sure I was safely out of the way before you got him here, could you?' he demanded. 'How long has it been going on, Poppy? How often has he been coming round when I'm not here...?'

Suddenly Poppy had had enough, her shock giving way to pain as she retaliated bitterly, 'Why should *you* care? You're never here and—'

'And Chris, of course, is. What did you do to get him here—pretend you needed a cousin's shoulder to cry on? What exactly are you hoping for, Poppy? You know he doesn't want you.'

'Yes, I do,' she agreed starkly, her eyes registering her anguish as she mentally added, And, much more importantly, neither do you.

'Chris came here to talk to me about Sally,' she told James quietly, her anger subsiding under the weight of her pain. 'He's concerned because she wants to start a family when they'd agreed that they would wait for a while.'

'A family... Is that when you told him that she's not the only one to want his child...? Is *that* why he told you that you were very special to him...?'

Poppy couldn't conceal her small flush as he repeated the words Chris had said to her.

'Chris just came here for advice…as a cousin,' she told him shakily.

'A cousin! Is that why you were in his arms?' James asked sarcastically.

'James, where are you going?' Poppy protested as he pushed past her and into the hall.

'To get what I came back for,' he told her grimly.' Knowing how much you dislike coming home to find me here, I left in too much of a hurry and forgot some papers I need and so I had to come back for them.'

Poppy heard the door slam as he went into the small room he used as a study. She was still standing in the kitchen when he walked back in.

'James, we need to talk,' she told him bravely. 'We can't go on like this.'

'So what do you suggest we do? Get a divorce?' he demanded savagely. 'Get out of my way, Poppy,' he advised her angrily, 'before I do something we'll both regret.' He paused in the doorway to turn round and tell her brutally, 'And I warn you now, if you do ever find a way of persuading my brother to fulfil those adolescent fantasies of yours, I promise I'll make the pair of you sorry you were ever born. You don't really love him, Poppy; you don't *know* what real love is.'

No, I don't love him, Poppy agreed silently, listening to the engine of his car fire as he started it, the tears pouring down her face. I love you.

And, as for real love, she knew what it was to feel it but she certainly didn't know what it was like to receive it. 'What do you suggest we do?' James had challenged her. 'Get a divorce?' Did that mean that he was regretting their marriage, that he wanted to bring it to an end?

Unable to endure the loneliness of her own home, Poppy spent the rest of the weekend with her parents, explaining away her pale face and preoccupied manner by admitting wanly that she was missing James, which was, after all, the truth—or at least part of it.

On Monday morning, although she had a splitting headache, brought on, she suspected, by having spent half the night crying into her pillow, she insisted on going into work despite her mother's suggestion that she stay at home, but by mid-morning the pain in her head had become so intense that she finally gave in and told Chris that she intended to go home.

'You can't drive,' Chris told her after one look at her too pale face. 'I'll take you. When is James due home?'

Poppy turned away, unwilling to admit that she didn't know. She could have found out easily enough, she assumed, by asking his secretary but her pride wouldn't allow her to betray how little she knew about her husband's movements.

Chris had just pulled out onto the main road when it happened. He had to stop to avoid a cyclist and the driver of the car behind them didn't realise what had happened in time and ran into the back of them.

Poppy felt the impact jerk her forward in her seat against the restraint of her seat belt, automatically crying out both against the sharp, searing agony and in fear for her baby, the pain catapulting her into a pit of smothering darkness as she slid into a deep faint.

The first thing she heard when she came round was the sound of an ambulance, although she didn't realise then that it was coming for her.

'Don't move, Poppy,' Chris urged her anxiously as she tried to struggle against the restraining belt.

At some point he must have got out of the car, Poppy recognised, because he was now standing beside the open passenger door, whilst another man, a stranger, peered in at her and blustered defensively, 'It was only a little bit of a knock… Can't have done that much damage.'

'She's pregnant,' she heard Chris hiss angrily back. 'My God, man, why the hell couldn't you have watched what you were doing?'

'Damn cyclist.' The man crumpled. 'It was all his fault.'

'I doubt that the police will see it that way,' Chris warned him grimly.

Poppy wished they would both go away and stop arguing. The sound of their voices was making her head hurt and she dared not even think about what that agonisingly sharp pain she could feel in her body might portend.

'James…James…where are you…?'

She didn't even know she had said the words out loud until the driver of the other car asked, 'Who's this James?'

'Her husband,' Chris told him sharply. 'And I wouldn't want to be in your shoes when he finds out what's happened.'

Poppy was shaking with shock by the time the police car and the ambulance finally arrived.

'Sorry, love,' the ambulanceman apologised as he gently helped Poppy from the car, refusing to let her walk, insisting she get on the stretcher instead. 'It's these roadworks, see; we couldn't get through them.'

'What happened exactly?' Poppy heard him asking Chris, and she could see the way he frowned when the policeman muttered something to him about the car having been pushed along the road for quite some distance.

However, there was only calm reassurance in his

eyes as he turned back to Poppy and told her gently, 'Best get you where they can take a proper look at you, love.'

'I'll come with you...' Chris began, but Poppy shook her head.

'No... There's no need; I don't want you,' she told Chris huskily. 'I want James...' Her eyes filled with tears she couldn't control, her whole body shaking with them.

Never mind me; what about my baby? she wanted to scream as the ambulanceman asked her if she was in any pain anywhere. The sharp pain she had felt before had subsided but the baby was ominously still and Poppy, who had felt exasperated some nights when she had been kept awake by its kicking, prayed desperately now for it to move.

The drive to the hospital seemed to take for ever and Poppy saw the concerned looks that the two ambulancemen exchanged when she was sick twice on the way there. The nurse who admitted her was kind as well as efficient, promising to get in touch with Poppy's parents and assuring her at the same time that babies were tougher than one thought.

'Let's get you sorted out first,' she told Poppy, adding, 'That's a nasty bump you've got on your forehead... does it hurt?'

Poppy, who hadn't even realised until then that she had bumped her head, touched her temple and winced as her fingers came away sticky with blood.

By the time her mother and father arrived she was tucked up in bed.

'Oh, darling...how do you feel?' her mother asked her anxiously as she hurried to her side.

'I'm all right,' Poppy assured her. 'It's the baby.'

She saw the look her parents exchanged and her anxiety increased.

'They keep telling me not to worry...that it's best to rest...but I haven't felt her kick for ages and I had this awful pain. I want James,' she told her mother bleakly.

'Chris is doing his best to find him, darling,' her mother tried to reassure her. 'He'd left the people he was visiting before Chris could get in touch with him and we can't get through to him on his mobile phone.'

'He won't use it in the car,' Poppy told her fretfully. 'He says it's too dangerous.'

The afternoon passed in a haze of examinations and hushed conversations out of her earshot which left her feeling increasingly anxious. The baby still hadn't moved and she was growing afraid that something might have happened to it. To her...to James's child, James's daughter.

Fresh tears rolled down her face. Her parents had volunteered to stay with her but she had sent them home. It was James she wanted. Only James.

She closed her eyes, whispering his name, her hands folded protectively across her belly. If only she had been holding their baby like that earlier, it might not have been hurt, she thought miserably.

She tensed as the door of her room opened, but it wasn't James who came in.

'Chris,' she said weakly in disappointment, subsiding back against the pillows. 'Where's James? Have you been able to contact him?'

'Not yet.' He tried to smile, but Poppy could see how anxious he was. 'Don't worry.'

He tried to comfort her, taking hold of her hand and patting it, but, weak from shock and fear, Poppy snatched it back, telling him crossly, 'Don't...don't; it isn't you I want, it's James.' As she started to cry harder she was distantly aware of Chris ringing the bell for the nurse and of her suddenly appearing and the two of them talking in lowered voices. She strained to hear what they were saying.

'She wants her husband,' the nurse told Chris. 'She's in a very unstable condition, and we're rather concerned about the foetal heartbeat…'

'We're doing our best to find him,' she heard Chris respond. 'He should have been back by now. God knows where the hell he is,' he added feelingly.

Poppy closed her eyes. James had gone; he didn't care about what happened to her. If anything should happen to their baby, he wouldn't even know and she would have lost them both. Without them, what was the point in her going on? She could hardly swallow past the huge lump of misery blocking her throat.

'They want me to go now,' she heard Chris telling her awkwardly as he responded to the nurse's brief nod and stood up.

Poppy didn't care if he stayed or went. Without James she was alone anyway, would always be alone.

At some point she must have drifted off to sleep. She knew that the nurse had administered some kind of sedative—'to rest the baby', she had told Poppy firmly when she had tried to object.

Now, as she opened her eyes, she realised that the headache and sickness that she had felt earlier had gone but that her body felt stiff and sore and the graze on her temple throbbed painfully.

The room was in darkness, but as she turned her head she realised that Chris was there, standing just inside the door, and that his arrival was probably the reason why she had woken up.

'Poppy...' Chris began, but Poppy turned her head away from him.

'Go away, Chris,' she told him quietly.

As she heard the door close behind him she let out a small sob.

'James...James, where are you? I love you so much,' she whispered under her breath. 'I love you both so much,' she added as she touched the still bump of her stomach. 'James...'

'Yes, Poppy, I'm here.'

The shock of hearing his voice made her stiffen and then turn her head so quickly that she winced in sudden pain.

'James!' she repeated in disbelief, her eyes fastening hungrily on his shadowy outline in the darkness, as though she was afraid to believe that he was actually there. 'When...? How...?' she began, trembling as he sat down next to her.

'Chris had left a message for me at home,' he told her sombrely, then emotion broke through the controlled tautness of his voice as he exploded, 'My God, Poppy, how—?'

'It wasn't Chris's fault,' she told him quickly. 'It was an accident; he...' She had started to shake violently, her finger picking anxiously at the coverlet until James reached out and took hold of her.

'You're cold,' he said, but Poppy shook her head, dismissing her own injuries as she told him quickly, 'James, it's our baby... I can't feel her kicking any more. They keep telling me not to worry and that she's all right...but how can she be all right when she's so still? Oh, James, I'm so afraid for her,' she whispered helplessly. 'She's so small, so vulnerable and I love her so much.'

'Chris said that you told him to go away, that you only wanted me. Is that true?' James asked huskily.

'Yes,' Poppy admitted, and raised her head off the pillow to ask him uncertainly, 'Where were you?'

'On my way to Italy…to the villa.'

'What…? Why?'

'You are not the only one to indulge in pointless fantasies, you know,' James told her obliquely. 'The only difference between us is that I've had a hell of a lot more experience at doing it.'

'Fantasies? What fantasies?' Poppy demanded uncertainly.

'Oh, the usual kind,' James told her gravely. 'That the woman I love loves me back, that she wants me, that in the darkness of the night, in the privacy of our shared bed, she turns to me and tells me that she aches for me to touch her, to love her and to go on loving her for ever.'

As she listened to him, Poppy's body started to stiffen in anguished shock.

'Who is she…this woman?' she asked shakily. James was in love with someone else. Why had she never guessed…realised…? 'Do I know her?'

'Yes, you know her,' James admitted, but he wasn't looking at her any longer, Poppy recognised. He was looking at her body instead.

'The baby!' she suddenly gasped in delight. 'She's moving… Oh, James, she's moving, she's all right, she's…' Even now Poppy couldn't bring herself to say the word 'alive' and to admit by saying it just what she had been dreading. 'Oh, James.' As she clutched his hand, happy tears poured down her face.

'Why did you want me with you and not Chris, Poppy?' James asked her as he reached out his hand and covered the small bulge.

'You're…you're my husband,' Poppy told him, unable to bring herself to look properly at him. 'My baby's—our baby's—father and…'

'And?' James prompted.

He wasn't looking at her. He was still looking at her stomach, which was perhaps why she suddenly found the courage to tell him.

'And because I love you,' Poppy admitted quietly. 'But I know that isn't what you want,' she added hastily. 'I'm not an adolescent any more, James. I do know now what truly loving someone means. If you want me to… to set you free so that you can go to her…to the woman you love…then I'll…' she said bravely, then stopped to bite down hard on her bottom lip as her emotion threatened to overwhelm her.

'Go to her? I'm already with her,' James told her softly.

'Already with her?' Poppy's heart started to thump heavily as she looked indignantly from the closed door to his face. 'You've brought her here…now…?'

'Oh, Poppy.' Suddenly, unbearably, he was actually laughing at her—laughing as he stood up and then leaned over the bed, gathering her up in his arms to hold her close and touch her tenderly.

'You're the one I love, the one I've always loved. Are you really so blind that you never knew it?'

'You love me…? But you can't,' she protested. 'You've always been so angry with me, so I—'

'Because that was the only way I had of defending myself, protecting myself from the pain of knowing that you only had eyes for Chris. I fell in love with you about the same time that you fell in love with him.'

'But if you love me, why—?' Poppy stopped, her face suddenly crimsoning.

'Why what?' James pressed.

'Why did you act the way you did after...after...? Why did you behave so coldly to me after we'd made love?' she asked him huskily. 'You must have known how much I wanted you.' Her colour deepened. 'I thought you were... I thought you didn't want me any more, that I'd disgusted you—'

'Disgusted me?' James interrupted her. 'Oh, Poppy, if only you knew what it did to me when you told me that you wanted me. You'll never know how close I came that night to telling you how I felt, but I couldn't get out of my mind the way you'd told me that you wanted me to be Chris...that you'd believed that first time that I *was* Chris.

'I stopped being intimate with you because I had no choice. I knew that it was only a matter of time before my control broke and I told you how I felt and I couldn't lay that burden on you. Not after everything else I'd done.'

'Everything else... What else?' Poppy demanded.

'Making love to you when I knew you couldn't really want me...when I knew that you were still a virgin and unlikely to be using any form of birth control...and, having done so once, being unable to resist repeating the offence and knowing when I did how it increased the likelihood that you would conceive.'

'I think I knew I had,' Poppy told him in awe, before admitting half-shyly, 'There was something—a feeling, a sort of knowing.'

'I didn't set out to force you into a position where you'd have to marry me,' James told her, 'but, once I knew the possibility was there, there was no way I was not going to use it. I told myself that it was me who'd made love to you, me your body wanted, even if your heart remained locked against me, and that somehow I'd find a way of making you see that you couldn't possibly want me so much physically without there being some possibility that you might come to love me.'

'I probably already loved you, even before…before we made love,' Poppy told him hesitantly. 'When I was young… Before… You were always… It was *you* I loved best then,' she told him softly, 'but somehow when I started to grow up…'

'Everyone goes through teenage crushes,' James told her gently.

'I can't understand how I ever thought that what I felt for Chris was really love,' Poppy said. 'When I look back now…'

She stopped talking as James bent his head and kissed her.

'James…? James?' she demanded, shaking his arm as she broke the kiss.

'What is it?'

'I want to go home,' she told him unsteadily. 'Please make them let me go home…with you…'

'Are you sure?' James asked her quietly, searching her face and then cupping it in his hands to kiss her— holding her as though he simply couldn't bear to let her go, Poppy recognised with a sense of wonder.

Now that she knew the truth it amazed her that she had not seen it for herself. The love she had thought could never be hers was there, displayed in his every touch, his every look. It wasn't just with words that love was communicated, Poppy knew with sudden wisdom.

Looking back, she could see that it was perhaps no wonder that she had responded physically to James the way she had that first time they had made love; her body had recognised the truth that her mind had been too stubborn and perhaps a little too immature to want to see. There was no point in even trying to compare what she felt for James with the feelings she had had for Chris.

Chris!

She gave James a rueful look.

'I was horrid to poor Chris,' she told him solemnly.

'Good,' James replied unsympathetically, and then relented to smile lovingly at her.

'Do you think things will be all right with him and Sally,' Poppy asked him anxiously, 'now that she's decided she wants a baby?'

'Chris and Sally love one another; there's no doubt about that. They'll find a way of working things out.'

'I'm so glad you're here,' Poppy whispered as he bent his head to kiss her again. 'And so,' she added, 'is your daughter. Oh, James—' she clung to him, trembling slightly '—if anything had happened...'

'Don't,' he begged her. 'If anything happened to you, I don't think I could bear to go on living.'

The nurse clicked her tongue reprovingly when she came into the room and found her patient wrapped in her husband's arms.

'I want to go home,' Poppy told her.

'Well, I don't know about that,' she said disapprovingly. 'You're supposed to be resting...'

The doctor, however, when summoned by James, took a more benign view. There was no reason why Poppy shouldn't go home, just so long as she took things easy for a few days, he declared.

'Don't worry...she will,' James assured him, adding in an undertone to Poppy, his face mock-severe, 'Even if I have to stay in bed with her to make her do so...'

'No more business trips away from home?' Poppy

questioned James some twenty minutes later as he gently helped her into his car.

'None,' he assured her firmly. 'From now on Chris can handle those.'

'Poor Sally,' Poppy protested.

'Well, perhaps not all of them,' James allowed. 'But the only way I shall be working away from home in future is if my wife comes with me.'

'There's just one condition,' Poppy told him mockingly.

'And that is?' James demanded, his eyebrows lifting in a return of his old hauteur.

'That the head of the company and his translator get to share a double room, and a double bed,' Poppy purred. 'All in the name of financial economy, of course.'

'Of course,' James agreed, and then added in a husky voice as he saw the way Poppy was looking at him, 'You're supposed to be resting—remember?'

EPILOGUE

HOLLY JOY was born four days before Christmas, just in time for her already doting father to take her and her mother home with him to spend their first Christmas together as a family.

'She's perfect,' James told Poppy lovingly on Christmas Eve as he watched her feeding their small daughter. 'But not as perfect as you.'

Poppy laughed.

'I can remember a time when "perfect" was the last adjective you would have used to describe me,' she reminded him. She laughed again as Holly Joy squeaked her protest at having her enjoyment of her supper disrupted by her father's determination to kiss her mother but that laughter was soon stilled as she responded to the love and passion she could feel in James's kiss.

'Do you realise that I wanted our baby to be a girl because I saw it as a way of loving a miniature version of you?' he murmured, and Poppy, listening to his confession, felt tears forming as she understood just how much her husband wanted—had always wanted—her love.

Around her neck she was wearing the creamy pearls which James had given her to celebrate their baby's birth, and amongst the presents which had arrived for Holly Joy from her aunt Sally had been a handmade

silver bracelet in an unusual design of flowers and ribbons, rather like a bridal wreath.

Poppy had also received from her a bouquet of flowers which she'd instantly recognised. How long ago it
seemed now since she had caught Sally's wedding bouquet and yet, in reality, it was barely ten months.

'It didn't seem appropriate to send you this when you
and James married; I don't know why,' Sally had written on the accompanying card. 'But now it does. Two
down, one to go...'

Poppy laughed as she showed James the card.

'Well, she may have got her way with me,' she told
him, 'but she's not going to find it so easy with Star.
She really is anti-marriage and anti-commitment. Still,
two out of three isn't bad.'

'Mmm,' James murmured, gathering her in his arms
after she had put Holly back in her cot. 'Right now I've
got far more interesting things I want to do than talk
about Sally's manipulation of superstition.'

'Such as?' Poppy teased.

'Come here and let me show you...'

Laughingly she did.

* * * * *

Too Wise to Wed?

PENNY JORDAN

PROLOGUE

ANOTHER wedding celebration. Star scowled as she studied the elegant invitation before throwing it onto her desk.

She was very tempted to make some excuse not to go—but if she did her friend Sally was bound to pounce on her absence as a sure indication that she, Star, was afraid that the old-fashioned superstition that Sally had practised on the occasion of her own wedding might have some potency to it after all.

Which was all nonsense of course. Just because the other two women who had caught Sally's bridal bouquet along with her had within six months of Sally's own wedding become brides themselves, it did not mean that she, Star, was going to fall into the same trap. No way. Not ever.

She scowled again, even more horribly this time. The fact that Poppy, the other bridesmaid at Sally's wedding, had got married had not come as all that much of a surprise to Star, but the announcement that Sally's stepmother had also married—just a small, private wedding—and was now holding a celebration party with her new husband for all his friends and relations in America... Uneasily, Star stared out of her study window. It so happened that business was taking her across to the States so she could, in fact, make it to the party, and if she didn't go...

If she didn't go Sally would tease her unmercifully about being afraid that there was something in that stupid, old-fashioned tradition that whoever caught the bride's bouquet would be the next to marry.

But weddings were not her thing at all—she had only gone to Sally's because Sally was her oldest and closest friend. After all, she had attended far too many of her father's to have any faith any longer in the durability of the supposedly lifelong vows that people exchanged in the heat of their emotional and physical desire for one another, their compelling need to believe that those feelings would last for ever.

No, weddings, or parties to celebrate them, were quite definitely *not* her scene, and marriage even less so.

But, that being the case, what *had* she to fear in going to Claire's party? Wasn't she, her will, her determination, stronger than any foolish superstition? Of course she was, and, just to prove it, throwing open her window, Star took a deep breath and said firmly and loudly, 'I am not going to fall in love. I am not going to get married. Not now. Not ever. So there.

'Now,' she muttered as she closed the window, ignoring the startled and slightly nervous glance of the elderly lady walking across the lawn in front of the apartment block, 'do your worst, because, I promise you, it won't make any difference to me and it certainly won't change *my* mind. Nothing could. Nothing and *no one.*'

CHAPTER ONE

STAR surveyed the crowd of happy well-wishers surrounding the recently married couple with cynical contempt.

How many of those exclaiming enthusiastically about the happiness that lay ahead of Claire and Brad now that they were married could truthfully put their hands on their hearts and swear that their marriages, their permanent relationships, had truly enriched their lives, had truly made them happy?

If they'd known what she was thinking they would no doubt have questioned the ability of someone who had never been married and who was so vehemently and vocally opposed to any kind of emotional commitment to pronounce on the state of marriage at all, much less to criticise it, but Star believed that she had access to far more experience of what marriage actually was than most of them would be able to boast.

'Star. Claire said you were going to be here.'

Silently Star suffered the enthusiastic hug of her oldest friend.

Sally's voice voice muffled slightly by the thick, smooth, shiny sweep of Star's dark red hair as she continued to hug her whilst telling her, 'I'm so pleased about Ma and Brad, I just wish she wasn't going to be living so far away. It was a wonderful idea of Brad's family, wasn't it, to organise this post-wedding get-together and to invite us all over to share it?

'Has Brad confirmed officially yet that you're getting the PR contract for the British distribution side of things?' Sally asked as she released her.

'Not yet,' Star told her calmly.

'But you are going to get the contract,' Sally insisted.

'It looks likely,' Star agreed sedately.

'There's only you left now,' Sally teased her friend, changing tack. 'Out of the three of you who caught my bouquet, two are now married, despite the vow that all of you made to stay single.'

Star gave a small, dismissive shrug.

'It was inevitable that Poppy would marry James once she had got over her adolescent crush on Chris, and as for your stepmother...' Star looked thoughtfully towards Claire, who was standing arm in arm with her new husband, her head inclined towards him as they exchanged a small, intimate smile.

'You can stop looking at me like that,' she warned Sally firmly. 'I'm afraid *I* fully intend to be the exception to the rule, Sally. I intend to stay very firmly single and free of any kind of long-term emotional commitment.'

'What if you fall in love?' Sally probed spiritedly.

Star gave her a contemptuously bitter look.

'Fall in love? You mean like my mother, who has fallen in love so many times that even she must have lost count, and who uses that state as an excuse for submerging herself and everyone close to her in a swamp of emotional chaos? Or were you meaning that I should, perhaps, follow my *father's* example and show my "love" by begetting children whose existence becomes virtually forgotten when he moves on to a new love and a new commitment?'

'Oh, Star,' Sally protested remorsefully, reaching out to touch her friend's slim, tanned wrist in a gesture of female sympathy. 'I'm sorry. I—'

'Don't be,' Star interrupted her crisply. 'I'm not. In fact

I'm grateful to both my parents for showing me reality rather than allowing me to believe in a false ideology. All right, so *my* parents might have taken to unconventional lengths the modern view that we each have a right to pursue our emotional happiness, no matter what the cost, but tell me honestly, Sally, how many couples *you* can name who remain genuinely happy in their relationships once the initial gloss has worn off.'

'You're such a cynic,' Sally complained on a sigh.

'No,' Star punched back. 'I'm a realist. I accept what, at heart, most women know but cannot allow themselves to accept—that the male human being is genetically programmed to spread his seed, his genes, just as far as he physically can, to impregnate as many women as he possibly can, and *that* is why he finds it biologically impossible to remain faithful to one woman.

'And that is also why, in my opinion, if a woman wants to be happy she has to adopt his way of life, to enjoy herself sexually when it suits her and not him, to choose her sexual partners because they please her and to refrain from becoming emotionally involved with them, and to remember, if and when she chooses to have a child, that the chances are that she will be the sole emotional support to that child—!'

'Oh, Star, that's not fair,' Sally interrupted her sadly, wincing when she saw the sardonic eyebrow that Star raised in silent mockery to her protest. 'All right, I know that there *are* men like your... Men who do... Men who can't be faithful to one woman,' Sally agreed. 'But not *all* men are like that.'

'Aren't they? But then you would say that, wouldn't you?' Star asked her grimly. 'After all, you've got a vested interest in believing it, haven't you?' she added. 'Speaking of which, how are things between you and Chris at the moment?'

'They're fine,' Sally told her quickly.

Star knew her so well. Too well at times. Star knew how

to get under her skin and pinpoint those small, tell-tale areas of vulnerability. She always had done and it didn't even help Sally to remind herself that Star's mode of defending herself and her own vulnerability was to go on the attack. Sally knew how much Star hated any reminders, any discussions about her emotional history, and how prone she was to fending them off by targeting her 'attackers' own weak points.

Not that her relationship with Chris was weak or under threat in any way, Sally hastily assured herself. It was true that just lately Chris had been working longer hours and away from home rather a lot, but...

Sally, suddenly realising that Star had switched her attention to someone else, turned round to see what had distracted her and was rather puzzled when she could see nothing out of the ordinary.

'I must go,' she told Star. 'Chris will be wondering where I am.'

'Mmm...' Star agreed, steadily returning the appreciative interest of a man standing several yards away.

He had been watching her virtually all afternoon, despite his outward absorption in the woman clinging determinedly to his side.

She had two children with her, both of them petite and fair-haired like her. She was quite obviously their mother. Was he their father? Star gave a small shrug. What concern was that of hers?

She was not the kind of woman who deliberately made a play for another woman's man, enjoying the challenge of taking from and competing with her own sex, but neither did she necessarily believe that it was up to her to be the guardian of someone else's relationship.

As a young adult in her late teens and early twenties, she had gone through a phase of sexual experimentation with a variety of short-lived partners. But these days she was ex-

tremely choosy—too picky, in fact, or so she had been told—
and she was very strict about adhering to a certain set of rules
and standards that she had evolved for herself—not, perhaps,
the same rules that society hypocritically pretended to live by,
but she stuck to hers and they were important to her.

For a start, her partner had to have a clean bill of health and
a willingness to prove it. And he certainly had to understand
that all she intended to share with him was her sexual self.

She had no inhibitions or hang-ups about the physical side
of her nature. Why should she have? If nature hadn't intended
a woman to enjoy sexual pleasure then she wouldn't have
equipped her with the means to do so, and, that being the
case, it was more of a sin, in Star's book, to deny herself that
sexual pleasure than to enforce on herself a set of antiquated
rules which had been imposed on women by men to preserve
their own self-bestowed right to enjoy their sexuality whilst
denying women the right to enjoy theirs.

Last but not least, her partner had to accept with good
grace the fact that once the sexual excitement of their relationship had faded it was time for them both to move on, although not necessarily, in her case, to another lover.

These days she spent more time in bed alone than with
someone else, and, if she was honest with herself, she had
grown to prefer it that way.

When her father had walked out on her mother and she had
witnessed the financial and emotional devastation that his absence had caused, despite her youth, she had made herself a
vow that the same thing would never happen to her, that she
would never allow herself to depend financially, or indeed in
any way, on anyone other than herself, and that, unlike her
mother, she would not keep on falling in love and remarrying in the forlorn hope of finding someone to fill the empty
space in her life...in herself...

There were no empty spaces in her life or in her, Star had

decided triumphantly three months ago when the arrival of her twenty-fifth birthday had prompted a mental stocktaking of her life.

'Mom, I need the bathroom...'

Star frowned as her attention was abruptly refocused on the small family group that she had noticed earlier by the shrill, insistent voice of one of the children.

The man with them—their father, she assumed—was, she observed, more interested in catching her eye than acknowledging his wife's attempt to capture his attention.

'Clay, Ginny wants the bathroom,' Star heard her telling him.

'Then take her,' he responded impatiently, shaking his head when the woman tried to insist that he went with them.

The look he gave Star as his wife gave in and walked away from him with their children across the lawn of Brad's large family home—built on the shores of the lake around which lay the small American town where he and his family lived and to which he had brought his bride, Sally's stepmother—was one she had seen in very many pairs of male eyes before his.

Barely waiting until his wife and children were out of sight, he started to make his way towards Star.

Star did nothing. She simply stood still, watching and waiting.

He *was* quite attractive, she decided judiciously, though not so attractive as he obviously believed, but then she quite enjoyed a certain amount of confidence in a man, as well as that very obvious streak of selfishness, provided he did not bring it to bed with him.

A selfish lover was not to her taste at all.

As he came towards her she did not, as another woman might have done, exhibit any self-consciousness. There was no need for her to raise flirtatious fingers to the silky dark red satin of her hair which today she was wearing loose over her shoulders in a smooth, polished, immaculate fall. Nor did she need to check any other details of her appearance or draw attention to her sensuality.

The simple silk and linen dress that she was wearing had been bought in Milan and it showed. It fitted the slender, elegant line of her body perfectly. That was to say, it merely hinted at the feminine curves that lay beneath it rather than hugging or emphasising them in the way that the dress worn by the woman who had been clinging so desperately and so unsuccessfully to the man's side had done.

Star never wore clothes which drew attention to her sexuality—there had never been any need for her to do so—not even in bed, where the only thing she wanted next to her own skin was that of her lover.

Behind her she could still hear the querulous voice of the child and the equally irritated response of her mother.

Star's make-up, like her hair and her perfume, was understated. Her father might not have given her his physical support or indeed his financial support during her childhood, but he had given her his excellent bone structure, and by his absence he had also given her the opportunity to witness, at first hand, the folly of trying too hard to please his sex.

Not that she would ever have been tempted to try to appeal to this particular specimen of it, she decided, abruptly changing her mind about her admirer's potential as she observed the smug satisfaction in his eyes—and the lack of humour or intelligence. She might not want to form any kind of permanent or emotional bond with a lover but she enjoyed the spine-tingling ritual of foreplay as much as any other woman, especially when it was spiced with intelligent conversation and laughter.

As she broke eye contact with him with a coolly dismissive look that told him he was wasting his time, she realised that she could still hear the whiny voice of the child behind her and her mother's reproach as she demanded, 'Oh, Ginny, why did you say you wanted the bathroom if you don't? Your father… Oh…'

Star frowned as the woman's tone of voice changed, all its former irritation and lethargy replaced by an almost breathless note of sexual excitement and warmth as she exclaimed, 'Oh, Kyle! Where did you come from? I didn't see you. Clay is—'

'I know where Clay is. I've seen him,' Star heard a coolly incisive male voice interrupting, and she could tell from the way he drawled the words that he knew exactly what Clay had been doing and, moreover, did not approve.

The voice sounded interesting but the man, Star suspected, who not really her type. He sounded far too disapproving and moralistic.

She was just about to walk away and refill her glass with the rather good champagne cocktail that she had been enjoying when a purposeful quartet comprising the two adults she had just heard talking plus the two children—or, rather, a slightly uncertain trio shepherded by an extremely large and very determined sheepdog in the form of a man who would normally have caused her more than a single heartbeat's recognition of his masculine appeal—crossed her line of vision heading towards the man who had just been trying to attract her attention.

There was really no comparison between the two men, Star decided. Clay now looked sulkily, almost seedily unappealing as he ignored his wife's outstretched hand and frowned impatiently down at his two children, whilst the man who had sounded so determined to remind him of his marital and parental status looked…

He looked like the very best kind of sexy American male, Star admitted to herself.

Tall, lithe in the way he moved, he had a sheen of good

health on his thick, well-cut dark brown hair and on his forearms where his flesh was exposed by the short sleeves of his
snowy-white T-shirt.

She didn't miss, either, the brief glance he gave her as he
restored and reunited the small family group—a look which
told her how thoroughly he disapproved of what had been
going on.

In a flash, the automatic flare of sexual awareness she had
felt was submerged by a much stronger flare of resentful anger
as she recognised what he was doing. The fact that she herself had already decided that she wasn't remotely interested
in the sexual invitation being handed out to her was forgotten
as she rose to the challenge of his interference.

Just what the hell did he think he was doing? Star asked
herself wrathfully. She had a deeply rooted resentment of
other people trying to make her decisions for her, to control
her life for her, especially her sex life, and if he thought for
one moment that if she'd really been interested in Clay she
would have allowed *him* or that theatrical piece of byplay of
his to stop her…

Frowning, she started to turn away, shrugging aside her
irritation.

It wasn't like her to let anyone get under her skin so easily, especially a male anyone…and especially a male anyone
whom she didn't even know and with whom she had barely
exchanged more than one assessing glance.

Her frown deepening at the realization that she'd let herself waste time thinking about a man whom she was hardly
likely to see again, Star was startled when the subject of her
thoughts suddenly appeared in front of her, blocking her path.

Star focused cool aquamarine eyes on him without smiling.

'We haven't been introduced yet,' he began, smiling at her.

His teeth, Star was surprised to see, did not possess the
uniform perfection that she had grown used to seeing in

American adults. In fact, one of the front ones had a small but very definite chip in it. His smile was slightly lopsided as well, making him look vaguely boyish—something which might appeal to those members of her sex who enjoyed having someone to mother, Star decided scathingly, but she personally preferred her men to be totally and uncompromisingly adult, thank you very much.

'No, we haven't, have we?' she agreed in answer to his comment, with a pointed and wholly unfriendly baring of her teeth, but as she made to sidestep him he stepped with her, still blocking her path.

Star stepped the other way and again he followed her.

'You're in my way,' she told him sharply.

'Your glass is empty,' he commented, ignoring both her comment and her hauteur. 'Let me get you another drink.'

'Thank you, I can get my own drinks *and* anything else I feel I might need,' Star told him evenly.

To her surprise, instead of being offended, he laughed.

'Ah, you're annoyed with me over Clay,' he said, knowingly shaking his head as he added, 'I'm sorry about that, but you would have been rather disappointed. He isn't—'

'Really? You certainly are a very perceptive man,' Star marvelled sarcastically, 'if one look is all it takes for you to know immediately exactly what another person wants.'

'He's a married man,' he returned quietly, the good humour dying from his eyes. His eyes were a very deep, dense blue, shaded by thick dark blunt lashes which, for some odd reason, Star felt compulsively tempted to reach out and touch to see if they felt as soft as they looked.

'Yes, I rather assumed he was,' Star agreed. 'Which was what attracted me to him in the first place,' she added with blithe disregard for the truth. No one, but *no one* had the right to make her decisions for her and she was determined to make sure that this interfering would-be knight in shining armour was made aware of that fact.

'Married men make by far the best lovers,' she went on in deliberate provocation. 'They're normally so grateful to have a receptive, responsive woman in their bed after being frozen out sexually by their wives that they're only too willing to please, and, of course, once the fun is over you can send them home.'

'Fun? You think of sex as fun—something recreational like baseball?' he questioned sharply.

'Yes,' Star agreed, pleased to have pierced the armour of quiet self-assurance that he seemed to wear so easily and so irritatingly.

'Don't you?' she challenged him mockingly.

'No,' he retorted immediately, 'I don't. So far as I am concerned, sex without emotion, without love, without all the things that bond two people together, is like a flower without perfume, initially appealing but on closer inspection a disappointment.'

'That depends, surely, on your outlook?' Star argued, adding when he looked questioningly at her, 'On whether or not you *want* your flower to be perfumed. Some people *don't*; some people are allergic to perfume.'

Trust her, she was thinking ruefully. Outwardly this man, whoever he was, had all the male attributes that most appealed to her. Pity that he'd had to go and spoil it all by opening his mouth and voicing his opinions. An amusing thought suddenly occurred to her, making her eyes sparkle warningly. He deserved to be punished a little for his interference and his high-handed, moralistic manner and she certainly deserved to have a little fun.

She couldn't remember the last time she had devoted her energy to anything other than her work. Her last relationship had been over for— Oh... She was startled to realise that it was almost two years since she had told Jean Paul that their long distance affair was over.

She had been celibate for two years! Amazing... Oh, yes, it was high time she had some fun.

So he didn't believe in sex without emotion, did he? Well, she didn't believe him. No doubt he found it a good line with which to blind other women to the truth, but she was not like other women. No man *really* wanted commitment... No man *really* wanted a woman's lifelong love. Oh, he might tell you he did at the start of a relationship, but sooner or later he would revert to type—to want the challenge of someone fresh, someone new. Star had seen it happen so many, many times.

Yes, it would be amusing to teach this man a lesson, to let him believe that he had deceived her with his insincerity, and even more amusing to bring him to the point where he was forced to admit just how good sex could be—for its own sake—and she *would* make him admit it; Star was determined on that point.

'It's normally my sex who express those particular views,' she told him, letting her voice soften and become slightly husky, her eyes sending deliberately sensual messages to his as she played with her empty glass. Then she breathed, 'Perhaps I will have that drink after all.'

It never mattered how blatant you were or how insincere, Star reflected grimly as he fell into step beside her, guiding her through the crowd to a hovering waiter with a full tray of freshly poured cocktails. Men fell for it every time, greedily swallowing bait that surely in reality should have choked them.

There hadn't been a man born yet whose sexual ego didn't outweigh his brains, she decided as she accepted the full glass he was handing to her.

As she took the brimming glass from him a few drops fell onto her skin. Laughing provocatively, she made to lick

them off, and then, looking straight into his eyes, offered him
her wrist instead and whispered suggestively, 'You do it...'

To her chagrin, instead of taking up her sensual invitation, he produced a large white handkerchief and carefully
dried her skin, telling her quietly, 'I'm afraid it's going to
stay slightly sticky. Did any spill on your dress? It might—'

'No, my dress is fine,' Star told him angrily, snatching her
wrist away from him, her skin burning slightly with an emotion that she realised with shock was humiliation.

No man...*no* man had ever reacted to her like that...re-
jected her like that, and this one was certainly not going to
be allowed to be the first.

Stifling her pride and staying where she was instead of
turning on her heel and storming away from him proved
harder than she had anticipated, but somehow she managed it.

'Are you a member of Brad's family?' she asked him,
subtly studying the contours of his body as she waited for
him to reply.

Those muscles were certainly solid enough. What did he
do? she wondered. Something that involved being outdoors
a good deal of the time, perhaps.

'No, I'm not. Are *you* related to Claire?'

He sounded more polite than genuinely interested but Star
refused to be put off.

'No. I'm actually a friend of Sally, Claire's stepdaughter,'
she explained. 'In fact we've been friends since our school-
days; but I'm not just here as a friend—I'm here on business
as well. I'm a consultant and Brad's been asking my advice on
how to improve the image of their British distribution arm...'

A slight exaggeration of the truth but justified in the circumstances, Star excused herself. She was not normally given
to exaggerating her own importance—in any area of her life.
It was not normally necessary and she recognised that she was

being far more forthcoming, supplying him with far more information about herself than she would normally have done.

But then this was not just about sex, just about meeting an attractive and very sexy man and wanting to go to bed with him, it was about proving a point, about confirming one of life's realities, about making him back down and admit that he was lying when he pretended to be so emotionally correct and right on!

Engrossed in her own thoughts, Star missed the sudden, startled flare of recognition that darkened his eyes as he listened to what she was saying.

'So...you won't be attending the family dinner later this evening, then,' Star commented, and offered temptingly, 'Neither shall I.'

In point of fact she *had* been invited but she knew that Sally and Claire would understand if she didn't go.

'No... No, I shan't,' he was agreeing, his impossibly dark blue eyes—in a woman Star would have instantly suspected coloured contact lenses but something told her that this man would never fall victim to such vanity—meeting hers and causing her pulse to race a little faster. Oh, yes, he was quite definitely her type, physically at least.

'So both of us will be at a loose end,' Star prompted. She was beginning to wonder if she had imagined the intelligence she had seen in his eyes earlier, he was so slow on the uptake.

'Yeah, I guess it looks as though we will...' he agreed in a slow drawl.

'We could have dinner together,' she persisted, 'at my hotel; I'm staying at the Lakeside,' she added, mentioning the town's most luxurious hotel.

'The Lakeside...' He glanced at his watch—a plain, no-nonsense affair with a worn leather strap, Star noticed. 'I could meet you in the foyer at eight?'

'Eight will be fine,' Star assured him, wondering what on earth she was letting herself in for.

She said as much to Sally a few minutes later when her dinner date had excused himself and she had bumped into her and Chris walking across the lawn.

'I hope I don't have to work as hard in bed as I had to do to get him to have dinner with me,' she told her friend feelingly.

Sally laughed, although Star could see that Chris looked slightly uncomfortable. Men didn't like it when a woman was sexually aggressive, it made them feel uneasy...threatened.

'Where is he?' Sally demanded. 'Point him out to me...'

'I can't; he's disappeared,' Star told her as she searched the crowded lawn.

'Perhaps he's got cold feet and decided to make his escape,' Chris suggested.

Star gave him a cool look.

'If he has, there are plenty of others to take his place,' she responded.

She could see Sally biting her lip and giving Chris a warning look as he opened his mouth to say something else, but she waited until Chris had excused himself and left them on their own before telling her friend gently, 'It's all right Sally, you don't have to protect me from Chris. I know he doesn't approve of me.'

'It's not that,' Sally protested. 'It's just...'

'It's just that he doesn't like it when a woman behaves like a man?' Star suggested.

'You deliberately try to give him the wrong impression,' Sally defended her husband. 'You make him think...'

'Make him think what?' Star taunted her. 'I make him think that I like sex...that I like men.'

'But you don't, do you?' Sally countered swiftly, shocking Star into silence. Then seizing the advantage she had gained, she continued, 'You don't really like men at all, Star; you de-

spise them. You think that all men are like your father,' she
added sadly, 'and they aren't. They—'

'No?' Star fought back. 'Tell me that again in ten years'
time, Sal!'

'Oh, Star,' Sally protested under her breath as she watched
her friend stalk off.

'Where's Star gone?' Chris asked his wife a few minutes
later as he rejoined her. 'Off on another manhunt?'

'Oh, Chris, she isn't like that. Not really,' Sally protested.
'She just…she's just so vulnerable, really. She was hurt so
badly when her father left her mother and rejected her, trying to claim that she wasn't his child, and then there were
so many bad relationships in her mother's life, so many love
affairs that went wrong, that it just reinforced her belief that
men can't be trusted. She tries to pretend she doesn't care—
she even jokes that she can't remember any more how many
step and half brothers and sisters she has got because there
are so many of them—but deep down inside, I know that she
does care, that she—'

'You're far too soft-hearted,' Chris told her lovingly, curling his arm around her and swinging her round so that they
were face to face. 'I don't know whether it's all this fresh air
or not, but suddenly I am very, very hungry.'

'Hungry…?' Sally gave him a startled look. 'Chris, we've
only just eaten that wonderful buffet; you can't possibly—'

'Who said anything about being hungry for food?' Chris
whispered in her ear. 'It's *you* I'm hungry for… Mmm…and
you taste very, very good as well…'

'Chris!' Sally protested as he started to nibble her ear, but
she was laughing as she tried to push him away.

On the other side of the lawn someone else observed them.
He had been watching too when Star had been with them,
had seen her stalk away from Sally in obvious high dudgeon.

It was funny, but although he had heard quite a lot about

her both from Sally and from Claire he still hadn't recognised who Star was until she had made that comment about doing some PR work for Brad, Kyle acknowledged.

Listening to Claire and Sally describing her and her background as they'd explained the events surrounding the throwing of Sally's wedding bouquet and the trio's avowed determination to remain unwed despite having caught it, he had felt mildly sorry for the unknown Star and, if he was honest, a little smugly self-satisfied that he was too well balanced to share her warped outlook on life—and he could have done, given his own family history.

His mother had regularly dumped him on whoever she could find to take charge of him whilst she went off with her latest lover. His father had finally and unwillingly taken him under his own roof whilst making it clear how little he wanted him. But happily the bitterness which could have tainted the whole of his life had never been allowed to take root, had in fact been washed away, flooded out by the outpouring of love he had received from his stepmother's older sister, the woman who had become a surrogate mother to him and whom he still gently mourned.

But now...now he had met Star, had witnessed at first hand the powerful, turbulent, magnetic pull of her sexuality, had felt his body respond to it and to her! And it had responded to her... Was still responding to her, if he was honest.

Intellectually he might be aware of all the pitfalls involved in following through on what was running through his head right now, but physically...

He had seen the look she had given him when he had stopped Clay from making his play for her, and the even more contemptuous one she had sent him when he had informed her of his views on sex without emotion. He suspected he knew exactly why she had been so determined to get him to have dinner with her—and it didn't have anything to do with any desire to get him into bed. He only wished that he could say the same about his own motives in accepting.

Right now the thought of all the ways he would like to pleasure her if he had her spread out on a bed underneath him was driving him wild, with the kind of ache that was rapidly becoming a sharp urgency.

For starters he certainly wanted to see that smooth hairstyle all mussed and soft and those challenging sea-green eyes hazy and dazed with the joy of what they were both experiencing, and he surely wanted to feel those full, firm lips quivering eagerly beneath his, clinging to his, whilst he slowly stroked her silky skin. Oh, yes, he surely wanted that.

He wanted to peel her clothes from her body and share with her that spiralling, giddying, breathtaking climb through the delicately, deliberately erotic foothills of shared foreplay, across the plateau of escalating desire and then on to the heights where they could look down on the rest of the universe and momentarily believe that they were superhuman, immortal; but for that it was necessary to reach out and share yourself mentally and emotionally as well as physically and Star had made it more than plain that that kind of intimacy was not on her agenda.

And he had spoken the truth when he had told her that, to him, sex without emotion was like a flower without perfume, and he felt as sad and compassionately sorry for someone who had been denied the ability to experience that emotion as he did for someone who had been denied the gift of sight.

Of course, there had been occasions when he had been growing up when he had thrown himself wholeheartedly into the experience of exploring his sexuality, but since then there had been only two serious relationships in his life—one with a fellow student whilst he'd been at college, which had ended shortly after their graduation by mutual consent, and another which had been over for several years now and which had ended when he had moved from New York City to set up in business here in this quiet, sturdily American small town.

He remained on friendly terms with both his ex-lovers and was godfather to both their eldest children.

It had been the death of Grace, his 'surrogate' mother, that had prompted the heart-searching which had led to the ending of his New York relationship, bringing about as it had the admission that the emotion which he felt for Andrea had become that of a close friend rather than a lover. She had begun to feel the same way, she had confessed when he had finally brought himself to broach the subject with her.

He had promised himself when he'd left New York that the next time, the next love, would be his last, his for all time and beyond time, and, perhaps because of that, or perhaps simply because he was older and wiser and maybe tired too, he had found himself reluctant to embark on any new relationship, sensing that ultimately it would not fulfil his need to form a lifetime bond with that one special woman who would accept him and love him as he was and for what he was, as he would her.

He knew that many of his friends considered him to be something of an idealist. Well, why not? He wasn't ashamed of his feelings, his needs. Why should he be?

And it was only very, very rarely now that his body reminded him that sometimes physical desire and emotional need did not run comfortably in harness with one another—so rarely, in fact, that he couldn't actually remember the last time. So rarely...that it had been tricky getting himself to admit that his determined restoration of Abbie and her two little girls to her roving husband's side had had less to do with supporting her than with satisfying his own need to see if the luscious, long-legged redhead whom Clay was making such determined eye contact with looked as good from the front as she did from the back.

She had...unfortunately for him.

He glanced at his watch. It was time he left. He had some paperwork he wanted to get through. He had just about made his way to his car when Brad suddenly materialised at his side.

'Kyle!' he exclaimed, smiling at him. 'Did you get to meet Star? I meant to introduce you to one another since you'll be working closely together once you take over from Tim Burbridge in Britain... I still haven't formalised the details of her contract with her yet, but from what I've seen of her work there's no doubt in my mind that she'll do a good job for us.

'Tim Burbridge is taking a month's leave from the end of next week, as you know, and I'd like the two of you to meet beforehand so that he can hand over things to you; of course, you'll be staying on to work alongside him once he's back at work... I think you'll find him very co-operative and open. He understands how important it is for us to bring our British distribution network up to the same high standards we have over here in the States...

'It won't be easy, though,' Brad warned him. 'One of our biggest problems is recruiting the right calibre of technician. Not so much on the technical side—they all have the necessary skills for the job; no, the problem is more on the motivation side of things, from what I can see...'

'Mmm...I've been thinking about that,' Kyle responded. 'I think some kind of in-house training scheme coupled with incentive awards might be one way around the problem... But, of course, first I'll have to discuss things with Tim,' he added diplomatically.

'Well, that's something you and Tim and Star can work on together,' Brad told him. '*Did* you get to meet her?'

'Not exactly... Not officially.' Kyle was deliberately vague.

'Well, I'll make sure that the two of you do get a chance to get together before you fly out to Britain,' Brad promised him.

'You know how much I appreciate what you're doing for

us, don't you, Kyle?' Brad asked his friend. 'So far as I am concerned, the distribution network you've set up for us is one of the prime forces underpinning our success. It doesn't matter how good a product is; if you can't get it to the customer when and where he wants it and install it and keep it in good working order, it doesn't matter a damn how good it is.'

Kyle gave a small shrug. 'It works both ways,' he reminded Brad. 'No matter how good a distribution and servicing network is, it can't operate efficiently without a reliable product.'

'We make a good team,' Brad told him, 'and I can't pretend that I'm not hoping you'll be able to help us turn the British side of our business around and bring it into line with our home market success.

'Will you be joining us for dinner this evening?' Brad asked him as Kyle started to unlock his car.

Here was his chance to get out of his dinner date with Star, Kyle acknowledged, and he would be all kinds of a fool... asking for all kinds of trouble if he passed up on it.

Ten minutes later, driving towards his own lake-shore home, contemplating the brief, negative shake of his head and polite words of excuse with which he had responded to Brad's question, he grimaced to himself.

OK, so he was all kinds of a fool!

CHAPTER TWO

It took Star an unusually long time to prepare for her dinner date with Kyle. It was not like her to dither over what to wear or to question the effect she was likely to have on her date; she dressed to please herself and not anyone else, and yet, for some reason, she found herself eschewing the loose silky cotton dress she had originally decided to wear in favor of a much more sophisticated and slinky one-shouldered black jersey number that she had added to her packing at the last minute on some odd impulse.

Like today's silk and linen dress, she had bought it in Milan where they knew all about the subtle art of emphasising a woman's sensuality rather than her sexuality.

It was not a dress that a man would immediately and necessarily see as provocative. It skimmed the curves of her body rather than clung to them, but the way it exposed the smooth, warm curve of her shoulder and bared one arm, the way it highlighted the fact that one needed a well-toned body and precious little underwear to show it off made it the kind of outfit that bemused men with its subtly sensual message and automatically had every other woman in the room narrowing her eyes warily.

To complement the dress Star had swept her hair up into a smooth chignon and put on heavy, almost baroque dull gold earrings plus a single, matching dull gold bangle.

She was just about to apply her favourite perfume when something stopped her, and, instead of touching it lavishly to her pulse points, she sprayed a small cloud of it into the air and then walked slowly into it. This way the fragrance would be so elusive and subtle that anyone wanting to know if she was truly wearing it would have to move very close to her—very close indeed.

Smiling with satisfaction, she picked up her bag and headed for the door, pausing for a second before turning back and quickly spraying the bed with the same delicate perfume.

So, he liked his roses to be perfumed, did he...? Well, to-night he certainly wouldn't have any complaints. Still smiling to herself, Star stepped out into the corridor.

Whoever had been responsible for the interior design of the hotel was obviously a fan of the *Gone With the Wind* era and had a very romantic streak, Star decided, because the bank of lifts, instead of being situated in the foyer, was actually located on a balconied mezzanine area above it so that one's entrance into the foyer had to be made via a sweeping, curved staircase.

There were, of course, amenity lifts situated discreetly to one side of the foyer, but there was no harm in taking advantage of the props which had so usefully been loaned to her, Star reflected as she paused at the top of the flight of stairs for a moment, firmly refusing to glance downwards in the direction of the foyer to see if her dinner date was there to observe her, before moving elegantly down the stairs in a very fair imitation of the arrogantly graceful prowl that she had seen top models adopt at prestige fashion shows.

Kyle did see her, his brain grimly reinforcing what it had already told him. She looked, he acknowledged as he studied Star's elegant descent from the shadows of the mezzanine, much as he might have imagined some fabled Greek goddess to have looked—almost slightly inhuman in the perfection of her feminine mystery, her profile sculptured, her gaze remote, her body… Hastily he forced himself not to think about exactly what that sleek, fluid stretch of matt fabric was concealing.

He was not surprised to see, when he checked the foyer, that virtually every other man there was watching her, mesmerised by the strength of her sensuality and her own indifference to it.

As she reached the last stair he started to walk towards her. For a second Star almost didn't recognise him. For some reason she had expected him to look as he had done earlier in the day and for a moment the sight of him wearing not a white T-shirt and jeans but an immaculately cut dinner suit threw her.

It made him look taller, broader and somehow more remote, more inaccessible…more…formidable.

Giving herself a small inward shake, Star dismissed such unproductive and over-imaginative thoughts. He was still the same man, whatever he chose to wear, whatever outward image he might try to present; inwardly he was just like all the rest of his sex and, like them, sooner or later, no matter how much he might try to deny it, he would prove himself to be as faithless, as worthless as the rest.

'Never make the mistakes I've made,' Star's mother had told her emotionally in the first throes of her grief and anger after Star's father had left. 'Never trust a man, Star…any man… They'll only hurt you in the end.'

Star, six years old at the time, had taken her mother's words to heart and learned from them—unlike her mother, who had gone on allowing her emotions to rule her life and then regretting it.

He was only a few feet away from her now—more than close enough for her to be able to look right up into those astonishingly dense dark blue eyes.

Gravely he returned her gaze—without allowing his to slide downwards to her body. Star allowed her eyebrows to rise a little as she mentally awarded him a point for his subtlety.

'We still haven't introduced ourselves,' he announced as he stepped towards her. 'Kyle...Kyle Henson,' he told her, extending his hand.

'Star...Flower,' she told him wryly, adding with a small, dismissive shrug, 'A small folly of my mother's and not, unfortunately, her only one.'

'I'm sorry, I don't quite follow you,' Kyle said.

'It was a joke.' Star shrugged. 'But obviously not a very good one. I was trying to say that my mother's larger folly was not so much in the choice of my name as in the choice of my father...'

'Ah... You don't get on well with him.'

'Well enough,' Star countered. 'Or at least as well as any of the other half a dozen or so offspring he has fathered... and perhaps rather better than most. You see, I have the distinction of having known him the longest and therefore having had the greatest time in which to grow accustomed to his...foibles...'

'You don't like him,' Kyle suggested.

'No, I don't *like* him,' Star agreed. 'So go on,' she mocked as they walked towards the restaurant bar. 'Tell me how shocked you are by my undaughterly emotions and how devoted you are to your own wonderful parents... They are wonderful, of course,' she added, giving him a thin smile.

A man like him would have wonderful parents: a mother who adored and cosseted him, had brought him up to think he was the most wonderful human being that ever lived. And his father would have been stern and silently proud of the boy-child he had produced, reinforcing with everything he did the growing child's belief in himself and his invincibility, his right to live exactly how he chose.

'No, as a matter of fact they weren't,' Kyle told her evenly, and then, before she could cover her shock, asked her, 'Are you always this open and frank with strangers?'

'No,' Star told him, giving him a deliberately seductive half-smile. What she had been intending to do was to shock him a little bit, needle him slightly, but his quiet denial of her comment about his parents, coupled with his obvious lack of any intention of expanding on what he had said, had caused her to change tack. If she couldn't shock him into taking notice of her, then she would have to seduce him into doing so.

In the bar they both ordered spritzers before sitting down to study the menus they were handed.

Although Star was well aware of the interest she was exciting amongst the other diners, she gave no sign of it, and Kyle, who was watching her, wondered wryly how long it had taken her to grow the outer skin of cool self-confidence that she armoured herself in.

That remark about her parents—her father—had been deliberately provocative and he sensed that he had caught her off guard with his response to her taunting comment about his own family background.

Despite the information about herself that she seemed to hand out so freely, he sensed that she was an extremely private person, deeply protective of her innermost self.

'So,' Kyle invited, putting down his menu and smiling across the table at her, 'tell me more about this interesting-sounding family of yours.'

'Interesting?' Star raised her eyebrows and gave him a wry look. 'My mother is currently in the throes of a traumatic love affair with the son of one of her oldest and closest friends. It's supposed to be a secret but, of course, it isn't. My mother couldn't keep a secret if her life depended on it and she certainly can't seem to see that what she's doing is bound to lead to disaster. She's bound to lose her friend, and as for her toy-boy lover…'

'You don't approve?'

Star looked at him. He had surprised her with his invitation to talk about her family. Normally, in her experience, the subject most men preferred to discuss was themselves. Star wasn't used to being asked such unexpectedly intimate questions. One of her strongest character traits was a refusal to deal in any kind of deceit—a fact which put her at a disadvantage now, she recognised, as she found it impossible not to reply honestly to Kyle's questions.

'It isn't a matter of whether or not I approve,' she told him. 'It's more a matter of knowing what's going to happen, of knowing that someone else is going to have to pick up the pieces of the mayhem that my mother's emotional overload always causes…'

'That someone perhaps being you?' Kyle probed.

This time Star could not answer. The anxiety and sense of guilt she had felt as a child, listening to her mother, watching her go through the turmoil of a series of destructive relationships, was something that even now, as an adult, she found impossible to discuss.

The fear she had experienced then, the sense of being alone with no one to turn to, the panic at knowing that she was her mother's emotional support rather than the other way round still sometimes surfaced to attack her present-day, adult self-assurance, even if nowadays, outwardly at least, she had learned the trick of transmuting it into angry contempt for her mother's way of life.

'Why don't we talk about you?' she suggested softly. 'I'm sure that would be far more…interesting…'

Lifting her glass to her lips, she looked across at him as

she took a slow, deliberate sip, letting her lips stay slightly parted whilst she looked at his mouth.

At first she thought that her deliberate sensuality had had no effect on him, and then, to her delight, she saw the small, betraying movement he made, the slight shifting of his body, as though suddenly he wasn't quite at ease with himself.

'There isn't much to tell,' Kyle responded, and Star smiled to herself as she caught the slightly roughened edge to his voice and knew what had caused it.

No matter what he might be trying to tell her, she suspected that he was far from lacking in sexual experience, and from what she could see of it she could sense that his body had just the kind of sensual appeal she most liked.

Star did not believe in being a passive lover and, whilst not having any specific desire to be dominant or aggressive, she did like to be able to take the initiative to touch and taste the man in bed with her, to reach out and stroke his skin, to discover where and how she could most arouse him, even to tease him a little bit sometimes, testing his self-control. And something told her that Kyle would be very self-controlled.

'My parents split up before I was born. My mother had never wanted a child. Her ambition was to be an actress.'

Star frowned as she heard not condemnation in his voice, as she had expected, but, instead, compassion. He felt compassion for a mother who had rejected him? A tiny feather-brushing of unease—no more—disturbed the deep waters of her conviction that all men were the same, that all men were, in essence, her father—a feeling so vague that it was easy for her to dismiss and ignore it and tell herself that Kyle was even more devious than she had first suspected and adept at manipulating the vulnerability of the female psyche.

'Unfortunately she died before she could realise it,' Kyle continued. 'An undiagnosed heart defect. Before her death, though, there had been...problems...and ultimately my father agreed to take me in and bring me up alongside his second family... I was very lucky...'

'How—in being allowed to grow up alongside them?' Star enquired mockingly.

He couldn't deceive her. She knew all about how it felt to watch the father who didn't want you favouring some other child whilst you looked on in impotent grief and rage.

'In a sense, yes,' Kyle told her evenly, ignoring her sarcasm. 'You see, my stepmother had an older sister who... Well, let's just say she was a very, very special person and she kinda took me under her wing...helped me to understand... to develop a proper sense of myself...taught me what it was like to be loved and valued...and that's something I guess every child, and every adult too, needs...'.

'Here endeth the first lesson,' Star taunted softly under her breath, but if Kyle had heard her he wasn't responding to her taunt. Instead he was looking at the menu.

'Would you recommend the sea-bass?' Star queried with mock-feminine deference.

But Kyle refused to be drawn, commenting only, '*I* certainly like it.'

'Well, then, I'll just have to try a taste of yours, won't I?' Star flirted, refusing to give up.

It was only a matter of time, Star told herself confidently. With time and persistence she would be able to prove to her own satisfaction that underneath the disguise of chivalrous knighthood that he chose to wear he was just as untrustworthy, as selfish and careless of other people's feelings as the rest of his sex.

Not that it was going to be all hard work getting him to back down from his claim that, for him, sex meant nothing without emotion. Unlike men, she did not need the crutch of self-deceit for her ego. It wasn't simply to prove a point that she intended to challenge him—and to win. She had already acknowledged the heightened buzz of sexual awareness that being with him was giving her.

The *maître d'* was hovering, waiting to take their order. Star's mouth curled in a small feline smile as she chose one of the vegetarian options, her smile deepening as Kyle ordered the sea-bass. Before handing the menu back to the *maître d'* he murmured something to him that Star couldn't hear.

Several minutes later, as a waiter escorted them to their table, Star was amused to see the way the other diners watched them whilst trying to pretend that they were not doing so.

'We seem to be causing something of a stir,' she murmured dulcetly to Kyle as they sat down. 'I wonder why...?'

'Oh, no, you don't,' Kyle countered evenly, smiling at her. 'You know perfectly well that there isn't a single man in the place who has been able to take his eyes off you since you came down those stairs.'

Kyle wasn't quite sure how he expected her to react to his comment, but the sudden warm peal of totally genuine laughter she gave as she acknowledged the truth of his comment made him realise that she was not as predictable and true to type as he had originally assumed, and that whilst with a little conscious effort he should be able to withstand the sensual heat of her deliberate come-ons to him, resisting the effect of that wholly natural laughter and the rueful intelligence in her eyes was going to be much, much harder.

So it was with relief that he observed her revert to type, and he was thrown as she asked him softly, 'Not a *single* man... Does that include you?'

'I'm as visually attracted to a beautiful, sensually dressed woman as the next man,' Kyle replied drily.

It was not exactly the reaction she had hoped for but it would do—for a start, Star told herself as the waiter brought their starters.

Star had ordered mussels, which she picked up with her

fingers and ate with a deliberate, almost greedy relish, triumphantly conscious of the fact that although Kyle affected
not to be he was acutely aware, as he ate his way stoically
through his seafood platter, of the sensuality in the way she
was eating.

When she had had enough she licked the juice from the tips
of her fingers with deliberate enjoyment, enthusing, 'Mmm...
that was delicious.'

There were several mussels still left on her plate and as
she made eye contact with him she picked one up and held it
out to him, offering, 'Here, why don't you try one?'

His calm, 'I already have, thank you,' as he indicated the
empty shells on his own plate, would have caused a lesser
woman to retreat in a self-conscious fluster of embarrassment,
Star acknowledged, but she was not so easily discomposed.
Why should she be? She knew already that he wanted her.
Now it was simply a matter of making him admit it.

As she smiled into the bemused eyes of the young waiter
who had come to take their plates, she mentally congratulated
herself on her inevitable victory and settled back to enjoy the
rest of the game.

Their main courses arrived and were served—her own
very appetising vegetarian dish and Kyle's sea-bass.

Star waited until they had been served before recommenc-
ing her attack, pouting slightly as she eyed her own plate and
then Kyle's.

'The bass *does* look good...' she began.

There was something in the dark blue steadiness of his
gaze as he returned her eye contact that wasn't, somehow,
quite in line with his predictable, 'Would you like some?'

'I thought you'd never ask,' Star responded softly, already
leaning towards him, reaching out with one hand to hold his
wrist as he lifted his fork towards her mouth, when out of
the corner of her eye she saw him make a small gesture to-

wards the *maître d'* and then saw, to her chagrin, their waiter hurrying towards their table, carrying a small portion of the sea-bass.

She could see Kyle watching her urbanely as the waiter served her with the fish, all her earlier good humour and sense of triumph evaporating in the smouldering fury of knowing that he had not only anticipated her move but very skilfully sidestepped it as well.

Star wasn't used to men rejecting her sexual advances; she wasn't used, in fact, to having to make them. It wasn't normally necessary and for a moment the sheer shock of having the tables so neatly and unexpectedly turned on her held her completely silent.

'So you're a PR consultant,' Kyle commented as he calmly ate his own fish.

'Yes,' Star agreed coolly. 'I trained with one of the large London agencies and then decided to set up on my own...'

'It's a very stressful and competitive business, especially—'

'For a woman?' Star supplied challengingly for him.

'For anyone,' Kyle corrected her. 'Especially when you're working on your own.'

'I like stress...and competition,' Star told him. Was he trying to find out if she was involved with someone? If she had a partner...a backer...another man in her life? Determinedly she pushed her chagrin at his refusal to respond to her flirtatious teasing over the fish to one side. If he was interested in finding out if there was another man in her life then that was a good sign.

'And I'm certainly far from being the only woman to set up in business on her own,' she added.

'True,' he agreed. 'They do say that the type of person most likely to succeed in business on their own is one who enjoys taking control of their own life.'

'And you don't approve of the female sex wanting to take control?' Star asked softly, feeling that she was getting back on firmer ground.

'Not at all,' Kyle contradicted her. 'It's just that I often wonder if it isn't so much a need to take control of their own lives as a fear of being in a situation where they are not in control that is the real emotion motivating such people—a fear of making contact with others, of being open to them... and vulnerable to them...that drives them into isolating themselves—'

Star stared at him across the table as he broke off to shake his head as the waiter offered him more wine; she was torn between an aggressive desire to deny what he was saying and a passively wary one to ignore it.

'I own and run my own business too,' she heard him saying as the waiter left, 'and...' He started to frown as he realised that she had stopped eating, and asked her solicitously, 'Didn't you like the bass, after all?'

'The bass is fine,' Star told him stonily, 'but the conversation isn't.'

Kyle gave her a thoughtful look.

Those dark blue eyes really were dangerously deceptive, Star acknowledged. The extraordinary depth of their colour tended to make one focus on that, rather than on the intelligence behind them.

Suddenly she felt extraordinarily tired. Delayed jet lag, she told herself. She had a meeting with Brad in the morning, for which she needed to be fresh and alert. The last thing she needed was to spend the evening with some pseudo new man whose idea of foreplay was to psychoanalyse her. But she couldn't retreat now without getting at least some tacit admission from him that he did want sex with her; her pride wouldn't let her.

She thought quickly and then decided what to do.

'I'm sorry,' she apologised faintly, 'but I'm not feeling very well.' She gave him a softly rueful look. 'I wonder if you could help me to my room...?'

'Of course.'

Star could see him frowning as he quickly summoned the waiter.

'Would you like me to arrange a house call from the hotel's doctor?' he asked her concernedly.

Star shook her head.

'No...no...it's nothing, really... Just delayed jet lag mixed with too much sun this afternoon,' she explained. 'Nothing a good night's sleep won't put right...'

He had certainly been very efficient at settling their bill and getting them out of the restaurant with the minimum fuss and delay, Star had to acknowledge a few minutes later as they waited for the lift.

Once it arrived and the doors opened Star gave a delicately nervous shiver before reluctantly stepping inside.

'I know it's silly but I don't really like them,' she confessed only semi-untruthfully to Kyle as she stepped inside.

'It's a perfectly natural feeling,' he assured her as he followed her in and waited for her to tell him her floor number. 'I doubt there are many of us who actually enjoy being confined in such a small space, if we're honest about it.'

When the lift came to a halt at Star's floor Kyle politely stood back to allow her to precede him out of the lift before falling into step beside her.

Star deliberately waited until they were outside her bedroom door before starting to search her bag for her passkey, and then, when she did find it, she deliberately let it slip through her fingers so that Kyle had no option but to bend down to retrieve it for her, thus allowing her to close the small gap between them so that when he stood up again they were virtually standing body to body.

As she looked at his mouth Star deliberately let her own lips part slightly, her voice softly breathless as she thanked him for her key. She leaned forward, letting her body sway provocatively against his, her eyes starting to close on a small, whispered breath.

It was inevitable, of course, that he should respond to her, his head bending towards hers as he reached out to take hold of her.

It wasn't just triumph that she could feel as her small ploy worked, Star acknowledged. The pleasure warming her body was not purely that of victory. She could feel his body against her own now, satisfyingly male and hard-packed with muscle. His skin smelt clean and fresh and she was already anticipating how good it would be to give in to the feminine urge to bury her fingers in the thick darkness of his hair when they kissed. And she knew that he would kiss well. His mouth had already told her that. She looked at it now, not needing to fake the look of sensual appreciation in her eyes as she lifted them to meet his.

She would be generous in victory, she decided dizzily, very generous, when she showed him just how good it could be, when she made him admit that he wanted her—and she *would* make him admit it.

She saw the way his eyes changed as he felt the full warmth of her breasts pressing against his chest and a sharp thrill of arousal ran through her as she saw the dark burn of desire igniting his gaze.

'Kiss me,' she whispered compellingly to him as she finally closed the small space between her own mouth and his and placed her lips on his.

He responded immediately, as she had expected, his arms tightening around her, his mouth reacting to the soft pressure of hers whilst she teased him a little bit with delicate butterfly kisses which ended, as she had known they would, with his opening his mouth over hers.

She had been right about him being good, she decided dazedly several minutes later. It wasn't fiction any longer that she felt slightly light-headed and needed to cling to him for support, and there was certainly nothing faked about the way her heart was racing, nor the growing tumult of sensation threatening to flood her body.

She couldn't remember the last time a man had affected her so powerfully or so immediately. In fact, she didn't think there had ever been such a time…nor such a man. And she knew that he was equally affected. They were standing body to body after all, and there was no mistaking or concealing his own, very male arousal and response to her, even if he had tried to move discreetly away from her—but Star was perfectly well aware that her own body was betraying *her* as flagrantly as his was him.

The fluid fabric of her dress could not possibly conceal the taut peaks of her nipples, but Star was not ashamed of nor embarrassed by her body's response to him. Why should she be?

She was even tempted to lift his hand and place it on her breast so that he could experience for himself the effect he was having on her, but there was no need for them to rush things. They had the whole night ahead of them and there was something to be said for drawing out the pleasure of mutual discovery and its even more pleasurable culmination.

There was no doubt in Star's mind that his mouth would feel every bit as good against her body as it did against her lips and that when he finally placed it against her naked breasts and slowly caressed each sensually aroused peak the pleasure she would experience would more than compensate for the control she was forcing herself to exercise now.

And besides…

Besides, it had been a long time—a long, long time—since

she had last experienced something like this, since she had last been held and kissed by a man who seemed to read her mind and her desires so exactly that all she wanted to do was cling to him and let his mouth...

With a tiny little moan, Star moved closer and opened her mouth beneath his, inviting him to deepen his kiss with the thrust of his tongue, her body quivering with aching arousal as she waited for him to do so...and waited...and waited. Confused, Star opened her eyes.

Kyle had stopped kissing her now and his hands were cupping her face.

As she read the message in his eyes, Star's own eyes widened, at first in disbelief and then in anger, her hands dropping to her sides as he kissed her lightly on the mouth once and then a second time a little more lingeringly. But even as she made to return to his arms he was gently releasing her, saying quietly but oh, so firmly, 'I'm sorry...'

Sorry... He was sorry! Star couldn't believe it.

Confused and wrought-up by the messages her body was sending her, Star couldn't control the sharp-toothed bite of her shocked chagrin and the dismay that followed it as she exclaimed, 'You're *sorry*!'

How dared he do this to her? How dared he hold her, touch her, *kiss* her as though...as though...

Struggling to contain and control her emotions, Star took a deep lungful of air, trying to find a suitably acerbic response to his unbelievable withdrawal. But all she could think of was how his body had felt against hers, how she could have sworn he wanted her, how she knew that he had been aroused and that men, in her experience of them, did follow up on that kind of arousal, especially when...especially with her...

As she looked in furious disbelief from his mouth—stiffening her body against the treacherous memory of just how good it had felt to have it moving against her own—and up to his eyes Star realised that the expression she could see in their navy blue depths was not one of male sexual triumph as she had expected but instead a totally unfamiliar mix of warmth and compassion.

Compassion... He felt *sorry* for her. How dared he...? How dared he?

Immediately her defensive reflexes, honed over the years until they were needle-sharp, sprang into action, her spine straightening, her head lifting, her eyes flashing a fierce message of warning and pride as she stepped back from him and told him icily, with a disdainful shrug, 'Don't be. After all, I'm hardly missing out on the world's most exciting sexual experience, am I? You aren't the only man to feel threatened and emasculated by the strength and honesty of a woman's sexuality... I suppose I should have realised what kind of man you were when you tried to hide behind that claim that you could only have sex with someone you "lurved",' she taunted him mockingly. 'It's the classic get-out for men like you, isn't it...?'

She gave him a falsely compassionate smile and touched him contemptuously on the arm as she added,'We can't all be the same, of course. But it must be hard, I know, for a man to admit that he's only got a very low sex drive. Thanks for warning me about yours before things went any further. There's nothing more disappointing for a normal, healthy, sexually motivated woman than a man who can't...whose libido doesn't match hers...'

Before she turned away from him and swept into her room Star paused to look tauntingly into his eyes, but, to her surprise, instead of betraying the chagrin and anger she had expected—after all, no man could endure having his masculinity, his sexuality called into question, especially by a woman—he was just standing watching her steadily.

* * *

The man was an idiot...a total blockhead. Star was still fuming half an hour later as she slipped between the cool, fresh sheets of her hotel bed. He had to be to have behaved the way he had.

She knew that he had been turned on, aroused, when they were sharing that passionate kiss; she had felt the unmistakable hardness of his body against hers.

When sleep eluded her she thumped the pillow angrily, refusing to admit that it wasn't so much Kyle's calm expression of his lack of any desire to take things to their natural sexual conclusion that was keeping her sleepless and furious as her own unwanted excess of desire.

How could she, a sophisticated, experienced woman in her mid-twenties, who had had no trouble at all in remaining celibate for over two years, suddenly want one man so much that her body ached as painfully as though she had succumbed to a virulent fever?

With a small, fierce groan she closed her eyes angrily, willing herself to go to sleep. She had a busy day ahead of her tomorrow, starting with an early-morning meeting with Brad, and that was what she ought to be concentrating on, not some pathetic apology of a man whose claim to some hypothetical high moral ground was simply a cloak to conceal his real lack of libido.

It was just over half an hour's drive from the hotel downtown to the lakeside home that Kyle had bought when his distribution business had first become successful.

A little further up the lake and rather more isolated than Brad's home, the clapboard house had virtually been on the point of falling down when Kyle had bought it.

He had done most of the restoration work himself, enjoying the challenge of not only practically rebuilding the old house but also scouring the neighbourhood for the replacement materials he had needed to do so.

It had amused him the previous summer to be approached by the features editor of a local prestige publication who wanted to run a piece on the house and the restoration work he had done on it.

It hadn't just been his home that the features editor had shown an interest in either. She had been an attractive, vivacious brunette with a sensational sense of humour to match her equally sensational figure and Kyle had had to remind himself pretty sternly of the vow he had made to himself.

An ambitious college graduate, she had made it plain that all she was looking for was a summer romance before she headed for New York and fame. But he had done the New York thing and discovered that, after all, he was really a small-town guy at heart, with small-town values and beliefs and, if he was honest with himself, which he tried to be, happily content that that should be so.

Friends teased him about the fact that he lived alone in what was so obviously a family home, but he simply smiled good naturedly, laughing with them.

Only Kyle really knew how important his home was to him and how much he had felt in need of somewhere that was his own, of roots, of stability and continuity, after the confusion and pain of his early childhood.

Knowing that he had too much on his mind to sleep, he parked the car and walked down to the lake following the shoreline, his mouth quirking into a rueful smile as he recalled the angry insult that Star had flung at him outside her bedroom door.

If only she knew. Not since his turbulent teenage years had he experienced such an overwhelming surge of sexual desire.

Just standing there in the hotel corridor kissing her, he had already, in his imagination, removed her clothes, stroked the satiny softness of her skin, felt the soft feminine tremble of her body as he cupped the warm, full globes of her breasts, marvelling at the contrast between their creamy satin fullness and the dusky rose-brown of their areolae and the taut nipples that crested them, just as he had already felt the way she'd moved against him, her eyes closing, her body swaying and straining closer to his hands and mouth as he gave in to his desire to touch and taste the sweet femininity of her.

He knew exactly how it would be. How she would cry out in sharp pleasure as he kissed the quivering softness of her throat and then moved lower over the creamy slopes of her breasts and lower still until a taut nipple was his captive, drawn into the hot suckle of his hungry mouth, he equally its prisoner as he felt himself yield to the sensual power of his desire for her.

Yes, it had been a long time since a woman had affected him so intensely, so overwhelmingly, so sexually...and so emotionally.

There had been a moment after he had released her when he had looked into her eyes and seen beyond the outraged anger of her pride to the hurt bewilderment behind it and had had to fight with himself not to step forward again and take her in his arms and hold her there.

If he had done... If he had done, right now his body wouldn't be aching so hard that he was practically grinding his teeth with the intensity of it. But there was more to being a man than satisfying a sex urge... Much more, even if Star Flower did not appear to think so.

One day he would... He had already turned round and started to retrace his steps, but now abruptly he stopped and stared out across the lake's deceptively placid surface. One day he would what?

Right now he ought to be thinking of ways of calming the situation. Tomorrow morning, when Brad formally introduced him to Star and told her that they were going to be working together in Britain, she wasn't going to like it; she wasn't going to like it at all.

CHAPTER THREE

'AND one vital aspect which I'd particularly want you to focus on in any campaign is the reliability not just of our systems but, even more importantly, of their installation and maintenance.'

Star raised one eyebrow as she swiftly made a brief note of what Brad was saying to her. She had done her homework very thoroughly indeed before coming over to the States to meet with him and that homework had included interviews with those who had already had Brad's company's air-conditioning systems installed. A complaint from many of them had concerned the delays and problems that they had experienced in getting the systems installed and running efficiently.

'Is something wrong?' Brad asked her thoughtfully now, seeing that raised eyebrow.

'From what I've heard, there seems to be a problem with the installation and back-up system in Britain,' Star told him unhesitatingly. 'And, that being the case, I wouldn't have thought it was a good idea to focus any PR campaign in that particular direction.'

'We have had problems in that area,' Brad agreed, 'which is one of the reasons why I'm hiring you to come up with a campaign which will improve our image in that area...' He paused as his intercom buzzed, excusing himself to Star whilst he answered it.

'Yes, that's fine, Jan,' Star heard him saying warmly. 'Tell him to come right through.

'I am aware of the problems and I have taken steps to correct them,' Brad continued to Star, 'and for that reason I've asked a friend and business associate of mine, who owns a highly successful business over here, to help us out by going over to Britain and seeing what he can do to improve things over there, so far as the installation and service side of things is concerned...

'I've actually asked him to call by this morning so that the two of you can meet. You'll like him. He's—' Brad broke off as the door opened. 'Ah, Kyle!' Star heard him exclaim warmly. 'Good... Come in and meet Star.'

'Star...' Brad began as Star fought to control her consternation.

But Kyle forestalled him, saying calmly, 'Star...Ms Flower and I have already introduced ourselves to one another.'

They might have introduced themselves to one another, as he had put it, but he had certainly made no mention of who exactly he was, nor of the fact that there was every chance that they were going to have to work together, Star fumed as she gave him a glitteringly insincere smile.

Now she understood what had motivated him last night. Quite plainly, knowing who she was, he had decided that he didn't want to become sexually involved with her, to allow her to have any kind of upper hand or control of the situation when he knew that they were going to have to work together.

She, regrettably, had not had the benefit of that particular piece of information, and if she had done...

'I'm sure that the two of you are going to work very well together,' she heard Brad saying.

She could feel Kyle looking at her, almost willing her to look directly at him, but she refused to do so, keeping her gaze fixed rigidly instead on a point several feet away whilst she said with as much calm as she could muster, 'I understood that I would be working with Tim Burbridge.' She was referring to a relative of Claire's. 'I thought he was in charge of the British side of your distribution network.'

'Yes, he is,' Brad agreed, 'but, as you've already mentioned yourself, there have been problems in establishing the standard of installation and back-up service we pride ourselves on giving our customers, and as Tim would be the first to admit, whilst he has no problem selling the units to customers, he is finding it difficult to recruit the right kind of technical people to follow through from his sales, and that's where Kyle comes in.

'Not only does Kyle have a firsthand knowledge of just how our units should be installed and maintained but he has also built up States-side the very best installation and service team we have ever used.'

Star's mouth twisted in a slightly cynical smile as she listened to Brad singing Kyle's praises.

'The British employee's psyche and attitude to work is not necessarily the same as an American's,' she announced coolly. 'What works here in America will not necessarily work in Britain,' she said challengingly, looking directly at Kyle for the first time, the warning look in her eyes telling him that what had happened last night was now in the past and that he would be a very foolhardy man indeed if he tried to make any capital out of it now.

'That's true,' he agreed, answering her, 'and I appreciate that there will be certain...cultural difficulties to overcome...'

'Which is, hopefully, one of the ways in which you will be able to help Kyle find the right approach,' Brad intervened.

Star's eyebrows lifted as she pointed out coolly, 'I'm a PR consultant, not a sociologist.'

'Yes, but you've already highlighted our main area of weakness,' Brad was quick to tell her, 'and I suspect you're far

too intelligent and independent a woman not to have formed
certain conclusions and views on how the problem can best
be resolved.'

What Brad was saying was no less than the truth but his
praise immediately made Star feel wary and suspicious. Men
did not, in her experience, praise women unless they wanted
something in return.

Brad and Kyle were obviously close friends and she wondered suspiciously if it was, perhaps, in their minds to place
any blame for any potential failure on Kyle's part to achieve
the same success in Britain as he had done in the States on
her shoulders, or rather on the shoulders of her PR campaign.
It was not, after all, unheard of for men to use such tactics—
gamesmanship, they called it; plain underhand was a more
honest description in her book.

'It's my job to promote the company from a PR point of
view,' she told Brad firmly. 'Or at least that's what I understood the contract I signed earlier to say.'

'Yes, of course,' Brad agreed politely. He looked slightly
puzzled, causing Star to wonder if she might have misjudged
him and even been guilty of a little paranoia, but where men
were concerned a woman couldn't be too careful, she reminded herself. Look at the way Kyle had withheld from her
the fact that he already knew that they were going to be seeing each other again.

'I know you're flying back home today,' Brad told her,
'but Claire wondered if you'd time to have lunch with her
and Sally before you left. She said to tell you that she'd pick
you up at your hotel at noon.'

There was really no way Star could refuse. Sally was,
after all, her closest and oldest friend and during her turbulent teenage years her home and her stepmother had provided
Star with the kind of warmth and stability that her own home
life had lacked.

Ten minutes later, as she left Brad's office, she couldn't bring herself to look directly at Kyle. Gritting her teeth, she walked past him, her head held high.

All right, so he might very well have stolen a march on her and was no doubt right now enjoying that sensation—enjoying knowing that he had rejected her, enjoying the superiority and sense of power he probably felt that gave him—but she was damned if she was going to give him the satisfaction of letting him see that she was aware of his triumph.

'Come on, the champagne's already on ice,' Sally announced, pouncing on Star as she walked into the hotel foyer. 'You did sign the contract, didn't you?' she asked, frowning slightly as she saw how grimly preoccupied Star looked.

'Yes, I signed the contract,' Star confirmed.

'Star, what is it, what's wrong?' Sally began, confused. 'I thought you'd be over the moon. You said yourself that this would be the biggest contract you'd had; you were so excited about it and—'

'It's nothing… Just a bit of jet lag,' Star lied, forcing herself to smile. What was the point, after all, in advertising her sense of ill-usage? Sally wouldn't really understand. She had never shared Star's feelings about the perfidious nature of the male sex.

'Claire's waiting for us in the dining room,' Sally explained, taking hold of Star's arm as she added, 'No, not this way. We've got our own private dining room courtesy of Brad. He's a darling, isn't he? But then American men *are* sweeties, aren't they? Just look at Kyle…' Sally closed her eyes and gave a small, ecstatic sigh of deeply feminine approval.

'If it wasn't for Chris, I think I could fall for Kyle in a big way—a *very* big way,' she emphasised. 'He's got that something about him that tells you you could rely on him utterly and completely, hasn't he? You just *know* that he's the kind of man who would always be able to get a taxi and produce an umbrella when it rains.'

'Oh, yes, irresistible,' Star replied sarcastically, trying to hold onto her temper as she listened to Sally eulogising on Kyle's supposed virtues.

'You don't like him, do you?' Sally guessed. 'But Star—'

'Personally, I prefer my men a little less homey and a little more sexy. All right, then, a lot more sexy,' she told Sally recklessly. 'And—'

'Oh, but Kyle *is* sexy,' Sally interrupted her to protest. 'He's very sexy,' she insisted. 'Anyway, enough about him. How did your dinner date with that guy go last night?'

Star murmured something non-committal, her expression clearly revealing that she didn't want to talk about it.

'Look, Star,' Sally said gently as she saw the familiar stubbornness tighten Star's mouth and recognised the look in her eyes, 'I know how you feel about men and I *do* understand, but just because your father—'

'Just because my father what?' Star demanded dangerously.

Sally gave a small sigh and tried again.

'Not all men are the same. Look at Chris…and Brad…and James… And Kyle is—'

'The kind of man who claims he can only have sex with a woman he feels emotionally bonded to,' Star interrupted her savagely, and added vehemently, 'He's lying. I know it and I mean to prove it, to make him—'

She stopped speaking, abruptly aware that she had been letting things get out of control and allowing herself to be swamped by her emotions.

'Star,' she heard Sally appealing softly, but she refused to respond to her friend's plea, turning her head away when Sally suggested gently, 'I can see that you and Kyle obviously haven't quite hit it off, but don't you think you could be overreacting a little bit…? He really is one of the most

genuine men…people I have ever met and everyone else, including Brad, has a very high regard for him; he says he's
the most honest and straightforward man he's ever known—
very highly morally principled and completely a man of his
word, whilst, at the same time, always having the ability to
see the other person's point of view and to treat them compassionately.'

'Brad would think that—he's another man,' Star sneered,
her body stiffening in rejection of what Sally was trying to
tell her.

But, even whilst her body language was challenging Sally
to continue to oppose her, inwardly her stomach had started
to churn in a long-familiar mixture of pain and fear made
highly toxic by a generous inclusion of panic as she fought
to hold onto her beliefs and her self control.

A long, long time ago she had first experienced that same
volatile cocktail of destructive and painful emotions when
listening to her mother denouncing her father. Then she had
fought fiercely to deny and reject what her mother was saying,
convinced that she was wrong, that her father loved them—
that he would never leave them, and she had been wrong.

But she was not wrong now. She was not wrong about Kyle.

And somehow she would find a way of proving, not just
to herself but also to those like Sally who doubted her judgement, that she *was* right.

Somehow she would find a way of exposing Kyle's hypocrisy for what it was. It would be her own personal crusade,
her own private war.

'Well, perhaps Kyle just isn't your type,' Sally was saying
diplomatically, obviously anxious to smooth things over. 'According to Brad he's an idealist and a romantic. It's a shame
that there isn't anyone special in his life,' she added musingly.
'I suppose the kind of woman that would be most likely to

appeal to him is someone soft and gentle, someone he could cherish and protect, and that's not you at all, is it?'

'No, it certainly isn't,' Star agreed shortly.

'Well, we'll just have to see if we can't find him someone suitable at home,' Sally chattered on. 'Any suggestions?'

'Sally, I'm a PR consultant, not a dating agency or a marriage bureau,' Star snapped. 'I'm sorry,' she said when she saw Sally biting her lip. 'I'm just feeling a bit on edge.'

'A *bit*!' Sally exclaimed, feelingly. 'When Claire told me that Brad was definitely going to offer you a contract I thought you'd be on top of the world. After all, you've talked of nothing else for weeks.'

'I know,' Star agreed contritely.

What Sally had said was true. When she had first discussed the possibility of organising a PR campaign with Brad and Tim in England she had told Sally that if Brad did give her a contract it would be the biggest step forward in her solo professional career that she was ever likely to take.

She had worked on big accounts before but only as part of a team, and her clients now were, in the main, small, fledgling businesses very much like her own. The mere fact that she would be working with such a male-dominated business would also add the kind of gravitas to her business portfolio that she might otherwise have spent years trying to achieve. It wasn't just a matter of the additional income she would earn, it was the fact that doors to other business opportunities would open for her if she mounted a successful nationwide campaign for Brad's company.

She knew that she had a strong flair for her work and that her ideas were innovative and fresh. To have Brad confirm that, not just verbally as he had done this morning but materially as well in offering her a contract, should have filled her with exultation and pride, but instead all she could think of was the fact that Kyle wasn't going to be an unwanted memory that she could leave behind her when she flew home but a very intrusive presence in her life, and that no matter how hard she tried to ignore him...

Star started to frown. There were always two ways of looking at a problem: one was to see it as an obstacle to be overcome, something that used up valuable energy and time, the other was to look at it in a more positive light, to turn it into something that could be used to one's own advantage.

She remembered how seethingly angry she had been at the way that Kyle had managed to turn the tables on her and how much it had galled her knowing that she would have to walk away, allowing him to cling to his false piety and morality, secretly laughing at her, but the fact that he was going to be working in Britain, even if only for a short time, meant that she would have a second chance to prove herself right, to make good her angry claim to Sally that he was not the knight in shining armour that Sally believed.

'I'm sorry if I don't seem very enthusiastic,' she apologised to Sally, acknowledging that. 'I suppose I still haven't quite taken it all in.'

'Well, it's only natural that you'll worry a little bit about it now that the initial euphoria's worn off,' Sally comforted her. 'But at least you'll have Kyle on hand to turn to... I know that Tim's a dear but he isn't exactly... He doesn't...' She paused and made a small face.

'I doubt very much that I shall have much contact with Kyle,' Star returned crisply as Sally indicated the door which led to their private dining room. 'After all, it is Tim Burbridge who is in charge of the distribution side of things and Kyle's role is only peripheral to my work, so I—'

'Oh, but Tim won't—' Sally began, only to break off as her stepmother opened the door and exclaimed warmly,

'Star, my dear! Come on in!'

* * *

By the time she boarded her home-bound flight Star's mood had been mellowed by the delicious surprise lunch that Claire had given for her and the equally delicious vintage champagne she had consumed.

She settled herself in her seat and closed her eyes, opening them again when she heard an attractive male voice enquiring, 'Er...mind if I sit here next to you?'

Thoughtfully Star subjected him to a brief inspection. He was certainly good-looking but for some reason she felt less than enthusiastic at the thought of enduring several hours of heavily seductive flirtation.

Refusing to return his smile, Star claimed untruthfully, 'I'm sorry, that seat's already taken by my mother.'

Whilst Star was crossing the Atlantic, Kyle was standing at the window of his office in one of the town's most prestigious blocks, staring frowningly through it.

It would be a simple enough matter to pick up the phone and tell Brad that he had changed his mind; that he couldn't, after all, help him and fly out to Britain; it was, after all, what all his instincts warned him to do—but he already knew that he wasn't going to make that phone call, that he couldn't bring himself to go back on his agreement to help Brad.

He had known, even before they had met this morning, that Star would not forgive him easily either for last night or for withholding from her the fact that he'd known that they would be working together—two strikes against him already. One more and he would be totally and completely out of the game, which, where a woman like Star was concerned, was surely his safer and saner option, he comforted himself.

So why, then, was he so reluctant to embrace it...? As reluctant, in fact, as Star assumed he had been to embrace her—assumed so erroneously, so very, very erroneously. If only she knew...

Thank the Lord she didn't, he mused; he was going to have enough problems to contend with as it was.

CHAPTER FOUR

IN THE fortnight following her return from America Star was too busy professionally to have any time to spend working on her campaign to prove that Kyle was not the saintly, exemplary male that he liked to pretend he was.

Her hectic schedule culminated in an overnight stay in London whilst she attended a trade fair with one of her clients—a young and very talented interior designer. Having persuaded a highly acclaimed local builder of prestige houses to allow Lindsay a free hand in the interior design of one of his show houses, Star had then used her contacts to get the house featured in the new homes supplement of one of the national dailies.

As a result, not only had the builder sold every single one of the houses on his small, exclusive development but Lindsay had also been inundated with new commissions and couldn't heap enough praise on Star for what she had done.

'At least let me redesign your flat...as a bonus,' she begged Star now as they travelled home together in Star's car, Star at the wheel.

'I'm very tempted,' Star acknowledged, 'but there's the problem of where I would live and, more important, where I would work in the meantime.'

'Mmm...I'd forgotten for a moment that you work from home,' Lindsay said and added curiously, 'Wouldn't you prefer to rent an office somewhere and keep your work separate from your private life?'

'My work *is* my private life,' Star told her and meant it. 'And I can see no point in passing the expensive and unnecessary overheads involved in maintaining a fully equipped office on to my clients when I can work just as easily from home and be there on hand whenever they need me. My flat has two good-sized double bedrooms and it was no hardship to convert one of them into an office.'

'Mmm…Carey's built your flat, didn't they?' Lindsay asked her.

'Yes,' Star agreed. 'That was how I first came into contact with them. I went to look at the site when I first saw the flats advertised. At that stage Frank Carey was planning to build one-bedroom apartments plus some slightly larger flats with one double bedroom and a box room… I pointed out to him that so far as most people were concerned a box room served only one purpose and that was for the storage of junk and that he'd sell the properties far more easily if he cut down on the number of flats by one and increased the floor space of all the others to include a good-sized double bedroom.

'He refused to listen to me at first…'

Frank Carey was a man in his early sixties who had been in the building trade since he left school and was, it had to be said, just ever so slightly tinged with an old-fashioned attitude towards women, to put it politely. Lindsay, with her own experience of just how stubborn he could be, asked Star curiously, 'How did you manage to get him to change his mind?'

Star grinned at her.

'I persuaded twenty of my friends to make interested noises about the rest of the flats with a proviso that he increased the size of the box room.'

'And it worked…? He didn't suspect?' Lindsay asked, awed. Star laughed.

'Oh, yes, he guessed what I was up to all right, but in the end he gave in, and out of the twenty people who originally showed interest in the flats he eventually got seven sales.'

Whilst Lindsay stared at her in round-eyed respect, Star gave a small, self-deprecatory shrug and told her, 'That, like getting your designs featured in the national press, was more good luck than anything else. However, when Frank eventually offered me a good discount on my own flat, I didn't turn him down.'

'I suppose *I* ought to be thinking of moving to somewhere smaller and more easily manageable,' Lindsay acknowledged dolefully.

'It's definitely over, then—your marriage?' Star queried.

She knew that Lindsay and her husband had split up several months earlier. Her husband, from what Lindsay had said and from what Star had read between the stilted lines of explanation that she had been given, was apparently unable to accept the sudden success of his wife's business and the fact that she was now the major breadwinner in their small household.

Star had only met Miles Reynolds briefly. He was, according to Lindsay, a hugely gifted and under-appreciated set designer. Star had found him sullen and inclined to try to put down his long-suffering wife.

It had been his decision to move out, because, or so he'd complained, it was obvious that Lindsay's business success had gone to her head and now meant more to her than he did.

Lindsay had begged him to come back but Star had urged her not to give in to his emotional blackmail and to leave him to stew in his own sulks.

Now it seemed that the marriage was definitely over.

'You'll have to take care, when you file for divorce, to protect your ownership of the business,' Star warned her now.

'Divorce?' Lindsay gave her a shocked look. 'Oh, no, I don't think...' She lapsed back into silence, unwilling to admit to Star, whose views of marriage and men she now knew very well, that she still loved her husband and that there were times when, despite the fact that she knew he was behaving both childishly and selfishly, she missed him and ached for him so desperately that she was quite willing to give up the business completely just to have him back.

Only her common sense kept her from telling him so, and she knew that Star would be as little able to understand how she could continue to love him and to accept him as he was, faults and all, as Miles was to understand how important the stability afforded by her own business success was to her and her hopes for the future, for the family she had hoped they would one day have.

'Remember,' Star warned Lindsay as she dropped her off outside her front door, 'no more freebies, no matter *who* asks for them; you don't need them any more...'

'No,' Lindsay agreed meekly, bit her lip. Then she temporised, 'Well, only the sitting room at the new centre they're opening in town for the over-sixties. They deserve it, Star,' she protested when she saw Star's expression. 'They've worked hard all their lives and they deserve a bit of comfort and care now; besides, I've already promised.'

Giving her a dry look, Star put her car back in gear. Some people were just too soft for their own good, she thought.

Once home, as she went through her post, she reran her answering machine to listen to her messages. Most of them were non-urgent; she tensed as she listened to one from her mother detailing the most recent instalment in the saga of her current romance. Star sighed as she heard the indignation mounting in her mother's voice as she described the confrontation with her friend over the discovery that she, Star's mother, was deeply embroiled in an affair with the friend's still-not-quite-twenty-one-year-old son.

Shaking her head, Star wound the tape on. She would call her mother later.

There was a message from Tim saying that he wanted to discuss with her the story-boards that she had dropped off with him the week before.

These outlined the basics of a possible nationwide advertisement that she had thought of running to bring the company's product into the public eye.

What she had in mind was to use a similar theme to that of a certain very successful coffee ad, by planning a set of ongoing ads that linked together in instalment form to make a story.

The first depicted the overheated atmosphere in an industrial setting without the benefit of any air-conditioning, coupled with the arrival of a visitor from a competitive business which had the benefit of Brad's air conditioning units. To inject a little humour into the situation Star's story-boards had depicted several of the extras in various states of undress. She intended to follow the first ad up with a second showing the coolly competent visitor offering the name of their air-conditioning supplier, but his rival deciding to use a cheaper and less reliable X brand.

Into the resultant chaos would walk the cool, important female buyer whose business both firms were competing for, at which point the X brand units would break down, allowing the user of Brad's air-conditioning to sweep her off to his own cool and well-ordered factory where the deal could be agreed in true ad fashion with a clinch. At this point there would be a tongue in cheek stating that there was only one situation where an efficient air-conditioning system could be too efficient. The elegant female buyer would purr, 'And is this how you turn it down…? Ah, yes… Goodness, it seems hot in here…' Her hand would reach out to stop the man's from turning it up again as she whispered, 'I have a better idea,' and reached behind her to undo the halter-neck tie of her top.

So far Star had only presented Tim with the first segment of the story, hoping to whet his appetite for the rest.

What she hoped to persuade him to do was to agree to a nationwide TV campaign. She had done her costings and was convinced that a successful campaign would fully justify the costs involved.

It wasn't just Tim whom she would have to convince, though, she reminded herself; it was Brad as well.

Having checked her diary, she rang and left a message on Tim's answering machine to confirm that the appointment he had suggested for the following morning was convenient.

As she left home the following morning, Star noticed that the 'TO LET' board for the flat adjacent to her own had disappeared, and she wondered briefly what her new neighbour would be like before concentrating on more important matters.

They were having an exceptionally good summer and the town was full of people in casual, brightly coloured clothes.'

Star, in contrast, was quite formally dressed in a subtle beige pleated silk skirt and a contrasting cream silk longline sleeveless top. Her skin tanned well despite the colour of her hair, going a warm peach rather than a deep bronze, and she was sardonically aware of the interest that she was creating amongst the male motorists at the garage when she stopped for petrol.

Resolutely refusing to make eye contact with the most persistent of them, she went to pay for her petrol. The garage sold basic groceries along with sweets and ice cream, and, whilst she was waiting to be served, on impulse, Star reached into the freezer for an ice cream—the kind that came on a stick and was covered in chocolate.

Having unwrapped it and disposed of the wrapper on her way back to her car, she had just unlocked the door when she heard a male voice to one side of her. 'Very sexy... It's really turning me on and making me hot, watching you suck that.'

Inwardly furious, but refusing to be intimidated or to show any kind of embarrassment or self-consciousness, Star turned round and looked coldly at him.

Middle-aged and besuited, he looked for all the world like the 'Mr Average' respectable family man he no doubt claimed that he was, and Star had no doubt that his wife would immediately have denied the very idea that her husband could behave so offensively.

He was still leering at her and now he was looking at her breasts, Star observed, and she removed the ice cream from her mouth and told him with acid venom as she pushed the melting ice cream onto the front of his shirt, 'Here—perhaps this will help you to cool down.'

Let him explain that to his wife if he dared, she thought.

As she spun round on her heel and got into her car she noticed that the garage forecourt was now empty apart from the obnoxious man's saloon and a sturdy four-wheel drive which had drawn up at the other side of the pumps.

As she drove off she glanced at her watch. She had plenty of time to make her appointment with Tim. Mentally she rehearsed the argument that she had prepared to counter the objections she suspected he would have to such a high-profile and expensive campaign.

From his hired four-wheel drive, Kyle watched thoughtfully as Star slammed her car door and started her engine.

He had seen her crossing the forecourt as he had driven into the garage and had been on the point of walking over to speak to her when he had witnessed her confrontation with the other driver and overheard what he had said to her.

There was, in his book, no possible excuse for the other man's behaviour, but he wondered what it was about certain people that caused them to attract to themselves situations which could only reaffirm their distorted views and suspicions of others. Was it, perhaps, due to some powerful cosmic force which had as yet to be scientifically identified? he mused fancifully as he went to pay for his own petrol. He doubted it.

He had been in Britain less than a week and had already discovered that although the climate was reputed to lack a certain warmth its people did not. Sally and Chris in particular had made him very welcome. Star, he suspected, would greet his arrival with considerably less enthusiasm.

'I don't think Star realises that you're actually going to be taking over from Tim,' Sally had confided to him the previous evening when she and Chris had invited him round for dinner. 'I know she can seem a little difficult—' she had begun in defence of her friend, but Chris had interrupted her acerbically.

'She's a man-hater, a real ball-breaker...'

'Oh, Chris, that's not fair,' Sally had reproved her husband. 'Star had an awfully difficult childhood,' she had told Kyle. 'She adored her father and the way he rejected her was so cruel...

'Well, you already know the story,' she'd finished awkwardly as Chris had given a derisive snort.

Then Chris had demanded, 'Can we please talk about something a little more pleasant than your socially dysfunctional friend?' He had proceeded to tell Kyle, 'She's like one of those spiders—the ones that destroy their mates after they've been bedded by them. And they talk about men being sexually predatory...'

'Chris, that's not fair,' Sally had protested defensively.

'Oh, come on,' Chris had retorted, then had quickly explained to Kyle Star's complete rejection of the idea that catching Sally's wedding bouquet could alter her decision never to marry or commit herself to a relationship.

'It's only because she's so desperately afraid of being hurt again the way her father hurt her, don't you agree?' Sally had appealed to Kyle.

'Yes,' he'd confirmed. 'You've only got to look at the animal world to see how often the need for self-protection leads to the masking of fear by an outward show of aggression.'

He mentally recalled that conversation now, and about the way Star had crushed the ice-cold remnant of her bitten ice cream against the obnoxious man's shirt.

As she waited in Tim's outer office, Star noticed that several changes had been made since she had last seen it—all of them an improvement, she noted approvingly as she observed how the pile of untidy, ancient magazines on the coffee-table had been removed and replaced by fresh, glossy ones and how, in fact, the whole waiting area had been changed around and now had far more comfortable, up-market furnishings, plus a self-service coffee and cold drinks machine and a TV screen showing a video of the American factory, including various technical specifications and details of the air conditioning units they made.

There was even, Star saw with some surprise, a display of fresh flowers, and the lighting seemed better, less harsh and yet at the same time giving more light.

Tim's middle-aged secretary-cum-receptionist smiled as she saw Star studying her surroundings and commented, 'Quite an improvement...'

'Very much so,' Star agreed, and glanced at her watch before asking, 'Do I have time for a cup of coffee before I see Tim or...?'

'Oh, no, it won't be—'

The other woman broke off as the door to the inner office

opened and a well-remembered American voice announced calmly, 'Star, it's good to see you again. Won't you please come through...?'

Kyle! Star stood up warily.

'My appointment was with Tim...' she began challengingly, but Kyle was already taking hold of her arm and drawing her into the inner office, leaving her with no alternative but to go with him.

Immediately they were inside, as he turned to close the door, she shook herself free of his hold and demanded, 'Where's Tim?'

'On leave,' Kyle responded quietly.

'On leave...?' Star stared at him. 'For how long?'

'It hasn't been decided yet. Brad felt that he would benefit from a month, possibly six weeks...'

Six weeks!

'So who's taking his place whilst he's away?' Star asked, but she suspected that she already knew the answer.

Even so, her heart plummeted as she heard Kyle say, 'I am.'

'But that's not possible; you can't be,' she protested, an unfamiliar sensation burning her face as she realised that her own gaucherie had made her colour up betrayingly. '*You* aren't employed by the company,' she amended. 'You're *not* a salesman. I was told that you were coming over here to sort out the technical side of things. If I'd known that I'd...' She paused.

Kyle told her calmly, 'I'm sorry if you think you've been misled; it certainly wasn't intentional...'

'But you knew before you came here that you were going to be taking over from Tim?'

'Standing in for him, yes,' Kyle corrected her. He paused and frowned slightly before continuing. 'I don't want to break any confidences but I'm sure that Tim wouldn't mind you knowing that the reason he's taking this period of extended leave is because he wants to update his management skills. On Brad's recommendation he's flying out to the US next week to take several courses at a specialised and very highly acclaimed personal development centre over there.'

'I see. I can't understand why Brad didn't tell me any of this before I signed the contract.'

'Perhaps he thought it wasn't important,' Kyle told her.

Behind him Star caught sight of her story-boards. Shrugging aside her anger at being caught off guard by Kyle's unexpected disclosures, she gestured towards them and said curtly, 'I'd better take those with me. Obviously the PR campaign will have to be put on hold now until Tim returns.'

'Why should you think that? On the contrary,' Kyle corrected her with maddening authority, 'Brad is keen for it to go ahead as quickly as possible. However...' he paused and looked from Star's angry face to the story-boards behind him '...whilst I can see the direction you're planning on taking with the campaign, I do have several problems with what you're proposing.'

Stonily Star glared at him. She had anticipated having one or two small tussles with Tim over the campaign, primarily over the ambitiousness and cost of what she was planning rather than anything else, but she had been reasonably confident of persuading him to add the weight of his consent to what she wanted to do when she ultimately put her proposal forward to Brad.

'If you're worried about the cost...' she began, but Kyle shook his head, not allowing her to continue.

'The cost isn't an issue at this juncture, but what does concern me is the degree of sexual stereotyping and the smutty, even pornographic slant to the ads. At home this kind of sexual innuendo, and indeed harassment, would never get past the censors and I—'

Star couldn't believe her ears.

'You're crazy,' she interrupted him angrily. 'There is nothing smutty about my work, and as for it being *pornographic*... How dare you suggest...? Might I remind you that my campaign is targeting the British market—a market which you are not, after all, familiar with? I can assure you that my campaign would have no problems with the censors here, and, as a matter of fact, a recent national campaign run on similar lines for another product has—'

'The coffee campaign,' Kyle interrupted her grimly. 'Yes, I know. I may not as yet be familiar with the British market, but I have been doing my research. That campaign, so far as I have seen, did not portray semi-naked male and female bodies in poses which might be considered more suitable for a crude seaside postcard.'

Star stared at him, almost too furious to be able to give vent to the angry words jamming her throat. 'My campaign has been carefully planned and thought out and is directed at a specific target market. It's a parody; it expresses tongue-in-cheek humour. It's a joke...'

'A joke? To portray a group of hard-working men stripping off to be taunted and mocked by their female colleagues? Would *you* think it a joke if the roles were reversed and it was a group of women removing their clothes to be leered at and catcalled by their male co-workers...?'

Star had heard enough.

'Oh, for goodness' sake!' she exclaimed, darting behind him to start gathering together her story-boards, her face flushed with fury.

'Don't think I don't know why you're doing this,' she told him cuttingly. 'I bet you just couldn't wait to get over here and start making things difficult for me, could you? Don't think I don't know that this is your way of getting back at me because your male ego couldn't take the fact that—'

'That what?' Kyle challenged her, his eyes suddenly so

steely and compelling that Star found herself unable to drag her own gaze away from them.'That I declined to take you up on your offer of sex? Hasn't anyone ever told you that the male animal likes to do his own hunting?'

'You claimed that you were different from other men,' Star reminded him, valiantly fighting back.

'No, I didn't say that,' Kyle corrected her. 'A psychiatrist would have a field day with you, you really are a textbook case. The young girl-child, abandoned and rejected by her father, who grows up to become a man-hater as a means of rejecting and separating herself from her pain. It even shows up in your work. Don't you *ever* get tired of it, Star? Don't you *ever* want a holiday from finding new ways to punish and ridicule the male sex?'

'My personal feelings have nothing to do with my work,' Star denied.

No one had ever spoken so forthrightly to her, or so brutally. So much for the chivalrous nature that Sally had insisted Kyle possessed.

'And neither have mine,' Kyle informed her quietly.

Their glances locked, and Star discovered to her chagrin that she was the first to look away.

For all his apparent amiability there was something as tough as hardened steel inside Kyle. Something…some belief in himself that he would not allow anyone to breach.

She wasn't going to give up so easily, though. She was convinced that her campaign would work. The trouble with Kyle was that he didn't understand the British psyche, the British sense of humour.

If necessary she would take her work to a higher authority, consult Brad direct… Either that or wait until Tim came back.

Drawing herself up to her full height, she glared haughtily at Kyle, burning him to cinders with the full furnace-blast of her contempt as she told him, 'I think, in the circumstances, it would be better if I put the campaign on hold until Tim returns. I can't—'

'No.'

'No...?' Star stared at him.

'Oh, I know what you're thinking,' Kyle told her. 'You think you can wheedle your way round Tim and get him to give his agreement to your proposals, but it won't work. Brad is anxious to get things moving as quickly as possible. He's given me the authority to take on board any extra help I think I might need in doing that if necessary.'

Any *extra* help. Star gave him a suspicious, narrow-eyed look. Was he threatening to go over her head and employ someone else to run the PR campaign?

'I have a contract,' she reminded him, just in case he had forgotten.

'Indeed,' Kyle agreed blandly, 'and I think if you read it you will discover that there are certain time clauses in it and certain contractual agreements which include the right of the company's representatives to veto your work...

'I do understand how you feel about my sex, Star,' Kyle added, more gently, 'and why you're letting your prejudices distort reality... Have you ever thought that counselling might help you to get things more into perspective, to let go of the past and—?'

'Go to hell,' Star told him rudely, picking up her work, her muscles straining against its weight as she manoeuvred herself towards the door.

When she reached it she turned back and looked at Kyle, determined not to let him have the last word or to feel that he had vanquished her in any way...*any* way!

'I don't care what you say, Kyle, you *are* just like all the rest of your sex—quite happy to cheat and lie, to deceive and hurt people, to do *anything* just as long as it allows you to do what you want to do—and I'm not deceived. I know what you're really like and I'm going to prove it to everyone else as well...'

Kyle had started to frown as he listened to her passionately angry outburst, looking not at her any longer but down at his desk. Only when she had finished did he raise his head again, his expression unreadable as he commented calmly, 'I see. So it's war, then, I take it...?'

'To the death,' Star vowed, and meant it.

CHAPTER FIVE

STAR was still fuming over Kyle's criticism of her campaign when she arrived home, and carrying the heavy story-boards upstairs to her second-floor flat did not help to improve her temper.

The communal landing which she shared with the other residents was not really designed to accommodate a woman of five feet six and weighing just a tad over eight stone plus two unwieldy, rigid pieces of board just that bit too deep to fit comfortably under her arm and too long to fit within her arm-span, and Star cursed under her breath as she banged her elbow on the wall.

She knew, of course, that it would have made much more sense for her to carry the boards upstairs singly instead of trying to move them both together, but she was still so infuriated by what Kyle had said to her that she just wasn't in the mood for behaving logically.

Once inside her own flat she inspected her elbow and grimaced as she realised that she had broken the skin. By to-morrow she would have a terrific bruise there—one of the penalties of her particular type of skin colouring, something else to count as a black mark against Kyle. Well, he wasn't the final authority and she would show him that *she* wasn't going to let him push her around. Quickly she looked up Brad's number, her fingers curling impatiently around the receiver, her voice crisply firm as she asked the telephonist who answered her call for Brad.

'I'm sorry,' the girl apologised, 'but I'm afraid he isn't available.'

When Star asked when he would be available and learned that Brad had taken Claire on a honeymoon trip sailing round the Virgin Islands, she thanked the girl and replaced the receiver.

No wonder Kyle had felt so confident about rejecting her work. He must have known that she wouldn't be able to go over his head to Brad.

She frowned as she heard her doorbell ring, and went to open the door.

Sally was standing outside and her eyebrows lifted questioningly as she asked, 'What's wrong?'

'I've just been trying to ring Brad,' Star told her. 'But he isn't there.'

'No, he and Claire are spending some time sailing around the Virgin Islands,' Sally confirmed. 'Lucky things... What did you want him for?' she enquired curiously, her attention distracted by the story-boards propped up against the wall. 'Are these for the campaign?' she asked Star interestedly. 'May I have a look or—?'

'Go ahead,' Star told her curtly.

'Mmm...*very* sexy,' Sally commented after she had studied them.

'Sexy? According to Kyle they're sex*ist*,' Star told her bitterly.

'He doesn't like them?' Sally asked sympathetically.

'He doesn't like *me*,' Star corrected her grimly. 'If I'd known that I was going to have to work so closely with him...' She pushed her fingers into her hair angrily.

'God, when I think how he must have been smirking to himself there in Brad's office, knowing that he was coming over here to take over from Tim and knowing, as well, that *I* didn't know. It wouldn't have mattered what kind of campaign I'd come up with; he would have rejected it.

'My campaign *is* good, Sally. I know it will work…'

'Mmm…well, couldn't you perhaps compromise a little… perhaps have just a little less emphasis on the…?'

She made a sketchy gesture in the direction of the story-boards, causing Star to demand suspiciously, 'What are you trying to say—that *you* think he's right…that *you* agree with him…?'

'No…of course not. I was just meaning that you could perhaps meet him halfway and—'

'Give in to him, you mean. Pander to his male ego. Let him think that he's *won*. Never!' Star told her fiercely. 'Men are all the same,' she proclaimed bitterly.

Sally sighed.

'Star, isn't it time you let go of the past?' she suggested gently. 'Kyle was saying only the other night that—'

'You were talking about *me* to *him*?' Star pounced on her words, her face suddenly flushing angrily. 'What were you saying? What did he say?' she demanded peremptorily.

'No, Star, it wasn't—' Sally protested, but Star wouldn't let her finish.

'No, don't tell me. I don't want to know. I don't care *what* he thinks about me or—'

'Look,' Sally cut in quickly, 'I only came round to tell you that we're having a barbecue next weekend so that we can introduce Kyle to a few people. It will be lonely for him living over here and you remember what I was saying about trying to find someone nice for him…? Well, what about Lindsay? She's on her own now, isn't she? And she'd be perfect for him. She's such a wonderful home-maker and so sweet and gentle, and now that her marriage is over—'

'It isn't over,' Star snapped. 'They're only separated, not divorced.'

She had no idea why the thought of Lindsay as a potential partner for Kyle should make her feel so...so...so intensely antagonistic—probably because she disliked him so much herself.

'You will be able to make it, won't you?' Sally was asking her. 'I know it's short notice but—'

'No, I won't,' Star told her shortly, and refused to meet Sally's eyes as she told her, 'I...I'm going to see Mother. I owe her a visit and—'

'It's all right; I understand,' Sally told her quietly. 'I'd better go; I'm going to visit a friend who's just had a baby boy. He's so sweet and everyone who meets him just adores him... even Chris. I think he's beginning to come round to the idea of us starting our own family...'

Star was surprised to find her eyes stinging with hot tears after Sally had said goodbye.

She knew that Sally had not believed her when she had claimed that she was going to see her mother, but it wasn't just that. Somehow, these days, their friendship just wasn't the same, and she knew who to blame. How dared Kyle take it upon himself to discuss her with *her* friends? And what exactly was it that he had said to them about her?

Fiercely she swallowed back her threatening tears and picked up the phone to ring her mother, leaving a message on the answering machine when there was no response.

Normally, she would have thoroughly enjoyed the opportunity to relax at one of Sally's barbecues and would have gone early to help her friend with the preparations, but now, thanks to Kyle, even that small pleasure was denied her. There was *no* aspect of her life that he hadn't somehow managed to invade, damage even, it seemed, to the extent of turning Sally, her oldest and closest friend, against her. Well, he hadn't vanquished her yet. She had promised him war, and war was exactly what he was going to get, Star decided, gritting her teeth. Beginning with her campaign...

So Kyle thought her work was sexist, did he? Well, perhaps she could find another way of getting her point across—something he would find easier to relate to...something he would find easier to understand.

Her mind buzzing, fuelled by adrenalin and the challenge of getting the better of him, Star started to work.

Three hours later, her arm stiff from the speed with which she had been working, she finally sat back and studied what she had done, her mouth quirking in a surprisingly youthful and wicked grin.

The first drawing was very similar to the first part of the story-board she had submitted for approval—a factory setting with the workers wilting listlessly in the heat. He was followed by a second drawing showing the same workers looking refreshed and working energetically after the installation of Brad's firm's air-conditioning system. Both scenes were being observed by a *Playboy*-type model.

However, the next pair of drawings bore no resemblance to those she had submitted for the campaign and were strictly for private viewing, Star acknowledged as she surveyed them in triumph; the first of the pair featured the same *Playboy*-type female, partnered in bed by a man whose features were a caricature of Kyle's—and even caricatured he managed to look unexpectedly attractive, Star noted with a frown as she wondered why her attempts to make his chin look weaker and his eyes less magnetic had not worked. He was lying on his back on the rumpled bed, his glance piously averted from his flaccid penis, whilst his partner told him happily that she knew exactly how to put things right.

The next drawing showed the pair of them in an extremely compromising position in the now deserted factory. The

newly installed air-conditioning unit was blasting out cold
air, but instead of smiling in triumph Kyle's pneumatic lady-
friend was eyeing his still unresponsive body dolefully, whilst
underneath Star had pencilled in the caption, There are some
overheated situations which even we cannot cool down.

What she had done was, Star knew, totally outrageous
and would, of course, have to be destroyed. But, even so,
it had been worth her aching wrist and the three hours that
she had spent working on it just for the satisfaction the result had given her.

Ridiculing Kyle had helped her to get back her sense of
perspective.

She still didn't agree with his criticisms of her campaign,
but at least now she felt able to reflect on them in a more de-
tached manner, her mind already examining various ways
in which she could tone down the elements of the campaign
that he had objected to whilst still keeping its essence. She
was still convinced that the campaign would work, that its
tongue in cheek humour would appeal to potential customers.

It was gone six o'clock. She hadn't had anything to eat
since breakfast and she had virtually no food in the flat either.
Fortunately, the local supermarket didn't close until eight.

An hour later, as she drove home, her shopping complete,
her mood was still triumphantly buoyant. Perhaps she could
attend Sally's barbecue after all, she decided—if only to prove
to Kyle that *she* wasn't going to let *him* come between her
and her friend.

She had just parked her car outside the block of flats and
retrieved her shopping from the boot when she was hailed
by one of her neighbours.

Amy Stevens was a widow in her early sixties, a small,
vague sort of woman who always set Star's teeth slightly on
edge, although she berated herself for being so unresponsive
to the other woman's obvious attempts to be friendly, telling

herself that it wasn't Amy's fault that she came across as being so irritatingly helpless and dependent and that she ought to be more sympathetic towards her loneliness.

'I've just been talking to your new neighbour,' she told Star now. 'Such a charming man. So polite and well mannered. He's an American.'

An American!

Star listened in foreboding as she looked from Amy's face to the blank window of the second-floor flat next to her own.

'He said he'd be staying for several months,' Amy confided, and then added, 'I told him how concerned I was about the fact that just about anyone can drive through the gates into our grounds and he agreed with me that we really ought to have proper security gates fitted.'

Star sighed. The installation of electronic security gates was one of Amy's hobby-horses. Her box of groceries was beginning to make her arms ache, so she used them as an excuse to escape.

She had almost reached the top of the stairs when she heard a door opening onto the landing, followed by the sound of decisive male footsteps crossing the marble floor.

She reached the top of the steps just as he started to descend them and for once she was grateful for Amy's need to chatter as she and Kyle came face to face.

His surprised, 'Star, what are you doing here?' as he automatically reached forward and took hold of her grocery box before she could protest caused her to bare her teeth.

She returned, '*I* live here, as if you didn't know...'

'No, actually I didn't,' he told her curtly, frowning. 'If I had... Which is your flat?' he asked her, glancing round the small hallway with its four doors.

'This one,' Star told him grimly, indicating the door closest to his own.

She already had her key in her hand and as she stepped

past him and unlocked her door she held out her arms for her groceries, but to her anger he ignored her, simply stepping past her and into her flat, announcing, 'I'll take these through into the kitchen for you.'

'No, thanks...' Star began, but he was already moving down the narrow hallway, leaving her with no option other than to follow him. She saw him pause as he passed the open door to her sitting room, openly appraising his surroundings.

Star had redecorated the whole flat the year before, choosing colours and fabrics which she felt most at home with—crisp, natural, crunchy linens, smooth, sensuous silks, clean cottons and soft wools, all in harmonising shades of cream and beige, her favourite colours.

Even Lindsay had been surprised the first time Star had allowed her to see all over the flat, marvelling slightly enviously at Star's gift for blending colours and fabrics.

'It's perfect!' she had exclaimed. 'But it just seems so... so unlike you...'

'What did you expect?' Star had asked her wryly as she'd watched Lindsay smoothing down the padded toile cover on her bed. 'A screaming mixture of clashing, angry colours?'

'No, of course not,' Lindsay had denied, but as her friend had studied the small pattern on the cream wallpaper that picked out the soft, muted dark red of the toile bedcover Star had seen that she was completely thrown by Star's choice of decor and Star hadn't felt it necessary to admit to her that her home, these colours, this soothing blend of fabrics and shades were, in fact, a reflection of that part of herself that she preferred to keep most private—that part of herself that was vulnerable and in need sometimes of the calm, soothing comfort of surroundings that provided her with the harmony and almost physical sensual comfort that she had missed as a child.

Sometimes, just to touch her fabrics, to feel their differing strengths and textures beneath her fingertips, to know that they all sprang from natural sources, was enough to soothe even her most turbulent thoughts and memories.

Normally, when she was expecting clients, she closed all the doors to her private rooms, and on their arrival ushered them straight into her work room, and now, as she watched Kyle studying her home, her defences immediately sprang into action so that when he turned to her and asked her quietly, 'Did you choose all this yourself?' she immediately lied.

'No... I have a friend...a client who's an interior designer. She did it.'

Why, when his immediate acceptance of her lie was exactly what she wanted, did she feel such an acute stab of unexpected chagrin at that acceptance?

'You can give those to me now,' she told him curtly, but she had forgotten that the door to her work room was open and that by moving she was almost deliberately inviting Kyle to look towards it and see the drawings that she had left on display.

She tried to close the door, but it was too late. He had already seen what she had done and was moving closer to inspect it more thoroughly.

Star held her breath as she watched him slowly examining all four drawings.

'You've got a good eye for caricature,' was all he said when he had finished. 'But not, it seems, for proportion.'

Proportion?

Star frowned, not understanding until he reached out and indicated her character's flaccid penis.

'I'm just an average-sized guy,' he told her lightly. 'I take a regular size ten or eleven shoe, that's all. I'm no superman!'

To her chagrin Star could feel herself starting to blush as she realised what he meant. If her male character was rather more than averagely well endowed, then she had not made him so on purpose, and, in fact, hadn't been aware of it until he'd pointed it out. A Freudian slip, some might say.

'And she certainly isn't my type,' he added. 'What made you choose her?'

'She's the complete opposite of me,' Star responded angrily before she could stop herself.

'Meaning?' he queried quietly, dangerously focusing on her, refusing to allow her to withdraw her gaze from his.

'I know exactly why you rejected my proposals for the advertising campaign, Kyle, and it has nothing to do with them being sexist,' Star told him angrily.

He was still watching her and for no reason she could name Star felt an odd thrill of high tension course hotly through her body.

'You and I are never going to be able to work together,' she cried out, frustrated by her failure to break free of his penetrating gaze. 'Your male pride, your shallow male ego will never allow you to forget that I showed you to be sexually incompetent.'

As she hurled the insult at him Star had the same sensation in the pit of her stomach as though she had stepped into a lift which had descended too fast, the shock of hearing her own words, of knowing how uncharacteristically out of control she was getting making her feel sick and weak, appalled by what she had said and by the frightening surge of her temper.

It was so unlike her; she was normally so calm and controlled, so logical and coolly incisive in everything she said and did, despite the colour of her hair. Losing one's temper was a sign of weakness, a sign of vulnerability, an admission of self-doubt; she knew that and yet it was too late now to step back from the precipice she herself had so dangerously created. Her pride left her with no other course than to take a deep breath and fling herself over it as she heard Kyle saying with ominous calm, 'Is that a fact? Well, for your information—'

'Whatever you want to say, I don't want to hear,' she cut him off. 'What exactly is it you're trying to prove, Kyle? You come over here...you move into my apartment block...you talk about me...criticise me to my friends, telling them—'

'Oh, no, I'm not letting you get away with that one,' Kyle interrupted her grimly. 'For starters, I'd already agreed to help Brad out over here long before I ever knew you existed, and as for me renting an apartment... It just so happens that the one I'd originally rented fell through—the owners decided not to go abroad as they'd planned, after all—and this was the only suitable vacancy the agents had on their books. If I'd known that you lived here—' He broke off and then told her acidly, 'Get a life, Star. Stop using your past and your father as a stick to beat the rest of the male sex with and an excuse for your emotional immaturity.'

'What emotional immaturity?' Star exploded, her self-control finally giving way beneath the combined pressure of Kyle's unexpectedly skilful attack and her own shock.

'Do I really need to tell you? You're the one who said that the only kind of intimacy you wanted to share with a man was a sexual one, that you were too afraid of the potential pain any kind of emotional intimacy might cause to risk—'

'I *never* said that,' Star interrupted him furiously.

'Not in so many words,' Kyle agreed with a shrug. 'But it's obvious that you *are* afraid—'

'No. That isn't true,' Star denied vehemently, shaking her head. 'It isn't true. And I don't... You can't... I want you to leave,' she managed to calm down enough to tell him shakily as she tried to control the way her body was starting to tremble inwardly as well as outwardly.

She started to turn her back on him, terrified of him seeing how traumatically his quietly voiced words had affected

her, but before she could he reached out and took hold of
her wrist, the expression in his eyes suddenly changing as
his thumb registered the too fast, nervous race of her pulse.

Her strangled, 'Let go of me,' was ignored as he insisted,
'Look at me, Star! Look at me!'

She wanted to refuse, but somehow she could not do so,
her gaze lifting angrily and defiantly to meet his as she tensed
her muscles against his mental invasion of her emotions in
much the same way as a nervous young virgin might have
tensed her body against a more physical intrusion.

'I'm right, aren't I?' he challenged her softly. 'You *are*
afraid of committing yourself emotionally to a man…to a
relationship…'

'Go to hell,' Star hurled inelegantly at him as she finally
managed to pull her wrist free. 'And get out of my flat…'

To her relief he began to walk back towards the front door,
but before he got there he paused, then turned round and simply looked at her, subjecting her whole body—from the tips
of her toes to the top of her head—to a slow, seeking inspection of such unexpected and open sensuality that Star actually
felt herself starting to curl her toes—an instinctive feminine
reaction to the effect he was having on her.

She had been appraised sexually by men before, many,
many times, but she had never experienced anything like this.
It was like comparing… It was like comparing sex to making
love, she acknowledged unwillingly as she heard Kyle saying
softly to her, 'And for your information, Star, I didn't walk
away from you that night because I didn't want you, but because I did. Just like I do right now. *Just* like I do right now…
Oh, yes,' he continued, when he heard her indrawn breath,
'right now there is nothing…nothing that the most primitive,
basic male part of me wants more than to pick you up and
carry you into your bedroom and lay your beautiful, naked

body beneath mine whilst I prove to you just how very, very wrong you are…'

'Really?' Suddenly Star was back on safer, familiar ground, her voice gaining strength and developing a cynically mocking undertone as she challenged him, 'So what's stopping you? Surely not the fear that you don't compare well with my…drawing?'

Star slid him a tantalising, slant-eyed look of laughing invitation but instead of taking her up on it Kyle shook his head and told her gently, 'No! *You* are…or rather your fear, your refusal to let yourself let go of the past and to stop punishing yourself for your father's faults. You aren't to blame because he wasn't there for you, Star. *He* is, and when the day finally comes when you can accept that, when you can share real intimacy with me instead of wanting to use sex as a means of punishing me for being a man, then—'

'Don't hold your breath,' Star advised him bitingly. Did he really think that she was stupid enough to believe in what he was saying?

When she could share real *intimacy*… Any woman who thought that she could do that with a man had to be a fool. It was like opening your door and inviting a thief to walk in and help himself.

As Kyle closed her front door behind him, Star's telephone started to ring. She went to answer it, frowning as she heard her mother's voice, her frown deepening as her mother explained that Star could not visit her over the weekend as she was going away with a 'friend'.

Her mother's coy use of the word made Star grimly demand to know just who her 'friend' was, but her mother, characteristically, refused to answer her.

Another man, Star guessed, but refrained from saying so.

Well, there was no way she was going to change her mind and go to Sally's barbecue now, she decided when she hung up. She would just have to pretend that she was still going to her mother's; after all, it wasn't as though she didn't have plenty of work to occupy her, she acknowledged as she glanced towards the drawings which had caused her such amusement and release earlier.

Now that the adrenalin buzz of excitement had drained away, leaving her feeling irritated with herself and deflated, she viewed the sketches in a different light, grimacing in distaste as she removed them and ripped them up. It had been a childish thing to do and something which she was now uncomfortably aware had, in a way, backfired on her and degraded her more than it had Kyle.

What it had also done, though, was give her several ideas on how she could subtly alter her original campaign. Quickly she retrieved her box of groceries and took them into the kitchen. Food first and then work, she promised herself.

And that was another advantage of working from home. There were no problems about working late into the night, nor did she have to get up early in the morning to get to an office. She could work all night and then drop into bed with the dawn if she wanted—and indeed had done so on occasion.

As she unpacked her groceries, she tried not to think about the fact that Kyle was now living right next door, his bedroom separated from hers by only a single internal wall.

His bedroom... Now why the hell should she be thinking about that...? Angrily she slammed the fridge door closed. There was no reason, none at all. She didn't want him...she just wanted to prove to herself that she was right... Not that she had any doubts on that score, she assured herself hastily. Of course she didn't. How could she have? No, of course she didn't... It was just...

Star cursed as she realised that she was trying to open

a carton of milk from the wrong side, and urged herself to concentrate on what she was doing, as milk spilled from the carton and down over her wrist onto the worktop.

CHAPTER SIX

STAR glowered ferociously at the sun shining through her kitchen window. The sky was a soft haze of blue and already, at just gone eight in the morning, she could feel the heat in the sun—a perfect day for a barbecue. Except that *she* wouldn't be going to it; *she* would not in fact be going anywhere, thanks to Kyle and, of course, her mother.

She could see the postman walking towards the apartment block; the contract gardeners employed to keep their small grounds neat and weed-free were already at work, the boxes of bedding plants that they were removing from their truck reminding Star that her own small balcony area and window-boxes needed attention. That at least was something she could do with her day in addition to working.

She heard her letter box rattle as the post arrived and padded barefoot into her hall to collect it, her body stiffening as she recognised her father's handwriting on a large square envelope that looked suspiciously as if it contained some kind of formal invitation. Not another wedding, she decided sardonically; surely even he had grown tired now of constantly changing partners?

It *was* a wedding invitation, Star discovered, but for her stepsister's wedding rather than her father's.

Emily was not one of her father's other children but the

eldest daughter of his second wife. Even after he and her mother had divorced, and despite the fact that she was not his natural child, Emily had stayed close to Star's father—much closer than she had done herself, Star acknowledged as she remembered her old childhood bitterness and resentment over the closeness that her father and Emily had shared.

Star could still remember the pain and resentment she had suffered on her rare visits to her father, when she had seen how differently he'd treated Emily from the way he'd treated her. She remembered how shut out and unwanted she had felt and how much it had hurt knowing that he loved Emily more than he loved her... Hurt... She frowned.

Now it seemed that the bond between Emily and her father was as close as ever since he was obviously hosting the wedding and giving Emily away.

Typically of her father, the invitation included a brief, handwritten instruction that she was to stay for the weekend and that he would book rooms for her and a friend, if she cared to bring one, at a local hotel. He explained:

Unfortunately we cannot put you up at the house as Emily will be staying, of course, along with her fiancé, and of course the twins will be down from university and both of them want to bring their current partner with them. So I know you'll understand...

Her father possessed a magnificent seven bedroom Georgian rectory which he had bought for next to nothing early in the eighties but Star could well understand that with so many children of his own, plus steps, there would indeed be no room for her. When had there ever been?

She remembered vividly how, on her first ever visit to him, he had had to go out and buy her a sleeping bag and she had had to suffer the indignity of sleeping on the floor of the landing of the small house he had been sharing with

Emily's mother. Emily, of course, had had her own room but
Star had been barred from sharing it because apparently she'd
frightened Emily.

She flung the invitation down on the kitchen table. She
wasn't going to go; why should she? Why should she once
again be made to feel the outsider, the unwanted interloper?
Let Emily play the adored and adoring stepdaughter if she
wished, but she was going to play it without her as an audience, Star decided grimly.

Suddenly the brightness of the sunshine irritated her and
she yanked down the blind over the kitchen window, blot-
ting it out.

She could well imagine what would be said about her in
her absence when she did not turn up for Emily's wedding,
but *she* didn't care, she told herself bitterly. Why should she?
When had any of *them*, but more especially her father, cared
about her?

After she had finished her breakfast coffee she reminded
herself that she was supposed to be visiting her mother—the
excuse that she had given Sally for not attending her barbecue—and that the last thing she needed was for Sally to find
out that she hadn't gone away at all. With Kyle living next
door, even if she hadn't seen anything more of him since their
altercation, it was more than likely that Sally would learn that
she had lied about her mother if she stayed in her flat.

Reminding herself that she needed plants, compost and
several other bits and pieces if she was going to spend the
late afternoon and early evening working on her baskets and
tubs, she decided that rather than purchase them from a local
garden centre she might as well take the opportunity to visit
a very highly acclaimed centre which specialised in the more
unusual plants and which was a good hour's drive away.

* * *

It was early evening when Star finally returned home. A quick search around the car park confirmed that there was—as she had expected—no sign of Kyle's four-wheel drive.

As she unloaded her car she tried not to think about how unsettling her day had been. The fine weather had brought out a good many visitors to the garden centre, families in the main—tight-knit, self-contained, exclusive units of mother, father and offspring.

Fathers had changed since her childhood; now they were far more involved with their children, far more physically affectionate with them. Seeing them today with their children had brought back the pain and misery of her own fatherless childhood—emotions exacerbated, she had no doubt, by the receipt of her father's note this morning. Despite what Kyle seemed to think, she did not need a counsellor—or anyone else—to explain her own emotions to her; she understood them all too well.

By now Sally and Chris's barbecue would be in full swing, their small garden filled with their mutual friends. They were a good crowd, sociable and entertaining, with a wide variety of interests and a very cosmopolitan outlook on life, and Star knew that she would have enjoyed being there with them. But, thanks to Kyle, she could not be.

No doubt right now he would be charming all the women whilst still managing to earn the respect of the men; she had seen how highly Brad thought of him. And no doubt Sally would have managed to introduce Lindsay to him by now. And Sally was quite right, of course—Lindsay *was* exactly his type.

Would he look deep into Lindsay's eyes and tell her that for him sex without emotion was like a flower without perfume? If he did Star could well imagine the effect it would have on her far too vulnerable friend. And when he drove

Lindsay home and she asked him in for a cup of coffee would he hold her and kiss her and then tell her—?

Stop it, Star warned herself angrily as she carried her plants up to her flat. Why should *she* care *what* he said to Lindsay or how her friend reacted? She cared because Lindsay *was* her friend, she told herself defensively. That was all... Her thoughts, her feelings were nothing to do with her emotions. The anger and bitterness that she could feel coiling so tightly in her chest were on Lindsay's behalf, not her own.

It took several journeys to carry all her purchases up to her flat and once that was done she opened the French windows onto her private balcony area and started to remove her display of pansies, whispering tenderly to them that they would be quite safe and that they would enjoy their new home in a protected corner of the flats' grounds which she had earmarked for them.

Once this had been done it was already past eight o'clock and beginning to grow slightly dusk, though the air was still warm. Star worked on. What, after all, was the point of stopping? What else had she to do other than to compose a note declining her father's invitation to Emily's wedding?

The pots were now complete. She had decided on a scheme of all white flowers this time, having seen a similar display in the corner of the garden centre. White... How bridal... Emily would be thrilled, she taunted herself, but in some countries wasn't white also the colour of mourning?

Mourning... Star sat back on her heels and closed her eyes. What the hell had she to mourn? Nothing, thanks to her wisdom in making sure she did not fall into the same trap as the rest of her sex and allow a man to steal her heart and then destroy her life.

At eleven o'clock she tucked the final plant into place. The balcony needed cleaning where she had spilled compost on it but she would leave that until morning, she decided tiredly as she opened the door slightly to allow some air into the sitting room whilst she stripped off her grimy clothes and showered.

Kyle frowned as he drew up outside the block of flats and saw the lights on in Star's flat. According to Sally, she was supposed to be away for the weekend.

His frown deepened as he got out of his car and realised that Star's balcony door was open. It would be an easy enough task for a burglar to climb up to it and break in; the locks were flimsy enough, as he had seen from his own, and Amy had told him only the previous morning that she was concerned about the lack of security.

He was just wondering what he ought to do when he saw Star's car. What was she doing at home? Had she, perhaps, come back unexpectedly and surprised an intruder? If so...

Kyle took the stairs two at a time, then rapped firmly on Star's door. Star heard it as she came out of the shower. Frowning, she pulled the belt of her robe a little more securely around her waist and went to the door. Chances were that it would only be one of her neighbours—Amy, more than likely, unable to sleep and come for a chat.

Her hair, wet from her shower, was wrapped in a towel turban-style on top of her head, and with her face free from make-up she looked, although she didn't know it, more like the solemn child she had been than the woman she now was.

As she opened the door the last person she was expecting to see was Kyle. He at least, so far as her imagination was concerned, was very cosily ensconced in Lindsay's home, no doubt offering her solace and comfort of a kind that made Star's upper lip curl in disdain just to think about it.

Only he wasn't. He was standing outside her front door. In her hall now, in fact, she recognised as he closed the door firmly and demanded tersely, 'Are you all right?'

'Yes, of course I'm all right. Why shouldn't I be?' she challenged him.

'Sally said you were going to spend the weekend with your mother. When I drove up and saw your lights on and the balcony door open, I thought you might have had burglars—'

'And so you knocked on my door, hoping that they would let you in,' she scoffed. 'Is that what you are trying to tell me?'

'No. I knew you must be here because I saw your car, but I thought...' He paused, raking his fingers through his hair, all too aware of how she was likely to react if he told her what had been running through his mind. A woman on her own... vulnerable...beautiful...and with the kind of temperament all too likely to push a couple of thugs into...

'What are you doing here, anyway?' he demanded instead. 'Sally told me that your mother lives down on the south coast.'

'Yes, she does,' Star agreed uncommunicatively. It was unfortunate that he knew that she hadn't been away but she would just explain to Sally what had happened, only changing the timing so that she could pretend that she hadn't realised her mother would be away until it was too late to change her mind about the barbecue, and, after all, so far as Kyle went she owed him no explanations. None at all.

'I was just about to go to bed—' she began, and then stopped as she saw it—the tell-tale mark of another woman's lipstick on his jaw... Lipstick on his jaw and... Her nostrils quivered fastidiously as she moved slightly closer to him and caught the scent of perfume on his clothes—Lindsay's perfume; she would have recognised it anywhere.

A sudden sense of fate having played into her hands, having dealt her all the cards she needed to win, made her feel almost dizzily reckless. Now was her chance to prove what she already knew. He had come here to her flat straight from another woman...from her friend with whom he had been sharing—if she was any judge, and she was—an intimate goodnight... A very intimate goodnight, she decided bitterly as she saw another lipstick stain, this time close to his ear.

Much as it went against the grain, the time had come for her to use a little subtle subterfuge. This was, after all, war, she reminded herself as she lowered both her voice and her eyes and murmured mock-dulcetly, 'It was kind of you to come and check that I was all right.' A contrite smile curled her mouth. 'I was just about to have some supper; would you like to join me or did you have enough at the barbecue?'

For a moment Star thought that he might have cottoned onto the secret meaning underlying her words. He certainly looked rather sharply at her but as she held her breath and waited he simply said, 'A cup of coffee would be very welcome.'

'A cup of coffee... Well, I think I can manage that.'

The balcony windows were still open and as she went to close them Star deliberately shook her damp hair free of its constraining towel; her cotton robe was only thin and with any luck the light from behind her ought to give him a pretty clear impression of exactly what it was concealing.

Star knew without vanity that she had a very sensual body—strong-boned and yet at the same time alluringly, femininely curved and delicate, her waist narrow, her hips softly curved, whilst her breasts were taut and firm, her nipples, now that she was standing in the cooling night air, suddenly stiff. A little too much so, she decided as she turned away from the window and made her way to the kitchen... It never did to overgild the lily, and in her experience men preferred to believe that only they could have *that* particular effect on a woman.

Male egos—how much damage they caused...how much pain and misery. If he responded to her sexual overtures now, it would prove beyond any shadow of a doubt—not that she had any doubts— that she *was* right about him, that beneath

that assumed demeanour of caring sensitivity he was just
as self-centred and untrustworthy as the rest of his sex, and
that his claim to want to make an emotional commitment
to a woman was just another male ploy designed to trick a
woman into trusting him.

If he was genuinely even one tenth of the man he claimed
to be, there was no way he would be able to respond to her
overtures having just, quite obviously, made love with Lindsay. But of course he wasn't what he claimed to be at all; she
knew that.

She walked into the kitchen, her body movements deliberately subtle and sensually enticing, and Star knew that he
was watching her as he followed her into the small, confined
space. As she filled the kettle she smiled at him and purred,
'Why don't you make yourself comfortable?'

He didn't look at her as he sat down but Star knew that he
had to be conscious of the firm yet seductively soft curves
of her breasts, which were now virtually on a level with his
eyes. There wasn't an awful lot of room in her small kitchen,
but there was no real need for him to move his outstretched
legs so betrayingly, turning away from her slightly as he removed his jacket and placed it over his thighs.

The invitation from her father was still on the table and as
she carried his coffee over to him she picked it up quickly.

'A duty invitation from my father—a way of underlining
the fact that Emily is so much more the kind of daughter he
prefers, all pliable sweetness and wanting to please...'

'Emily?' Kyle was frowning, Star saw, and she wished that
she had not made any reference to the letter and wondered
why on earth she had.

'Your half-sister?' he quizzed in that open, interested way
that Americans seemed to have.

'No,' Star snapped grittily. 'She's my stepsister. Louise,
her mother, was my father's second wife; they're divorced

now but Emily has always stayed in contact with my father. She claims she looks on him as her real father. God knows why, since he and Louise were only together for four years before he ditched her for a new, younger model—just long enough for her to produce the twins and for him to get bored.

'After Louise came Harriet—no previous convictions—sorry, children. That lasted five years and produced Anne and Sam and then...let me think...Gemma or Jemima. I can't quite remember.

'You see, by then the visits had trickled down to one or two a year. There wasn't any room, you see...not with all those children who needed a father so much more than I did... And, of course, I was such a difficult child, so disruptive with the little ones, not like Emily who was always so sweet and loving with them. They all adored her...all the wives...but they were all so alike...and all the best of friends... Tragic, really, in a black-comedy sort of fashion.

'And now it's Lucinda's turn. She and Emily are close friends. In fact I seem to remember being told that they were at school together, although I suspect that Emily might have been in a higher class. She's only three years older than me, you see, and Dad's taste runs to sweet, innocent young things.

'He must be getting rather tired now, I imagine, because they've been together three years, but then, of course, the triplets are very energetic—not easy for a man in his late fifties, although he does try not to show it.

'No doubt he'll fully enjoy the role of father of the bride, although Emily will have to make sure that he always believes that *he's* the most important man in her life, and he won't like it when she makes him a grandfather—'

'So you're not going to the wedding, then?' Kyle interrupted her quietly.

'Weddings aren't my style,' Star told him curtly, and added vehemently, 'No, I won't be going—not that I'll be missed.

It's only a duty invite. No doubt someone, probably Emily, has even had to remind him that I exist.

'The truth is that my father would like to believe that I don't exist. I'm not his kind of daughter, you see… I'm not the kind he can show off to his friends as his pretty, adoring little girl. Emily's much more suited to fulfilling that role than me.

'And then, of course, if I did go, there'd be the usual comments that I'm not fulfilling my traditional female role, that I'm not decorating the arm of some suitably impressive man—but not as impressive as my father, of course.'

Star suddenly realised that not only had she raised her voice above its normal level, cool pitch, but also that, shamingly, it was filled with angry emotion. What on earth was wrong with her? What had possessed her to reveal so much about herself—to *betray* so much about herself?

As Kyle watched the emotions chase one another across her face—anger, confusion, dismay, disbelief and, most telling of all, pain—he wanted to reach out to her, to take hold of her and make her whole again, heal all her hurts, show her that she was wrong, that she was perfect and fully worthy of being loved just as she was. *Just* as she was. And he also knew exactly how she would react if he tried, if he let her see how vulnerable he knew she was beneath that shield of prickly pride and acid cynicism that she used to protect herself.

He could see her so clearly as the child she must have been—an outsider…different…sensitive, and far too intelligent not to be aware of the prejudices and flaws in the adults around her.

'I could come with you to the wedding if you like,' he said.

The offer stopped Star dead in her tracks. She was already furiously angry with herself and thoroughly bewildered by her uncharacteristic behaviour, and Kyle's words had left her totally nonplussed and bereft of her normal ability to make a quick, defensive comeback—unable to do anything other than simply demand huskily, 'Why?'

Kyle had no intention of telling her why; instead he simply shrugged and answered, 'Why not?'

'I'm not going; there isn't any point,' Star said fiercely.

'Yes, there is,' Kyle contradicted her. 'He is your father; they are all your family—'

'I don't *have* a father,' Star told him flatly. 'Nor a family; and I don't want one either. I'm not going.'

'Just like you didn't go to Sally's barbecue tonight. Funny,' Kyle told her with deceptive gentleness, 'I hadn't thought of *you* as the type to run away from a situation that made you feel vulnerable. It just goes to show—'

'I did not run away,' Star interrupted him angrily. 'And nothing, no one makes me feel vulnerable.'

Her eyes warned him against continuing but Kyle ignored the fiercely challenging look she was giving him, telling her, 'If you really believe that, then you are lying, Star, and not just to me but, more importantly, to yourself, pretending—'

'Pretending!' Star had had enough. 'I'm not the one who's pretending,' she stormed at him. 'You're…'

To her horror Star suddenly found that she couldn't go on—that her throat was closing up, her eyes filling with tears. Tears… She never cried. Ever.

As Kyle saw first the disbelief and then the panic crossing her face as her eyes filled with tears and her throat muscles constricted, he decided that there was a time in every man's life when he could allow himself to stop listening to his inner voice of caution and act on his instincts instead.

Through the blur of her tears, Star saw him stand up and come towards her but didn't realise what he was going to do until she felt his arms come round her, holding her, drawing her firmly against his body, one hand securing her against him whilst the other rubbed her back in the same comforting way that she had seen parents comforting small children.

For some reason what he was doing, instead of restoring her to sanity, seemed to have the perverse effect of making her cry harder, in deep, gulping sobs accompanied by ridiculously childish hiccups, whilst his voice murmured soft words of comfort in her ear.

Men did not treat her like this, cuddling her and comforting her as though she were a small child; she did not behave like this—crying, clinging, wanting to be held, to feel secure...comforted...understood.

Understood. She stopped crying, her body tensing in rejection of Kyle's hold on it as she started to pull away.

Kyle, who until that moment had managed to make his body understand that on this occasion she was not a highly desirable and sensual woman but a very unhappy and needy child, was very quickly reminded by that same body that those deliciously warm and feminine breasts that he could feel and virtually see beneath her thin covering did not belong to any child. He warned himself of all the reasons there were for not allowing himself to feel what he was feeling right now and then promptly ignored them as Star lifted her face up to his, her lips parting, ready to deliver what he knew would be some scathing and furious criticism of his behaviour.

What was it about the combination of vulnerability and strength in a woman's face when it was wet with tears at the same time as her eyes were full of fury that evoked such an instant and age old male response? he wondered helplessly as he looked from her angry eyes to her softly parted mouth and gave up the struggle to resist the temptation in front of him.

Kyle kissed her, the unexpectedness of the warm pressure of his mouth on hers causing her eyes to widen in shock as she stared up at him in disbelief, her body motionless in his arms, as caught off guard as a young, untried girl.

She tasted wonderful, Kyle acknowledged, her mouth as sharply sweet as a delicious piece of fruit, tormenting his taste buds, making him want to take more and more.

Star blinked dizzily as he lifted his mouth from hers, touching her lips with the tip of his tongue. She looked at Kyle's mouth and then raised her gaze to his eyes, her own cloudy and confused. An involuntary shudder went through her body; she looked back at Kyle's mouth.

That look wasn't faked or contrived, Kyle knew; he doubted that she even knew what she was doing or the effect it was having on him, he didn't have to hear her whisper huskily, 'Kiss me,' to know what she wanted and she didn't have to ask him for it either. He was covering her mouth with his own even before she had finished saying it, kissing the way he'd wanted to kiss her right from the very start.

Star had ceased to exist on her normal plane from the moment she had discovered that she was going to cry. Now she was vaguely aware of somehow, somewhere along the line, stepping out of her normal persona, her normal behaviour, but it hardly seemed worth concerning herself about when the movement of Kyle's mouth on her own was filling her with the kind of physical sensation that would have made the explosion that led to the creation of the universe a mere nothing.

When her head fell back against Kyle's supporting arm to allow his mouth easy access to the taut line of her throat, she whimpered in fierce, excited pleasure, digging her nails into the strong muscles of his back and raking it passionately as she shivered beneath his caress, her breasts lifting, their nipples taut and dark and clearly visible beneath their thin covering.

She was kissing him too, hungry, biting kisses interspersed with the shallow, frantic sound of her breathing, making Kyle want to wrench the thin covering off her body and slide his hand between those long, slender legs to find out if her womanhood had that same delicious, succulent moistness as her mouth.

He wanted to touch her with his fingers and to carry the scent and taste of her to his lips, to lick the flavour of her from them and then kiss her whilst he still had the taste of her in his mouth, to make her know that once the immediacy of their shared desire to come together was sated he wanted to repeat that intimacy by replacing his fingers with his mouth—and if there was any possibility that she might share his desire and similarly want to explore and know him, then...

Star whimpered deep in her throat as she felt the pulsing ache inside her body grow to a heated throb. She couldn't wait much longer. She had never wanted a man with such... such intensity, such overwhelming insistence.

Her hands moved down over Kyle's body, his mouth silencing her small purr of satisfaction with a kiss of fierce male hunger as she felt the hard surge of his erection. She didn't want him like this, quickly and frantically, the pleasure gone almost before she could enjoy it. She wanted...she wanted...

Dragging her mouth from his, she told him huskily, 'Not here... In bed... I want...I want you in bed, Kyle... All of you, not just...'

He seemed to understand without her having to say any more because he was already turning towards the door, letting her guide him to where she wanted him to be, taking control only when she opened the bedroom door, pulling her back into his arms and kissing her deeply, using his tongue to show her the pleasure his body would soon be giving her, giving them *both*, as he pushed her robe off her shoulders and explored her body blindly with a delicate fingertip touch that left her shuddering and clinging achingly to him.

However, when she reached towards him and tried to undress him, he pushed her gently away and told her softly,

'No, not yet... I want to look at you...see you...know you first, Star.'

She had no inhibitions about her body and felt no shame about her sexuality or her needs, and yet for the first time in her life, as he took a step back from her and silently, lingeringly let his gaze rove over her body, she knew what it was to experience uncertainty and insecurity—so much so that she actually found that she was holding her breath, wondering, worrying that... And then she looked into his eyes and her pent-up fear leaked away on an unsteady lurch of sharp emotion.

'Star...' She could hear in the husky, shaken timbre of his voice all that she wanted to know—his awe, his desire, his adoration of the perfect femaleness of her.

Her confidence returning, she waited for him to come to her, to take her in his arms, and he kissed her slowly and lingeringly as he picked her up and carried her towards the bed. By the time he reached it his mouth had travelled as far as the tiny hollow at the base of her throat. By the time he lowered her onto it he was caressing the smooth slope of her breast. By the time she was actually lying on it his mouth had reached the rigid peak of her nipple, and she expelled a long, slow moan of satisfaction as his gentle caress became firmer, stronger, his kiss turning to a rhythmic suckle. Blindly Star reached for him, her hands tugging at his shirt, and then she smelt it...that unmistakable scent of another woman's perfume.

It was like free falling without the security of a parachute, knowing that only pain lay ahead, that there was no escape from it. No hope of any safety. And with her knowledge of that pain came shock, anger and panic.

There was no need for her to do any more. She had all the proof she needed. She had been so right to mistrust him. These and a hundred other thoughts she didn't want to acknowledge raced through her brain, her body awash now with confused emotions and sensations.

Valiantly she tried to recover her lost ground, to convince herself that what had happened had all been part of her grand plan, that she had known what she was doing all the time, that she had simply pretended to want him, that she had never really been in any danger of losing control.

As he felt her body stiffen in rejection of his touch, Kyle lifted his head to look at her.

'Thank you,' Star told him, 'but there's no need for you to go any further. You've already proved my point for me… proved that I was right about you…'

'Right about me?' Kyle could see the antipathy glittering in her eyes and hear the contempt in her voice but he had no idea what it was he was supposed to have done.

'You're a fake, Kyle,' Star told him triumphantly. 'A liar… a cheat…no different from the rest of your sex… You didn't want just sex—sex without emotion—remember?'

Kyle closed his eyes and held onto his self-control—just. Now he understood. He knew what was happening, what she was trying to do. Self-preservation, self-protection was all very well and his compassion helped him to accept her need to deny what was happening between them, to reject the emotions that he was pretty damn sure she felt as strongly as he did in favour of the safer alternative of mere physical need, but he was still a man, after all, and right now…

'Star,' he told her firmly, 'there's no way that what we're experiencing…*sharing*…could ever remotely be described as "just sex". I understand that it's difficult for you—'

'No?' Star cut across him bitingly. 'So it wasn't sex; what was it, then? Love?' she challenged him mockingly. The harsh tone of her voice jarred but Kyle refused to allow her to force him into a fight.

'I don't know,' he told her softly. 'But what I *do* know is

that there was a hell of a lot more going on between us just
then than the mere physical arousal of two bodies—'

'Really? Well, you should know. I suppose you said the
same thing to Lindsay, did you?'

'Lindsay?'

He was an actor, Star acknowledged, she had to give him
that, but then of course he would have to be able to carry off
the kind of act he liked to put on.

'Yes, Lindsay,' she repeated tauntingly. 'Remember her…?
She's the one you were with before me…the one whose lipstick you were still wearing when you came in…the one
whose perfume you are still wearing right now. Right here.'

She let her fingertips touch his throat and the open neck
of his shirt—the open neck she had further unfastened in her
desire to touch him and hold him, to—

The savage, raking pain that tore at her was surely far
too intense to be put down to mere anger against men and
their perfidy, their deceit… But determinedly she ignored
that knowledge and instead tried to find release from it by
digging her fingernails into his skin purposefully, painfully
before releasing him, her mouth curling in disdain as she told
him, 'You smell of her perfume… Of her…'

Those last two words weren't true, but Star didn't care.
She wanted him to know how completely he had betrayed
himself, how utterly contemptible she found him.

'And just for the record,' she added, determined now to
settle every single score, '*I* never really wanted you, Kyle…
not even just for sex. You're not my type. All I wanted was
to show you how pathetic you are and how easy it is to see
through your lies.'

Kyle had had enough. Compassion was one thing; allowing her crazy paranoia to go unchallenged and unchecked
was something else again.

'I do not lie,' he told her grimly. 'I don't have the need.

Neither do I have the need to create some fantasy world for
myself filled with fantasy villains because it's the only way
I have of trying to pretend that I haven't been hurt and that
I'm not afraid and vulnerable. *I* don't need to cling to the belief that all women are like my mother and that because she
didn't want me and she walked out on me that means that I
was to blame, that her inability to mother me lies with me.
Your father walked out on his marriage and you because—'

'It wasn't my fault… It's not true… I tried to be good, to
be what he wanted.'

White-faced, Star almost screamed the words at him as
the angry tears flooded her eyes.

'No, Star,' Kyle agreed gently, 'that's right—it wasn't your
fault—but deep down inside you don't really believe that, do
you? Just as you refuse to believe that you might just possibly be wrong…that I might just possibly have genuinely
wanted you, physically and emotionally…that I haven't lied
at all, that—'

'Go to hell,' Star screamed at him. 'How can you want
me when you've come to me from Lindsay's bed? I don't believe you.'

'No?' Kyle queried thickly, his patience finally snapping.
'Then try believing this…'

Star couldn't believe how quickly he overpowered her,
taking hold of her and imprisoning her flailing arms whilst
he silenced her furious protests with his mouth, kissing her
with an angry passion that excited a response inside her that
blasted apart her self-control and had her clinging to him,
fighting fire with fire, kissing him back with just as much furious sexual urgency as he was showing her, knowing that it
wasn't just the hard pressure of his hold on her that was weld-
ing her body to his, knowing that his visible physical arousal
only mirrored the inner secret ache of her own.

'I have not been making love to Lindsay… I have never,

would never go from one woman's bed, one woman's *body*,'
he emphasised, 'to another's.

'I could take things to their natural conclusion between
us now—take *you* now,' he told her rawly, 'and prove to you
just how wrong you are, not just about me but about yourself. God knows I want to. But if I did I would be breaking
one of the rules I've made for myself, which is never to touch
a woman in anger. But then you aren't a woman really, are
you, Star? You're just a hurt, angry child, wildly hitting out
at every man who comes near her because the one man she
needs to love her doesn't.'

His mouth smiled as he caught the warning hiss of her
indrawn breath but his eyes didn't. His eyes, Star registered
painfully, were completely blank of any emotion, and as he
released her and got off the bed she started to shiver with
reaction.

Her pride wouldn't allow her to conceal her body; instead,
she stood up and held her head up proudly, following him to
the door. When he reached it, he paused and turned to face
her. Was it her imagination or did a tiny muscle beat frantically in his jaw as he looked at her?

'And, for your information, the only woman that I...my
skin...my *body*...could possibly smell of tonight is you. I
wanted to fall asleep with the scent of you all around me.
The taste of you in my mouth. Did you know that?' he asked
her quietly.

To her shock he suddenly came up to her and bent his head
to kiss her naked breast before telling her thickly, 'I wanted
to taste you not just here but here as well.' And then, before
she could stop him, he touched her briefly but deliberately,
intimately, just where her body was still achingly moist and
ready for him.

Star couldn't stop herself from betraying her shocked reaction. It burned two bright red spots of colour high on her cheekbones and tightened her already over-taut muscles.

'Yes, I know,' Kyle said heavily to her. 'You want me to go!'

Speechless, Star watched him as he walked into her kitchen and re-emerged carrying his discarded jacket. She waited for what felt like a very long time after he had gone before walking unsteadily to her door to lock and secure it.

Nothing in her life, in her experience, had prepared her, *could* have prepared her for what had just happened... Nothing and no one.

CHAPTER SEVEN

'I'M REALLY sorry you had to miss the barbecue, you would have enjoyed it,' Sally sympathised as she handed Star one of the mugs of coffee that she had just made, settling herself onto one of the pair of garden chairs that she had drawn up on the patio overlooking her garden.

Star had planned to spend the whole day working but a phone call from Sally halfway through the morning, inviting her over for a coffee and a natter, had changed her mind.

'How was your mother?' Sally added solicitously.

She was fine, Star was about to say, but then she shook her head and admitted quietly, 'I never went to see her. She… she… There was a mix-up over the arrangements and—'

'Oh, Star, why on earth didn't you come round?' Sally chastised her.

'I…I wasn't really in the mood… I…I'm having a bit of a problem with this campaign for Brad…and I—'

'But you were so excited about it,' Sally reminded her.

'Yes, I was,' Star agreed, 'but that was before…'

'That was before you realised you'd be working so closely with Kyle?' Sally suggested. 'Oh, Star, I wish you could… I wish the two of you had hit it off better,' she amended tactfully. 'He was a real hit with everyone on Saturday.'

'Really?' Star tried to keep her voice flatly uninterested and non-committal, but she knew that she had failed when she saw Sally frown. Part of her itched to tell Sally the truth about her precious, wonderful Kyle, to tell her how he had come straight to her bed, her arms from Lindsay's, but another part of her—a new, unfamiliar, illogical part of her—shrank from revealing to even so close a friend as Sally just what had happened.

'Mind you, I still haven't managed to find anyone for Kyle,' Sally admitted ruefully. 'I introduced him to Lindsay and the two of them were chatting for simply ages. I even saw Lindsay fling her arms around him and give him a kiss at one point and I thought... She disappeared shortly afterwards but Kyle stayed on, although not for much longer.

'However, Lindsay rang me the day after to tell me that, thanks to the heart-to-heart conversation she'd had with Kyle, she'd realised how much Miles meant to her and how much she wanted to save her marriage and so she had gone straight home and telephoned him to tell him so.

'He apparently had been feeling exactly the same way and the upshot of the whole thing is that they've decided to give their marriage a second chance. She was even talking about them starting a family,' Sally added slightly wistfully.

Kyle had been having a heart-to-heart with Lindsay about her marriage. Kyle had *not* taken Lindsay home... Lindsay had kissed him out of gratitude and happiness. Kyle and Lindsay had *not* been lovers. He had *not* come straight from Lindsay's arms, from her bed to her own.

'Star...what is it? Are you feeling all right?' she heard Sally asking her anxiously.

'Yes, yes, I'm fine,' she assured her friend.

'You look dreadful. I thought you were going to faint, you went so pale,' Sally told her.

'I...I've just been a little tired; this campaign...I've been...'

'Why don't you talk to Kyle about it?' Sally suggested practically. 'Perhaps he could—'

'No.' Star cut her off sharply, firmly changing the subject by asking her, 'Have you managed to change Chris's mind yet about the two of you starting a family?'

It was no secret to Sally's friends that she wanted a baby.

'I'm still working on it,' Sally admitted. 'I know we both agreed that we wanted several years together before we even started thinking about a family, but since both Poppy and Claire have become pregnant... It isn't that Chris doesn't want children; it's just that he feels we're not ready for them yet. I know what he means, but I just feel so...'

'Broody?' Star supplied for her dryly.

'Well, yes,' Sally confessed. 'We're off to Italy at the end of September, Poppy and James are lending us the villa for a month and I'm hoping to work on him then.'

'Perhaps he feels that having a baby is becoming more important to you than he is,' Star suggested.

Sally looked shocked. 'Oh, no...he couldn't think that... could he?'

'You have become rather obsessive about it,' Star pointed out.

'Mmm...a bit like you with this thing you've got about men in general and poor Kyle in particular, do you mean?' Sally came back slyly.

'I've got to go,' Star told her quickly, and finished her coffee. 'I've got a deadline to meet...'

'So have I,' Sally said mischievously. 'I want to be pregnant by Christmas...'

After she left Sally, Star didn't go straight home, despite the fact that she had spoken the truth when she had said that she had work to do. Instead, she drove aimlessly along the country lanes outside the town, trying to bring some kind of order to her chaotic thoughts.

Even she couldn't refuse to accept that Sally had been telling her the truth. An unfamiliar feeling of panic seized her, her hands literally shaking as she held the steering wheel, a sense of foreboding and unease rushing threateningly towards her like thunderclouds in a summer sky—menacing, obscuring, gathering on the horizon.

It just wasn't possible that she had been wrong about Kyle. She couldn't have been. She knew that. All that rubbish he had mouthed about needing love and commitment, about finding sex empty and meaningless without them—it was just a clever way of tricking a woman into lowering her defences; she hadn't been wrong about that. She *couldn't* have been. Her whole body was trembling now, fear invading her like a black miasma. But fear of what?

She remembered how badly her body had ached after Kyle had left her, how she had woken at dawn with it still aching and shreds of misery-inducing dreams still lingering painfully in her mind—dreams from her childhood in which she had been left abandoned and fearful, knowing that she had done something dreadfully wrong as she cried out after the angry, disapproving faces of the adults around her, who ignored her pleas for them to remain, turning instead to leave her…to punish her.

She had rationalised her feelings, of course: her aching body had quite simply been the result of sexual frustration. It had, after all, been a long time since she had last had any sexual satisfaction and she had never been embarrassed or ashamed about acknowledging her body's needs before, she had reminded herself angrily, so why should she be so now, just because it was Kyle who had aroused her? And as for her dreams… Well the cause of those had quite obviously been the letter that she had received from her father.

She still hadn't replied to it; the letter itself had disappeared and although she couldn't actually remember doing so she imagined that she must have thrown it away. She would have to acknowledge it, of course, and with the formal 're-grets' card and a wedding-gift cheque—after all, she already knew, didn't she, that her money would be far more welcome than her actual presence? It was just as well that the rest of her commissions had gone so well recently, she decided tiredly as she turned the car around and headed for home.

Her flat seemed unusually sterile and empty after the un-tidy busyness of Sally's kitchen. Her friend would make a good mother, Star acknowledged—unlike her. But then Sally had Claire to model herself on, whilst she... Her mother had hardly been the maternal type and had said frequently and openly in front of Star that her life would have been much easier without the burden of a child, especially since that same child's father had managed to evade all responsibility towards her.

The issue of children had never been one which Star had given much thought to—there had been no need. She had known almost all her life that she would not have any, just as she had known that she would never commit herself to a man. Kyle, of course, would want dozens of them and would adore and dote on them.

Kyle! Angrily she cursed herself under her breath. Well, she wished him joy of them and of the woman he would marry to mother them. Star knew exactly what she would be like, of course: the complete antithesis of her—small, sweet, loved by everyone who knew her, universally praised as a perfect mother and wife, docilely content to let Kyle take the lead in every aspect of their lives and to dutifully turn a blind eye when he chose to stray from his proclaimed path of virtue. And, of course, he would stray, but not with her, Star decided savagely as she brought her car to a halt outside her apart-ment block. Never with her.

The phone was ringing as she opened the front door, tantalisingly stopping just as she managed to reach it. So what? Whoever it was would no doubt ring back; in the meantime she had work to do, or rather she desperately wished she had work to do. Despite all her efforts to do so, she had not as yet been able to come up with a satisfactorily inspirational alternative to her original idea for Brad's campaign, something that enthused her sufficiently for her to feel that familiar bite of excitement that she knew she needed to bring out the best of her inventive mind.

The phone rang again. She reached for the receiver and stiffened as she heard her father's voice.

'Star...just thought I'd give you a ring to apologise again for not being able to put you and your friend up here at the house, but you know how it is. Everyone's going to be home for the wedding and we're already having problems fitting everyone in as it is. Mind you, you'll probably be far more comfortable at the George; I've booked you a suite for the night.

'We'll be having a small family dinner party here at the house on the Friday evening and of course the pair of you will be more than welcome to join us if you wish, although Kyle didn't sound too sure you would.

'Nice chap. Where did you meet him, by the way? He's obviously American... Must admit, it came as a bit of a surprise when he rang to confirm that you'd both be coming, but he explained that you were right in the middle of a big campaign—'

'Dad...' Star tried to interrupt him chokily, but she could already hear the sound of children quarrelling in the background and before she could tell her father that, whatever Kyle might have said, she had no plans to attend her stepsister's wedding he was speaking again quickly.

'Look, I must go... It's the triplets. Louise has gone out shopping and left me in charge. Look forward to seeing you both.'

'Dad...' Star tried again, this time with more desperation in her voice, but it was already too late—the line had gone dead; he had more important, more pressing matters to deal with than listening to her. When had it been any different?

Just what did Kyle think he was doing? she fumed silently as she replaced the receiver. Who did he think he was? What gave *him* the right to take it upon himself to telephone her father for *any* reason, never mind to accept an invitation that she had already decided to decline, and never mind including himself in it at the same time?

'I could come with you...' he had suggested casually, and at the time she had simply thought that he was trying to find another way of undermining her. Perhaps he still was. Why, after all, should he want to go with her?

If he had been a different man and it had been a different situation, his motives would have been obvious: a night away in a hotel would give him the ideal opportunity to try to seduce her; but, given the situation which existed between Kyle and herself, such a scenario was ludicrously laughable. Kyle would run a mile rather than put himself in a situation where there was any possibility of any kind of intimacy between the two of them; any thoughts of seduction entering his head were more likely to be centred on *his* fear that *she* might attempt to seduce *him*, rather than by any desire on his part to take advantage of her.

Take advantage! In spite of herself, Star laughed. What a thought! She couldn't imagine herself ever being in a situation where she might be the hesitant and uncertain recipient of a man's sexual intentions, the helpless, vulnerable female to his powerful sexual machismo, swept away by the force of the passion that his desire ignited within her, all fluttering pulses and eyes as she clung to him and pleaded with him for temperance.

What a farce. She had certainly never had to drag a reluctant mate to her bed, but then she had certainly never had to be coaxed against her will either. She either wanted a man or she didn't. If she didn't, she said so, and when she did...

When she did, she took great care to make sure that she was always in control, both of herself and her partner.

Just as she had been in control with Kyle the other night, a taunting voice mocked her. So much in control in fact that just for one heart-stopping, faith-shaking moment before he had turned and left her, when the effect of what he had said to her and what he had physically done to her had been so strong, she had actually wanted... What? To beg him to stay? No, never...never!

Never! The denial was still reverberating angrily through her head half an hour later as she slammed the receiver back in its cradle, having discovered from his secretary that Kyle was out of the office and not expected back until much later in the day.

She had phoned him to demand an explanation of just why he had taken it upon himself to contact her father and announce that they—*they*, mark you, not merely she—would be attending Emily's wedding, and she was now furiously aware that without any outlet for her pent-up rage it was going to be almost impossible for her to concentrate on her work.

She could picture the wedding now: Emily looking traditionally pale and feminine, clinging to Star's father's arm as she walked down the aisle of the small village church, then the reception in a marquee at a local hotel—not, fortunately, the prestigious hotel where her father had booked them a suite. Just who was he trying to impress? Certainly not her; rather, it was a subtle underlining of her position as family outsider.

Yes, she could visualise the reception—the noise, the confusion, the busyness, the heat. She stood transfixed, her eyes widening slightly as the mental images unrolled inside her head.

Noise, heat, cross children, tired, irritable adults, a buffet table groaning with wilting food, a tearful bride, hot, screaming babies slightly too plump, middle-aged aunts with flushed faces. Ah, but how different it all could have been if only the hotel management had had the thought to install air-conditioning...

Switch to a different scene: a twenty-first birthday party—dim lights, loud music, gyrating bodies, flat drinks, discontent and complaints, overheated tempers, overheated and over-excited young men resorting to cooling themselves and their screaming girlfriends with the aid of shaken champagne bottles and the hotel's expensive ornamental indoor waterfall... Again how different it could have been.

Four hours later Star flung down her pencil, eased her aching back and flopped back in her chair. It wasn't the kind of campaign that she had originally envisaged—not quite as tongue-in-cheek or provocative—but her drawings certainly got the point across and, what was more, she acknowledged, they showed a year-round usage of Brad's air-conditioning units and not simply their necessity in hot weather.

She had even managed to accommodate Brad's requirement to bring in the superior efficiency of their installation and maintenance service by showing a game show in which Kyle's engineers came out points ahead as the clear winners in a competition with a rival organisation. And there was quite definitely nothing either smutty or sexist in any of the ads, Star decided in tired triumph.

All she had to do now was get them past Kyle. *All...* As she pushed her hair wearily off her face, she wished bitterly that she were able to go straight to Brad with her proposals, but, of course, she couldn't.

Her stomach rumbled, reminding her that she hadn't had

anything to eat since breakfast. The phone rang just as she walked into the kitchen but it was not Kyle returning her call as she had anticipated, much to her disappointment—she was still spoiling for a fight with him—but Lindsay.

'I just wanted to let you know that I won't be around for a few weeks, and also that we are going to give our marriage another try.'

Your marriage… What about your career? Star wanted to ask her, but she forced herself to hold her tongue. Obviously, she decided bitterly, Kyle's point of view meant far more to Lindsay than hers.

She would certainly not have advised the other woman to make the first move; she would have told her to let her husband do that. After all, he was the one in the wrong. All Lindsay had done was prove that she was a successful businesswoman. If her husband's pride couldn't take that, then in Star's opinion that was his problem and not Lindsay's.

After Lindsay had rung off Star tried Kyle's office number again but wasn't surprised when there was no reply. It was, after all, past seven o'clock.

She would have to wait until he returned home and tackle him then. And tackle him she certainly intended to do, because there was no way she was going to allow him to get away with his outrageous behaviour—no way at all.

It was gone ten o'clock when Kyle did eventually come in. Star saw him pull up next to her own car, but the phone rang before she could intercept him. This time it was her mother, who had heard the news about Emily's wedding and wanted to have a long moan about the situation. Star cut her short just as soon as she could. She was not really in the mood to listen to her mother's complaints; she had complaints of her own to lodge, far closer to home.

She had just replaced the receiver when she heard the sound of Kyle's front door opening. Suspecting that he must be about to go out, she hurriedly opened her own front door, determined to stop him.

The smile he gave her was warmly disarming but Star was not deceived; he must have realised that it wouldn't be long before she discovered what he had done.

'I want to talk to you,' she told him angrily.

Her sharp ears just caught his ruefully murmured, 'Talk… That makes a change.'

It took a monumental effort for her not to respond. It infuriated her that he should somehow have managed to turn *his* refusal to have sex with her into a totally false assumption that *she* was desperate to have sex with him. There had never been anything personal in her determination to arouse him; all *she* had wanted to do was unmask him as the deceiver she knew him to be.

'If it's about the advertising campaign,' he told her quickly, checking his watch, 'I'm afraid—'

'No, it's *not* about the advertising campaign,' Star interrupted him fiercely. 'It's about—'

Downstairs someone had opened the entrance door, causing a sudden gust of wind to rattle the window on the landing and her half-open front door to slam shut.

Star frowned as the unexpected noise interrupted her and then gasped as she realised what had happened. She had been in such a hurry to intercept Kyle that she had neglected to put her door on the latch. Now it was not just closed but locked as well, with her on the wrong side of it, without her keys, without anything other than the clothes she stood up in. She looked disbelievingly at the door and then accusingly at Kyle.

'That's your fault,' she told him forcefully. 'Thanks to you, I'm locked out of my flat.'

'Thanks to me…?'

'Yes,' Star fumed. 'If you hadn't had the gall to interfere and telephone my father with that stupid message about us attending the wedding… *How* did you know where to telephone him anyway?' she demanded suspiciously, and then answered her own question, her eyes widening in disbelief as she accused him, 'You took my letter; you stole it. You—'

'Hey, hang on a minute,' Kyle interrupted her. 'I did no such thing. As it happens, I found the letter caught up in my jacket, and when I realised what it was—'

'You read it and—'

'I thought it would be a good idea to ring your father and introduce myself to him, explain what we planned to do.'

'What *we* planned to do?' Star was thoroughly outraged. '*We* planned to do nothing,' she protested bitterly.

Kyle looked pained. 'You'd already agreed that we should attend the wedding together.'

'I agreed no such thing.' Star could feel her face growing red with temper. 'You know what my father thinks now, don't you?' she almost howled in fury. 'He thinks that you and I… That we're… I'm not going,' she told him vehemently. 'You do realise, don't you, that he's booked us a suite, no less, and not two separate bedrooms?'

'Well, he did explain that they were a little short of space,' Kyle acknowledged, completely missing the point that she was trying to make. 'And, to be honest, I thought you'd prefer the hotel…'

'What I prefer is for you not to interfere in my life. You had no right. I'm *not* going. There's *no way* that you can make me,' she told him aggressively, before turning round to walk back into her own flat.

Only, of course, she couldn't, could she? She paused, mentally consigning him to the deepest, blackest depths of hell, and then gritted her teeth, turned round and told Kyle crankily, 'I need to use your phone…'

'I'm afraid you can't,' Kyle told her politely.

Star stared at him. 'What you mean, I can't? I've *got* to.

I've locked myself out of my flat, thanks to you. I need to ring a locksmith.'

'Doesn't anyone have a spare?' Kyle asked her.

'No,' Star told him. That was against the rules, of course. They were supposed to deposit a spare with a trusted key-holder, only she balked at the idea of anyone—anyone at all—having access to her most private domain and so she had never supplied one.

'I need to use your phone,' she repeated, but Kyle was adamant.

'You can't...'

'Just try stopping me,' Star challenged him angrily, marching past him and straight into his flat, where upon she came to an abrupt halt. The hall and the sitting room beyond were both completely empty.

'What's happening?' she demanded. 'Where's the furniture?'

'Gone,' Kyle told her ruefully. 'Apparently your late neighbours neglected to settle all their bills before they left and this morning the bailiffs arrived and removed their furniture...'

'*And* the telephone?' Star protested. 'But that's...'

Kyle shook his head. 'No, that's been cut off. Apparently they didn't pay that bill either. I've made arrangements to have it reinstated and to have new furniture delivered but unfortunately not until tomorrow.'

'They must have left something,' Star said weakly as she stared around the empty rooms.

'They did,' Kyle agreed. 'The bed,' he told her when she looked questioningly at him. 'I bought a new one. The one they left wasn't very comfortable.'

'The bed... That's *all* the furniture you've got...a bed...?'

'Well, they left the kitchen fitments as well,' Kyle informed her. 'So at least we can eat as well as sleep.'

'*We*?' Star glared at him. 'If you think I'm sharing a bed with you...' she began.

But Kyle reminded her, 'It's either that or the floor.'

'You've got a car,' Star pointed out. 'You could take me to a hotel.'

'I could, but I doubt that they'd allow you to book in...not dressed like that...not without any money.'

'Dressed like what?' Star glanced down at herself and re-alised that he did have a point. She had no shoes on, her feet were bare and she was wearing a loose, soft cotton top and an old pair of leggings—hardly the kind of apparel to inspire financial confidence.

'You could lend me some money; in fact I could stay here and *you* could book into a hotel room,' she told him.

Kyle shook his head. 'No way,' he told her firmly. 'This is my flat and my bed—a new bed, an extremely comfort-able bed, a bed I am not prepared to give up for a demand-ing termagant who—'

'Oh, very chivalrous,' Star interrupted him, angry colour scorching her face. How dared he refer to her as a terma-gant? She had every right to be angry with him after what he had done.

'I could go to Sally's,' she told him.

'You could,' he agreed, looking down at her feet. 'But it's quite a long walk, at least five miles.'

Star gritted her teeth. 'You're enjoying this, aren't you?' she challenged him bitterly, and the smile that curled his mouth and his open acceptance of her accusation did noth-ing to alleviate her rising temper.

'Do you blame me?' he asked her drily. 'After all, would *you* turn down an opportunity to put one over on me, Star... to have me at a disadvantage? Don't perjure yourself,' he ad-vised her kindly. 'We both already know the answer...'

He was right, of course, but that didn't make it any easier

to bear. How could she have been so stupid as to forget her keys or, at the very least, to put the door on the latch? She knew how, of course: she had been in such a steam of temper, so seriously determined to vent her anger on him, that she hadn't stopped to think. That nasty, niggling awareness that she was very much the author of her own misfortune couldn't be denied—at least, not to herself—but she was damned if she was going to admit it to him.

'If you hadn't made that idiotic telephone call to my father, none of this would have happened. Why did you?' she demanded.

'I thought it was what you wanted,' he told her innocently. He was playing with her, deliberately baiting her; Star knew that.

She breathed in slowly and tried to count to ten.

'Really?' She gave him a saccharine smile, her teeth snapping together audibly as she told him, 'I don't believe you; you're just trying to...'

'To what?' he queried. 'To do a little game-playing of my own...a little truth-outing? Aha. You don't like it when the boot is on the other foot, do you?' he taunted her as he saw the way her eyes flashed.

'What do you mean, "a little truth-outing"?' Star asked him grimly, ignoring his mockery.

'You said you wanted to have sex with me to prove that I was lying when I said I didn't want sex without emotion or commitment,' he reminded her.

'Yes,' Star agreed doggedly.

'Well, perhaps *I* have a little theory testing of my own I want to put into practice.'

'Theory-testing? What kind of theory-testing?' Star asked suspiciously.

'Well, now...' he drawled. 'I kinda think that that's for me to know and for you to think about, don't you?'

For once Star was bereft of any suitable reply; her mouth
opened and then closed again, her temper reaching boiling
point and running over it as she realised that somehow or
other he had wrestled control of the situation from her and
that there wasn't a damn thing she could do about it.

'I'm not going to let you get away with this,' she warned
him darkly when she had finally got her voice back. 'Whatever it is...'

To her chagrin, she saw that Kyle was actually daring to
laugh at her.

'You know what you need, don't you?' he advised her solemnly. 'A cool shower, a hot drink and a good night's sleep.'

He was treating her like an overwrought child, Star recognised as she contrasted his cheerful good temper with her
own impotent fury.

'What I *want*,' she told him through gritted teeth, 'is to
remove you from my life...permanently and preferably immediately...'

'Ah, but, you see, you were the one who invited me into
it,' Kyle reminded her.

'I invited you into my bed...not my life,' Star corrected
him, determined to have the last word.

'Mmm... Well, now it's my turn to invite you into mine...
What's wrong?' he asked when he saw the look that she was
giving him. 'I promise you, you have nothing to fear. Your
virtue is completely safe with me.'

Star glared at him. 'Don't be ridiculous,' she told him witheringly. 'And, for your information, I have *never* been afraid
of a man making unwanted sexual advances to me.'

She had intended her statement to be a contemptuous put-
down but somehow or other she must have missed her mark,
she decided as Kyle responded gently, 'No, I don't suppose
you have.'

CHAPTER EIGHT

IRRITATINGLY, Kyle had insisted that there was no way she could go to bed until she had had something to eat, and, ignominiously, Star had been so hungry that she had practically fallen on the simple meal of scrambled eggs and toast that he had made for her.

He was like a mother hen the way he fussed, Star decided waspishly now as he handed her a milky bedtime drink which she grimaced over before drinking. Not like a real man at all. Surprisingly the drink tasted delicious; she sniffed it suspiciously and accused him, 'You've put something in this, haven't you? Brandy...'

'The classic seducer's trick,' Kyle agreed solemnly, and then added, 'I'm surprised you never tried that one on me...'

'I was *not* trying to seduce you,' she reminded him. 'I simply wanted to prove...'

'Go on,' Kyle encouraged her. 'You wanted to prove...?'

'I've had enough of this,' Star told him, finishing her drink. 'I'm going to bed.'

She was undressed and in the shower before she remembered that she had nothing to sleep in—not that that would normally have bothered her; it was just that on this occasion... The thought of having to sleep in her bulky top was totally unappealing and as for her briefs... Well, she had already rinsed them out so that they would be fresh for the morning.

Wrapping a towel around her body, she went in search of Kyle. He was in the kitchen, predictably tidying up. What a man... Just as well they hadn't had sex; it would have been bound to be a disaster...

'I need something to wear,' she told him aggressively.

His eyebrows rose.

'Such as...?'

'Something,' she insisted. 'Anything... You must have a pair of pyjamas somewhere.'

'Nope,' Kyle denied.

'But you must have... What if you had to go into hospital?'

'What an optimist,' Kyle laughed. 'The best I can do is a T-shirt.'

'I suppose it will have to do,' Star told him ungraciously, following as he went into the bedroom and pulled open a cupboard door.

The T-shirt he handed her was soft and white and extremely large. She frowned slightly, remembering how snugly she had seen a similar T-shirt fitting him. She wasn't exactly minute and yet to judge from the width of the fabric she was holding...

She saw the way Kyle was watching her and stated crossly, 'I can't put it on until you've gone.'

Infuriatingly he started to laugh.

'Now I've heard everything,' he told her. 'You're quite happy to have sex with me—an act for which, presumably, you initially remove your clothes—and yet the mere thought that I might actually see your naked body throws you into a girlish display of maidenly modesty that wouldn't disgrace a virginal sixteen-year-old. Amazing...'

'No, it isn't; it's a perfectly normal female reaction,' Star corrected him, throwing him a look of vitriolic hatred.

How dared he laugh at her? How dared he... How dared he...how dared he *exist*? she fumed a few minutes later when he had gone, leaving her free to drop her damp towel and pull on his T-shirt. It was enormous on her. It was probably one he deliberately kept to impress women, she decided balefully. It was probably enormous on him too.

She yawned sleepily and burrowed deeper into her pillow. How much brandy had he actually put in that drink? she wondered. She yawned again, her body starting to relax. He had been right about one thing: this bed...*his* bed...was blissfully comfortable.

Well, she looked as though she was asleep, Kyle decided fifteen minutes later, cautiously opening the bedroom door. She ought to be; he had given her enough brandy to knock out a horse—an invidious tactic, but it was either that or risk spending the whole night with her arguing with him. What a woman.

He padded silently to the bathroom and stripped off his clothes before turning on the shower.

He wondered how long it would be before she guessed what he was up to. There was no need to question what her reaction would be when she did. He was playing a mite unfairly, he had to admit that, but then desperate needs called for desperate measures and he was certainly desperate. Any man would have to be to get involved in what he was getting himself involved in, but he was determined to show her that her antagonism towards his sex sprang not from the conviction she clung so determinedly and defensively to—that none of his sex could be trusted—but rather from her fear of the pain she had experienced when her father had left.

Once he could show her that with him she had nothing to fear... That his feelings...his love... That *he* would always... Hang on there, he warned himself. There was still a hell of a lot of ground to cover before she was ready to listen to that kind of talk from him—one hell of a long way to go.

He looked down into her sleeping face and somehow managed to resist the temptation to kiss the tip of her nose before throwing back the covers and quietly sliding into bed beside her—alongside her. Alongside, when what he would have preferred to do...where he would have preferred to be... Determinedly, he closed his eyes.

Star smiled happily in her sleep and snuggled closer to the male body lying alongside her own. Mmm...it felt so delicious...all that warm, soft, furry male body hair against her skin, and that lovely, tantalisingly erotic man smell—so totally unfamiliar...and yet somehow, deep down inside herself, she instinctively and immediately recognised a sense of being safe and warm and wanted, had an awareness of the rightness of being where she was and with whom she was.

She made a soft sound of pleasure and burrowed even closer to the source of all those wonderful feel-good sensations and emotions whilst Kyle held his breath.

He had woken up fifteen minutes ago, alerted to Star's unconscious "sleepwalk" across the gap that he had left between them by the unmistakable physical response of his own body to her proximity. For once, he was able to acquit her of any attempt to manipulate or manoeuvre him—*she* was quite definitely deeply asleep—and if he hadn't been finding it so damned hard to hold onto his self-control, or if he'd been a different type of man, he could have been giving himself a little bit of congratulation at the way Star's sleeping expression and her small sounds of pleasure betrayed how much she was enjoying her unwitting physical contact with his body.

His body or just any male body? Kyle frowned. Despite everything he had heard about her and everything she had told him about herself, Kyle had guessed that emotionally, where it really counted, Star was completely untried and untouched—virginal in that in her previous relationships she had always withheld her real, deep, inner self. And, as he had already told her, that kind of shallow pseudo-intimacy could never be enough for him. He held his breath as she burrowed even closer against him.

If this carried on much longer...! It had been difficult enough for him to resist her when she'd been deliberately and cold bloodedly trying to arouse him, but what she was doing now, with that sweetly sensual look of desire on her sleeping face... If she moved against him like that just one more time...

Kyle knew that he was audibly grinding his teeth as she still tried to get closer, pushing his arm out of the way, a small pout puckering her mouth as she tugged on his hand. Obediently he raised it and then dropped it again as he realised what he was doing, but somehow or other his hand had already found the smooth curve of her hip, and once there it was impossible for him to resist the temptation to stroke her skin, so soft and warm and alive, so womanly and desirable...so...so Star.

Outside the birds had started to sing. Star's pout dissolved into a dazzling smile as she rubbed her face against his chest, appreciatively breathing in his scent, nuzzling him and making soft, murmuring, cooing sounds of pleasure.

A man would have to be a saint to remain unaffected by what she was doing, Kyle acknowledged achingly. No studied, practised, deliberately calculated seduction could have had one tenth of the effect on him that her instinctive, artless, innocent betrayal of her desire to be close to him was now.

Somehow or other his gentle fingertip-touch against her skin had become a slow, lingering, rhythmic caress that had found the delicate, narrow indentation of her waist and moved beyond it to the full, rounded curve of her breast, just made to fit perfectly within the cup of his hand.

Star gave a softly voluptuous sigh and arched her spine.

Kyle groaned out loud. Star was touching him now, exploring the hard muscles of his back and moving lower, whilst the soft warmth of her breathing against his throat quickened. Against the hand that covered her breast he could feel her nipple swell and harden, just as his body was doing—just as it had been doing from the moment she'd started to move closer to him.

Reluctantly Kyle released her breast and started to ease her away from him gently, bending his head to kiss her forehead tenderly as he did so, only Star wouldn't let him go. Her hands clung to his shoulders and she was moving her body so that she was as close to him as it was possible to be, one long, slim leg wrapping itself firmly around him so that...

Kyle could feel the heat burning up under his skin as the T-shirt he had lent her rode up and he felt the warm, silky, bare length of her thigh pressing against him. He reached out, intending only to move her.

It was more than any man could be expected to stand... *any* man. With a smothered groan, Kyle gathered her closer, one hand sliding up under the T-shirt as he held her, the other lifting to push the soft mass of her hair off her face and slide along her jaw, cupping it lovingly as he bent his head to kiss her.

He kissed her once, very gently and delicately, a second time for no better reason than the fact that her mouth tasted so sweet and he was so hungry for her that he just couldn't resist it, and then a third time, deeper and longer, because, well, if a man was going to damn himself he might as well do the job properly, mightn't he?

Of course he might, and of course Star woke up. How could she not do?

Star was not in the habit of dreaming about being made love to and certainly not about the kind of lovemaking that included delicious, tantalising half-kisses that touched and awoke and inflamed her senses more intensely and erotically than any real, experienced kiss she could ever remember.

She didn't like having such dreams and, more specifically, she didn't like having such dreams about the one man who was least likely to want to participate in them with her. They made her feel angry and cheated...and...and vulnerable, as though there was something missing from her life—which was ridiculous; how could there be anything missing from the life that she had specifically and deliberately chosen and tailored for herself? Of course there couldn't be.

She tried to say the words out loud—a sure-fire mantra which had never failed to work in the past—only this time she couldn't actually say the words because something...someone was making it impossible for her to do so. Someone was kissing her; someone was...

Star opened her eyes and then closed them again on a dizzy wave of disbelief. Kyle was kissing her. Kyle was holding her. Kyle was lying so close to her that she could feel every single movement of his body against her own, every breath he took...every beat of his pulse... Every beat of his pulse...? Impossible. 'Impossible!'

She said the word quite clearly as Kyle lifted his mouth from hers in anticipation of her furious demand for an explanation of what he thought he was doing. And then he realised that no such demand was going to come, that she had in fact closed her eyes and snuggled back into his arms with a sigh of pure, feminine, seductive bliss, following her instincts and reaching up towards him, her hand on his jaw as she lifted her head off the pillow to close the small distance between them, her lips unexpectedly hesitant and searching as they caressed his own—more questioning than demanding, Kyle recognised as he kissed her back, his tongue tracing the shape of her mouth.

The immediate shudder of response that convulsed her

body surprised them both, Star's body tensing, her eyes opening as she waited warily.

She didn't like being responsive to him, Kyle sensed. Her body language told him that she wanted him to let her go, but he refused to respond to it.

'What's wrong?' he asked her softly. 'I thought this was what you wanted…to prove…'

'I've changed my mind,' Star snapped back at him, suddenly wide awake and made antagonistic by her realisation of what was happening to her and how vulnerable she felt. She was never the one to become so quickly and so intensely aroused—certainly not by a mere kiss. The sensation of wanting to be close to him…of wanting him…was alien and unfamiliar to her and she was afraid of it.

'Let me go,' she demanded tautly. 'I don't want—'

'You don't want what?' Kyle interrupted her softly. 'Me?'

He raised his hand and cupped the side of her breast, letting the tip of his thumb just touch the erect crest of her nipple whilst he told her gently, 'Liar.'

It was a case of being cruel to be kind, he told himself in justification of the stricken, panicky expression that he could see darkening her eyes. Instinct told him that she had never been in a situation like this before, never known what it was like to be afraid of her own sexuality.

Whilst she watched him her hands curled into two small, tense fists. Kyle bent his head and very gently kissed the centre of each breast, one after the other, his caress leaving the fine cotton fabric of his T-shirt clinging moistly to her skin.

He had never previously thought that there was anything particularly erotic about the sight of a girl wearing a wet T-shirt that was clinging to her otherwise naked breasts, but now, suddenly, there was a sensation inside him that was all male and entirely primitive. Before Star could stop him he had bent his head to her body again and this time there was no way she could control her fevered response to the sensation of his mouth dragging the slightly abrasive, damp fabric against the sensitivity of her skin.

Given that cerebrally the last thing she wanted was for him to continue what he was doing, it was perhaps a trifle contradictory for Star to give a little smothered gasp of pleasure and arch her body up against his mouth in deliberate incitement of a continuation of his mouth's sensual destruction of her self-control.

Star clutched at Kyle's shoulders, her nails digging into the hard muscle as wave upon wave of barely endurable pleasure swamped her. She was a sensual, sexual woman who had thought that she understood her body and was familiar with all of its responses, but this…!

This aching, overwhelming need was something else again and, as she had with everything else in her life which had made her feel threatened and vulnerable, Star fought against it, frantically trying to push Kyle away as his hands lifted her T-shirt and his mouth moved from her breasts to her ribcage and then lower, gently caressing and arousing every single inch of her skin.

Male desire, male urgency, male hunger—all of these she was used to, all of them gave her power and weakened the man who exhibited them. Male tenderness, male gentleness, male desire to give her pleasure—these were alien to her and she was both angered and frightened by them. They overwhelmed her, undermined her, made her want to reach out and hold onto the man caressing her, made her want to cling to him, to give the real essence of herself to him, and Star had never given anything of herself to any man, not since her father had abandoned her, not since she had realised that giving your love to a man meant being hurt by him.

Her love!

Star froze, the only movement in her body the small ripple

of sensation just under her skin where Kyle's mouth had been slowly caressing the smooth curve of her hip.

But she didn't love Kyle.

This need she could feel battling with her brain's fierce exhortation to her to push him away, to make herself safe, this desire to reach out and touch him, to feel his skin beneath her hands, her mouth, to hold him and wrap herself around him, to draw him deep, deep within her body and to hold him there—all this was nothing… It meant nothing. How could it when *he* meant nothing?

His fingertips stroked sensually along the inside of her thigh. How could she ever have thought that his refusal to touch her must mean that he was somehow sexually inadequate? she wondered. This man could do more to arouse her senses to a fever pitch of aching need with a single kiss, a single touch, than any other man had been able to using every kind of sophisticated foreplay that had ever been imagined.

His mouth trailed moistly along her hip-bone, following the fierce pulse-beat of need that was beginning to throb through her whole body.

He was, Star witnessed, as unconcerned about her viewing his own arousal as he was concerned about ensuring that she experienced every single sensation of her own.

In the dawn light she could see his body perfectly clearly through the sharply painful glitter of the tears which had, for some reason, filled her eyes and blocked her throat.

His body was everything that a man's body should be— well muscled without in any way becoming a caricature of over-developed and somehow totally non-sexual maleness, his skin warmed by the sun but not over-tanned, his body hair darkly silky, heart-lurchingly male both to her sight and her touch.

She wanted to reach out to him as she had never wanted to reach out to any other man, to touch him with her fingertips and her mouth, to know and explore him—not clinically and cold-bloodedly, with the single-minded purpose of arousing him, but for her own pleasure as well as for his and because she actually wanted the feel and the taste of him beneath her hands and her mouth. Oh, how she wanted them. Oh, how she wanted them…and him.

Star closed her eyes to block not just the weakness of her tears but, even more importantly, the sight of so much temptation.

But nothing could block out her senses, her mind…her heart, her vulnerability and the root cause of it.

'Stop it… I don't want this.'

Kyle heard the words but it took several seconds for their actual meaning to sink through the fierce thrill of aroused pleasure that the sensation of Star's wonderfully warm and responsive body beneath his mouth gave him. Every touch, every caress, every soft drift of his mouth released a small, frantic torrent of responsive quivers and movement. He had never known a woman so warmly and vibrantly alive, so sensually aware. Just holding her and touching her the way he was doing right now was more deeply, sensually pleasurable for him than any lovemaking he had known in the past.

The thought of how she would feel, how she would be when he eventually reached the hot, sweet heart of her was already making his heart pound with deep, heavy hammer-blows of surging longing.

He would take his time, draw out the moment of pleasure, kiss and caress every tiny bit of her, touch her gently with his tongue in that special, sensual and oh, so sensitive place, waiting until she was ready for him before taking her fully into his mouth and feeling her body dissolve in liquid waves of sensual release.

But she was telling him that she didn't want that. That

she didn't want him. Reluctantly Kyle responded to her rejection, her denial.

The moment he released her Star scrambled off the bed. Her legs were shaking so much that she could barely stand up. She felt sick and anxious and angrily frightened as well...

'No,' she said loudly, her body going rigid as she fought to reject her emotions. Kyle, who had been about to reach out to her, let his hand drop back to his side.

'I rang you several times this morning but there was no reply.'

'No, there wouldn't be. I wasn't there,' Star told her mother shortly.

It was less than an hour since she had finally managed to get into her flat with the aid of a locksmith who had exchanged the kind of knowing male look with Kyle when she had explained her predicament that set her teeth on edge.

And, of course, the commotion they'd caused had brought Amy out to see what was going on, and Star had been well aware of what was going through her mind when she had asked where Star had spent the night and Kyle had responded immediately, 'With me.'

Although why she should care or feel angry and self-conscious she had no idea...she told herself. Only, of course, she did, just as she knew exactly why she was so reluctant to explain to her mother what had happened.

It had nothing to do with any kind of embarrassment or guilt over the fact that she had spent the night with a man and everything to do with her own illogical behaviour and emotions. Even now she still couldn't believe what she had done. She, a woman who had always prided herself on being in control of her sexuality, for some totally inexplicable reason had suddenly become so overwhelmed by it, so afraid of it that she had had to take refuge in the kind of female behaviour that she had thought belonged solely to nervous young virgins.

No woman of her experience *ever* let things get to the stage that she had done and then said no. No woman…but she had. And not because she had suddenly had a change of heart and decided that she didn't want Kyle. Oh, no. Certainly not because of that… If only!

A change of heart! Star closed her eyes and tried to swallow past the huge, painful lump which had blocked her throat. How very appropriate that she should pick on such a phrase… How appropriate and how appalling…

'Star…? Star, are you still there?'

'Yes, I'm still here, Mother,' she responded huskily, dimly aware that her mother was in the midst of complaining about Emily's wedding again, but too preoccupied with her own thoughts to try to stop her.

'I was just wondering why on earth your father's making such a thing about Emily's marriage. It isn't even as though she is his child. Of course, he always did enjoy throwing her in my face…the child of the woman he discarded me for… making it obvious that she took precedence over you…'

Star sighed. She had heard it all so many, many times before. 'Perhaps he genuinely did prefer her to me,' she pointed out quietly to her mother. 'After all, she was…is…far more the kind of daughter he wanted.'

'Rubbish… He just did it to spite me. Well, it's just as well he didn't invite me. I couldn't have gone. As a matter of fact…'

Star frowned as her mother's voice faltered betrayingly.

'Well, I might as well tell you now… I shall be getting married myself. Very quietly, *very* quietly,' she stressed. 'And we'll actually be away on honeymoon the day Emily gets married.'

Star took a deep breath.

'I see,' she said as neutrally as she could as she tried not to visualise her mother standing side by side with the gangly, still not fully grown teenager who was her current lover, making what in Star's opinion was a total mockery of the sacred vows of marriage.

'And Iris... Has she become reconciled to you and Mark marrying or—?'

'Mark!' Her mother's response was immediate and shocked. 'Don't be ridiculous, Star. I'm not marrying Mark; he's only a boy, a child...'

Not marrying Mark. Hard on the heels of her relief Star felt her stomach start to churn with the familiar sensation of anger and anxiety that her mother so often caused.

'Not Mark,' she repeated slowly. 'Then who are you marrying, Mother?'

'Why, Brian, of course,' her mother responded impatiently, for all the world as though Star were a particularly dense child. 'Who else?'

Who else indeed? Star opened her mouth to remind her mother of all the other 'who elses' there could have and had been and then closed it again.

Brian Armstrong was one of her mother's oldest friends. He had known her before she had met and married Star's father and he had remained patiently and, so far as Star was concerned, unfathomably devoted to her in all the years since.

Whenever her mother was in trouble it was Brian she turned to. He was her rock, her one true friend, she had once laughingly told him in Star's presence, and Star, eight years old then, seeing the painful way he blushed and looked away, had been torn with embarrassment at witnessing such intense adult emotion and anger at her mother for causing it and for being oblivious and uncaring of what she was doing.

Brian had loved her mother for as long as Star could remember, but never once had her mother given any indication that she might return that emotion.

'Brian,' she said numbly. 'But Mother—'

'I know what I'm doing, Star,' her mother interrupted her firmly. 'I should have married him years ago but I suppose I wanted to show…to prove to your father that he wasn't the only one who could change partners whenever the mood suited him… I saw him not long ago, you know… He had those three children with him—the triplets… He looked so old… Poor man… I almost felt sorry for him.

'Brian and I are getting married in the Caribbean, by the way,' she told Star. 'So romantic… It's time *you* got married, Star,' her mother reproved her. 'I can just imagine how Louise will be crowing over the fact that her daughter is getting married first.'

'Mother…' Star started to protest warningly, but her mother was already announcing that she had to go and replacing the receiver.

Her mother remarrying…again. Well, at least she was marrying Brian and not Mark, Star reflected, which was probably the most sensible, the *only* sensible decision that her mother had made in her entire life.

Unlike her mother's, all *her* decisions were sensible and well thought out. She never acted on her emotions, nor allowed them to rule her. Never…

'And Kyle asked me to ask if you could come in to see him and bring whatever work you've managed to do on the campaign so far,' Star heard Tim's secretary explaining to her as she cradled the telephone receiver against her ear.

'Well, I haven't really got very much to show him as yet,' Star said untruthfully.

But Mrs Hawkins had obviously been primed by Kyle not to accept any put-offs, because she insisted, with quiet firmness, 'He has a free slot this afternoon at four and I know he's hoping to fly home this weekend to report to Brad.'

To fly home. Kyle was going to be away… How long for?

Just…just for the weekend or for longer…? Star didn't like the ominous way her heart lurched and then started to beat far too fast. Kyle had said nothing to her about being away.

But then, why should he?

'I'll try to make it for four.' She gave in unwillingly. It wasn't that she didn't have anything to show Kyle, she acknowledged ten minutes later as she started to gather together her new story-boards. She did. And it wasn't even that she was afraid of him rejecting her work. So what was she so afraid of, then? Kyle himself? Why should she be?

Her face burned as she recalled exactly why she felt so reluctant to face him. How could she account for her ignominious flight from his bed this morning? After all the things she had said to him…all the taunts…all the insults…that *she* should be the one to cry craven, to say stop… And why had she?

She shook her head, still not ready to answer that question, even to herself.

'Kyle will see you now.'

Star squared her shoulders and nodded tersely in acknowledgement of Mrs Hawkins's statement as she stood up and gathered her work together.

As Star headed towards Kyle's office his secretary reflected that she looked as though she was about to undergo a gruelling ordeal, rather like her own dreaded visits to her dentist, and yet, personally, Mrs Hawkins found working for Kyle one of the most serendipitous experiences of her entire working life. He had that American way with him of somehow getting things done, of removing obstacles and barriers almost instantaneously and yet, at the same time, always remaining calm and polite.

Tim was a lovely man, of course, gentle and thoughtful, but he *had* lacked Kyle's resolution, his ability to insist on high standards and good workmanship. Mrs Hawkins had noticed already the drop in complaints from their customers, just as she had noted and approved of the firm way in which some of their less than efficient fitters and technicians had been dealt with and the way far more stringent standards and checks had been established for those who had taken their place.

Kyle reached the door before Star did, opening it for her and ushering her inside, watching her gravely.

How on earth was she supposed to concentrate on her work, Star wondered wretchedly, when all she could remember, all she could think about was that this morning she had been in Kyle's bed, had lain in his arms, and his touch had taught her things about herself that she had never dreamed existed—things she wished passionately that she had not discovered existed?

How could she concentrate on her work when she was still trying to deal with the aftershock of those discoveries?

'I've rewritten the proposed advertising copy, taking into account your criticisms,' she began stiffly as she lined up the story-boards.

Even with her back to him, she could sense Kyle moving closer to her to study what she had done. Quickly she moved out of the way. Kyle had stopped in front of the first board and was examining it. Making sure she kept a safe distance between them, Star waited until he had examined all of them.

'I like it... It's very good,' he told her when he had finished.

'It doesn't have the same punch as the other ideas,' Star asserted.

'No, perhaps not,' Kyle agreed. 'It *is* gentler, less hard-hitting, but in my opinion that won't detract from its overall impact.

'Don't forget that in the main we're selling these systems to men, not women, and most men, although they might be loath to admit it, do feel intimidated by and are antagonistic to what they see as domineering or aggressive women—women in control of themselves and their own lives...'

'Now who's being sexist?' Star couldn't resist saying grimly.

'I didn't say those were *my* feelings,' Kyle pointed out.

'Your father rang me this afternoon, by the way,' he told her in a different voice. 'He wanted to check that we were definitely going to the wedding. He said he'd tried to ring you but that you were engaged.'

Star stiffened.

'What did you say?'

Kyle shrugged. 'I confirmed that we were going and—'

'What?' Star demanded in disbelief. 'You can't possibly want to go.'

'No? How could *you* know what I might want, Star?' Kyle asked her drily. '*You* don't even know what you want your-self.'

Star stood and stared at him. She could feel the blood draining out of her face and then flooding back into it again in a hot burning tide of self-conscious colour and she knew that she couldn't do a damn thing about it or what it betrayed about her.

'That's not true,' she managed to deny unevenly, and then, unable to bear it any longer, she moistened her suddenly dry lips with the tip of her tongue and told him angrily, 'That's typical of a man... Just because a woman says no when she...'

'When she means yes, or rather—'

'I did not mean yes,' Star denied. 'How dare you imply that I did? That's the oldest trick in the book so far as your sex is concerned—claiming that you know a woman means yes when she says no and using that as an excuse to force her—'

'*I* didn't force you to do anything, Star,' Kyle pointed out gently. 'I do understand, you know,' he told her softly. 'I know you were afraid—'

'Afraid?' Star tensed. 'What have I got to be afraid of?' she demanded acidly. Her eyebrows rose mockingly. 'You?'

Kyle cursed himself under his breath. He had said too much but he had spent the whole damn day thinking about her, worrying about her, wanting to go to her and yet guessing how she would react if he did. And he had been right. But, tempted as he was to let her off the hook, to make it easy for her, he couldn't let himself lose the small piece of ground he had won, for her sake as well as his own.

'No, not me,' he acknowledged. 'What you fear, Star, is yourself, or rather your own emotions. That's what you're afraid of—needing someone, wanting someone...*loving* someone...'

'Loving someone!' Star exploded scornfully. 'Oh, come on...please...'

She managed to make her mouth curl in a creditable display of contempt, but inside she was shaking so much that she dared not close her mouth in case her teeth started to chatter.

Panic—something she had spent virtually all her life suppressing and hiding from others—suddenly overwhelmed her and snapped the bonds she had used to tether it as easily and mockingly as the Incredible Hulk bursting out of his shirt. The incongruity, the ludicrousness of it should have made her laugh; instead she felt half-paralysed with terror.

'I'm flying out to the States on Friday,' she heard Kyle adding casually, just as though those few hauntingly destructive sentences had never been spoken. 'Why don't you come with me and we can take these—' he pointed to the story-boards '—with us to show Brad? He'll be keen to see what you've come up with while he's been away on honeymoon.'

'No...'

The panic hadn't just escaped into her body, it had es-

caped into her voice as well, Star recognised as she fought
to control it.

'I…I can't,' she stressed shakily. 'I…I've got some other
work I need to do…'

'All weekend?' Kyle queried.

'I don't work nine to five,' Star snapped back at him. 'If
something urgent comes up—'

'Of course,' Kyle agreed soothingly, walking past her to
his desk, where he picked up his diary and, to her consternation, told her cheerfully after studying it, 'Well, it doesn't
matter. I can reschedule my trip for after your sister's wedding, to fit in with you. Do you have your diary with you?'

'No, I don't,' Star told him through gritted teeth. 'And she
is *not* my sister.'

'But she is a part of your family, and your father is still
your father.'

'I'm not going to the wedding,' Star told him determinedly.

Kyle gave her a tolerant smile. 'Of course you're going,' he
told her in a kindly voice, adding more firmly, 'We're *both*
going. Now, about this campaign… I'd like for Brad to see
what you've come up with as soon as possible.'

'Then why don't you take the story-boards with you this
weekend? I could redraw everything on a small scale if you—'

'Fine,' Kyle agreed. 'I'll let Brad see this first version then
I'm sure he will want to go through the whole thing with you
himself,' he added. 'Could you also come up with some idea
of the kind of scheduling and media scope you envisage using
for the campaign?'

'A TV slot would have the greatest impact,' Star told him,
'but of course it would be expensive…'

'Mmm…I guess it would, but if it were timed to fit in with
us getting into place the new fitting and technical people
we're subcontracting to… Leave it with me. I'll have a word
with Brad about that whilst I'm over there—'

He broke off as the phone rang, excusing himself as he went to pick it up. As he answered his call Star started to gather together her work but even though she wasn't deliberately listening she couldn't avoid hearing the warmly excited female voice exclaiming in a transatlantic accent, 'Kyle, I've just heard that you're coming home! That's wonderful. You can be sure there'll be a warm—a very warm—welcome waiting for you...'

Star could hear Kyle clearing his throat before he said quietly, 'I'm not sure exactly what time I'll be flying in and so—'

There was a giggle and then Star heard her saying, 'Well, that's OK. After all, I've still got my key...'

Picking up the last of her story-boards, Star gave him a bitterly corrosive glare before opening the door and walking through it.

It was obvious that some women...some relationships were exempt from his proclaimed desire for emotional commitment and intimacy. Unless...

She stopped abruptly in the outer office and frowned so horribly that Mrs Hawkins wondered uneasily just what on earth was wrong.

Unless the woman at the other end of the telephone was someone special, someone whom Kyle *did* want to make a full commitment to...

Well, if she was, then what the hell had he been doing in bed with *her*? Star wondered angrily as she stamped out of the office and headed for her car.

CHAPTER NINE

'KYLE came round last night. He wanted to know if we had any messages for him. He's flying out to the States today.'

'I know,' Star told Sally shortly in a tone that warned her that it wasn't a subject she wanted to pursue.

But Sally either didn't pick up on that warning or chose to ignore it, because she continued, 'Oh, heavens, I nearly forgot—Kyle asked me to remind you that the two of you have still got to sort out a wedding present for Emily. Is there anything you want to tell me?' she asked mock-innocently.

'Nothing,' Star denied.

'I see,' Sally commented judiciously. 'One moment you detest the man so much that you can't stand the sight of him, the next he's going to Emily's wedding with you…'

'It was an accident…a mistake,' Star protested crossly. 'I told him there was no need for him to interfere, to get involved, but he wouldn't listen and now there's no way I can get out of going without looking… If I back out now, everyone is bound to think that it's because I'm jealous of Emily… because she was always Dad's favourite…'

'You mean because she always made a point of making *sure* she was his favourite,' Sally corrected her roundly. 'I've never been able to understand why men are so blind to that kind of manipulation and false flattery.'

'Haven't you?' Star asked her sardonically. 'It isn't their eyesight that's the problem, it's their ego.'

'Mmm… Well, as for people thinking you're jealous of Emily, she was always the one who was jealous of you. Why else do you think she made such a big thing of ingratiating herself with your father?' Sally challenged her when Star started to shake her head.

'She's everything that I'm not—the kind of daughter that Dad always wanted. Not that it really matters now,' she said.

'Mum's getting married again, by the way,' she added, and rolled her eyes slightly as she told Sally, 'In the Caribbean and to Brian, of all men.'

'Brian? Oh, but he'll be perfect for her,' Sally enthused. 'He'll spoil her and look after her—and you'll be able to stop worrying about her and don't pretend that you don't. I know you too well,' Sally challenged her. 'You know, your father really does have a lot to answer for, Star,' she told her more gently.

'Yeah… Me for starters,' Star mocked back.

But Sally shook her head and continued firmly, 'You know that wasn't what I meant. He caused both you and your mother a lot of pain; he—'

'Mmm…well, that's men for you.' Star shrugged cynically.

'No.' Sally corrected her, 'That's *some* men, I agree; some men *are* vain and egotistical and uncaring of the hurt they inflict on others, the damage they do to other people's lives, but then so are some women. Not all men are like your father, Star,' Sally told her. 'Look at Chris…and James…and Brad…and Brian. Look at the way he's gone on loving your mother—'

'Aren't you omitting someone from this list of supermen?' Star asked her wryly. 'Kyle,' she prompted, when Sally looked puzzled. 'Surely you weren't going to miss an opportunity to point out to me what a truly wonderful, caring, sincere specimen of male perfection he is? If I were Chris I think I might be getting rather worried.'

'Chris knows he doesn't have to worry about me falling for another man,' Sally retorted firmly. 'When is Emily actually getting married?' she asked.

'Next month,' Star told her.

'Mmm…a September bride… Have you decided what you're going to wear yet?'

'I haven't a clue,' Star informed her in a voice that said that she didn't really care.

'Doing anything interesting this weekend?' Sally asked her, changing the subject.

'Nothing,' Star told her. Kyle would be doing something interesting, though. Kyle would be doing something extremely interesting; at least, he would be if the owner of that husky, feminine transatlantic voice had anything to do with it.

Kyle—why on earth was she wasting her time thinking about him? And why on earth had she been so stupid as to give in to that ridiculous and unnecessary fit of panic the other morning, when, if she'd stayed, she could have proved beyond any shadow of a doubt that she had been right about him all along?

And what had he meant anyway by that comment he had made to her about doing some truth-outing of his own? What truth-outing exactly? What truth was there to come out, after all? None… None.

And of course she wasn't missing him… Why on earth should she be? He had only been gone a matter of hours, and even if he had been gone days…months…years…it wouldn't have made any difference—she still wouldn't miss him, she insisted to herself several hours later as she padded barefoot around her flat and tried to convince herself that the reason she was trying to work out the time difference between here and North America was simply in case Brad should try to get in touch with her to discuss her work.

In case *Brad* should try to get in touch with her, she emphasised mentally for the benefit of that small, jeering, disbelieving voice which refused to let her off the hook. For no other reason.

In America Kyle opened his front door and smiled lovingly at the small, dark-haired woman who was waiting for him, opening his arms wide to receive her as she hurled herself into them.

'And how's my favourite big brother?' she asked him teasingly when he finally put her down.

'Your only big brother,' Kyle reminded her drily.

She was the youngest of his father's second family and a gap of over ten years separated them, but she was the closest in looks and temperament to her aunt, his stand-in mother, and he would have loved her just for that if for nothing else.

'You've lost weight,' she accused him, 'and you're not smiling—not properly, with your eyes. Something's wrong. What is it?'

'Nothing—there's nothing wrong,' Kyle denied, but she shook her head.

'Yes, there is. What is it...*who* is it? Who is she?' She pounced on him with awesome female instinct, adding as she saw his face, 'Aha, so it is someone... A woman... *The* woman,' she guessed triumphantly. 'Who is she, Kyle? Do I know her?'

'No,' he told her, shaking his head, and added under his breath, 'And, the way things are looking, I doubt that you ever will.'

He hadn't intended her to hear him but she had and now she was by his side, frowning her disapproval and her scorn of any woman fool enough not to want her adored elder brother.

'Want to talk about it?' she offered, but Kyle shook his head.

He had Star backed into a corner and, like any cornered creature, she was desperately looking for an escape and wildly angry with it. Perhaps the kindest thing to do would be to give her that escape. But to what? He knew that he loved her and he was pretty certain that she felt something for him—something that wasn't just lust, even though he knew quite well that *she* would claim that it was.

He had a strong suspicion that her sister's wedding could prove to be the catalyst that pushed things one way or the other, that removed the barriers between them or re-erected them and made them even stronger.

He had unashamedly badgered Sally for as much information as she could give him about Star and her relationship with the rest of her family, and most especially her father, and he thought he understood just why Star was so afraid of allowing herself to love anyone, why she couldn't even allow herself to accept that such a concept as love could exist between a man and a woman.

Getting her to relinquish the shield of bitterness and rejection that she had forged to protect herself would be a painful process—for both of them. After all, what right did he have to interfere in her life?

'Tell me about her,' Kelly tried to coax him, but Kyle shook his head again. He knew his half-sister meant well but there were some things that were too private...too potentially painful to discuss with anyone.

His body, his brain, his mind might be here in North America, he acknowledged, but his heart, his emotions, his real, true essence were all in England with Star, and that was something that was too intimate, too personal to tell anyone. That could only be shared with one other person. Only she didn't want to hear… She was too afraid to let herself hear, he corrected himself tiredly.

'Hey, come back; you were miles away,' Sally accused Star. They were having lunch together in their favourite Italian restaurant and Sally had been regaling Star with the latest gossip when she had suddenly realised that Star was staring absently into space.

'Anyone would think you were in love,' Sally teased her.

'In love? *Me*? Don't be ridiculous,' Star retorted witheringly. But, curiously for Star, her face had suddenly become slightly flushed, Sally noted, and she couldn't quite look her in the eye.

Coincidentally Sally and Poppy had been discussing Star only the previous evening, Poppy laughing about the vow she and Claire and Star had made never get married.

'You've had two successes,' she had reminded Sally, 'but I doubt that you're going to get a third. Not with Star.'

Sally wasn't so sure, but she had kept her thoughts to herself.

'Have you heard anything from Kyle?' she asked Star conversationally now. 'I know he had to extend his stay in North America because Claire mentioned it the last time she rang.'

'No, I haven't. Why should I?' Star responded tersely. 'There's no reason why he should get in touch with me.'

'No, of course not,' Sally agreed soothingly. 'I just thought he might have rung to…to ask you to keep an eye on his flat…'

Star looked suspiciously into her friend's too innocent face but decided not to pursue the subject—not to think about the empty flat and the oddly painful feeling she had experienced the morning she had woken up and discovered that Kyle had not, as she had expected, returned. And she certainly didn't

want to think about the betraying phone call she had made
to Mrs Hawkins later on that same morning.

But why should she feel uncomfortable about making a
phone call—an enquiry about the whereabouts of someone
whom she was, after all, involved with in a business capacity? It was a perfectly normal and acceptable thing to do.
Naturally, she needed to know when Kyle was likely to return
since he was the person she had to channel her work through.

She didn't tell Sally any of this, though, and neither did she
tell her about the shaming way she had been rushing straight
to her answering machine to check her messages every time
she had been out, just in case Kyle had rung.

In love. Her! The very idea was ridiculous, derisible...
laughable... So why wasn't she laughing?

Star could see the light flashing on her answering machine
unit as she opened her workroom door, but she deliberately
refused to go and check it until she had removed her coat
and made herself a cup of coffee—like a child forcing herself to wait and not open the most special and exciting birthday present until last.

Coffee-mug in one hand, she sat down and ran the tape.
Her heart jolted against her ribs, coffee spilling down onto
the desk as her hand started to tremble, but when she re-
played the answering machine tape it was Brad's voice she
heard and not Kyle's.

Brad wanted her to call back so that they could discuss
her campaign.

Star put down her coffee mug and walked over to the window. Her throat ached and for some reason she found it difficult to swallow. The familiar view outside had become oddly
hazy and misty, but it wasn't until she blinked that she realised that her eyes had filled with tears.

Tears. Her! And for a man? Why? What was so special

about *this* man that he could have this effect on her, that he could make her feel...want...need him in all the ways she had promised herself she would never allow herself to want or need any member of his sex?

She gave a small shiver. Had she been a different kind of woman she might almost have been tempted to believe that there was, after all, something in that old superstition about catching the bride's bouquet. But it was all total rubbish, of course, and the kind of outdated mythology that had no place in a modern woman's thinking or her life.

She went back to her desk and picked up the telephone receiver and quickly dialled Brad's number.

Twenty minutes later, their conversation over, she let out a shaky breath of relief before punching the air in excited triumph. Brad had not only endorsed her proposals for the campaign, he had actually also allocated a more than generous budget to cover the cost of running her ads on TV.

There was still an enormous amount of work to be done, of course, and Brad had stressed that the timing of the TV campaign was vitally important and that it must coincide with the completion of Kyle's revamping of the technical side of things.

'To offer a service we can't follow up on would be counter-productive, to say the least,' Brad had told her.

'Suicidal,' Star had agreed.

'Kyle's due to fly back to Britain tomorrow,' Brad had informed her. 'He'll fix up a meeting with you to go over everything we've discussed and I guess he'll have his own input to make. It will make sense to have any actors who feature in your ads as service engineers dressed in whatever uniform Kyle decides his contract people will wear...'

'Mmm...' Star had agreed with him. 'And, of course, so far as the visual impact of a TV campaign is concerned, the colour of the technicians' uniforms or whatever could be very important. It has been proved scientifically that different colours cause different emotional reactions in people.'

Whilst they had talked she had made notes of the points that Brad had raised and now, as her initial euphoria subsided, she studied them.

This contract, this campaign, was the high spot of her career, a triumphant breakthrough, rewarding not just her persistence, her hard work and her single-minded concentration but also her gift for innovation and creativity—so why had Brad's confirmation that he fully endorsed her campaign left her feeling somehow empty and unsatisfied? Why was the once familiar thrill of succeeding somehow just not there?

Why, instead of feeling good about herself and what she had achieved, did she feel much the same as she had done as a child of ten years old when she had won an important scholarship, only to have her mother protest that it didn't do for girls to be too clever—boys didn't like it—and for her father to be too wrapped up in his new wife and family even to remember what she had achieved by the time he eventually got around to seeing her?

What was *wrong* with her? she asked herself hardly. She was an adult now, not a child. She had no need of anyone to praise and compliment her. She didn't need the approval and congratulations of others to make her feel good about herself... It was enough for her to know what she had done. She looked at the phone. Perhaps she could ring Lindsay and they could go out for dinner together, only no doubt Lindsay would be too busy now that she and Miles were reconciled.

What *was* the matter with her? she wondered irritably as she found her throat closing up on a lump of self-pitying emotion for the second time in twenty-four hours.

Perhaps she was suffering from some stress-related illness and that was what was making her feel so unfamiliarly weak and vulnerable. Yes, that was probably it, she decided quickly. What she needed was an early night and some decent sleep.

Star had just curled up in bed when the phone rang. Sleepily, she reached for the receiver, her whole body going into shock as she heard Kyle's voice.

'Star, are you OK?' she heard him ask intuitively as she drew in her breath and tried to clamp down on the tell-tale sensations swamping her. 'Have I rung at a bad time?'

'I was trying to get an early night,' she told him coolly, once she had got her breath back. 'What do you want...?'

'Do you mean you're in bed?' he asked her, ignoring the second part of her conversation.

'That is normally where I go when I want to sleep,' Star confirmed sardonically, and asked again, 'Why are you ringing, Kyle? What do you want?'

There was a brief pause and then Star nearly dropped the receiver when he told her huskily, 'If I told you you'd probably hang up on me...'

Kyle, flirting with *her*. Kyle, coming on to her. Star couldn't believe her ears.

The words 'try me' rose to her lips but she quenched them firmly and said crisply instead, 'Brad rang me earlier to confirm that he's happy with the campaign.'

In his office Kyle smiled ruefully to himself. Was Star backing off from a sexual challenge? Either he had made a lot more progress than he had dared hope—or a hell of a lot less.

'Yes. He's approved everything you want to do,' he said, without telling her how much time and effort he had put into persuading and convincing Brad that the expense of running a TV advertising campaign could be justified.

That was the main reason why he had stayed over longer than he had originally planned. It had taken all the will-power he possessed and more not to telephone Star before now, and

right now just hearing her voice was enough to make his body
ache so much that he had to grit his teeth against his need.

'Look, it's going to be late tomorrow when my flight gets
in and I was wondering if you could possibly do a little grocery shopping for me?'

Star was tempted to refuse but instead she heard herself
asking, 'What exactly is it you want me to get?'

'Oh, just the basics,' Kyle responded vaguely. 'You know—
milk, bread, that kind of stuff. It's going to be going on for
midnight before I get in. My sister gave me enough home
baked stuff to dangerously overload my luggage before she
left. Not that I'm complaining; it was good to have her staying;
it gave us an opportunity to catch up on one another's news.'

Star expelled a ragged breath. It had been his *sister* who
had been staying with him and not another woman, a potential lover!

'If you want to leave it in my flat, Amy has a key.'

He held his breath, hoping she would say that she'd wait
up for him, and then released it when she made no response.

Star didn't make any response because she was wondering why he had seen fit to leave Amy a key and not *her*, and
wondering as well why she should feel so uptight about it.

'Well, I guess I'd better go and let you get back to sleep,'
she heard Kyle telling her. 'Congratulations, by the way. Brad
was very impressed by your campaign, and with good reason,'
he told her generously. 'I know you thought I was being deliberately obstructive over your original idea, but I'm behind
you all the way on this one. You've got a very creative mind,
Star, a very special talent, and I predict it won't be long before you're making the big agencies very edgy and nervous.'

Star gripped the telephone receiver tightly and stared at
her bedroom wall.

Why? Why did it have to be *Kyle* who acknowledged her

success and paid tribute to her skills, and why on earth did she have to feel even more desolate and forlorn because he had?

Quietly and without saying another word she replaced the telephone receiver.

Kyle sighed as he followed suit. No doubt she had thought that he was being both patronising and sexist in congratulating her, but he hadn't meant it that way. *He* had no hang ups about a woman being professional and successful—in fact he applauded it.

Star frowned as she placed her bag of groceries on Kyle's worktop and opened his fridge door.

Inside were two cartons of long-life milk plus all of the other basic items she had assumed he wanted her to get.

Out of curiosity she checked the freezer, her mouth compressing as she saw loaves of bread.

Why had he made an expensive transatlantic call to ask her to shop for items he already had?

Perhaps he had forgotten he had them, she decided as she unpacked and put away her shopping.

The flat had been refurbished now but the plants in the kitchen and sitting room looked desperately thirsty.

Automatically she watered them, making soothing, clucking noises as she saw how rapidly they absorbed the moisture. Plants were, after all, living organisms that needed care and nurturing...just like human beings... She frowned again as her brain assimilated that thought. What was she trying to tell herself—that *she* needed care and nurturing...? Since when?

Quickly she finished what she was doing, but on her way out of the flat some impulse she couldn't resist took her not to the front door but to the bedroom. The bed was neatly made, with no sign, no imprint of Kyle's body on either the bed or his pillow, and yet she still went up to it, smoothing the fabric of the pillowcase with her fingertips, bending her head towards it and then picking it up.

She was still standing with it clasped in her arms when she heard the front door open. For a second she simply stood where she was, completely frozen, and then, in a panic, she dropped the pillow back onto the bed and hurried out into the hall to come face to face with Kyle.

'You're early,' she told him accusingly. 'You said you wouldn't be back until midnight...'

'I caught an earlier flight,' he told her cheerfully, looking over her head towards the open bedroom door.

'I...I was just checking to make sure everything was all right before I locked up,' Star told him quickly. 'I...I've put your shopping away.'

'Thank you.'

Uncertainly Star looked up at him, her mouth parting in a soft O of surprise as he bent his head and kissed her.

She heard the thud of his case as he dropped it and wrapped both his arms around her, and knew weakly that she really should protest, that such a lingering and almost lover-like kiss was scarcely necessary in acknowledgement of the simple, neighbourly task of getting his shopping. But instead she just stood where she was, letting the tender, persuasive warmth of his mouth dissolve the iciness which seemed to have lodged around her heart.

When Kyle finally removed his mouth from hers she opened her eyes and looked dizzily into his.

'I...I have to go,' she told him unsteadily.

'Yes,' he agreed gravely, reaching out and tucking an errant lock of her hair behind her ear. 'I think you do.'

Wordlessly Star watched as he opened the door for her and he waited whilst she walked across the landing to her own flat.

Once inside it, she closed the door and then leaned against

it, closing her eyes and breathing deeply. How *could* a single, simple kiss affect her like that. She felt…she felt… She didn't want to acknowledge or examine *how* she felt, she admitted shakily. She was too afraid of what she might learn.

Once Star had gone, Kyle walked into his bedroom. The pillow she had been holding lay in the middle of the bed where she had dropped it. Smiling, he picked it up and restored it to its rightful position.

CHAPTER TEN

'RIGHT, everyone... Last one now, everyone smile.'

Star could feel the tension in her jaw as her mouth widened in obedience to the photographer's request. What with the video and the formal photographs as well as the various family members wanting to capture their memories of the ceremony on film, it was a wonder that there had been any time for the actual formalities of the marriage itself, she reflected ironically as the photographer signalled that he was finished with them and the assembled family group started to break up.

Kyle, who had been standing beside her, laughed as one after another of the triplets ran towards him, demanding to be picked up.

'He's certainly got a way with children,' her most recent stepmother commented tiredly as she watched her offspring clamouring for Kyle's attention. 'Of course,' she added, 'they do really miss the input they would get from a younger and more physically energetic father. Has Kyle any children?' she asked Star inquisitively.

'I have no idea,' Star returned shortly, before turning her back on her. She had already seen the assessing and unmistakably feline look of interest that Lucinda had given Kyle. Perhaps it wasn't just the triplets who were missing out on input from a younger and more physically energetic man, she reflected, watching Lucinda's unsubtle attempts to get Kyle's attention.

Oh, yes, Kyle was certainly a hit with her family, she admitted, even her father was impressed. Wearily she massaged her temples; the tension headache that she had woken up with this morning had gradually become more unbearable as the day progressed.

Kyle had suggested that they travel down to the wedding the day before and stay over an extra night, but Star had rejected that idea, claiming that she was too busy to take the extra time off work. Now, though, she was paying the price for her stubbornness with an aching head and a fraying temper.

It had shocked her to discover how much her father seemed to have aged and actually physically shrunk since she had last seen him. Standing next to Kyle, he seemed so much shorter than the younger man and yet her childhood memories of her father were of an impressively tall, powerful-looking man.

He still retained his vanity and egotism, though, Star had decided cynically when he had insisted on being photographed surrounded by his progeny and his wives, both past and present, only her own mother missing from the line-up. Star realised now that he had not asked after her mother, and made a point of going over to him to inform him that she was to marry Brian. His reaction was brusquely dismissive.

'He just doesn't care,' she fumed after he had walked away and she had gone back to Kyle, who had witnessed the exchange from a short distance away. 'He never cared about either of us.'

'You're wrong,' Kyle corrected her decisively. 'I'd say he's actually rather jealous…'

'Jealous? No way. He was the one who wanted the divorce.'

'Some men can never really let go. Their vanity demands that they are the controlling force in a relationship, the most loved. It strikes me that you and your mother had a lucky escape, Star,' he added wisely.

'A lucky escape? What on earth do you mean?' Star challenged him.

'Look around you,' Kyle instructed her, 'and tell me what you see...'

'My father,' she responded belligerently.

'Your father and who?' Kyle questioned patiently.

'My father and his children...the ones he really wanted,' she told him angrily. 'The children he really wanted and their mothers...'

'Mmm. Shall I tell you what I see?' Without waiting for her to answer he continued, 'I can see a man who cannot bear to be ignored, who must come first—a man who is quite happy to manipulate and undermine those he claims to love to ensure that he is always the prime focus of their attention. Look at the way he plays one person off against another, the same way he played you off against Emily—the same way, in all probability, that he played you off as a child against your mother and vice versa.'

Star immediately opened her mouth to deny what he had said, her eyes mirroring both her shock and her outrage.

He forestalled her. 'It's human nature for us to want our parents to be paragons and perfect, Star, especially when our contact with them is limited. I know, I've been there and suffered the consequences. It can be devastating for children when they realise that the mother or father they love so much isn't perfect—devastating enough to turn that love to deep-seated resentment and even hatred.'

Star spun on her heel and walked away from him, angrily reacting to his comments in much the same way as she might have done to someone physically probing a painful wound with a surgical instrument, but thereafter she couldn't help observing how accurate his assessment had been.

Her father *did* encourage his different families to compete for his attention, he *did* manipulate chaos rather than encourage harmony between them, sometimes even between different members of the same family group, and she was shocked to realise that, whereas in the past she had always thought of herself as the lone outsider to the charmed, extensive family unit that he had formed around himself, there were in fact several others who shared her painful isolation and exclusion from the family fold.

Withholding his love and his approval and singling out one particular person at a time for this treatment was something her father was adept at, Star recognised. And she had also recognised something else which was even more disturbing, she acknowledged as she watched the way that Kyle encouraged the smallest of the triplets, the one who had held back as the other two had yet again rushed into his arms, to come forward, deftly hoisting one child onto his shoulders, leaving both arms free to gather the remaining two.

The look of relieved, grateful joy that radiated from the third small face made Star bite down hard on her bottom lip. What she had finally realised was that Kyle would never behave like her father. He would never willingly or wilfully hurt anyone, much less someone he professed to love. Kyle was different...Kyle was—

'Thanks...for coming.'

The hesitation in Emily's voice as she came to join her made Star quell her normal hostile response to her stepsister.

'You look beautiful,' Star told her, and meant it. 'Dad looked so proud as he walked you down the aisle.'

'Did he?' Emily gave her a surprised complacent look. 'He wasn't at all pleased when I told him that David and I were going to get married. David's been married before, you see, and John made a big thing about him marrying me on the rebound. He knew David's first wife and, according to him,

David was desperately in love with her. It brought it all back for me, of course—how desperately jealous I was of you as a child and how desperately jealous my mother was of yours.'

'*You* jealous of *me*?' Star stared at her. 'But *you* were always his favourite… You were the one he—'

'No, I wasn't.' Emily cut her off, shaking her head decisively. 'Oh, I know it may have seemed that way, but he was always comparing me with you, saying how much cleverer you were, how much prettier. Everything I did you had done before me and so much better—even though you were younger. Just as everything Mum did your mother had done before her and so much better.'

She pulled a wry face. 'I didn't want any of this, you know,' she told Star, gesturing towards the lavishly expensive marquee thronged with guests. 'I wanted to get married very quietly…for it just to be me and David…but John made such a fuss… He kept going on about the huge wedding that David and Naomi had had and what people were going to think and say if we didn't do the same. He wanted me to have all the children as attendants, you know—*all* of them,' she stressed meaningfully, 'including you…'

'What?'

Emily laughed as she saw Star's look of revulsion.

'I told him you'd never agree—thank God. And of course you know what he's like—he had to make a big thing of it, claiming that I didn't want you because I'd always been jealous of you and then insisting that if all his children couldn't be included then none of them should be. Not that I minded. I was more than happy with David's two nieces as my bridesmaids.'

'I should think you were,' Star said feelingly, unable to stop herself from mentally counting up all her father's children and then looking at the triplets who were still with Kyle.

'I know; it doesn't bear thinking about, does it?' Emily murmured, reading her mind.

'No, it doesn't,' Star agreed.

They looked at one another and then burst out laughing, the laughter in Emily's eyes suddenly turning to bright tears as she reached out and hugged her fiercely, saying emotionally, 'Oh, Star, I so much wanted you as my sister, but somehow we never got it quite right did we?'

'No…no, we didn't,' Star said grimly, and then to her own surprise she heard herself saying, 'But that doesn't mean that we still can't.'

'No, it doesn't, does it?' Emily agreed, giving her another fierce hug.

'Ready to go?' Kyle asked a few minutes later, deftly avoiding a would-be rugby tackle from someone's child as he crossed the hotel lawn to join Star.

Heavens, he was like a modern-day Pied Piper, Star decided in fascination; none of the children, it seemed, could keep away from him.

'What on earth is it about you?' she asked him distastefully. 'Your aftershave?'

'Nope.' Kyle laughed good-humouredly. 'Nothing special; I just like kids.'

'So I see,' Star responded disdainfully. 'Let's hope your wife, when you do marry, is equally enthusiastic; after all, she'll be the one who ends up playing the major role in their upbringing.'

'Not necessarily,' Kyle corrected her. 'I'm quite happy to be a house-husband father if things work out that way.'

Star digested his statement in silence as he drove them back to their hotel. Her tension headache had spread to her neck and the muscles of her shoulders and upper back now and she instinctively tried to ease the stiffness out of them.

Kyle frowned as he saw her discomfort and asked her in concern, 'Are you OK?'

'I've just got a bit of tension, that's all,' Star answered him brusquely. She wasn't used to anyone showing concern about her health; her relationships with men had never included that type of intimacy.

'Don't worry, I know just the thing for it,' Kyle assured her as he turned into the drive that led to their hotel.

'So do I,' Star snapped.

Typically Kyle refused to take offence or retaliate, simply smiling at her as he parked the car. Uncharac-teristically, Star let him take the lead in dealing with the receptionist.

The day had drained her both emotionally and physically— as she had guessed it would—but for very different reasons from those she had imagined.

She was amazed at how easily and how dispassionately she had been able to watch her father ignore her and turn to fuss with the triplets instead. And she had felt for them, rather than experiencing her normal sense of humiliation and shame at being passed over in favour of her father's other children.

Their suite was large and comfortable, with two bedrooms and bathrooms and a shared sitting room. Star, like Kyle, carried her own overnight case, and she was just about to put it in her room when Kyle told her quietly, 'I've arranged for the bill to be made out to me; we can split the cost later. I thought you'd prefer it that way rather than have your father pay.'

She stopped and stared at him, unable to say a word, her eyes filling with quick, irrational tears, and virtually stammered a low, 'Y-yes…thank you…I would.'

How had he known that she would feel like that? she marvelled as she walked into her room. That she would want…? She put down her case and closed her eyes. From the other side of the half closed door she heard Kyle saying, 'I've or-

dered a room service meal—if that's OK? I didn't think you'd
want to bother going down to the restaurant, but if—'

'No...no, that's fine,' she assured him wearily. Her head
had started to ache really badly; all she wanted to do was to
get undressed, have a warm, relaxing bath and then lie down.

She closed the bedroom door and started to remove her
suit.

'Star?'

Groggily Star opened her eyes. She was lying on her
front. Kyle was standing at the side of the bed, looking down
frowningly at her. Her room was in semi-darkness and as she
glanced automatically at her watch she realised that she had
been asleep for over two hours.

'What happened to dinner?' she demanded huskily, wincing as she moved and discovered that the tension from her
headache had remained in her neck and shoulders.

'I cancelled it,' Kyle told her drily. 'We can always reorder
later. How do you feel?'

'Lousy,' she told him feelingly.

'Perhaps I can help; where does it hurt?'

'What are you doing?' Star demanded breathlessly as he
placed his hand on the bare skin of her naked shoulders and
gently started pressing the tense muscles.

'Giving you a massage,' Kyle responded easily. 'It's a
proven fact that it's just about the best way to relieve stress-
induced tension.'

'A massage!' Star started to sit up and then subsided as she
remembered that she was completely naked.

'I don't need a massage,' she tried to protest crossly, but
her body was telling a different story as it positively revelled
in the sensation of Kyle's fingers easing the knots of tension
from her taut muscles. Star tried to tell him to stop but her

demand was muffled by the pillow as Kyle pressed more firmly into the knotted tissue.

'No wonder you've got an aching head,' he told her wryly. 'The whole of your back feels like it's virtually seized up. Breathe deeply and slowly,' he instructed her, 'and we'll do this properly; you feel like you need it.'

She felt like she needed what? Star wondered edgily. If it had been another man she would have been highly suspicious of that type of comment, but Kyle, of course, was different.

'There you go, tensing up again,' she heard Kyle complain as her body reacted to the message that her brain had just given her. Kyle was different. Kyle *was* different.

An odd sensation, a combination of breathlessness, light-headedness and exhilarated relief, burst upon her, causing her to feel somehow as though she had just laid down an extraordinarily heavy burden that she had been forced to carry. She opened her mouth to tell Kyle about it and then closed it again as her habitual protective caution reasserted itself. As she turned her head she saw a neat pile of clothes on the chair next to her own and recognised that they were Kyle's.

'Just stay right where you are,' she heard him instruct her before she could ask what he was doing. 'I'll be right back.

'Here you are; you can lie on this,' he announced several seconds later as he emerged from her bathroom carrying a huge bath towel. 'I haven't got any massage oil but I guess this will do...'

'Massage oil?'

Star's head whipped round. Kyle was standing beside the bed holding what looked like a courtesy bottle of some kind of body oil. He had stripped off to his underwear—a pair of snugly fitting black briefs.

The sight of a man in his underwear was not one that Star normally found in the least erotic. In her opinion men looked sexy either fully dressed or wearing nothing at all; a man wearing briefs and, even worse, his socks in her view looked totally unalluringly and ardour-dampeningly coy. But in Kyle's case...

She gulped and tried to look somewhere else. From the way her pulse was starting to race it was just as well that he hadn't stripped off completely, she thought.

'I don't think this is a good idea...' she started to say, but Kyle refused to listen.

'It's OK, I know what I'm doing,' he told her. 'I had a lot of practice when I was in my teens.'

'Thank you,' Star told him through gritted teeth, 'but I do not want to hear an account of your youthful sexual adventures...'

'My youthful sexual adventures? What have they got to do with this?' Kyle asked her. 'Like I was saying...I had a vacation job one summer, working for the coach of the local hockey team. He swore by a thorough massage for relieving heavy bruising and muscle strains... He was the one who taught me how to do it...

'It's a pity we don't have a proper table, but I suppose the bed will have to do,' he added, whipping away the duvet before Star could protest.

Unlike him, she *had* removed all her clothes, and for some reason she did not feel in the least mollified when Kyle tactfully draped a small towel over the rounded curves of her behind.

'Now try to breathe slowly and deeply and just relax,' he instructed her.

'Just relax'. And how on earth was she supposed to do that when he—? Star stiffened in startled surprise as she felt him start to knead not her shoulders as she had expected but her foot.

'It's my back that's stiff, not my feet,' she protested.

'Your whole body is stressed out and tense,' Kyle informed

her firmly. 'Now keep still and just relax. A good massage should be a pleasurable, enjoyable experience...'

Star looked back over her shoulder suspiciously but Kyle's head was bent as he concentrated on massaging her calf and she couldn't see his expression—couldn't see *his* and quite definitely didn't want him to see *hers*, she acknowledged as she fought to suppress the very definite quiver of sensation that shot up her leg and which she knew perfectly well had nothing to do with the efficacy of a good massage and everything to do with the efficacy of the massager.

By the time he had reached the top of her thigh, Star was both gritting her teeth and curling her hands into two small, agonised fists beneath the controlling protection of the pillow.

'I don't understand it,' she heard Kyle protesting. 'It just doesn't seem to be working. You're every bit as tense as you were when I started...'

On the contrary, Star could have told him, it was working only too well, but in a rather different way from the one he had obviously envisaged.

'Well, there isn't much point in going on, then,' Star said in relief, but Kyle shook his head.

'No, my guess is that what you need is a whole course of treatment with a qualified physio...'

'You're probably right,' Star agreed. 'I'll organise something.'

'I'll just try and see if I can free some of the tension from your back,' Kyle told her, adding, 'You'll have to move further down the bed, though, so that I can come to that end and work that way...'

Work that way...? Work what way? He surely didn't mean...?

But apparently he did, and Star smothered a small, protesting groan as Kyle pushed the pillows out of the way and positioned himself on the bed in front of her. Did he *have* to kneel there like that? she wondered indignantly. And if he did...if he did... Dizzily she closed her eyes. Weren't men past the youth of their teens and twenties supposed to lose muscle tone and develop pot-bellies, especially those of them who were desk-bound executives?

Kyle didn't... Kyle hadn't...

'You really are in a bad way,' she heard him complain as he leaned over her and placed his hands on her back. 'You're actually twitching.'

Twitching... He would twitch if he... She smothered another groan as his fingers stroked slowly over her spine. She didn't know which was having the more destructive effect on her self-control—the sensation of him touching her or the sight and scent of him. The sight at least she could blot out, but the scent...his scent...

There was no masking the shudder that tormented her as Kyle worked his way over her back, and it was almost a relief when he found the flat, hard lump of knotted muscle which had formed as a direct result of her tension and worked on it, causing her to gasp with pain.

'It's all right,' he assured her soothingly.

All right? Oh, of course it was all right, Star decided helplessly. After all, all he was doing was reducing her to a helpless, gibbering wreck of agonised female desire—an aching, tormented, thoroughly aroused bundle of female cells and hormones.

As she ground her teeth against the moan of arousal that she could feel rising in her throat, Kyle asked solicitously, 'Did that hurt? Sorry...'

Star had had enough.

'No, it did not hurt,' she told him forcefully, wrenching herself out of his hands.

'Turn over, then,' Kyle suggested, 'and I'll—'

Turn over!

Star closed her eyes. 'I can't,' she told him in a small, mortified voice, and then added despairingly, 'Kyle, will you please put some clothes on?'

'On.' He was actually laughing wickedly at her, Star recognised as he released her. 'I kinda hoped you were going to ask me to take them off.'

'Off?' Star tried to sound quellingly acerbic but she knew her voice was trembling and she knew her body was as well.

'Yes, off,' Kyle said encouragingly as he gently but firmly turned her over and bent his head to kiss her gently, but not so gently that the effect didn't ricochet, rampaging from one end of her body to the other, Star noted in despair as she tried to resist what was happening to her. But how could she resist when, instead of assisting her, Kyle was just making the situation worse by continuing to kiss her?

She tried to say as much but the movement of her lips as she tried to form the words somehow or other gave Kyle the idea that she actually wanted him to continue kissing her and in the end it was simply easier to be acquiescent—easier and oh, so very much more pleasurable.

Kyle was still stroking her skin but his touch was very definitely a sensual and deliberately erotic caress now.

'Have you any idea what you've just been doing to me, how much you've been turning me on?' he whispered into her mouth as he opened it with his tongue.

'Tell me about it,' Star moaned back feelingly, her whole body shuddering with delight as his open palm slid over her breast, the tip of his thumb rubbing tormentingly against her nipple.

'Mmm…you taste so good,' she heard him telling her appreciatively as he nuzzled his way down over her throat and between her breasts.

'So good,' he repeated far more hoarsely as his tongue circled her navel and her towel was removed.

Star had thought of herself as sexually sophisticated but there was nothing sophisticated about the way she was reacting now, she recognised—about the way her whole body, but most especially her thighs, had started to tremble, about the sensations and emotions that gripped her as she felt Kyle's mouth open and move down over her body.

Such intimacies…such emotions surely belonged to true lovers and should be exclusively *their* domain but there was no denying her need to respond to and reciprocate the intimacy of Kyle's lingering oral caress.

Helplessly, she reached out to him.

For a moment she thought that he either didn't truly comprehend or didn't want to respond to her own need but after a second's hesitation he removed his briefs and watched her, his expression unreadable as she moved her body and then bent her head towards him.

He felt hard, powerfully hard to the touch and yet at the same time very humanly vulnerable. He didn't move but Star was aware of his quick indrawn breath as she placed her lips against his thigh and slowly started caressing him.

She wasn't sure which of them shuddered more deeply when she finally touched him with her tongue, delicately rimming a circle around him, but she knew that her own reaction to the feel and taste of him was so intimately powerful and explosive that she could actually feel her body tightening in sensual urgency.

'Star!'

The hoarse sound of her name was enough to make her pause and look at him. His face was slightly flushed, a dark burn of colour highlighting his cheekbones and his eyes. Star trembled, as shaky as a newborn colt, when she saw the look in his eyes.

'I want you,' she told him helplessly, unable to stop herself from responding vocally to the look he had given her.

'Nowhere near as much as I want you,' he retorted fiercely. 'Nowhere near as much.'

She had always known instinctively that there would be strength and power in those arms, in that body—but what she had not guessed was that that strength would empower her and allow her, for the first time in her life, actually to enjoy her own vulnerability, to feel that it was safe for her to allow someone else to take control, to know that she could trust him…that she was safe with him…

She cried out to him when he eventually entered her, unaware of what she said, unaware of having told him that she loved him, unaware of anything other than the almost violent surge of pleasure that engulfed her as the tight circle of her need snapped.

Star had known physical pleasure before but she had never known this emotional completeness, never known such overwhelming joy in the aftermath of any previous intimacy, never wanted to hold and be held by any previous partner the way she did with Kyle.

But then she had never loved anyone as she did him, had she…? She had never loved anyone at all…until now… Until Kyle.

Star woke up in the middle of the night suddenly and sharply aware that Kyle was no longer there in bed with her. Her eyes searched for him in the darkness and found him, standing motionless in front of the window, his head bent, his expression sombre and almost brooding. In a flash Star guessed what was wrong, what must be on his mind. Her love for him overwhelmed her. Immediately, she got out of bed and padded over to him, touching him gently on the arm.

'Kyle…'

He looked silently down at her.

'I know what you're thinking,' she told him, 'but it…it isn't like you think… I wasn't… I didn't…'

She took a deep breath, her voice soft with emotion as she told him, 'You haven't really broken your vow…about not having sex with someone but only making love… Not really.' She paused; this was so very difficult for her. Her pride alone was enough of an obstacle to overcome, never mind the fact that she was stripping away her defences and allowing Kyle to see her so nakedly vulnerable. She could see that he was frowning.

'Star…' he began, but she placed her fingers over his lips and gave him a look that was both fiercely determined and touchingly appealing.

'No…please let me finish,' she begged. 'This isn't easy for me. It goes against everything I've always believed in, everything I've always said and done, but I can't let you think—' She stopped and swallowed and then said huskily, 'It just wouldn't be fair… It wasn't just sex,' she told him bravely. 'What we did…what we *shared*,' she emphasised, 'was…' She swallowed again, moistening her nervously dry lips. 'We *did* make love with emotion and involvement,' she told him, looking down at the floor, unable to look directly at him any longer. 'At least I—'

She stopped.

'You what?' Kyle challenged her sharply, his voice sounding slightly rusty—probably because he was feeling so bad about what had happened, Star decided sympathetically. It was still such a new emotion to her, this sense of feeling for someone else, of wanting—no, needing—to put him first, to put his happiness above her own.

'I made love,' she told him firmly, finally managing to lift her head and look squarely at him. 'I…I made love and I— Kyle, Kyle…what are you doing?' she protested as he suddenly swooped and picked her up in his arms.

'What am I doing?' he repeated, his eyes and his mouth warm with laughter and with something else as well, Star recognised as her heart suddenly started to bounce against her chest wall like a rubber ball on elastic. 'What I am doing,' he said, 'is taking you back to bed where I fully intend to keep you until I get a verbal repetition of that statement you just made and where I intend, as well, to give you my own response to it, both vocal and physical.

'Now tell me again,' he demanded as he lowered her onto the bed and gently but firmly held her there.

'Tell you what?' Star queried, tongue-in-cheek.

'Tell me,' Kyle insisted between deliciously erotic kisses, 'what you know damn well I want to hear.'

'That I made love?' Star repeated huskily, keeping her gaze fixed on him. 'That we didn't just have sex? That for me that—?'

'No,' Kyle corrected her softly. '*We* made love. This time and every time,' he promised her. 'And the reason *we* made love is because we *do* love... I love you and...'

'I love you,' Star whispered shakily to him. 'Kyle, I love you,' she repeated, reaching out to shake his shoulder as she tried to communicate her own sense of wonder and awe at what she had so recently discovered.

Kyle watched her indulgently before pulling her into his arms and telling her provocatively, 'I know you do... I knew it all along.'

'You...you what...?' Star tried to protest, but Kyle took the expedient measure of silencing her by kissing her and kissing her...and kissing her.

Star snuggled closer to him.

'Mmm...'

'Mmm...' Kyle agreed as he lowered her back against the bed.

EPILOGUE

'AND to think that if I hadn't told you the night of Emily's wedding that it wasn't, at least on my part, just sex between us—because I hated to see you looking so…down, because I realised that my love for you was far, far stronger than my need to win and make you think that I'd triumphed because you'd broken your vow—none of this would have happened,' Star told her husband lovingly as she reached up and kissed him.

They had been married very quietly earlier in the day—a church ceremony with only their closest friends present. Sally, bloomingly pregnant and joyously happy, had escorted Star down the aisle in lieu of her father—Star's own decision. She had explained to her father that in view of their complicated family history and the fact that not all of Kyle's family could fly over for the ceremony they had decided against an ultra-traditional wedding.

Her mother had been there, with Brian, and so had Brad and Claire. Her father, characteristically, had sulked and announced that he would not be able to attend as a mere guest since he and the family were going away on holiday.

'Don't let it hurt you,' Kyle had told her gently when she had read her father's letter.

'It doesn't,' Star had responded simply and truthfully. 'He *is* still my father and always will be, but I see him differently now; I see him as he is and not as I want him to be, thanks to you. It doesn't hurt any more, Kyle,' she assured him. 'You have healed all my hurts.'

Emily and David had also been at the wedding. A friendship, a closeness that Star could never have envisaged existing even as short a time as twelve months ago had developed between her and her stepsister.

Sally and Star's friendship had strengthened and deepened too and Sally had already intimated that she wanted Star to be godmother to her soon-to-arrive baby.

'I can't promise to be a traditional wife and mother like Claire and Poppy,' Star had warned Kyle the night before the wedding. 'I can't change the person I am.'

'Star, I don't want you to change,' Kyle had told her firmly. 'I fell in love with you as you are. I *love* you as you are,' he had stressed.

Now, in the privacy of their honeymoon-suite bedroom, listening to her reflecting on that all-important night they had spent together, Kyle started to laugh.

'What are you laughing for?' Star demanded.

'I don't think I dare tell you. Not until after we've consummated our marriage; that way at least you'll have to wait to divorce me instead of merely getting an annulment...'

'*What* are you talking about?' Star asked warily. By now she knew all about his quirky sense of humour and how much he enjoyed teasing her.

'That night you're talking about,' he told her more seriously, 'I wasn't brooding about the possibility that I might have broken any promises to myself...'

'Yes, you were,' Star insisted. 'I could see it in your face. You looked so...so sad, so despondent and I knew what you must be thinking. I knew how important your insistence on not having sex without love was to you.'

'Yes, it was important,' Kyle agreed candidly. 'But never

anywhere near as important as you. And besides,' he added softly, taking her in his arms, '*I* already knew that *we* had made love and not merely had sex...'

'What?' Star struggled to break free of him as she glared up at him. 'How could you possibly have known that? Even I—'

'You told me,' Kyle interrupted her gently. 'You told me when I was loving you how much you cared, how much you needed me...how much you loved me...'

'Did I?' Star looked uncertainly at him, inwardly digesting what she had just learnt. 'Oh,' she said, and then added, 'So there was no need for me to... I didn't have to... I could have...'

'There was no *need*,' Kyle agreed. 'But that doesn't mean that I didn't and don't appreciate what you did and said, my darling, nor that I don't realise how difficult it must have been for you to overcome all those inbuilt prejudices and fears.'

He bent his head and kissed her and then withdrew his mouth a breath away from hers as she struggled to speak.

'Well, if you weren't looking so unhappy about that, then what was bothering you?' she asked him curiously.

'You,' he came back promptly. 'You might have told me you loved me in the heat of the moment, so to speak, but I knew how much you'd hate revealing something which you would see as vulnerability and how much you'd resent me for being the cause of it. I didn't just want your loving...your *love* in bed physically...I wanted it wholly and completely and I wanted you to want me in the same way. If I looked despairing it was because I was wondering just how the hell I was going to achieve that kind of miracle, and then you solved the problem for me...'

Just before he bent his head to resume kissing her, his attention was caught by something on the small table next to them. He reached out and picked it up, holding it out to Star for her inspection as he whispered in her ear, 'It's the room-service menu. It's got sea-bass on it. Want some?'

'Hmm... I'm not so sure... Perhaps I should just have a taste of yours,' she responded provocatively.

They were both laughing as Kyle picked her up and carried her towards the bed.

The bouquet arrived with the room-service waiter and the sea-bass. Attached to it was a small card on which Sally had drawn a small cartoon character punching the air in triumph and written the words, 'Yes! Yes!! Yes!!!'

Laughing helplessly, Star showed it to Kyle. 'Strange things, these old superstitions,' Kyle told her, his words muffled through their shared kiss. 'It doesn't do to treat them lightly or to mock them. You just never know what might happen.'

'No,' Star murmured back happily, 'but I think I know what's going to happen now!'

* * * * *

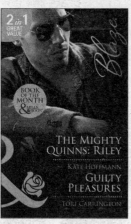

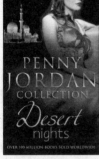 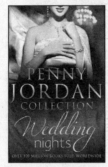 

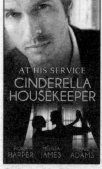

Special Offers

Every month we put together collections and longer reads written by your favourite authors.

Here are some of next month's highlights— and don't miss our fabulous discount online!

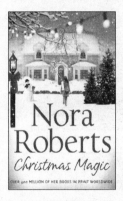

On sale 5th October   On sale 5th October   On sale 5th October

The World of Mills & Boon®

There's a Mills & Boon® series that's perfect for you. We publish ten series and, with new titles every month, you never have to wait long for your favourite to come along.

Blaze®

Scorching hot, sexy reads
4 new stories every month

By Request

Relive the romance with the best of the best
9 new stories every month

Cherish™

Romance to melt the heart every time
12 new stories every month

Desire™

Passionate and dramatic love stories
8 new stories every month